INTRODUCING...

HOBART FLOYT
an unassuming Terran Everyman, drawn into a maelstrom of intrigue, avarice, and the possibility of sudden death.

and

ALACRITY FITZHUGH
an irreverent, young knockabout spacer with an enigmatic past and a dubious future.

These two partners-in-peril flit from planet to planet—exploit to exploit—in the first of a new series of exciting adventures.

REQUIEM
for a
RULER of
WORLDS

Brian Daley

A Del Rey Book

BALLANTINE BOOKS • NEW YORK

A Del Rey Book

Published by Ballantine Books

Library of Congress Catalog Card Number: 84-91792

ISBN 0-345-31487-5

Manufactured in the United States of America

First Edition: May 1985

Cover art by Darrell K. Sweet

To Lucia, with love, thanks, and admiration.

CONTENTS

ACKNOWLEDGMENTS

My gratitude to Lil and Ron Drumheller for their kindness and interest.

I'm also much beholden for the contributions of Owen Lock, who's been endowed by Destiny with all the things that define a truly great editor: a touch of the poet; perception; imagination; expense account lunches; an understanding, good-humored wife named Arleen; and most importantly, a convertible couch.

"... and let him be cast forth, into the exterior darkness."

MATTHEW 22:13

PROLOGUE

IN THE TIME OF THE THIRD
BREATH

STORMCLOUDS FOR MY WINDING SHEET, CASPAHR WEIR thought with approval as his chair floated out over the meadow.

A towering black front was rolling toward him, outlined in blue-green by Guileless Giles, the larger of Epiphany's two moons. That he'd helped nature along, ordering his meteorological engineers to shape the night's tempest, didn't detract from Weir's enjoyment. He was accustomed to arranging things to suit himself. And, he'd decided, a person as close to death as he could be forgiven a little theatricality. Certainly his life had been filled with high drama, triumphs, and defeats.

He wondered what they'd say about him when he was gone. Perhaps a paraphrasing of an ancient Earth barb, one of his favorites: *He was never more popular than when he died.*

Fifty light-years inside what had, within living memory, been a special corner of hell, Director Weir—sometimes

known as Weir the Defender—touched a control on the arm
of his chair. It descended slowly toward the meadow's
thick, tangled carpet of ribbon grass. By craning his head
a bit—panting with the effort, feeling dizziness assail him
again—he could see his home, stronghold, and palace,
Frostpile.

It was a lofty dream-megastructure, veined like intaglio
and lighting the night. Frostpile was composed of domes,
turrets, and spires; citadels like shark fins; outlying forms
that often put visitors in mind of moored dirigibles cut from
crystal.

Begun almost thirty Standard years earlier, it wasn't quite
completed yet. A pity...

Director Weir winced as the chair jostled the least bit,
settling onto the oily ribbon grass. He automatically reached
for a control to make built-in medical apparatus mute his
pain. But the control wasn't there; he'd chosen to soar forth
from Frostpile in his old chair, unencumbered by machinery
that was fighting a futile holding action.

At least this is a seat of power, he thought, *and not a
flying geriatrics clinic*. Its arms, of beautiful teak from
Brimstone, worn by his hands and the years, comforted
him. The chair had served him for a decade before the
damned sawbones and his sister had browbeaten him into
using an airborne deathbed.

He smiled his chagrin at his own absentmindedness and
took his hand away from where the missing control ought
to be, lowering it into his lap slowly, trembling with the
effort. No pain interdiction tonight! No message blockers
or neuroinhibitors; no dulling drugs. He wanted to experience everything, even the pain; it was time to die.

The deathwatch had already summoned together loved
ones, friends, and allies, along with others for whom he
had little or no regard. If it made them feel better to gather
there on Epiphany, the Director had no objection so long
as they left him in peace.

Doubtless enemies in many places were keeping their own shadow-vigil. The repercussions of his death would be felt far beyond the relatively small volume of the nineteen systems he ruled.

His momentary twinge had been swallowed up in the deep, steady aching he'd endured for so long. Now he watched the stormclouds roll in, right on schedule. He nodded without realizing that he did. His engineers were expensive, but they were the best—and they asked no questions.

He knew he could trust them to keep their mouths shut, too. Good girls, even though Sonya's eyes had been brimming over when he'd given the order. Everyone knew his fondness for good, bracing weather. *At least*, he tweaked himself, *you're fond of it now that you don't have to campaign in it anymore!*

The black avalanche of clouds engulfed the sky, spreading and advancing. As he watched, it blotted out The Strewn, the gemwork open-star cluster that ornamented Epiphany's night as though a divine hand had sown seeds plucked from the First Light. Lightning danced among the clouds, green-white, followed by thunder; the air freshened with ozone.

On Old Earth—now shunned, mocked, having turned her back on her progeny—on Old Earth his age would be reckoned at ninety-three. In that time he'd been slave, murderer, outlaw, rebel, and conqueror. Hated and loved, he'd never quite believed that he deserved either.

Weir had brought along a small sound unit. Almost missing the control in his trembling, he put finger to touchpad. Music surged, sinister but lush and high-flown.

It was the overture to an opera written long ago on Transvaal, a world that Weir had been about to draw into his expanding sphere of influence. A thinly disguised metaphorical tale sponsored by that planet's government, it had been composed by a young genius who'd unleashed his full powers. Weir was portrayed as a kind of Mephistopheles who was defeated in the course of the story.

But Weir took a perverse pleasure in the grand and undisguised majesty of the music, the unrestrainedness of it. The young composer had died in the final battle for his home planet. Weir's forces took over, doing away with the slave trade that had thrived there and executing most of the plutocrats who'd run the place.

He loved the music, though, and was amused by it. He was not as evil as he was often portrayed, he was convinced; nor was he as virtuous.

He longed to stand and stretch, fill his lungs with the charged air, but his body had long since failed him. Perhaps on one of the truly advanced worlds, one that had missed the dark age after the sundering of the old interstellar unity and the end of the Second Breath of humankind, he could have had more years of life. But the new techniques were unavailable within his jurisdiction, and he refused to leave it. That had left him infirm, wed to the sustaining machines.

Until tonight.

Still, he'd extended his influence, played his part in the great conflicts and struggles that had given birth to the Third Breath of the human race.

"The Third Breath!" It was a labor even to murmur the words, but a joy nonetheless. He loved their sound, he who ruled nineteen star systems and wore an owner's code tattooed into his skin, and a subdural implant that broadcast it.

The Third Breath, no longer being born but passionately alive. Change and growth and light; he welcomed them. *Strange attractors.* A habitual musing came to him as his thoughts wandered. *Strange attractors . . .*

When Weir realized he was no longer alone, he was half dreaming of a girl he'd known for a brief moment in his youth. Her brown hair, ringlets of it, with its highlights of gold, had flown in the wind of a landing field. Her eyes, black and deep, had reflected the glare of a binary stellar system and held everything else to themselves—at first.

They'd come to love one another. For nearly eighty years, he wondered what had become of her, and never, for all his efforts, had been able to find out.

Then, emerging from his reverie, he saw the figure. Many in Frostpile were waiting with him, waiting for death. This was one such.

He said wearily, "Please go. I want to be—"

"You've altered your last will and testament. Why?"

Although no more than the residual image of his onetime self, muddled with age and pain, Weir was instantly cautious. "It doesn't concern you. No one's business but my own."

The interloper's tone put danger in the air, like the lightning's ozone. "It might be everyone's business, Caspahr. An Earthman. A *Terran*! What have you bequeathed him? Why are you bringing him here?"

Weir looked up craftily. "You mean 'her,' don't you?"

The figure moved closer. The wind was cold now, the lightning flashes more frequent, the thunder louder. "The cunning hasn't left you, Caspahr." A right hand came up; a glittering pinbeam pistol was pointed at the old man. A left hand exhibited a medical styrette.

Weir almost laughed at those, but hid it; a near-century of experience had made it a reflex to keep his options and advantages hidden as long as possible. He'd been victorious so many times, and on such a scale, that people tended to forget his defeats. Weir never did.

"No," the intruder went on, "'he' is the correct pronoun. That much I know. What have you given him?"

The pain was growing in Weir again, and he felt a little dizzy. He grunted, shifting in his chair, then gasped with the passing torment of even so minor an effort. He'd been lucky to make it from his bed to the chair.

"You'll be there for the Willreading. You'll find out then," he wheezed.

With a rasp of exasperation, the other stepped closer, the styrette before him. "You'll tell me in any case."

"A memory release?" Weir allowed himself a hacking laugh, forcing it a bit. It devolved into a gargling cough, and the old man tasted blood. It wouldn't be long now.

"Ahh, I see," the dark figure breathed. An injection would be futile, producing only coma or death. The styrette disappeared, leaving the pinbeam. "But why Earth? *Why?*"

Weir shook his head, almost drunkenly. "Poor Old Terra. Why *not?*" He knew it was a feeble deception. Still wed to his machines, he'd have managed something better, but the music and the approaching thunder were too loud. He was nearly chattering with the cold, and racked with pain. It was growing difficult even to assemble a coherent thought.

I'm only an old man who wants to be left alone! he thought. But few things in his life had come easily, and he saw now that his death would not.

"I am engaged in locating his name now; I shall have it soon," his unwelcome visitor said. "What I don't understand is your purpose. You've always claimed to despise Earth."

"I hate the Earthservice. I've nothing but pity for Terra itself." He gathered the warm, salty blood in his mouth and spat; in the dark, his enemy didn't see the crimson. *Merciful Fates preserve you, Functionary Third Class Hobart Floyt!* Weir thought. "I wish Terra well."

But it might not come out well for Floyt, particularly if he were unaware that he had a dangerous enemy moving against him. Weir now regretted the lack of instrumentation in his old chair; no built-in alarms or commo, and the old man had purposely left his own comband behind. He began fumbling with the buttons of the player, shutting off the music, hoping to surreptitiously record something the other said. But the intruder impatiently took the instrument out of his hands, put it aside, and began adjusting the pistol. The storm was nearly upon them.

Of course. Weir couldn't simply be left; there was the

off chance he would live long enough to tell someone that there was an assassin in Frostpile. But the pistol, adjusted to very low power, maximum dispersal, and held close to Weir's failing heart, would fool any but the most exacting coroner, even if there were an autopsy.

Fighting from a corner, as he had so many times before, Weir coldly dismissed any chance of his own survival. Instead he concentrated on the need to leave evidence, somehow, that he hadn't met a natural end. His hand fell on the chair's lift control. The intruder yelled a curse, raised the gun.

The old chair hesitated a bit, rising. Weir waited for a bolt from the pinbeam, which hadn't yet been completely adjusted. A wound from the weapon would serve his purpose; so would the intruder's secreting of his body to conceal the evidence of a violent death. In either case, others would know that an investigation was in order, and that precautions must be taken to safeguard the Inheritors. The old man took the only course of action available to him.

The chair's hesitation gave Weir's foe a chance to leap forward, dropping the pinbeam, grappling. The chair slewed around under their weight. Old, long unused, it sank to kick up tangles of ribbon grass. Then the safeties cut in, and it stalled.

Weir's heart was fluttering in his chest like a dying bird. Blood ran from his nostrils and mouth. His head lolled, then wobbled half erect. His assailant had gathered up the handgun again but held fire, watching the old man.

Weir arched backward in sudden agony. A minute part of him was content that he'd provided as best he could for the well-being of his little realm of nineteen stellar systems. But he also thought, *Poor Hobart Floyt!*

He seemed to be watching a blinding white light, his torment retreating. Then he passed from life into death.

The intruder felt for a pulse and found none. Weir was slumped in his chair. The storm struck; rain falling in windblown sheets. Frostpile was a luminous white faerie city in the distance.

The assailant returned the player to Weir's lap, pondering. What could the inheritance left to an obscure Earther possibly be? *What machinations had Weir set in motion?*

CHAPTER 1

THE ROAD NOT TAKEN

THE YEARNING'S TOO BIG FOR THE LEARNING. HIS FATHER'S words came back to him as Alacrity Fitzhugh gazed down into the abyss. The cold, eternal solidity of the granite blocks around him and the Earth beneath him brought back that observation about the Third Breath of humankind.

Sol's light had already brightened the peak of Huyana Picchu, high above and to the left. Now it touched Machu Picchu itself, casting long, vapor-filtered rays among the broken walls of the ages-old Inca fortress city. Looking down, he saw mist breaking as it rose off the dark serpentine of the Urubamba River more than half a kilometer below him.

He inhaled it, a unique moment. Alacrity had overcome tremendous obstacles to make his way to Earth and secure permission to walk its land, to see its seas and skies. A time of decision was drawing near; he wanted to feel connected to something larger than himself, something kindred, while he pondered. No surprise, then, that the words should come back to him.

"The yearning's too big for the learning," his father and

captain had said. "Too big for measurement and too big for poetry. The wishes and dreams are always there, in most of the sentient species. But comes a time like this, when the dreams suddenly feel like they're within reach—then an upwelling comes, too big for the normal boundaries of life."

That seemed like poetry to Alacrity, and measurement, too, the thing his late father had said.

A fine, tenuous moisture, an evaporating cloud, was all around Machu Picchu, but it would be a clear day. Alacrity eagerly anticipated seeing the Andean snowcaps from this spot. The weather was being cooperative; now if only the damned groundlings would follow suit.

The site, in what had been Peru before the Terran Unification, was one of those he'd wanted most to visit, one of the oldest. There were few enough left, thanks to the Human-Srillan War.

Giza was radioactive glass; the Parthenon had been hit during the last, mutually catastrophic Srillan attack—what the Earthers called the Big Smear. Jerusalem was gone, Shih Huang-ti's tomb, Mecca, Bethlehem, and Dharmsala. The old religions were only historical oddities here.

Srillan military thinkers, like their human counterparts, tended to target population centers in that war. Aside from the people who'd been annihilated, most of Rome and its treasures had been vaporized, and New York with its newer but still precious history. Sian and Moscow, Brazilia and Sydney, the same. The attack was so suicidal that surviving, lower-rank Srillan officers, upon their surrender, had been unable to explain the actions of the High Command, all members of which were dead. The belated arrival of the Spican fleet had turned a Srillan Pyrrhic victory into an utter disaster, but the curtain had been rung down on the Second Breath of humankind.

Long ago. More than two hundred Terran years.

Now, the Hawking Effect was bringing sundered humanity together, along with the other sentient races. The upwelling mentioned by Alacrity's father had been building for nearly eighty years. People across human space were beginning to feel that they had a real opportunity to seize a place in history, power, glory, riches—some great destiny or perfect fulfillment.

And some of them might even be right.

Alacrity drew Terran air into his lungs, tasting its strangeness, feeling the immense weight and timelessness of the Inca-carved stone. Several of the sacred llamas meandered through the deserted site, stepping delicately, dipping long necks to graze and coming erect again warily. The fog rose toward the city's ruins to disappear in the light and growing warmth.

Alacrity was like any number of humans—though the Earthers would call him *alien*, he knew resentfully—who knew little more about their origins than that the human race had begun there, on that hard-luck, xenophobic little planet.

The thin air two and a half kilometers above sea level was chilly, making him want to cough. He was more accustomed to the richer atmosphere of a starship than to any other. It had been so in his family for generations.

In the eight days he'd spent crisscrossing the planet, Machu Picchu had brought him closest to something he'd been hoping for—a kinship with his species at large, the groping beginnings of understanding of his place in the scheme of things.

The Inca Trail lay behind him as well as before. Old when Terra's space age had begun in humanity's First Breath, it was still passable. He'd descended to Machu Picchu through the Inca Gate, down decayed and tilted stone steps. He planned to leave over Huyana Picchu.

Alacrity resettled the Earth-style shoulder bag that contained the few personal articles he'd brought with him, none of them of offworld origin. He wore clothes a Terran history buff would favor for the visit: serape, jacket and trousers of imitation llama and vicuña, and rope-soled sandals.

Under the serape, though, he wore a hooded shirt, the hood pulled up. A pair of polarized wraparound glasses covered his eyes as well; he was trying his best to pass as an Earther for very good reasons.

Now he set his foot on the first step toward the laborious, rather dangerous trail up Huyana Picchu. Behind him, a harsh voice called out in badly pronounced Interworld Tradeslang.

"You! *Alien!*"

The spell had been broken. Earth was no longer the place of racial origins; it was only a hostile, almost closed world. Alacrity pivoted slowly, so as to give no provocation. Earthers were quick—even avid—to take offense, resentful of outsiders.

An Earthservice Peaceguardian stood there, and from the looks of him, the blood of the region ran strong in him. In those rugged mountains, one of the last habitable wild places on the globe, a few people had managed to avoid mass housing, forced emigration, and cultural assimilation. But the Earthservice was still in control. The short, thickset, barrel-chested man wearing lieutenant's tabs on his shoulders looked very much the trained Peaceguardian, humorless and severe, his holstered weapon and other equipment gleaming from harness carriers. The brassard on his helmet shone.

The Peaceguardian stepped up to him, pointing a white-gloved finger. "You're the offworlder, Spacer-Guildsman Alacrity Fitzhugh."

Little point in denying the statement. The lieutenant was glancing now from Alacrity to a hand-held screen, undoubtedly comparing the offworlder's long, pale face to that of his visa registration ID. Alacrity gazed down at him from his lanky 197 centimeters. He answered as cooly as he could, "That's correct, officer," in clear Terranglish. "How may I be of service to you?"

The peacer glared up at him through his tinted helmet visor. Here in Machu Picchu no antioffworlder slogans flashed from holoprojectors or blared from PA systems. But the fortress was itself a reminder of a greatness gone by and of the fact that Earth was avoided by all but a few extra-terrestrials and derided by most.

Two more Peaceguardians appeared from behind massive stones. The lieutenant continued to address Alacrity in barbarously accented Tradeslang, ignoring the fact that they had Terranglish in common. "You're to leave here *now*. Your visa has been voided. You will return to the spaceport and leave Earth."

Alacrity responded carefully. He was only twenty-two Standard—Terran—years old, but he'd been through tight situations on dozens of worlds, and in between. He knew better than to show anger.

"Why? I've done nothing wrong. This has to be a mistake."

"Negative! Witnesses saw you at old sites. You climbed the stelae and broke off pieces. You poked around sacred places with instruments. You desecrated; you vandalized."

Alacrity did his best to keep his temper; if he lost it now, the feces would really hit the flywheel. But he couldn't stop himself from snapping, "That's not true!"

The cop only scowled harder. "The testimony has been sworn. You *will* leave." He pointed to the Urubamba, far below, where there was a tiny village and a tubeway station. "The next cartridge leaves in just over an hour," he growled. "Be on it."

Thinking, *How would you like a face-ectomy, you little shit heap?* Alacrity stared at the lieutenant. But one of the other peacers had his palm on the butt of his pistol, and his partner was hopefully fingering a pair of nunchaka; the offworlder didn't voice the proposal.

Alacrity was, of course, unarmed, and had no desire to have his skull cracked or a kneecap burned off. The spacer spoke with the self-restraint he'd learned over a relatively short but singularly eventful life as a breakabout—a star rover. High movers, those who followed his trade were sometimes called, or go-bloods.

"There was no desecration. Earthservice visa briefings warned against it. I complied."

"The witnesses gave testimony."

Lines appeared around Alacrity's mouth. "What witnesses? I want to speak to them."

The lieutenant spat at Alacrity's feet, missing by millimeters. "You see no one. You go back to the spaceport and leave Earth soonest." One of his subordinates sniggered.

"Do you have any idea what that visa cost me? In time and money and effort?"

Visas *had* to be available, at least theoretically, to keep up appearances. Even Terra had no desire to be branded a closed world. But obtaining one had been an expensive, frustrating ordeal, and time-consuming into the bargain. Still, drawn by tales of Old Earth and the urge to tour humanity's Homeworld, the breakabout had persevered when other offworlders had scoffed and Earthservice functionaries and bureaucrats had rebuffed him.

Perhaps that had had something to do with his upbringing, son of two starship officers, grandson of another, born in transit, with no birthworld. But his patience with the delay and the bleak life of the closely guarded spaceport enclave had been nearly exhausted when, almost miraculously, the visa had been granted.

Roaming the planet, he'd been alternately exhilarated and disillusioned, proud and ashamed, puzzled and thrilled by revelation. *Only to come to this! Never to see the Forbidden City, the Serengeti, or Angkor Wat! Or the remains of an evolutionary climb millions of years long.*

He sighed. "At least let me send for an aircar. It'll be faster than the tubeway; I'll be gone that much sooner."

The peacer's smirk was ugly. "You go by cartridge! Who d'you think you are, an Alpha Bureaucrat? Bad enough you'll ride *beneath* our Earth; you won't foul her skies!"

Transportation up and down the mountain was usually provided by a bucket railcar. But with malicious satisfaction, the attendant told Alacrity that line wasn't in operation, even though the breakabout had seen it running only a half hour earlier.

Nothing for it but to plod down the unpaved switchback road on foot. He balanced his shoulder bag from long practice, and panted along in the thin air. The Peaceguardians, used to the road, followed without discomfort. The single vehicle that passed, a surface-effect truck, sped downhill in a swirl of dust. Alacrity halfheartedly tried to flag it down; the driver and his assistant showed white, hating smiles as they left him in their wake.

Alacrity coughed and spat out dust, then resumed trudging. The peacers spoke among themselves, laughing coarsely at jokes shared in some language Alacrity didn't understand.

The young offworlder left off his silent cursing of Terrans and his own luck and began worrying about his dilemma. He could see little to do except obey the peacers; there was no other authority to which he could appeal at the moment. The truckers' reaction proved that word of the allegations against him had already spread. He began to feel better about the cops' presence.

He glanced at the proteus on his wrist. He'd been moving as quickly as he could; now he began to slow, not wanting to spend more time than necessary in the village.

He gradually descended toward the little bubble of the tubeway station, in the middle of the collection of angular, pressformed buildings that were the quarters of the locals. The station faced a plaza layered with windblown dust and debris. It was still murky down there.

A crowd had gathered, twenty people or so. Not many showed the strong racial characteristics the lieutenant did. Centuries of interbreeding and acculturation, emigration and immigration had seen to that. The majority of the men and women there might have been from any broad mixture of Terran genes.

Many of them were dressed in clothing like Alacrity's, modern reproductions of attire from the past, a custom encouraged by Earthservice. Others wore coveralls, worksuits, or the uniforms of the guide staff. Nudging one another and pointing up toward him, they watched the breakabout approach and muttered among themselves. None displayed weapons as such, but many had tools or equipment that would serve nicely: torque bars, energy probes, and heavy spanners. Alacrity approached them slowly.

Over the smooth white bubble of the tubeway station a luminous Earthservice Infoprop displayer flashed: EARTH IS OUR MOTHER—TERRA FOR TERRANS. Another, smaller displayer registered two minutes until the next cartridge.

The breakabout stopped and turned to the Peaceguardians. They were wandering away in different directions; the crowd showed no such inclination. Alacrity called out to the lieutenant, but the man entered the peacers' little HQ-barracks building and the door segments spiraled in, shuttering.

Alacrity took a step toward it, then stopped. He was unlikely to find any help there, and the displayer now read less than one minute to cartridge arrival. Settling his bag, preparing himself, he strode toward the station, unarmed but not defenseless.

The crowd gave way before him, and his hopes rose; he could see through the station's viewpanes that the tiny waiting area was unoccupied, as was the platform beyond. He willed himself not to break into a sprint.

But as he was about to step through the station's entrance,

the displayer changed to read: NEXT CARTRIDGE DUE IN 1 HOUR 00 MINUTES.

Alacrity whirled instantly, without bothering to wonder how they'd rigged the displayer. The crowd was ringing him in. No cops were in sight.

An old woman came forward, her face gaunt and loose-skinned—smoothing collagen treatments were not for the Terran masses—but her eyes vigorous with hatred. As the lieutenant had, she spat at him, a pitifully weak attempt, the spittle barely clearing her lips. Somewhere behind her, a man yelled in vehement Terranglish, "You're not getting away that easily, *alien!*"

There were snarls of agreement, an unintelligible shout or two. Alacrity put his shoulders up against the wall of the station. On the peacers' HQ a displayer now read: TEMPORARILY UNMANNED—USE EMERGENCY COM-BOX. He wasn't surprised to see that the security monitors were dimmed and motionless, deactivated.

A snarley-ball sailed out of the crowd in his direction, as did a bottle. The bottle was no trouble to dodge; he'd been star-trained. But the snarley-ball, used by naturalists and hunters on many worlds to snare small game, exploded into a puff-sphere of wavering, sticky streamers.

Alacrity ducked as the blossoming, translucent strands drifted toward him, scooped up the fallen bottle, and underhanded it into the snarley-ball. Attracted by microfields, the adhesive streamers gathered around, enfolding it. The snarley-ball looked like a feeding anemone.

The cloud of strands was carried to the dust by the weight of the bottle, and Alacrity kept clear of it, as did the crowd, but still it hemmed him in.

They taunted and jeered him in the same language the peacers had used. He evaluated his chances of charging back up the road or plunging into the undergrowth, but decided that neither plan held much promise. The locals

were used to the terrain and altitude. And even if they didn't
run him down, he had nowhere to go.

So he stood erect, facing them. They froze, suspicious,
hands curled into claws or balled fists, or clutching make-
shift weapons. He swung his gaze around the arc of angry
faces.

"I've done nothing wrong. Why would I want to come
light-years and light-years just to desecrate your sacred
places? And alone, and unarmed? Does that make sense to
anybody here?"

They'd heard him out, but showed no belief or inclination
to listen further. The tallest among them, a burly man with
thinning, sandy hair, hefting an excavator in two huge hands,
took a step toward him. Alacrity reconsidered running for
it. He'd been in quite a number of hand-to-hand combats,
had lost what he considered to be far too many of them,
and hated the possibility of having that happen again.

The Earther gave an upswing of his head, pointing at the
breakabout with his chin, to address him. "We have heard
from . . . we've heard what you did. We *know*."

"Someone misled you. Who told you these lies?"

"*You're* the liar, *alien*!" the man grated.

"Alien? *Alien?*" Alacrity roared, as much for fury at the
unbelievable stupidity of the word as in reaction to the
danger of the moment. "I'm as human as you are! I paid a
small fortune for this jaunt; I fought your hidebound Earthservice for weeks for my visa! Who would do that just to
desecrate *his own ancestors' birthworld?*"

They still showed him their resentment and malice, but
held back from attacking. He took a step away from the
wall, then another. It was like being in the eye of a hurricane,
and for a moment the breakabout and many others there
thought that violence had been averted. Then a stone was
hurled by someone to his left. Alacrity caught the forward
sweep of the thrower's arm, just at the edge of his peripheral
vision.

He threw himself sideways, and the missile glanced off the station. A wiry, crazed-looking Earther darted toward him and clawed at the breakabout's wraparound glasses. They went flying as Alacrity shoved the man away. His burning glare held the others at bay. "You blind, idiotic damned Earthers!"

A low sound of shock and amazement went through them; he realized that they could see his eyes.

The words were muttered: *alien*; *offworlder*. He gazed at them with wide, oblique eyes, their huge irises an unearthly, radiant yellow streaked with red and black. *"Mutant!"* he heard. *"Freak!"*

Then they were closing in on him. The excavator raised, the tall man advanced. "Earth is for *humans*!" he said harshly. The implement hissed through the air.

Alacrity bobbed, leaning away. The Terran's weight and the momentum of the swing carried him off balance; Alacrity helped him along with a shove.

Terran hatred of non-Earthers had been nurtured by Earthservice psychprop and by the hardships and deprivations of the two centuries following the Human-Srillan War. Earth, which had only remained livable by accepting the charity of other worlds, was humiliated by their condescension. And so the Homeworld had withdrawn into galled isolationism and brooding nostalgia for its vanished glories.

With an assortment of shrieks, gnashing of teeth, and various obscenities, the crowd closed in on Alacrity, fanning out to forestall his escape. They inched toward the breakabout warily, having seen that he was quick.

Alacrity straightened all at once and, ripping open a compartment in his bag, jammed his hand in, groping. He plucked out a metallic object, a thing of tarnished metal with a tubular barrel and bell-like mouth.

"All right, just get back," he ordered menacingly, "or I'll blow the whole sad lot of you into dog fodder, or whatever the phrase is!"

They wavered, intimidated by his tone and manner, and the lethal, dull shine of the object he held. But the wiry man yelled, "They told us he wouldn't be armed! It's a trick!" and whipped a jimbo-wrench at the offworlder, who managed to evade it. Alacrity's hand squeezed convulsively on the object it held, which filled the air with a soulful honk!

Alacrity smiled in a sickly fashion, lowering the antique automobile horn he'd managed to persuade an old woman on Pitcairn Island to sell to him. He'd hoped to be able to take it offworld with him. The wiry man charged Alacrity, as did his neighbors, bashing and belaboring the offworlder. Many of them got in one another's way, and one even became entangled in the strands of the fallen snarley-ball.

The remainder, though, swung and kicked at him, reaching for handholds, dragging at him. He bucked and spun, hammered and kicked, trying to plunge free. One of the villagers landed a blow squarely to his back, a young woman of considerable beauty with heavy, blue-black hair and high cheekbones. She wielded a forced-air excavating tube with some skill. He lurched, nearly falling.

Two more tried to pile on to bring him down. They only succeeded in pulling away his shoulder bag and serape and ripping down Alacrity's hood.

Seeing his hair, some of them cried out in surprise and even greater wrath. It was long and thick, growing in slate-gray waves, shot through with silver strands. It grew halfway down his spine, like a mane. The mob took it as further proof of his nonhumaness, and redoubled its zeal.

The wiry man ran at him again. Alacrity somehow freed a hand to keep the fellow at bay with a fistful of his own uniform. Fumbling, the Terran, brought up a force-probe, its tip crackling with a full charge. The breakabout chopped at the wrist holding it, missed, and spun as he was borne to the ground by the combined weight and efforts of the Earthers. The writhing mass turned as it went down; the force-probe spat and sizzled as it struck the left side of a tall, sandy-haired man.

He screamed as the probe flared and blazed. Alacrity struck the plaza's surface with a thud, but heard the sounds. Then a fist struck his cheek a glancing blow, and another skimmed by his right ear. Boots, sandals, and bare feet thumped at him as he did his best to protect himself. People threw themselves across his legs to immobilize him, and then he heard the faraway chirpers of the Peaceguardians jarring the air.

The wiry man was still trying to reach Alacrity's chest with the force-probe, but the breakabout yanked a hand free and slammed the heel of it up under his chin, then chopped at his throat. As the Earther fell aside, the chop missed and the black-haired woman came into view again, raising her forced-air tube high. The peacers' chirpers were nearer, sounding at ear-splitting intensity.

Alacrity somehow deflected the woman's blow, and she lost her footing, toppling toward him. Through the gap in the melee, he saw for an instant part of the station's displayer: TERRA FOR TERRANS. These less-than-animals were welcome to it, as far as Alacrity was concerned.

When the young woman clawed at his face, he gripped her to him in a clumsy headlock, causing her neighbors to relent in their attack, fearful of hitting her. He took the opportunity to knee the wiry man in the jaw.

Then, as if by divine intervention, the peacers were at the outskirts of the brawl, breaking it up, pulling people away. But before they could work their way in to Alacrity, a youth, practically a boy, brought a millennia-old Incan stone pestle, a smooth stub of rock, down on the breakabout's head.

CHAPTER 2

THE CHOSEN

THE MESSAGE HAD BEEN ETCHED INTO A ROCK AT THE SIDE of the pressbounded roadway by some anonymous cyclist now generations dead: 2 KM UPGRADE.

Sweating over the randonneur handlebars, Floyt didn't let it deceive him; he'd pedaled the route before and knew that the warning was nearly a full kilometer shy of the mark. An error or a bit of mischief by one of the ancients; that, or the lay of the land had been changed when the Srillans brought havoc to Terra in their final raid, two hundred years before.

Lowering his head, Floyt settled into a practiced, determined cadence, the muscles of his legs working easily even though he was tired from a long afternoon's tour. It was the first time he'd gotten to do any cycling in two months.

Having slept later than intended on his precious rec-day, he'd expected to find only tired, leftover bikes remaining at the Earthservice Recreation Bureau substation. Not at all interested in the sport, he'd forgotten that everyone who could get to a screen or projector was watching the Earth-wide Soccer Cup game (Antarctica vs. Truk Islands, a grudge match).

So Floyt had been able to check out a gleaming new machine, a true joyride; he'd changed from his planned route, an easy one, to a challenging afternoon's travel.

The incline grew more pronounced and his breathing harder as he churned up the hill. The road was better than most, uncracked and therefore uncluttered by weeds or grass, even though rural highways received no maintenance from Earthservice. Little surface travel took place between population centers, except for a few hikers and cyclists, amateur naturalists, and similar eccentrics.

Floyt was just over 175 centimeters tall, rather stocky, with green eyes and the powerful legs of a lifelong bicyclist. He had close-trimmed brown hair and beard, with a good deal of gray in both. He wore cycling shoes, shorts, and singlet, with safety helmet and fingerless gloves. He was not known for standing out in a crowd.

The perspiration seeped down from his sweatband, into the scabs covering the scrapes on his cheek and temple put there by Arlo Mote during a party two days earlier. Mote worked in the same data management center with Balensa, Floyt's contracted spouse—Floyt preferred the ancient term "wife," but it was very much out of vogue just then—and was a Hemingway revivicist, the most ardent and overbearing Floyt had ever met.

Floyt's leg muscles began to complain at the workout he was giving them, but he persisted. Cycling was the only real exercise he got, his only chance to push his body to its limits and get in some solitary thinking time. He dug in, pressing down on a pedal with one foot, lifting against a toe clip with the other, then reversing the procedure. Though he'd resolved not to think about it, his mind strayed back to the fight two days ago at the data center's semiannual rapport/morale mixer. Balensa had insisted that Floyt accompany her to what had actually started out as a rather

modest affair. Nevertheless, Arlo Mote and a few other
buffs had come costumed as their chosen personae, a not
uncommon practice on preterist Earth.

Only a few light intoxicants were served; no limited-use
drugs or severe mood-alterers. Still, Mote had somehow
contrived to become belligerently drunk. Dressed in ersatz
safari clothing, he'd paid elaborate attention to Balensa,
quoting Papa's writings at some length, with a good deal
of slurring, as though they were his own.

Mote lived in a role-playing commune centered on the
"Lost Generation" between the first two world wars. The
commune provided activities and facilities to the Earthservice Rec Bureau on a part-time basis; Mote was involved
in many of the dramatic reenactments and roundtables, and
Floyt supposed that that gave the man a certain romantic
patina in the workplace. Balensa herself had been raised in
an extended-family/academic-group concentrating on the
Italian Renaissance; occasionally she alluded to the great
passion in her soul.

Floyt had already concluded that some of it had been
vented in Mote's direction but, in his easygoing way, made
no issue of it. Overreaction in such a situation was frowned
upon by Terran society in general and Earthservice psych-
counselors and Peaceguardians in particular. Floyt was surprised at the intensity of the resentment he'd had to suppress,
though.

But at length even the good manners and restraint required
by the close quarters in which most Terrans lived had worn
thin. Objecting to Mote's pawing of Balensa, Floyt reflected
that it was too bad he couldn't mail the ersatz Hemingway
a gun, so that the man could consummate his impersonation
by blowing his brains out.

Coming up the long hill toward the crest, legs trembling,
Floyt felt satisfaction in the fatigue he'd worked up, but the
memory of the fight still made him wince.

Mote had further goaded him with barely veiled insults

to his avocation, the tracing of genealogies. More, the man had provoked him with what was ostensibly a manly embrace, but in reality a humiliating mauling, and everyone there understood it.

Mote's revivicism had led him into antisocial behavior; it also sparked, in some fashion, a like response from the usually mild-mannered Floyt. It was as if some Terran ancient out of his genealogies were reacting, rather than Floyt himself.

He'd shoved Mote away hard, his first violent act since the age of twelve, nearly thirty years before. The fight had then become inevitable.

Arlo Mote had brought his cherished boxing gloves with him, of course; he was wont to tote them about slung casually over his shoulder, since displaying an elephant gun was something the Peaceguardians wouldn't permit. He and his little circle of hangers-on occasionally put on bouts at the role-playing commune, though the word was that none of them was a particularly good boxer.

Mote liked to joke that he was always hoping to run into a Max Eastman revivicist, for a decisive match; Floyt had always hoped that Mote would run afoul of a Jack Dempsey buff who'd play a leathersynth lullaby all over his face and skull.

The gloves being there, though, the crowd immediately began to clamor for a match. The idea alone was titillating because a fight unsanctioned and unsupervised by proper officials carried the heady intoxication of sin.

Floyt quickly found himself being laced into the clumsy, peculiar-feeling gloves as Arlo Mote stripped off his safari jacket, with its ammunition loops and dummy rifle rounds. Floyt stared at the avid faces and overbright eyes as the crowd formed a ring around them.

Only Balensa tried to stop the fight; she was obviously worried about both men. That stung Floyt, making him determined to go on with it.

Arlo Mote had naturally dabbled in boxing. Most people present had only a vague idea of the rules, gleaned from centuries-old motion pictures and stories. Floyt began to tremble, but not simply from fear of being injured. He hadn't grown up in a role-playing commune or historical preserve, or in an upper-bureaucrats' enclave. He'd been raised in a mass-dwelling complex, back in the days before crèche indoctrination and improved surveillance techniques had made Terran society quite so tranquil.

He'd run the great corridors in a roaming troupe, as had so many children, riding the transways and playing forbidden, sometimes lethal games in the chuteshafts. As the gloves were being laced on, he remembered the last time he'd been involved in violence.

A boy from another troupe had insulted a girl in the one with which Floyt roamed as a peripheral. Floyt's troupe caught up with the boy when he was alone. Floyt, the youngest, hadn't done much of the stomping and rib-kicking, sick with it even while it was going on. He'd quit the troupe and the corridors, turning inward.

Then the memory passed, and Mote was coming at him. But the revivicist had made a mistake; by unconscious identification with his idol or by natural disposition, he'd drunk far too much for a man in a boxing match.

Floyt had managed to block or evade most of Mote's punches and even land a few of his own. The gloves were thumbless, pillowlike, the only sort Earthservice would approve; little damage had been done on either side.

Then Mote must have remembered a little something from Hemingway's life; using his greater weight, he bulldozed Floyt into a corner and scraped the eyelets and laces of his glove across the smaller man's face, trying for his eyes.

Floyt barely saved himself by burrowing his head against Mote's slick, gray-haired chest. The eyelets had abraded and lacerated his cheek and temple, but he scarcely felt the pain or heard the screaming, shrieking workers. He did recall, later, hearing Balensa crying out to Mote, begging him to stop.

Now Floyt fingered the wounds; with accelerated healing treatments, the scabs were already peeling away.

It would've been poetic justice to beat Mote at his own game somehow, like one of the ancients in the pugilistic fantasies of the motion picture era. But there'd been no poetry that day, and Floyt had only a limited notion as to how to go about such a feat. Suddenly furious, he'd flung his arms around the barrel torso and brought his knee up sharply.

Onlookers went berserk, some in an almost sexual frenzy, others looking ill. A few had only seen Floyt break the rules, though most knew that Mote had done so first. One or two thought that what they'd seen *were* the rules.

But it was to the groaning, curled-up Arlo Mote that Balensa rushed. Floyt recognized then that he'd brought an end to his spousal contract in the most atavistic and inane way he could possibly have imagined.

The sun was westering beautifully, a red ball among glorious orange and purple clouds, as he came to a stop at the crest of the hill, drawing deep breaths and watching.

He glanced for a moment to his bare wrist. He'd left his accessor at home so that no one could contact him. That act of omission might result in his being charged with a misdemeanor if Earthservice became aware of it and decided that he had no viable excuse for taking himself out of communication. He didn't care; he didn't want to receive Balensa's contract termination decree over an accessor.

He soon had his wind back, and the evening breeze began to feel chilly. Earthservice Functionary 3rd Class Hobart Floyt pushed off, cruising downhill toward the Atlantic Urbanplex and home. Where beforetimes the click-song of the coasting bicycle had lifted his heart and charged his spirit with a wild yet serene freedom, that day it gave him no joy; Balensa would be waiting at home with the decree.

He asked himself repeatedly what the point of living was.

Floyt reluctantly handed in the beautiful bicycle. Dawdling, he took a leisurely cleanup at the Rec Bureau substation before changing into rec-day attire. Though Balensa was—had been—after him constantly to dress as Benvenuto Cellini, he preferred a comfortable old Edwardian suit.

The passenger transways and chuteshafts were unusually empty; he supposed that postgame celebrations were still in progress. Truk had trounced Antarctica.

For the first time he wondered who'd be required to move out of the apt. Maybe the Housing Division would require both spouses to vacate; the apt was large for the quarters allotment of unattached functionary thirds. The prospect of once again commuting between a bachelor's cubicle and his workplace was so depressing that Floyt began thinking about applying for implant medication.

The media-environment dwellings of Earth's golden age were gone forever, he knew, but he often longed for the lost days when work could be done at home. Earthservice rationales spoke of the efficiency of centralization, and of socialization, but many nursed the unspoken suspicion that other reasons were the true concern. Authority and its trappings had to be displayed, and served.

Floyt, immersed in these thoughts, almost passed her by without a sideways glance.

"Excuse me, sir? Citizen?"

She was standing near the cul-de-sac off a chuteshaft alcove where the large urbanplex map was located. She had a lost look about her and held a scrap of paper.

The woman was a true heartpulse, taller than most men, tall as an offworlder, with coppery skin and swirling black hair in an arrangement that looked windblown yet artful.

She wore sheer beige body swathings, glint anklets, minimal soleskins, and a high choker of tourmalines.

He realized that he was gawking. After some initial fumbling, he got out, "Yes? *Me?*"

It could be no one else; no other pedestrians were nearby.

"I'm more than a little turned around, I'm afraid. If you wouldn't mind..." She gestured vaguely at the map cul-de-sac.

"Of course."

Floyt felt an involuntary tingle of excitement as he entered the cul-de-sac with her. The map niches in the older plexes were rather secluded; he himself had kissed a girl or two in them as a young man.

He got a grip on himself. She simply wanted directions. No doubt a woman so attractive was tired of flirtation, especially from middle-aged men who were out of practice. *Don't make a fool of yourself, Hobart!*

Still, the exotic scent she wore made him giddy as he accepted the scrap of paper. After she'd thanked him, his gaze stayed on hers a half second too long, while he admired her clear green eyes and high-arched brows and full, glistening lips. He felt vaguely unfaithful until he remembered that his marriage was about to be terminated.

He bent to the map. She was standing behind him; he couldn't stop himself from breathing deeply, inhaling her perfume. He was certain that she was an actress or dancer.

He pointed to the map. "You see, we're right here. It's easy to get turned around in those lower interchanges, I know."

He referred to the paper, eyes flickering for an instant's glimpse of long, beautifully formed legs that were bewitchingly posed. His glance returned to the map.

"Now, you take a right turn here at the thighs, and then you—" He gasped in horror at his slip, turning instantly to apologize. It saved him. She had a medical styrette in her hand, poised to thrust home. She was so surprised by his sudden whirl, though, that she hesitated for a critical instant.

Gorgeous, statuesque women do not lure strangers into out-of-the-way places to give them flu shots! He knew instantly that he was in danger, probably deadly danger. The Hobart Floyt who reacted to it was some entity of reflex with whom the conscious man was quite unacquainted. He threw himself back flat against the map and the styrette just missed his shoulder.

Before she could recover, he shouldered past her, stumbling clear. She came after him again. He pulled over a recycling can, bouncing it into her path and scattering trash. She struck her shin on it, falling, but she'd nearly cornered him.

He shouted for help as, evidently used to this sort of thing, she sprang up to cut off his escape. She didn't look unnerved by his yelling.

"Stop! Get back!" he hollered as they maneuvered, he to evade or defend, she to close. "What're you doing? You've confused me with someone else!"

"Come here, you damn groundling!" she said under her breath. He had no time to spare for being flabbergasted that she was an offworlder. She was the first he'd ever seen in person.

A crumpled beverage cup bearing Antarctica's colors had left a puddle on the ground, and Floyt faked left, toward it. Countering him, the woman stepped into the spilled drink; her soleskinned foot slid.

In the instant it took her to regain her balance, Floyt dodged right, for the opening she'd left, at the same time snatching up the waste can and throwing it. She blocked, but the can struck the styrette, triggering it. A narrow jet of liquid *puff*ed into the air.

He couldn't make a break for it; if she brought him down from behind, she'd finish him.

Just then the chuteshaft opened, discharging a boisterous

party of soccer fans. The woman knew when to cut her losses; she backed out of combat range and dashed from the cul-de-sac.

By the time Floyt cautiously rounded the corner, she was gone from sight and the corridor was filling with rollicking sports buffs. There were no Peaceguardians to be seen. The best thing to do, he concluded, was return to his apt before anything else happened. He had to take a last look at the scattered trash and the beverage slick to convince himself that it had really happened.

She must've *mistaken me for somebody else*, he said to himself. There just wasn't any other explanation.

CHAPTER 3

PAROLED TO THE STARS

ALACRITY FITZHUGH HAD LOST CONSCIOUSNESS WITH NO expectation of waking up, but he opened filmed-over eyes and looked out at a distinctly clinical room.

He groaned, fighting down nausea, completely disoriented. He blinked. His harsh breathing hissed between locked teeth. The nausea passed after a few moments, and he realized that he didn't feel too terrible aside from the wooziness; he had the instinctive sensation that considerable time had passed.

Waking up at all was against the odds, he decided, and it would have been in a detention cell or prison treatment center, if anywhere, that he'd have expected to find himself.

This place, though, was neither. It reminded him more of a Srillan hospital he'd been in once while recovering and awaiting a hearing after a crash, some of the most civilized hospitality he'd ever received. He was acquitted, rightly, of all charges, but found out later that if he'd been judged guilty, the death sentence would've been carried out by the same concealed equipment that had ministered to him so faithfully.

The recollection made him uneasy. He glanced around. An abundance of medical apparatus was apparent in the room, but it was all tucked into wall nooks or folded back into floor or ceiling, inoperative. His was the only bed.

He could see no windows or viewpanels in the blue-white, deathly silent place, and no ventilation grills, though the air seemed fresh enough. He was under no restraint, and the single door was unguarded, at least on the inside. Floor, walls, and ceiling radiated soft light, sufficient without being too bright.

He sat up, moving his arms and legs experimentally, exploring his ribs and head. No fractures, no concussions— not even a bruise. Not surprising in a modern medical facility, but he was on Terra—or anyhow, that was the last place he remembered being.

A light sheet covered him, and he was naked. He'd slept in grav-bunks, flotation hammocks, and suspension fields, but this arrangement was the sort he tended to prefer. He tried to piece together the last things he could recall. The fight came back vividly; he felt quite lucid.

The door slid open. Alacrity looked up, expecting Peace-guardians, Earthservice bureaucrats, medical personnel, or investigators. Instead, a man of medium height and rather athletic build entered; he was tanned and handsome in the fashion that Earthers still referred to as Mediterranean. His hair was dark and straight; the ends of his carefully trimmed mustache curled around his mouth.

He was dressed all in carefully tailored black, looking distinguished rather than dashing: a billowing shirt with long, ruffled cuffs, high collar with ruff, tapered trousers, and gleaming shoes. He also wore a sleeveless manteau, open at the front, and a satiny sash wound around his flat, slender midsection.

The man looked to be in vigorous middle age. His eyes were light brown; the breakabout thought them to be direct and extremely observant. He stopped near the foot of the bed. When he spoke, it was in an unhurried, full voice, in formal, well-accented Terranglish.

"You're in an Earthservice Special Clinic, Alacrity. You suffered concussion, multiple contusions, and shock, along with various fractures, sprains, minor wounds, and blood loss, but all of that's been mended, or nearly so. It's fourteen-thirty hours or so, local time, Alacrity. Do you mind if I use your first name, or would you prefer 'Guildsman' or 'Master Fitzhugh'?"

"N-no. No. That's fine." Alacrity tried to rouse his thinking equipment and get a grip on things. His treatment and recovery indicated impressive medical resources, as good as any he could recall having seen. The kind available to the select few, or to no one at all, on most worlds.

The man in black had anticipated most of his initial questions; Alacrity waited.

His visitor went on, "I am Citizen Ash. Earth's executioner."

Alacrity had heard about the man from offworlders who'd visited Terra and from the few Earthers who'd been willing to talk to him. And some mention of the office had been made in the meager guides and pamphlets issued by Earthservice.

Trying not to show his shock, Alacrity remarked, "Very fitting name." Dust to dust. He was too numb to feel afraid.

Ash nodded. "But it's also a type of tree once believed to be a wellspring of life."

Alacrity wondered how many times Ash had pointed that out to people. He looked the executioner over. The man didn't appear to be the type to come into the room unprotected, even though the breakabout could see no weapons or defensive devices on him. Escape didn't strike Alacrity as likely.

A discrepancy occurred to him. Why would the Earthservice spend so much time, effort, and technology on the recovery of an offworlder only to execute him? Perhaps it was another obscure Terran perversion.

"I heard some of your psychprop babble: 'Earth has few capital crimes in these enlightened days.'"

"Do us both a favor and stop showing off," Citizen Ash bade Alacrity as he sat on the foot of the bed.

Terra *had* reduced its crime rate drastically over the centuries, by behavioral engineering and drastic punishments, enlightened alternatives and others not so enlightened—and by ruthless enforcement. Few serious crimes were committed on the Homeworld, and only a minuscule number of those were committed by people who could not or would not be dealt with in some fashion that Earthservice was willing to regard as rehabilitation—even if the process turned the perpetrator into a mildly retarded houseplant.

But for those very few occasions when the law demanded death, Terran society met its obligation in the person of Citizen Ash. The executioner was virtually autonomous within Earthservice; he was responsible for final case review and actual carrying out of sentence. Headsman, hangman, pusher of the button, or whatever—Alacrity wasn't even sure how the man actually performed his office.

But the breakabout did know that the position carried with it powers of investigator, detective, defense and prosecution, judge, jury, and appeals court, with extraordinary powers reserved to it alone. Even Alpha Bureaucrats showed respect for—and at times fear of—the courtly, courteous man. Ash had met his primary obligation many times during his long tenure.

Suddenly Alacrity remembered the tall man's final scream as the force-probe had found him.

"I didn't kill that man," the breakabout said softly, without undue drama; he assumed Ash had heard every variation on the not-guilty plea.

The Terran made a fist, cocked out the knuckle of his

index finger, and put the side of it to his pursed lips, staring into space for a moment. Alacrity waited.

At length the other said, "It is a little over seventy-nine hours since the killing occurred, Alacrity; sentence was passed just over two hours ago. I would not be here if the case were an open-and-shut matter."

Alacrity jackknifed upright in bed. Ash never even flinched; he appeared to have no misgivings about being in danger. It reinforced Alacrity's conviction that the executioner was well protected from any violence.

"Then what . . ." Alacrity made himself defer to this pensive grim reaper.

Ash smiled, impressed. "The depositions and testimony of those present and of the Peaceguardians all agree, as does the deathbed testimony of the deceased."

"Deathbed testimony? He was dead before the fight was over. He *had* to be; I heard him when—"

"You've been found guilty of murder, young man."

"I had no trial!"

"You've had all the trial to which an offworlder is entitled under Earthservice legislation."

Alacrity now gathered himself, hidden defenses or no, for a leap at Earth's executioner, to die in a scatterbeam or blaze-field rather than heave out his life in a gasbooth or drool away his last moments under lethal medication.

Ash held up a palm to him before he could, saying, "However, *I* am not satisfied that you're guilty."

When he realized how much he would have to relax, to uncoil, in order to look unthreatening, Alacrity could only give the executioner an abashed shrug.

Ash went on quietly, "I am intervening in your case. The court did not simply rush to judgment; it broke all previous speed records. I find that for some reason no surveillance monitor records were made of events in the plaza that morning. Moreover, only one witness claimed to have seen you actually use the force-probe. And the instrument itself, incidentally, had been stolen from an excavation site in the fortress ruins."

He held up an imager that depicted the wiry little man who'd tried to murder Alacrity and killed his fellow Terran instead. Alacrity yelped, "That's him! That's the dungbug who—"

"This man, too, is dead. Shortly after recording his testimony he fell from one of the trails on Huyana Picchu." Ash tucked the imager away. "I'm told such things are known to happen there."

"Will you listen to what I'm trying to—"

"Offworlder, you are an imbecile!"

Ash had risen to his feet, so angry that Alacrity thought for a moment that the executioner was going to hit him. The breakabout shut up; it struck him as a wise thing to do.

"Don't you think I can see that it's too pat?" the Terran continued in a more subdued voice. "And you, you young jackanapes, walked right into it. But something went wrong. I don't believe that there was supposed to be a death that day."

He sat again, leaning toward the breakabout. "But the case, as such, is unassailable, at least in any length of time to be of meaningful help to you."

"Then what're you doing here? Letting me pick how I go out?"

The handsome face grew contorted and blood-dark in an instant, the voice raspy with anger. "If you're so inclined." He rose and paced, to turn his eyes away from the offworlder.

"Other options are available," he continued over his shoulder. "Radical behavior modification, permanent imprisonment under Earthservice utilization, and so forth. But the guilty party has the right of refusal."

He turned back. "Would a star-man choose those?"

Alacrity considered. A forebrain shampoo, or life at hard

labor or as a laboratory animal on a blighted, hate-ridden little planet, with no hope of pardon or parole?

"I suppose you're . . ." Alacrity's head snapped up. "Wait a second. You didn't come here just to tell me this, and you didn't come here because you like me or because you know I was framed. You came here because unless something's done, *you're the one who's gonna have to push the button!*"

He could see that he'd hit dead center. Earth's executioner had never shirked his duty, but neither had he ever been placed in a dilemma like the present one. "Stop playing with me and tell me the rest, or by God in the Void, you'll either have to kill me or quit your office!"

Ash's face colored in unspeakable wrath, then cleared as suddenly, and he gave a bark of laughter. "New Earthservice legislation allows me—us!—a third way. You would be obliged to leave Terra. An Earthservice department, Alacrity—our largest—keeps track of the planet's every resource, including those offworld. Some of those offworld resources can be claimed by Terrans, for the benefit of all, but Earthers no longer have the knack for travel among the stars. They often come to grief, even within the solar system."

Alacrity acknowledged that with a nod. The risks were high, even for veteran breakabouts.

"We are initiating a new project, Project Shepherd," Ash continued, "to recruit qualified guide-escorts. I can commute your sentence. One mission for Project Shepherd, a round-trip, and you're quits with us."

"Only one?" Alacrity blurted before he could stop himself.

Ash gave his thin smile again. "In this case, *I* make the determination as to how many missions are to be required of you. The minimum, of course, is one. If you qualify, that is."

Alacrity switched from shocked relief to indignation.

"*Qualify?* To nursemaid an *Earther*?—no offense. Look, I realize that you don't know much about me, but I've been—"

"Indeed?" Ash broke in. "'Fitzhugh, Alacrity'—let's just skip the aliases, shall we?"

That was fine with Alacrity. Ash resumed. "'Birthplace unknown. Variously claimed or reported to be any of numerous planets and nonplanetary settlements. Most often specified as starship *Cavorter* in transit between Njarl's World and Hallelujah. No records available. Parents thought to be deceased.

"'Member, not in particularly good standing, of the All-Worlds Merchant Spacefarers Guild, Spican Aerospace Workers Alliance, Pan-Stellar Pilots Union, and many lesser, kindred organizations. History of frequent arrests, on a variety of planets, satellites, and other locations, including space vessels in transit.'"

Ash paused, studying the lanky, pale offworlder; the large, almost glowing yellow eyes and the flowing gray mane with its strands of silver. For all his differences from mainbreed Terrans, he was quite youthful-looking to have such a spotty past.

"Alacrity, what would you do if you were dining with Srillans and your host suggested that it was getting late?"

The breakabout vaulted off the bed in a swirl of sheet and began an animated, prancing shuffle around the center of the room. Ash watched interestedly.

Alacrity postured in grandiloquent style. He sang through his nose in imitation of the ebullient Srillan form. "*Ning-ning-a-ning!*" he cock-crowed. He danced around the executioner, addressing the song to him as though Ash were the hypothetical Srillan host.

"Let us all now praise Lord Ash, *ning-a-ning*! For his generous hospitality"—he struck a pose, a waggish aside to his invisible audience—"(don't let the door strike you in the rump!) *ning-a-ning!*"

He resumed his declamatory posture. "For this marvelous repast"—and again the aside—"(were all the toxic waste dumps closed?) *ning-ning*! For his thoughtfulness (it's so seldom you see utensils chained to the table!) *ning-a-ning-a-ning*!"

He stopped. Ash wasn't amused; Alacrity remembered, too late, how much Terrans hated the Srillans for what they'd done to Earth.

The executioner asked, "What would you do if you encountered, er..." He consulted his memory again. "An Adjustor on the planet Wendigo?"

Alacrity's expression went blank. His eyes unfocused. "Encounter? *How?* There's no one there, citizen; *no one*! If I remember that and behave accordingly, she may be indifferent to me and pass by."

"And the Parade of Initiates on C'que's Nest?"

"Steer a wide course around it. By parsecs, preferably. The hatchlings are always hungry, and their elders aren't inclined to deny them anything that day of the year. Well? Satisfied?"

"Quite. You're well qualified."

Alacrity sat on the bed, nodding smugly. "Damn right. You couldn't find a better..."

He looked up again, facing Ash. He said slowly, "You couldn't find a better escort on Earth if you tried all day. That's what this is all about, isn't it?"

"I believe that to be the case, Alacrity, but I can't prove it. At least not now. The sentence commutation covering Project Shepherd applies to lesser crimes as well as to homicide. Inciting to riot, for example; disturbing the peace; aggravated assault."

"They needed a babysitter, so they gave me a visa and arranged for trouble." He looked around the room suddenly. "Hold on; is anybody, uh..."

Ash motioned a dismissal. "No one monitors my conversations if I don't allow it."

"Nobody scroodles with Citizen Ash, huh?"

"Let's stay with the subject; I haven't much more time. A Terran named Hobart Floyt must go to Epiphany to claim an inheritance at the Willreading of Caspahr Weir, and return to Earth with it for disposition by the Earthservice Resources Bureau."

"Epiphany..." Alacrity frowned. Few outsiders ever made planetfall on Weir's personal world. The breakabout had heard rumors about the fabulous Frostpile and about Weir himself, even though a little nineteen-system realm was barely a spit in the ocean. Alacrity had already made up his mind but continued to probe, from reflex and for sheer love of it.

"What's the inheritance? What am I going to be guarding?"

"Floyt, at the very least. Beyond that, no one knows yet. A pittance, perhaps, or the deed to a planet."

Alacrity squinted at him. "I can't think of many reasons Earthservice would trust me, saving only one, citizen."

Ash nodded. "There's a proviso. That's why you're in an Alpha Bureaucrats' clinic."

"Conditioning!" Alacrity clenched his fists and prepared again to jump the executioner.

"Stop!" Ash had his palm up again. "There'll be no enslavement, Alacrity; no altering. My word on that."

Alacrity found himself listening.

"You escort Floyt to Epiphany, stay with him for the Willreading, which, with its attendant ceremonies, shouldn't take you more than a few days. Keep him safe, then return him with his inheritance. And that will be an end to it, insofar as you're concerned."

"And all I have to put up with is a little brain-changing, hmm?"

"There'll be no tampering, Alacrity. The modifications will only ensure that you keep your end of the bargain. I've let it be known that I will tolerate nothing beyond that."

"Out to Epiphany and back . . ." Alacrity said to himself, as though he hadn't decided. "You win. But just don't forget: we've *both* been scroodled, good and proper. Me because I was bugtrapped; you because you're sentencing an innocent man."

"I have no intention of forgetting it."

"Why aren't you trying to find out who did it to us?"

Ash looked at him for five seconds or so. "When I leave here, I will fly directly to the cell of a young woman who's been sentenced to death. She admits her guilt but refuses any alternative. She isn't as fortunate as you in having another way out. I will try to dissuade her from choosing execution, but I don't hold much hope. There are other cases, more than my office can properly deal with. And the backlog's growing worse. You're not the highest priority on my list, not anymore."

Alacrity said nothing. Ash was about to leave again when he remembered something. "By the way: your surname, 'Fitzhugh.' It's of ancient derivation, like mine. But I doubt it's your real one. What made you pick it?"

Alacrity grinned. "It was given to me a long time ago. My name's a *pun*, Citizen Ash. In your precious *Terranglish*."

CHAPTER 4

FIRM OFFER

FLOYT DREW A DEEP BREATH WHEN HE REACHED HIS APT
doorpanel. "Open," he said to the pickup mesh; the lock
snapped back, and the doorpanel slid aside.

He trudged between the neat stacks of boxes and cases
that held a good part of the family's possessions. They were
piled in the hallway because Floyt had appropriated the hall
closet as a tiny workspace. Into it he had crammed a chair
and minuscule table, desk-model accessor, and the accumulated reference materials and data of years of research.
Balensa was fairly tolerant of the arrangement, in that he'd
ceded her most of the rest of the apt.

And there'd been considerably more room once Reesa
had moved from her alcove. The seventeen-year-old was
engaged in a work-study program in pursuit of an advanced
degree, deeply involved in a somewhat romantic recreation
of a Pleistocene tribal group. Her parents were quite fond
of her, but had been relieved when she'd relocated to the
school dormitory in Lapland. Leaving flint chips in the
hygiene chamber to ambush bare feet, singeing the carpet
with sparks struck during firemaking attempts, and the aroma

of artificial animal grease had severely tested her parents' affection. She'd been rather hurt when they'd drawn the line at joining her in primate grooming behavior; Balensa in particular had been dismayed at the thought of searching her family for vermin.

Floyt grew alert when he realized that someone was in the modest living room with Balensa—a female whose voice he didn't recognize. And it was no tête-à-tête, for the stranger's voice was cold and formal, even hostile.

There was an expectant pause in the conversation. They were looking his way when he appeared.

Balensa seemed subdued but vexed. She was still an attractive woman, petite, with chestnut hair, an unlined face, and the figure of a teenager. She was dressed in a reproduction, an Italian style from the latter fifteenth century, of synthetics posing as stiff, densely patterned blue velvet interwoven with gold, its V-shape front showing off her slenderness to good advantage.

The other woman was unknown to Floyt, but seeing her gave him a start of dismay. She wore a well-tailored office suit and the pleated brown robes of an Earthservice supervisor. He concluded at once that the corridor incident had been picked up by Peaceguardian surveillance equipment.

He forgot his emotional disarray, worried now that he'd been remiss in not reporting the trouble at once, that he'd violated a regulation and was in trouble for it. But he couldn't understand why such an encounter would merit the attention of a full supervisor, even granted that it involved an off-worlder.

At about forty, she was extremely young for supervisor's rank. Though tall and severe, she wore her long auburn hair loose. She looked him over with cold brown eyes.

"We've been wondering when you'd get home," Balensa said with a touch of nervousness. "Supervisor Bear has been waiting for nearly an hour. Why weren't you wearing your accessor?"

"Greetings, Citizen Floyt," the supervisor said before he could become bogged down in explanations or excuses. Her tone was rather steely. "I'm Supervisor Bear, of the Resource Recovery Division. You and I have something to discuss."

Floyt moved into the room warily, clearing his throat. She'd addressed him as "citizen" instead of the more formal "functionary," so that might be a good sign. Though he was theoretically free to address her the same way, he would never have dreamt of doing so.

"I—I was going to report the attack as soon as I arrived home, Supervisor. I wasn't sure of the procedure, but I thought it would be safer than if I—"

Bear seemed to gather her self-restraint. *An hour or so with my wife has doubtless taxed it*, Floyt thought. Even a supervisor's cloak wouldn't have deflected all of Balensa's curiosity. Clearly, the subject of contract termination had been tabled by Balensa for the time being.

"Citizen Floyt," Bear interrupted, "be so kind as to sit down, if you will. My time's in rather short supply. Won't you have a drink?"

Floyt refused the drink and perched himself warily on the least comfortable seat in the living room. Balensa was artfully arranged on the sofa, while Supervisor Bear had, of course, taken the cloud-rest lounger.

On the center table a small bottle of premium Scotch, and a setup stood on Balensa's best imitation-silver tray. The refreshments had undoubtedly been obtained from the apt's service unit with Bear's allotment code; the machine would've ignored such an order given with his own or Balensa's code. Even in his agitated state, he registered the purchase with a twinge of envy—and resentment toward the service unit as well as Bear.

Balensa edged forward, intent on the supervisor. "You'll pardon me now," Bear said, "but it's necessary that I speak to your spouse in private. Perhaps you'd care to visit your rec-center or take a stroll. An hour should suffice."

Balensa looked as though Bear had hosed her down with ice water. "But, but—that is, as spouse, I think I have the right to know what it is—"

Bear let some peevishness creep into her voice. "The needs of Earthservice come first, and right now one of those needs is confidentiality. You're forcing me to use my rather limited time unproductively."

Balensa was up in a rustle of stiff costume, stalking for the door. "And, citizen..." Bear added. Balensa halted. "Keep utter silence about this visit; this is an official warning. And don't press your spouse for details. You'll be briefed at the proper time."

Thoroughly put to rout, Balensa exited. Bear took another sip from a drink that was mostly melted ice. Floyt was completely bewildered and still shaken by the assault, but with a supervisor doing the investigating, it would be wiser to wait and learn what he could, tailoring his account and explanations to the circumstances.

"Citizen Floyt, your hobby is genealogy," Bear began. "You're quite knowledgeable about Terran and offworld lineages and histories."

He nodded mutely.

She seemed about to go on in the same vein, then digressed to ask him, "How did you come to be so expert? The subject has little to do with your assignment as an information accessor/interfacer."

"I was introduced to genealogy during a collating assignment about eight years ago. It caught my interest."

Bear gestured toward the hall closet. "Your spouse showed me your cubby."

"I use my rec-time allotment to interface with the information systems, Supervisor." It was all perfectly legal, but he suddenly wondered if he'd done something wrong. There were so many Earthservice regs; it was impossible to know them all. "And sometimes I do research at the workplace, but only during breaktime. And I always charge it to my code . . ."

Unconcerned with minor details, she was making a rejecting motion. "Your work has been reproduced off-world."

He felt himself blush. Interest in offworld things was considered eccentric, if not suspect. "I contributed a few trifles to the data banks. Some offworld accessor noticed them and offered Earthservice a repro fee, or so I was told."

"They were more than trifles. Three separate, comprehensive genealogies and two monographs." It was true. And the money involved must have been considerable, he'd always assumed, because a microscopic sum had actually been passed along to him, though Earthservice assessments on offworld earnings were all but total.

"Some of this business apparently came to the attention of a man named Caspahr Weir," Bear was saying cooly, with a proper disdain for offworld things. "He was interested in his misbred origins, I suppose. At any rate, he died recently and saw fit to leave you a bequest in his will."

Floyt was severely staggered, but first of all by that name. Weir! That Weir should've taken notice of Floyt's work gave him a mixture of pleasure and embarrassment, so much so that he almost missed the last part.

"Bequest?"

"You heard me correctly. You're mentioned in the will of a man who was director—monarch, really—of nineteen stellar systems."

"I don't know what . . . what I should—"

"By provision of the will, all heirs—'Inheritors'—must gather at Weir's home on a planet called Epiphany. There you'll attend a Willreading, which is to take place in approximately three weeks. Failure to appear will mean forfeiture of all claim to your bequest. The Earthservice intends you to be there."

All that had gone before was a gentle overture to the

shock waves that began to crash through Floyt's nervous system. Offworld! Without realizing it, he poured himself a tumbler of straight Scotch and drank. He gagged. "I can't."

"Why?"

"Why? Vertebrae deficiency: I haven't got the backbone for it."

"That's as may be, but go you will. We don't know what the bequest is, but the opportunity must be taken."

"But it might be worthless! The cost of fare alone would be..." He paused for a moment and wondered if Earth-service expected *him* to pay his way. No, impossible; the price would be more than a Functionary 3rd Class earned in a lifetime. Several lifetimes.

He gulped. If the Earthservice picked up the tab for his fare to Epiphany, only to find that his bequest was of little or no value, would the bureaucracy be willing to unpocket for a ticket home?

"Interstellar passage has been provided for by Weir's executors." Bear smiled thinly. *"Round-trip* passage, citizen."

Under the circumstances, Earthservice had nothing to lose by sending him—except perhaps an easily replaceable Functionary 3rd Class.

The drink trembled in his hand as Floyt thought of the perils of offworld travel. Earthservice never stinted in stressing those to Terrans: injury, disease, death in uncounted forms, enslavement, and the possibility of being stranded forever in some fashion, unable to return home across inhuman distances.

The thought of danger reminded him of something. "An offworlder tried to kill me on my way home, Supervisor. Or at least she tried to do me more than a little harm."

Bear examined him fixedly, but she seemed to believe him. He answered her rapid-fire questions, finding to his surprise that exact details of the encounter had already become blurry. He sipped at his Scotch as she thought for a moment.

Then she activated her own accessor, a more sophisticated and ornate model than any he'd ever seen up close. When she keyed it, he was unable to hear a sound from her hurried conversation. When she signed off and he could hear again, she said, "There's little chance of finding her now, but a search will be made for your assailant."

"But she's fairly conspicuous."

"Her appearance has probably changed radically in the past hour. Now let's keep to the subject. I must say, for a citizen with such a high compliance quotient, you're being irksome."

"Sorry." He'd never heard of a compliance quotient before and wasn't sure he liked having a high one, but he obediently restricted his questions to the matter before them.

"Supervisor, how can I possibly hope to get to Epiphany, much less bring home some inheritance, whether it's of any value or not? I've no experience; I'm not trained for that sort of thing. This is insane!"

Bear answered, "We at Resource Recovery have provided for that. You'll be part of a new pilot program: Project Shepherd."

"It sounds very pastoral. Under other circumstances, I'd be reassured, but the demographics for Terran casualties during offworld travel are disheartening."

"True enough, citizen. Recovery of offworld resources claimable by Terran citizens has that drawback. But we can't let Terrans simply forfeit opportunities to claim payment, dun debtors, collect winnings, or—as in your case— accept inheritances. Imagine the value of even a minor part of Weir's wealth! Citizen Floyt, do you believe, as I do, that we owe Earth our all?"

"I . . . that is—"

"I knew you would! It's *our* Earthservice, after all; yours and mine!"

Naturally, thought Floyt. What with the planet's severely limited resources, every Terran was a ward of the Earth-

service and—all but a few—an employee as well. Floyt
didn't mention the open secret that Earthservice was controlled by a tight hierarchy, supervisors among them, with
Alpha Bureaucrats at the pinnacle.

She was looking at him with arch expectancy. He hastened to chorus, "Of course, Supervisor."

"Then you'll want to do your share," she said in a flat
voice, eyes staring into his. He knew then that there'd be
no avoiding it short of exposing a live power source in the
hygiene chamber and taking a high-voltage bath.

He sighed, "Might I ask just what this Project Shepherd
is?"

"It's *my* project," she said grandly, chin high. "We'll
provide you with a suitable escort, someone experienced in
the difficulties and dangers of star travel. A guardian, a
guide—a shepherd."

"Oh. How long will I be gone? And my escort—who is
he? Or she?"

Bear became curt. "You'll meet your escort quite soon
and go through a brief orientation. You'll also be given your
letter of Free Import."

"Free Import?"

"Yes. But all that will be explained in good time. In the
interim, put your affairs in order at home and at your workplace. Then hold yourself in readiness." She stood, and he
did too.

"There's one more thing, citizen." She'd left a shoulder
bag at the end of the sofa. Now she opened it and drew out
a wide, flashing band of some golden-red alloy. "You're to
wear this, beginning immediately."

He took it from her in astonishment. It was a belt of
placques so heavy that they dragged at his hand. Each was
decorated with cryptic characters and odd symbols. And
each bore the same device, a broken slave's collar. The
craftsmanship was superb; the placques glittered and chimed
as they struck one another.

Deeply engraved on the back of the buckle was the name HOBART FLOYT.

"It's an Inheritor's belt," Bear explained. "The executors' instructions require that you wear it from now until the Willreading." Her eyes lingered on it covetously. "It's too bad it can't remain here while you're gone."

She looked him in the eye. "Did I mention that it appears to contain some mechanism we don't understand?"

Floyt was foursquare opposed to putting it on, but she glared at him pointedly. With a sigh of surrender, he drew the belt around his waist and clasped the buckle. It closed with a heavy click. It was a perfect fit.

"It wouldn't shut for me," she said absently, her gaze fixed on the flashing, barbaric splendor of the thing. "It wouldn't shut for anyone. We didn't dare tamper with it."

Floyt considered that. "It perhaps read my DNA code? Or pore pattern or—but no, how would offworlders have known those?"

Bear gave him a hard stare then, without answering, turned to the door. "I'll be in touch with you when I've picked the person I want to serve as your escort. Precisely the person I want."

When she was gone, he removed the belt and examined it, reading his own name again, running his fingertips across the letters. It was odd to think that the artifact had crossed light-years. His heart sank once more at the thought of the danger and hardship the Inheritor's belt represented.

He stood looking at it for a long time there in his cluttered hallway, and reflecting upon his high compliance quotient. Resignedly, he replaced the belt around his middle.

When he clasped the buckle, it engaged with a sound of finality.

CHAPTER 5

VOLUNTEERS

FLOYT HAD FINALLY WRAPPED UP HIS WORK. IT TOOK HIM longer than it should have; his mind was elsewhere. He'd spent a good deal of his time distracted by fear of what was to come—of a thousand horrifying forms of death or mutilation, and of never being able to return for any of an almost infinite number of reasons. Inventing new and even more terrifying possibilities seemed to be the only thing at which his mind could work with complete clarity.

He damned Earthservice in his heart. He raged silently against Casphar Weir. He hated Balensa and anyone else who didn't share his bad fortune. He condemned the job assignment that had long ago brought him into contact with genealogies.

He'd been able to ignore his immediate superiors' unspoken resentment—that was one small consolation. No one, peer or boss, even mentioned the Inheritor's belt he now wore throughout his waking hours. Word had obviously been passed that Floyt wasn't to be questioned or bothered.

His fellow workers had wished him well, in ones and twos, briefly and surreptitiously, on his "new assignment."

Supervisor Bear called just as he'd completed his conscientious efforts at an orderly departure, instructing him to return to his apt within the hour.

Now Floyt, Balensa, and Bear were in the little living room again; Balensa was quite cheery.

"Citizen Floyt may be gone for some time," Supervisor Bear was saying. If she seemed warmer to his wife, she was no more cordial to Floyt himself. "In the meantime, Earthservice will provide for you and your daughter, homefront heroines in a new kind of struggle."

Balensa touched up her hair; Bear couldn't have taken a tack that would have appealed to her more. She was dressed in an outfit that would have been appropriate for marrying into the Borgia family. Claiming the guest seat, Bear occupied couch center. Floyt had tried to keep himself out of the spotlight.

Now Bear leaned toward Balensa, who sat beside her. "During Citizen Floyt's absence, you and your daughter will receive a special hardship allocation." She made a pass like a magician over a hat. "Quarters and consumption allotments equivalent to those of a Bureaucrat Fifth Class, in recognition of your sacrifice."

Balensa was more than elated; she could hardly wait to see her husband go. Under the circumstances, Floyt couldn't much blame her. With the new situation occasioned by Weir's will, all thought of dissolving the marriage had of course been dropped, and, with an overly cheerful superficiality, Balensa was once again his wife.

"Of course," Bear cautioned, "we'll be counting on you to make yourself available for psychprop interviews, public service spots, morale campaigns, and so forth."

Balensa agreed fervently. Floyt knew Bear would get gallant, stoic, silently overjoyed support from that quarter. He also suspected that one of the people who would benefit most from the whole episode was Arlo Mote.

Floyt had had little time for personal preparations; somehow or other Earthservice had selected his guide-escort within a day or two of his first interview with Supervisor Bear. Now a huge plainclothes Peaceguardian waited outside the apt door. He or a colleague had accompanied the new Inheritor everywhere outside of workplace or home since Floyt had put on the belt. Floyt felt himself more prisoner than hero of the public weal, but no further attempts had been made to waylay him.

Floyt put a hand on the modest travel bag he was to take with him. Bear and Balensa had both assured him that his precious files and genealogical data would be safe. He was disinclined to believe them, but that hardly mattered to him by then. He worked at achieving a dulled, fatalistic acceptance of the fact that he had no choice but to go to Epiphany.

"This person who's to travel with me," he said abruptly, "who is . . . he? She?"

"*He*," Bear clarified. Balensa, whose countenance had suddenly filled with concern over the possibility of a female escort, now brightened.

"A veteran spacer named Alacrity Fitzhugh," the supervisor added. She knew her own inner relief—that after things had gone so terribly awry at Machu Picchu she'd been able to put them back on course again.

She'd been almost giddy with her own daring in the aftermath of that calamity. Fitzhugh had seemed an ideal candidate despite the fact that she'd been able to discover almost no truly reliable background data on him. What mattered was that he was, though young, a seasoned and widely traveled breakabout who'd survived dangerous situations and thrived in alien surroundings.

Perhaps as important, as a member of various guilds and unions, he could deadhead aboard almost any ship on which his principal, Floyt, might book passage, saving Project Shepherd enormous expense. That was critical; the project's disastrous pilot mission had depleted the major part of its funding. Even if Bear had wanted to hire a qualified escort and pay his transportation costs, rather than flimflamming him into it, her funding wouldn't have allowed it, and the Alpha Bureaucrats were hardly of a mind to give her more money.

Until the fantastic luck that was the Weir legacy, which promised to make real her all-consuming desire to be an Alpha, her most likely mission scenario had involved dispatching a Terran spaceport worker to Mars for a paternity suit. The man had fathered a child by a female shuttle navigator, a Martian citizen, and their son had grown into a prodigy on the eerie Martian glass harmonica, becoming the rave of the planet. Under Martian filial law, the father had a right to share in the earnings, but round-trip passage for one to Mars would have taken a fearful bite from Bear's budget, and the outcome of the suit was far from a sure thing.

Despite that, it had been her best hope against cancellation of her project; she'd *had* to do something fast. And so Fitzhugh had been granted his visa; after studying his itinerary, she'd arranged for the mob and the incident.

Then, like a miracle, literally out of the heavens, Weir's executors had contacted Earthservice. The will not only promised the possibility of a major inheritance but provided for Floyt's round-trip passage. The expense of such a mission would be negligible. The Machu Picchu operation had gone ahead as scheduled, and the functionary had been duly conscripted.

Supervisor Bear still fumed at the fanaticism—and just plain bad luck—that had led to the villager's death. The matter of commutation no longer lay with the bureaucrats with whom she'd made secret deals. It rested with Citizen Ash. Like almost everyone on Earth, she dreaded any involvement whatsoever with the man.

Suddenly much more had been riding on the outcome than her ambitions. Bear had been at risk of being charged with crimes that would bring her under Ash's jurisdiction.

Compared to that, even Project Shepherd was of secondary importance.

But she had reasserted her icy self-control, moving quickly and decisively. She convinced or coerced those who were already involved into helping her in a desperate cover-up, framing Alacrity Fitzhugh for the killing. It had entailed the slaying of the real killer, in order to keep him from recanting his perjured testimony, and insuring by various means that no other witness would speak up.

Ash had commuted the breakabout's sentence. That was both a help to Project Shepherd and an unnerving hint that the executioner thought there was more to the killing than did the court that had found Fitzhugh guilty. Bear had gone forward with her plan nonetheless; she couldn't afford not to. However, she'd tabled, indefinitely, pending plans to entrap other escorts.

She rose from Hobart Floyt's couch, the stiff pleats of her cloak of office rustling. Floyt and Balensa automatically stood. "And now, Citizen Floyt, we must be off." To Balensa, Bear added, "The household liaison team will arrive at the beginning of next shift."

Floyt's wife and the supervisor embraced and kissed like family. Floyt resignedly took up his bag and fell in behind Bear as she swept through the doorway.

Ash entered the room with a drawn, tense Floyt at his side. Supervisor Bear followed a circumspect pace behind and to the left.

The decor had been chosen to aid Floyt's peace of mind, not Alacrity's; it looked not at all like an advanced conditioning facility, but, in deference to fashion, resembled a chamber from the planet's vaunted past, a Victorian drawing room. The functionary became visibly less nervous when he entered.

Alacrity felt differently. *Prism-trimmed lampshades, tasseled pillows, and red-plush loveseats don't have any busi-*

ness here, he thought huffily. No doubt the antimacassars were wired.

He and Floyt eyed one another. The breakabout saw a subdued little groundling—well, short, anyway. But he *did* look solid. *No wonder these poor marks are happier hiding in distorted reveries and vanished glory. No wonder they can only find courage in mobs.*

Floyt saw a cocky, glowering young alien, not realizing that the breakabout was irritated in part by having to wear a patient's disposable suit. The adhesive seams had a way of coming open at unpredictable times, or stubbornly remained closed when it was least convenient. Alacrity was sick of sudden drafts striking his posterior in the middle of a conversation, or hopping around the lavatory engaged in desperate conflict with the crotch seam. Little wonder Floyt thought him surly-looking.

Floyt, educated by Earthservice psychprop, saw what he'd expected: a not-quite-human with no respect for Terra or her past. Arrogant, no doubt, in his sole talent, which was to hop here and there around the void, contemptuous of Earth, uncaring that the virtues and nobility of the race had been fostered *here*, on *this* planet. Interesting in a freakish way, perhaps, with those eyes and the silver-gray mane, but a mongrel still and all.

Supervisor Bear offered terse introductions of the three conditioning techs, wishing to attract as little attention to herself as possible. Chief Behavioral Engineer Skinner was a heavily muscled, white-bearded man who'd adopted his name from that of one of his childhood idols. With him were his assistants, Clinicians Subutai (a tall, freckled, brown-haired woman, attractive in a rangy sort of way) and Scism (a thin, balding man with a pronounced squint and quite the darkest skin Alacrity had yet seen on Terra).

Bear gave them all a basilisk smile. "I trust you'll all get along satisfactorily." She left before Alacrity could make out much more about her than the fact that he hated her.

Subutai and Scism retired behind what looked to be a Chinese screen, replete with dragons and landscape motifs, to a hidden monitoring station. Alacrity saw no guards or security system, but had no doubt that both were nearby. He was sitting on the very edge of a heavily upholstered wingback chair. Skinner invited Floyt to sit in another near it, then said, "Please, do sit back in your seats, citizens, and I shall—"

"I'm not one of your damned citizens!" Alacrity glared at Floyt. Behind the screen, Subutai and Scism smiled and nodded to one another over their instruments.

Skinner smiled blandly. "You're right. I beg your pardon, Alacrity. Now, both of you, please try to relax."

Floyt complied as best he could; Skinner's appearance, dress, and manner were all calculated to reassure an Earther, and that helped. Alacrity edged back unwillingly, spine in contact with the crimson velvet, but sitting bolt upright. Pickups in the chairs fed more data to the clinicians.

Skinner began a rambling explanation of why they were all there. The breakabout interrupted, almost in monotone. "Hold it. I promised I'd go through with this, but I never agreed to pretend to like it. Or to be genteel." He turned to Floyt; Subutai and Scism read some interesting data from both chairs. "And I won't pretend to like you, either."

Floyt was studying Alacrity as though he were something for which there ought to have been a vaccine. "If you *should* begin to approve of me, let me know, Fitzhugh. I'll change at once," he replied calmly.

Viewing the readouts, the hidden clinicians smiled, well pleased. Their chief made calming gestures; his two subjects settled down. Alacrity saw that he must surrender to the inevitable; Floyt obeyed Earthservice, as he had all his life.

Citizen Ash spoke up; the others were surprised to realize how inconspicuous he could be when he wished. "I must leave you now. Hobart, Alacrity: good luck to you both. I pray that you return soon." He turned to go; Alacrity called out to him, and he paused.

"What happened to the girl?" the breakabout wanted to know. "The one you were going to talk to when you left me? The one with no third way out?"

"I will see her again, a last time" Ash's face was a mask. The clinicians noticed strange peturbations in their readings. Then the executioner was gone.

Skinner began to rebuild the mood he desired, furious with the disruption but not even daring to consider criticizing Citizen Ash. He rubbed his hands together heartily. "Now then, gentlemen, shall we begin?" Alacrity decided that, if the opportunity should ever present itself, he would knock Chief Behavioral Engineer Skinner's dong to the deck.

"You've both been briefed on the therapy you're to undergo here," Skinner began. He ignored the breakabout's bitter snort of derision. "Basically, it's a standard procedure. Citizen Floyt, you're aware of how common its use is in, ah, somewhat different circumstances here on Terra. Alacrity, you have no doubt encountered standard conditioning techniques, eh?"

Alacrity scowled. "I roger 'techniques,' all right." He also knew of places where it was possible to have behavioral programming erased or counteracted. He grinned wolfishly.

"Good!" Skinner replied, too genially. "Now, the one major problem we have is that of time. The provisions of Weir's will require that all Inheritors be present for the reading; this means that you must depart for Epiphany in slightly over two days.

"So instead of a full course of treatment, you'll only have time for a rather abbreviated conditioning, concentrating on your task. That is, going to Epiphany, claiming the inheritance, and returning with it to Earth. Obviously, this involves certain priorities."

Alacrity made a sour face, glancing aside at a reproduction of a Remington painting. One of the priorities would *not* be his own welfare.

Floyt was expressionless; Skinner looked forward to analyzing the readings being recorded by Subutai and Scism, to find out just what it was the man was feeling.

"Priorities. You, Alacrity, will see to it that Hobart performs his mission and returns safely. Hobart, it's necessary to place all emphasis on your mission. Understand, please, both of you: this will *not* make you feel like some sort of automaton. It will seem reasonable and desirable that you do what is required."

"How about *him*?" Alacrity broke in with a head motion at Floyt. "How do I keep him from doing some vapor-brained damn fool Earther thing or other and getting us into trouble. *Who's gonna be in charge?*"

Floyt went rigid with anger; he gave the breakabout a direct and unswerving stare. Embarrassed, Skinner hastened to add, "Er, you'll *both* be enjoined against provocative conduct. But this is hardly the time to go into that, eh?"

Alacrity's eyes dropped first, away from Floyt's unwavering glare. Maybe there was a little something to the guy after all. Too, he was disturbed by what Skinner had said. He had a premonition that, in a typical Earthservice reflex, the two unwilling companions were to be turned into some sort of *committee*.

"And now to work!" Skinner trumpeted, clapping his hands. Floyt looked back to Alacrity, wanting to clarify matters then and there, but the breakabout was fast asleep in his chair, Subutai and Scism having cut in its soporific field.

Floyt spent the better part of two days in conditioning-pseudosomnolence while Earthservice told him what he was to do. His loyalty to Terra and long-fostered resentment of things alien were bent toward a commitment to mission completion.

Motivation was hardly a problem for the behavioral engineers; it was more a matter of fine-tuning Floyt's xenophobia so that he could endure offworld travel and contacts. His conscious acceptance of the idea was fragile enough; his underlying fear and aversion were nearly off the scale.

While he was under, they brought in medical teams for his immunization and adaptive treatments, from Earthservice's point of view, the most expensive part of the mission. It might prove needless, in which case it would be eliminated from future Project Shepherd missions, but Supervisor Bear could not afford to have anything go wrong. Alacrity, of course, had received equivalent or superior treatment long ago.

Floyt did spend some waking time. A little groggy, he was given general orientations on interstellar travel and conditions in human space, those in the realm of the late Weir in particular.

He was also lectured on the reasons for Earthservice's actions. But his opposition to travel couldn't be eradicated, only submerged. It wasn't difficult at all to insure that he be prudent.

Getting the Earther to accept companionship with Alacrity was something else again. It was probable that Floyt would on occasion have to bow to Alacrity's judgment, or at least weigh it impartially. That required the tearing down of some of his distaste for aliens, which the clinicians did very carefully, considering the short time they had. They made sure that among aliens Alacrity was considered a unique exception. They wanted the remainder of Floyt's prejudice to stay intact.

Alacrity, younger and more resilient, didn't wake up again for over forty-eight hours. He had to be imbued with the desire to accompany, protect, and cooperate with Floyt. They had little enough to work with, especially after his experiences at Machu Picchu.

But they *did* have Floyt. The team deemed it best to create and stress a personal loyalty. In the process, they encountered a tremendous defensive blockage surrounding and sealing off the breakabout's past, origins, and upbringing. The two clinicians thought it natural, a protective mechanism of some sort. But Skinner felt that it was too strong, and must have been painstakingly constructed. He was intrigued and mightily tempted to probe it, but there was no time.

To cultivate the synthetic bonding, the team used recordings from Floyt's sessions on Alacrity. Their evaluation of the psychodynamics involved prompted them to emphasize Floyt's vulnerability, though the man actually displayed a surprising streak of self-reliance. They played it against the breakabout's rather easily provoked sympathy for an underdog or victim. The by-product, they knew, would be a certain contempt for Floyt's perceived weakness. The clinicians were willing to accept that.

They knew that they'd made progress early on the second day. Heavily medicated, Alacrity sat in a recliner viewing a tape of Hobart Floyt while a hypnofield worked on him. The recording, made in the course of the functionary's sessions, had been edited and orchestrated masterfully to portray Floyt as a likable but frightened man caught up in a dilemma beyond his understanding or abilities.

Suddenly the clinicians heard Alacrity mumbling. The team leaned closer, straining to hear.

"Poor sonuvabitch . . . poor little sonuva . . ."

Chief Behavioral Engineer Skinner broke into a beaming grin.

The time limit forced the team to discontinue its regimen, though there hadn't been nearly enough conditioning for a deep, completely reliable treatment. The team's disclaimers were ignored; Floyt *must* be present for the Willreading.

Alacrity was groggily led back to the bogus drawing room

by an aide. Floyt was already waiting, along with Skinner and his crew. The oriental screen had been removed; a surprisingly modern and compact control console glittered in the corner.

The conditioning team seemed so relaxed and jocular that it depressed Floyt and made him somewhat bitter, even though he knew he had to carry out his mission for the good of Terra. But the behavioral engineers would get to stay behind, among the true children of Terra, while he, Floyt, must venture out among the mongrelized, mutated, and crossbred offworlders.

Then his conditioning cut in, though it felt to him quite simply as though another thought had occurred to him. He was filled with a warm glow at the thought of all the good that he might be able to do with his inheritance.

Swaying for a moment as the aide released his arm, Alacrity stopped. Skinner and company raised the breakabout's hackles; they'd left his nervous system jangling and played out.

Then he spied Floyt. A wave of compassion swept through him. Poor little sonuvabitch!

A last attendee showed up, Supervisor Bear, looking triumphant. She gave the seated Floyt a pat on the shoulder, gazing down on him benignly. "You've done well, Hobart. From this point forward, physical hardships will be few."

On a jaunt to Epiphany and back, with somebody out to get him—or us? Alacrity marveled at her knack for lying. But he felt a sudden resolve to see to it that the Earther *did* make it. After all, none of this was really Floyt's fault either. The conditioning made him feel that way so strongly, he knew, but a good deal of his real self was in there someplace too.

Floyt made some halting reply. Though he'd gone through far lighter treatment than the breakabout, he was still a bit disoriented.

Bear turned to Alacrity. The subzero cordiality only made

him loathe her more. "You have a rare opportunity to atone for your crime by doing something worthwhile. I trust you'll show gratitude and make good use of it."

"If I had my way, Bear, there'd be a filter in every urethral duct to eliminate your type."

A shade paler, Bear launched into a general pep talk. The others listened deferentially, but Alacrity, anger smoldering, looked around the room restlessly. Then he noticed that, eyes still on Bear, the little clinician, Scism, was edging toward the console. He covered the movements of his hand with his body as he reached for the controls.

As punchy as he was from the things that had taken place since Machu Picchu, Alacrity had nonetheless picked up a fair idea of how the console worked, his normal reaction in encountering new machinery. Scism seemed about to give a lethal twist to the control governing energy influx for Floyt's chair.

Alacrity *ejected* from his chair, hurling himself across the room at Scism. The clinician whirled the dial; Floyt yipped in pain and surprise, stiffening. Scism faced Alacrity, aiming a slender, glittering tube his way.

The breakabout never even slowed down; Floyt was injured but, for the moment, still alive. Alacrity tried to dodge, meaning to try a flying tackle, hollering for the others to help.

Scism was faster than he looked. The beam caught Alacrity full in the face, stretching him headlong on the rich, imitation-Persian carpet.

He only lost his sense of time for a moment; it felt like no more than seconds later that he came to, battered and sore, staring up at the replica chandelier.

Paralyzer, stungun, whatever they call them on Earth, he realized; he couldn't have survived anything else at point-blank. At that, the gun must've been set at low power. He still felt as though somebody had dialed up a couple of extra gravities. He strained, raised his head.

First he saw Floyt's face, wearing a strange mixture of perplexity and amazement. Bear was next to him, still wearing her bland expression over a certain gloating. The team stood in a loose circle, peering down.

Skinner was taking his pulse manually. "Jus' 'n ole-fashioned doctor, huh?" The patient yanked his wrist free.

Scism gazed down sympathetically; Subutai was murmuring psychometric observations into a recorder. Alacrity congratulated himself sourly on having fallen for another Earthservice setup.

"Did I pass, you mucus wads?"

"Magnificently," Skinner acclaimed. He helped Alacrity up, knowing the breakabout would be too weak to take more than an ineffective imitation of a punch or kick at him. "Sorry we had to do it, young man, but that was your final test."

"I would say you're in dependable company, Citizen Floyt," Subutai observed.

Alacrity saw from the look on Floyt's face that he'd been as much taken by surprise as the breakabout.

Then, brows knit, the functionary faced Bear and Skinner. "That was a vicious, unnecessary thing to do." In his confusion and anger, he thought back to the woman who'd attacked him with the styrette. Another Earthservice ruse, a test? Of what?

For the first time, Bear's countenance grew troubled. Floyt's asserting himself, particularly for the offworlder, was no part of her scheme. The team was watching the functionary intently.

"Forget it," Alacrity said to Floyt in disgust. "We've got a ship to catch."

Alacrity wanted their leavetaking to be inconspicuous—secret, if possible. However, that didn't dovetail with Bear's plan to make the pilot mission a shining achievement and propaganda victory.

And so the waiting room at Earth's last remaining spaceport, closed to the public, was filled with recording teams and their equipment. All material would be heavily edited later on, naturally. In the event that this mission came to a bad end too, the recordings could be disposed of. The first *successful* mission would be the one palmed off on Terrans at large as Project Shepherd's initial one.

"Make sure you have the letter of Free Import," Supervisor Bear reminded Floyt for the third time. "In fact, let me see it."

He sighed and extracted it. The Earthservice letter of Free Import was a rare document; few Terrans had even heard the term. The one-page form, bearing Floyt's name in glowing characters, cited regulations of which he was totally ignorant. It authorized him to return to his place of residence—presumably with his inheritance—without hindrance or interference from Earthservice customs officials or Peaceguardians. What with the many interbureaucratic rivalries and feuds, Bear was taking no chances on having to share Project Shepherd's thunder with anyone, or having the bequest or its proceeds diverted from her own budget.

He carefully resealed it into an inner pocket of the awkward anticontamination suit he wore. The suit, like almost everything he was to take, had been provided by Earthservice psychprop analysts. It was decked out with medical gear, urine and excreta reservoirs, decontamination kits, and testing paraphernalia. It was armored against radiation, and its cumbersome helmet, which Floyt carried under his arm, had arrangements for eating, drinking, regurgitation, and purging of nasal cavities and ears. Provision had even been made for keeping the wearer's eyes clear of discharge and the like.

The anticontamination suit had an airpack and heating

and cooling equipment but, as Floyt had already discovered, no apparatus for dealing with an itch on the wearer's calf.

Just as Earthservice intended, Floyt looked as if he was bound for a radioactive wasteland teeming with demented plague carriers—which, Alacrity thought, looking at him, was exactly the way the breakabout felt about Earth.

Of course, Floyt's wife and daughter were present. Seduced by the luxuries and perquisites that she too could share in her father's absence, Reesa had set aside the tailoring of a pseudodeerskin wardrobe. Balensa wore her finest; Floyt found himself staring at her even though it hurt.

Reesa and Balensa's comments and responses had been composed for them by Bear and her psychprop director. They showed great affection for Floyt and profound concern for his safety; the audience had to be reminded that offworld travel was risky and uncomfortable. Mother and daughter made evident their pride and the fact that they couldn't wait to have Floyt home, a hero of Terra. They were modest about their own home-front courage.

Alacrity sat in a corner, much ignored, which was fine with him. Earthservice didn't want to make much of the offworlder's role in the mission.

"I'm going along in case he needs his excreta bag changed," he'd deadpanned to one pickup, and that had been that.

He looked different now from the young man Bear and Floyt were somewhat used to. Earthservice had reclaimed his warbag from a spaceport lockbox. He wore a blue-gray shipsuit, a bit faded and worn, its ship-patch and insignia mounts bare. It had numerous carry-loops and cargo pockets on hips, legs, arms, and chest. A high collar, worn open, concealed a hood. The full-body insert for heating and cooling was a compact bulge in his right hip pocket. Instead of soft ship's shoes, he wore a pair of pathfinder boots he'd bought on So Far, comfortable despite their knee guards and protective reinforcement.

Next to him, his warbag held just about everything he owned. Reesa appraised him from across the room, noticing the slim build and broad shoulders and his height. The strange hair and tawny, wide, oblique eyes interested her. She wondered how he would look in a deerskin loincloth. She began to drift his way, but was intercepted by a vigilant psychprop assistant director.

Alacrity had been keeping an attentive eye on Bear. Now, seeing her alone, he walked over to her purposefully, the pathfinder boots making little sound on the glossy floor.

"What about my other things—you know? When do I get them back?"

"They've been given to the shuttle crew. They will be returned to you on Luna."

Alacrity swore. "Listen, do you want me to keep your boy safe or not?"

"Those are the rules!" She walked off, leaving him scowling.

A warning hooter indicated that the lunar shuttle was about to lift. Recording crews were ready to immortalize the moment. Reesa and Balensa were suddenly and bravely holding back tears. There would be little coverage of the vessel's actual liftoff; such things were considered vulgar.

Alacrity shouldered aside the lackey who was reaching for his warbag. He grabbed it and led the way with wide strides, focusing on no one. He trod heavily, making the boarding tube resound hollowly. The white-painted lock gaped, its rescue and safety stencils in red.

A bored crewchief leaned on the lock. He had the soft, pallid, gravity-beset look common to Lunarians. No charming attendants or luxury class on the Earth run; Terra was lucky that the Lunies kept the route open.

The crewchief ticked off Alacrity's name against a passenger manifest on his hand-held screen. Floyt was still embroiled in his leavetaking, the sound of it echoing down the boarding tube.

She was a superannuated vessel, a headboarded ship called *Mindframe*. The passenger compartment was drab and sparse. There were only two or three other passengers, unremarkable and quiet, apparently content to tend to their own business. Alacrity secured his warbag and glanced through a viewport.

Earth's last spaceport. It was a sad, mostly abandoned place of empty gantries and decaying hangars, neglected and moribund. Beyond the perimeter he could see the plains of Nazca, suitably vacant and forbidding.

Only a once-weekly shuttle and occasional freighters connected Terra to the rest of the universe. No starship was permitted to make planetfall.

Alacrity walked back to the lock. At the opposite end of the boarding tube stood Floyt with Bear and his family crowded around him. The recording teams were in a feeding frenzy, circling and angling for good shots, doing their best to miss nothing. *Mindframe* was near liftoff time, and the Lunies were in no mood to hang around the Terran gravity they so disliked for another take. Alacrity watched the happy scene, arms folded across his chest.

"Our hopes and prayers go with you, Citizen Floyt. A grateful Terra looks forward to your return." Supervisor Bear showed her profile to best advantage.

Floyt was unmoving, gaping down the tube. He hadn't taken his cue, so Bear pushed tentatively against his shoulder. He didn't budge. The recorders were still running.

"We thank you for your selfless devotion to the cause of Terran well-being," she improvised. In her mind, the music that would accompany this part of the documentary and psychprop spots was reaching a crescendo. She urged him on with her hand again, harder.

Floyt dug in his heels. Alacrity watched with interest. Balensa and Reesa ad-libbed an endearment or two, but they were plainly distressed. The medical equipment and other gadgetry attached to the anticontamination suit rattled as the supervisor tried to shove the functionary along without appearing to.

Balensa and Reesa had relapsed into silence. The struggle at the head of the tube was becoming more energetic. Without breaking her profile, Bear made a minute hand signal.

The crews stopped recording and someone acknowledged, "Clear!" Supervisor Bear placed both hands on Floyt's shoulders, pushing. Still silent and expressionless, he braced one hand against the tube's entrance and refused to move. The psychprop director and his assistant rushed to help, setting their shoulders against Floyt's back while Bear, teeth gritted, pried at his fingers.

With a mighty, concerted effort, the three bulled Floyt loose from his position and, legs churning, propelled him down the tubeway. They stopped one another halfway. Floyt, arms windmilling, equipment clattering, flailed onward in a barely controlled stumble, his helmet bouncing along behind him.

Alacrity was obliged to catch him as the Terran collided with him in the shuttle's lock. The Lunie crewchief yawned and duly noted Floyt's arrival. Floyt shook off Alacrity's hands, eyeing the breakabout and shaking his head fatalistically. "There's two born every minute."

CHAPTER 6

THE SOCKWALLET LASHUP

BUCKLED INTO HIS WIDE, DEEPLY CUSHIONED ACCELERA-
tion chair, Alacrity went to sleep right after *Mindframe*
raised ship. The brutal Earthservice conditioning had taken
more out of him than he'd let himself show on Terra. Besides,
he hadn't yet riddled out the conflicting feelings of protec-
tiveness, resentment, and forbearance he felt toward Floyt.

The plains of Nazca dropped away beneath them, allowing Floyt his first aerial view of the Nazca Lines, made by
Terrans millennia before the recorded beginnings of human
flight. The lines formed enormous totemic symbols, but only
for an observer flying high overhead. The Lines were one
of the reasons the Nazca spaceport had been selected to be
the planet's last functioning one.

Like all Earthers, Floyt was a member of the Church of
the Terran Spirit, at least nominally. But he found himself
too distracted by his difficulties to meditate very much upon
the Lines.

Mindframe climbed quickly through the atmosphere. The
headboarded skipper lost no time in adjusting the ship's
gravity to the accustomed lunar one-sixth Standard. Floyt

shifted uncomfortably in the bulky anticontamination suit. He was still trying to deal with the dread and apprehension threatening to overwhelm him when he too fell asleep.

Alpa Bureaucrat Stemp had titular superiors in the Earthservice organization, but they existed for cosmetic purposes, mere figureheads. He had in truth only a handful of peers, and the Alphas were answerable only to themselves as a group.

It was generally assumed that the Alpha prefix stood for exalted rank, talent, and achievements. But for Stemp and his circle, it represented their position as Earthservice's apex-predators.

Stemp had disposed of several minor matters: reallocation of protein distribution, suppression of certain fundamentalist tracts, and denial of permission for a 1960s revivicist festival due to the antiauthoritarian sentiments of that era. He had also taken his nap.

Just then he was attending to a very low priority issue, condescending to permit Supervisor Bear to enter the vaulted vastness of his office, that she might deliver her progress report.

She showed him a strained smile and wore a much different air from the one she'd employed with Floyt and the others. Stemp's whim had kept her waiting for more than two hours, but she was all sweetness and light.

Her most attractive feature, her long, burnished brown hair, shone. Stemp braced himself for another dose of her effusiveness. Bear didn't fail him.

She spoke too quickly, too animatedly, too ingratiatingly. Project Shepherd was entirely her venture at this point, of course; Stemp didn't want to be too closely identified with it, in case it should end in failure. If it succeeded, she would naturally receive a portion of the credit and praise he would garner, and he would reward her. That was the order of things.

But there'd been that first-mission fiasco, so Stemp was still keeping himself distanced from Shepherd. No Alpha forgot for a moment the fact that the predators occasionally fed on one another.

Onward plowed Bear, fairly glowing. She'd come to Stemp's attention and been permitted her very brief, vague glimpse of the sweep and majesty of the Alphas' power. She lived only for the time when she would join them. She was one of many aspirants.

It took only a few mild proddings from Stemp to get her to abbreviate her report. She told of Alacrity's recruitment—scrupulously avoiding any mention of her own part in it, though Stemp would almost certainly have an inkling of that. She went on to Floyt and the mysterious offworld inheritance—

"Weir?" Stemp burst out, suddenly sitting upright, coming out of a half doze, eyes bulging. "Great Holy Terra! *Weir?*"

Supervisor Bear's stomach did a fancy change-step, and her heart threatened to fibrillate. "Was your research team asleep?" Stemp demanded. "Weir has never been anything but a vexation to us!"

Bear swallowed. "I was aware of a certain lack of cordiality between Weir and Terra's offworld reps and contacts. There didn't appear to be anything else prejudicial." She saw her entire career being cycled down the sanitary conduit.

Stemp had regained mastery of himself, half closing his eyes. "How high was the clearance level on your project?"

"B-Beta clearance, sir." What could she have missed, she wondered—unless it was Alpha-access material? "Your study group approved it, Alpha Bureaucrat Stemp. And it was passed by the Overview Board." Approved, Project Shepherd had become Bear's own bailiwick; she'd lost no time insulating it from outside scrutiny and interference.

Nevertheless, Stemp was linked to the project. Although he was pretending to use his information displays, which were shielded from her view, he was lost in thought. Bear couldn't imagine what would make so petty and distant a potentate as Weir dangerous to Earthservice. She tried not to fidget as she waited.

At length, Stemp rapped, "Very well; I want an in-depth project report at once. And keep me informed of all developments. Communication, information, rumor, *anything*. Understood?"

She nodded vigorously, maintaining the prescribed eye contact throughout. "That's all." He pretended she was no longer there.

Bear slunk from the office, resisting the urge to run. When she was gone, the Alpha let out his breath in a sustained blast. He drummed his fingers in thought, head bowed. This Project Shepherd business could well put him in jeopardy.

And sometimes the apex-predators fed on one another.

When Floyt awoke, he saw from the cabin displayer that safety harness was no longer required and passengers were free to move around the cabin. He'd heard that passengers were sometimes permitted to visit the cockpit of a spacecraft, and so he unbuckled himself clumsily, still encumbered by the anticontamination suit. In the light gravity, he rose with elaborate care, his equipment rattling.

Alacrity, still apparently asleep, said, "Ho?"

"Yes?"

"Would you please get rid of that ridiculous fart incubator? The Lunies will laugh themselves sick. Besides, it'd attract attention in Lunaport."

As Floyt struggled out of the suit, he looked at the other passengers. There was nothing remarkable about them. Earthservice investigators had run rigorous checks on them, as well as the crew, to minimize the chances of trouble. On Luna, things would be much riskier.

Stowing the suit, Floyt paused for a moment to look at

the Earth. It was a broad blue-and-white arc astern, making him feel queasy; he continued forward.

The cockpit hatch was open. Floyt looked through and froze in mid-step. The pilot and copilot, a heavyset middle-aged woman and a barely postpubescent boy respectively, were strapped into safety recliners, seemingly asleep. They were headboarded, their implants relaying instructions to *Mindframe*.

There were manual controls as well, and these responded to the silent commands. It was as if ghosts were manipulating the touchpads and switches; monitors and indicators flashed in all colors, ignored. There was ceaseless, disembodied activity.

A surveillance monitor swung to focus on him. A synthesized voice asked politely, "Is there any problem?"

"No, I . . . no. Thank you." He retreated, flustered, from the haunted cockpit and its corpselike residents.

"Spooky, isn't it?" Alacrity said when Floyt returned to his seat. "I don't much care for headboarders either." He thought it better not to tell the Terran any of the gruesome tales about what happened if a headboarder became mentally unhinged.

"Here." Alacrity handed Floyt an elastic, pouchlike affair with a fastening strap.

"What's this?"

"Put your valuables in it—money and travel documents. Then put it on, between your calf and knee, pouch facing inward, under your pants." He smiled at Floyt's surprise. "Keep your eyes open and stick close, citizen. This is a *starport* we're headed for. If you don't know what that means, you will in about three hours."

Studying Luna's cold, pockmarked face on their approach, Floyt saw that the final Srillan raid had left Earth's moon almost completely untouched.

"Anyway, almost everything's underground," Alacrity

observed. "The surface is either empty or looks like a gar-
bage dump."

Mindframe settled into a subsurface hangar, and a huge
slab-door rolled closed overhead, while a debarkation tube
stretched out to leech onto the shuttle's airlock.

The two had their minimal baggage in hand, and Alacrity
insisted on presenting the anticontamination suit to the shuttle crewchief, since they had no further use for it. He didn't
mention that he'd sold the suit. The cash was already in his
upper left arm pocket.

The Terran followed the breakabout through the tube,
shuffle-hopping in the fractional gravity, taking to it quite
handily, delighting himself until he realized that he wasn't
supposed to be enjoying any part of his assignment. Alacrity
paused by the airlock at the tube's end, signaling for Floyt
to hang back while the other passengers queued up at the
customs chutes.

The Earther was content enough with waiting, testing his
newfound skill with little bounces and skips. Carrying small
cargo boxes and personal baggage, *Mindframe*'s crew moved
past them, graceful and free in its native gravity. The headboarded pilot and her copilot greeted Floyt courteously, as
if they'd met him while awake.

The crew presented themselves to the customs agents;
the other passengers had been passed through quickly. Now
Alacrity moved to get into line, with Floyt close behind.
The customs agent who checked out Floyt's documentation
examined him a little curiously; Earthservice functionaries
weren't known to travel offworld for any reason. But the
man marked Floyt's ID packet and, after a cursory look
through it, his bag as well.

Alacrity was still standing before an agent in the next
chute, Floyt saw. After the agent had finished with the
breakabout's documents and warbag, he lifted a large wooden
case from behind the counter.

Alacrity opened the case's fingerprint lock. Floyt went

over to see what was going on. The breakabout drew out a coiled band of red-brown leather.

It was a heavy, machine-stitched gunbelt with shoulder strap and holstered pistol. Alacrity opened the holster strap and drew the weapon, with a bit of effort, the metal clinging to the leather. He drew the ponderous handgun and set it down carefully on the counter.

"Officer's weapon?" one of the customs inspectors asked.

"Captain's Sidearm," Alacrity corrected, pointing to a gleaming insignia on the holster. The harness was a variation on the ancient Sam Browne belt. The breakabout slung it over one shoulder.

One inspector entered the gun's serial number into a data-search terminal. Others examined his documents, both paper and info-wafer, suspiciously. "It was my father's," Alacrity added.

It was a weapon that would make an impression on anyone, weighty and matte-black, wide-muzzled and ominous. It had a curved basket-guard to protect the user's hand from energy backlash.

More interesting, to Floyt, was the sturdy rib running from muzzle to handguard base. It was a deflector, like the ones on primitive Terran firearms, for warding off edged or blunt weapons. This one was notched and dented in several places. The Captain's Sidearm had contoured grips of yellowed ivory mounted with worn crests of some sort. The crests resembled a florid Maltese cross superinscribed on a celestial arc.

Alacrity went to one end of the counter with the inspector-in-charge. They had the hardwood box and the Captain's Sidearm, and the breakabout was speaking earnestly to the Lunie. The other customs agents conspicuously ignored the conversation.

Alacrity reached to the pocket on his upper left arm, and lunar metal-foil currency changed hands. The inspector-in-charge nodded, and an underling entered serial numbers into the data unit. Alacrity had a temporary carrier's permit. The customs agents disappeared behind their superior, eyeing the cash in his hand. Alacrity tucked the hardwood box into his warbag, gathered up bag and gunbelt, and sauntered back to Floyt.

He stopped to don the gunbelt, adjusting the old-fashioned buckles and settling the strap that fit over his left shoulder. "As soon as we can, Floyt, we'll pick up one for you, something easy to fire, that you can hide under your—"

"I will not carry a weapon."

"Listen, this is a starport. And Epiphany might not be safe either."

"I *won't*!" Earthservice psychprop had been emphatic about that from infancy. Alacrity saw that there was no appealing the decision for the time being. He skip-shuffled for the exit. Floyt trailed him with a growing surety of movement.

They threaded their way along a winding tunnel marked in Terranglish and Tradeslang. It was well lighted and comfortably warm. The air smelled of hydroponic and aeroponic growth. They emerged into a place designated "Billingsgate Circus," named centuries before by some homesick cockney. It was an enormous rotunda, some two hundred meters across, set beneath Luna's surface and roofed by a transparent dome.

Due to glaring signs and holos on the circus, it was difficult to see anything through the dome. The place was a costume-jewelry box of shops, brothels, stalls, saloons, hotels, places of worship, clinics, shady-looking places claiming to be schools, casinos, and dance halls.

Banks of machines vended everything from on-the-spot blood tests to disguises, and raucous autohucksters, like robotized barrow boys, were everywhere.

Lunies of every age and sort abounded. Their dress ranged from nudity with polychromatic skin film to latter-day Byzantine neo-Nipponese to the mode known as "sex gladiator." Floyt in his understated Earther slacks and the matching tunic that concealed his Inheritor's belt, and Alacrity in his shipsuit, attracted no notice.

Local residents had a suggestive, even provocative way of moving in their light gravity—by Terran standards, at any rate. They sucked and chewed on pacifiers impregnated with their favorite drugs, or paused to sniff from inhalers. They masticated hybridized betel nuts and coca leaves, popped spansules, or licked chemically enhanced sweet-sticks.

Floyt gaped at a major corridor called Petticoat Lane, the main spaceport red-light district. Its blazing, graphic advertisements offered things illegal even to mention on Terra. Near the two was an extravagant-looking cabaret called, simply, Sorbition. Among its flashing messages was one assuring the public, LOWER LIFEFORMS SERVED—WHAT'LL YOU HAVE? Alacrity gazed at it wistfully, but knew they couldn't stop just then.

Nor would there be time for Floyt to pick up another language or two at the local Pan Stellar Communications Institute franchise. Pan Stellar taught everything from Terranglish as a second language to the finger-palaver of Smack Dab and the neo-Silbo whistled in Tivoli's endless caverns. The techniques included mnemonic treatments, info implants, subliminal tutelary programs, and heuristic regimens.

It wouldn't take long, but it would have taken longer than they had. Still, Terranglish was fairly common where the two were bound, and many other languages were based on it and used loanwords from the Terran tongue.

A few non-Lunarians were also around, O'Neillers and other Solarians. Alacrity also spotted a number who were outsystem, and the nonhumans in the crowd were obvious. Floyt had often heard the term "bright-eyed and bushy-tailed," but never before encountered an intelligent being who lived up to the expression. His lip curled as a thing like a walking mushroom covered with feathers bobbed past. "I keep waiting to turn into a pillar of salt," he declared.

"Oh, this is just the action part of town," Alacrity said lightly. "Lunaport's got its monuments and parks and city hall." He watched a svelte young woman with a green-dyed topknot, wearing an extremely wide-mesh body stocking of the same color, sashay into an endorphin den. "Things are always a little looser around a spaceport."

Floyt checked the cheap proteus supplied him by Earthservice. His accessor, of course, was of no use away from Terra's data and computer-service networks and satellite links. "I suppose it's best we were getting to our lodgment. It's a place called the High Movers' Stop." Weir's executors had included provisions for quarters during the wait for transit. "Which way would that be, Alacrity?"

The breakabout answered, "Forget it; we're not going there. Too many people know we're supposed to."

"The Earthservice gave me definite instructions. It's settled."

"Hell's entropy! Will you forget Earthservice, Ho? We're on our own now, can't you get that through your turban?"

Several passersby noted the dispute without stopping. It wasn't much out of the ordinary in Billingsgate Circus. Besides, Alacrity had one thumb hooked in a gunbelt carrying a rather large pistol.

"See here," Floyt objected. "I'm tired and foul-smelling. I have no intention of wandering Lunaport until boarding time."

"Ho, how'd you like to check into the Stop and find another admirer waiting for you with a styrette, hm? Tired of living, are you, or just curious about the afterlife? We'd probably *both* end up getting terminal vitamin shots!"

Floyt half smiled despite himself. "Well, even at one-sixth gee, we're going to get pretty tired standing around here, aren't we?"

"I asked a few questions when I came through O'Neill V on my way to Terra. We've got a perfect place to moor down for a while."

"You have friends here?"

"Sort of. There's a Forager lashup out near Hubble City. That's for us."

Floyt yielded. They wove through the throngs, kangarooing and skid-stepping. Alacrity found a map sphere, then led Floyt off toward a tubeway.

When they'd boarded and found places on the insubstantial-looking seats, the Earther inquired, "Who are these Foragers?"

The capsule accelerated as Alacrity replied, "You'd call them, uh, Gypsies. Or beachcombers. Salvage and recycling experts. Nomads."

"Criminals?" Floyt couldn't stop himself from asking.

Alacrity's look hardened. "No. And neither am I. Listen, I know what they told you about me, but I'm a murderer about the same way you're a noble, fearless hero of the Terran weal, all right?"

Without turning a hair, Floyt answered, "Credit me with a little intelligence; Skinner and his team worked on me, too."

They both acknowledged a bit of common ground, Floyt with a half smile and Alacrity with a nod. Floyt went on, "So these Foragers roam the entire moon?"

"They go just about anywhere other humans go—any star system and in between."

Alacrity looked to the viewscreen at the front of the capsule. It showed the lunar surface beneath which they were passing and the ruins of the first boxtown. In its time, This End Up City, or "Upsie," as it came to be called, had been the largest ever to accumulate. But Upsie had been abandoned centuries before, ramshackled and used up during the first hundred years or so of human expansion.

Shipping containers of every shape and size, fabricated for cargo of all descriptions, had been jury-rigged as living quarters. Additional structures had been slapped together from whatever materials were available. This End Up City, like most boxtowns, had been a high-risk place to live.

Boxtowns were found all across human space still; Alacrity had lived in them and knew their subculture well. He watched until the place was no longer within range of the capsule's pickups, then turned back to the Earther.

"I've met Foragers before. These should be willing to take us in. We'll see."

The specter of the moon's first and smallest mass driver grew rapidly in the monitor, little more than skeletal remains, stripped and—rare for Luna—vandalized.

Clustered around the catapult head, though, were newer structures that struck Floyt as disharmonic and looking a bit unfinished, even though their design was strange to him and struck him as hodgepodge.

"This is our stop," Alacrity announced. They gathered their things as the capsule slowed and stopped, then stepped out onto a broad platform. The capsule whispered away on its rail-field.

The place had plainly been a busy depot at one time; now it looked forlorn. A few crates and containers were stacked here and there, along with old machinery, pieces of equipment, and scavenged parts. But most of the huge depot was empty, with just enough debris and general refuse to give it an air of decay.

Several men and women, young and fiercely suspicious, stood nonchalant guard. To Floyt they resembled some offworld update of Dickens's street urchins. They carried hammergun rifles, plasma lances, and scatterbeams. Half of them were crouched near machinery or other cover. The Terran concluded that they'd been forewarned of the capsule's approach—not surprising, he supposed, in such a pronouncedly technical society.

Carefully ranging to either side to give themselves clear fields of fire, the Foragers studied the new arrivals. They hadn't missed the weapon on Alacrity's hip. The breakabout lowered his warbag, and the Earther followed suit dubiously.

The guards were grimy and looked both hungry and dangerous. Floyt opened his mouth to invoke Alacrity's conditioning if he had to, in order to leave as promptly as possible. The breakabout spoke first, though.

"Which outfit is this?" he queried in loud, curt Terranglish.

"Who wants to know?" a thin young woman asked in the same language but with an exotic accent like nothing Floyt had ever heard before. Her straight brown hair was very close-cropped, her gray eyes canny and direct. She wasn't beautiful, Floyt thought, but attractive in her intensity and command of self.

"Shipwreck Mazuma," Alacrity answered. Floyt looked to him in open surprise, and the Foragers didn't miss that either. "I got that name from the Doghouse Outfit, from Freebie Giveaway himself. By spit and by split, divvies and blood. That was back on Blue Ribbon."

The Foragers glanced to one another uneasily. "Well?" Alacrity shouted, suddenly looking cantankerous. "I'm claiming my entitlements. What're you going to do about it?"

"What about him?" the woman asked, nodding toward Floyt.

"He's with me. I'm not asking for gens privileges, darling; just a place to locker." Floyt wondered why that made the woman blush angrily and the men chortle.

She approached Alacrity warily and offered her hand. The Terran didn't see the recognition technique as they clasped one another's wrists. Nevertheless, when they released, she nodded, saying, "He knows the get-in."

The rest relaxed just a hair, lowering weapons. "This is the Sockwallet Outfit," she informed them. Then, turning from them a bit, she spoke softly into a comclip concealed in the folds of her tattered scarf.

When she turned her attention back to them, she said to Alacrity, "Gunny's going to meet us at the main lock. He's our boss." She held out her hand again. Alacrity shucked his Sam Browne belt and handed over the Captain's Sidearm.

Foragers moved in and searched their baggage and persons with hands and surprisingly sophisticated instruments. They did it so thoroughly that Floyt almost objected until he saw that the breakabout, headstrong and quarrelsome as he might be, was accepting the inspection with good grace.

Half the guards remained behind. The two travelers were surrounded by their tatterdemalion escort and convoyed toward the lashup.

In a larger warehouse area beyond the platform, the newcomers saw much more equipment and cargo, salvage and scrap. It was all carefully sorted and tagged or stenciled, stacked, crated, and orderly. The jumble on the capsule platform had been camouflage.

The party skim-hopped up an incline toward the mass-driver's former control complex and catapult head. The members of the Sockwallet Outfit kept a sharp watch on their visitors. "How'd you fall in with the Doghousers?" the woman asked.

"Met up with them after they hit some trouble on the *Bragging Dragon* job."

She was impressed. "You too?" she asked Floyt. Having no idea what they were talking about, he simply told the truth. "No."

"What's *your* name, by the way?"

Alacrity answered for him. "Name's Delver Rootnose. He's not Forager, as you can see. Neither am I, really. We buddied a while ago."

Floyt held his peace, reflecting that Alacrity hadn't created a bad alias for someone interested in genealogies. "What do they call you, rig?" Alacrity asked.

"Simoleanna Coup."

"Simoleanna?"

"S'right. My father's name was Simolean Coup. And they don't call me Anna and they don't call me Mo. It's Sim. Got me, rig?"

"Sim. Got you."

The group sequenced through gates and open locks, up toward the lashup. The tunnel was vast, its floor, walls, and ceiling of seamless rockmelt.

They passed a trio of guards skip-sliding down to reinforce the detail at the capsule platform, and saw others posted, Foragers of all ages past adolescence, and both sexes. They were well armed, with energy weapons and flechette burpguns. Alacrity congratulated himself on picking the safest place on Luna.

They ascended to the outer door of the final airlock, which was secured shut. A monstrously obese man waited there; Floyt judged him to be of old-time Polynesian descent. He wore a gorgeous handmade sweater of off-white wool from Dunrovin and loose black pantaloons, with scarlet velvet slippers.

"Gunny, this is—"

He gestured Simoleanna to silence, gliding over to them like a balloon. He stopped before Floyt, jabbing a thumb into his quivering chest and announcing, "Gunny Readyknob is my name. What's yours, rig?"

"Delver Rootnose," the Earther responded promptly, not without trepidation.

The Sockwallets' leader looked to Alacrity. "And that'd make you Shipwreck Mazuma, huh?"

Alacrity nodded.

Gunny Readyknob went on, "Well, if you were *really* in Freebie Giveaway's outfit, you know what Freebie keeps up his right sleeve. Now what d'you think that would be, rig?"

Alacrity raised one eyebrow. "Freebie's got nothing up his right sleeve, Gunny. He's left-handed. That's where he keeps his neurosap."

Gunny switched to a language Floyt didn't recognize, filled with rasping clicks and aspirants. The Terran caught the rising inflection that made it a question, though. "Shipwreck" replied in the same tongue, finishing with the strangely Terranglish word "Shibboleth."

Whatever it all had meant, Floyt saw, it convinced Gunny Readyknob. He laughed monumentally, rippling, and plucked up Alacrity, placing a sound, smacking kiss on his forehead. The other Foragers guffawed; the breakabout endured it with a blush.

The guards slung arms. The whole group began to pass into the main airlock. Floyt's fears for his own safety had submerged his distaste for offworlders until now, but he found his revulsion for the grubby space tramps growing. Safety or no, he wasn't certain that he could tolerate their company in close quarters for long. Simoleanna Coup was eyeing Alacrity curiously. The breakabout seemed at ease.

The outer hatch, a gargantuan metal plug, swung shut, moving silently and smoothly. Floyt couldn't see how it was hinged. The lock had once been external, giving access to the lunar surface. It had fallen into disrepair and been stripped once the mass-driver had gone out of service. The Foragers had refurbished the lock soundly, though, and with great craftsmanship, connecting it to the lashup they'd established aboveground.

The Foragers were such meticulous engineers that there was no discernible change in pressure or sound as the hatch closed. The airlock was decorated with escutcheons, bow shields, and interior emblems from various spacecraft, like some medieval throne room.

Other members of the outfit were waiting in the lock. They closed in on Alacrity and frisked him again, thoroughly and with his silent cooperation. Floyt emulated his companion. The search was, again, complete but not rude. In the meantime the guards were handing over their weapons, which were stored in an arms room to one side of the airlock.

Alacrity's proteus was confiscated, as was Floyt's. "Part of the hospitality." The breakabout shrugged. Gunny laughed mountainously, but held on to the Captain's Sidearm, which seemed to raise no objections from anyone. The travelers' luggage, which had been examined once more, still wasn't returned to them.

"They've got to be cautious," Alacrity explained quietly to Floyt as the inner hatch swung open noiselessly. "If anything ever happened to a bubble or lock or seal, the whole lashup could go, and everybody in it."

They moved out under a soaring, crystal-clear dome thirty meters high. "God in the Void," Floyt said, borrowing Alacrity's oath.

Filtered by the dome, sunlight streamed down on them. Connecting tunnels radiated in all directions—none of the construction matching, nothing uniform—to the disparate structures of the lashup. The inner hatch was already swinging shut behind them. Keeping all interior hatches and doors secure was instinctive with the Foragers.

"Are the lunar authorities aware of all this?" Floyt asked Alacrity.

Gunny Readyknob had caught it. "We pay our taxes, Delver, and plenty of squeeze besides. And we mind our own business, too." Floyt supposed that would make anybody acceptable on the Moon.

The Sockwallet Outfit had built their lashup on the surface because, unlike Lunarians, Foragers preferred views and vistas, landscapes and the feeling of plenty of room. They built with whatever was available when they stopped somewhere. On their migrations, they took only themselves, tools and equipment to make their living, emergency shelters and weapons, personal belongings, and the sacred artifacts of the Outfit.

In the middle of the dome was a pole eight meters or more in height, a bizarre pylon made of many miniature charms and constructs, stylized faces, symbols, fetishes,

mementos, and trinkets, layer upon layer of them, fused
into a mass representing an informal history of the events
and fortunes of the Sockwallet Outfit.

Alacrity skimmed over to it, with Floyt in his wake. If
it could be avoided, Foragers preferred not to equip their
lashups, which were always temporary, with artificial gravity. The Terran was glad he took fairly well to the Moon's
one-sixth Standard.

The breakabout kissed his fingertips softly and laid them
against the strange column in a reverent gesture. Floyt held
back, sensing that he didn't have the prerogative. The reactions of Gunny, Sim, and the rest showed approval of both
men.

Gunny beckoned, and they passed from the dome into
the lashup itself. It had a haphazard look to it at first glance,
since it incorporated the forms of salvaged vessels and vehicle hulls, building shells, and parts thereof. But the construction was all first-rate craftsmanship. The muddled
architectural scheme had a certain consistency: variety and
disregard of convention.

The lashup was carefully designed for its environment,
but each of its component sections had a character and feel
of its own.

"C'mon in, rigs," Sim bade them, "and join the fun."

Below, on the depot platform, the guards went on alert
as another capsule arrived.

Its doors slid apart, and a tall, muscular man stepped
out. He had a heavy-browed, blunt-nosed face; his pink
scalp gleamed, hairless. He wore the loose plaid culottes
and pleated shirt favored by many Venerian businessmen,
and carried a slim attaché case, an expensive Aladdin model.

He was pulling on a stylish mandarin hat, eyes to the
ground. When he looked up, he stopped dead in his tracks.
The Sockwallet guards were amused that such an intimi-
dating face could show such bewilderment. They saw his

fear of them, and the dawning realization that he'd stepped off at the wrong stop, written clearly on the rugged countenance.

He heard the capsule doors closing and turned, lurching frantically to hold them open. Plainly unused to lunar gravity, he got his feet tangled.

One guard laughed, not unkindly, "Hubble City's one more stop, rig." The man grinned sheepishly and called thanks in Terranglish accented with Venerian Crosstalk.

But as the capsule pulled away from the platform, a change came over the muscular man's features. He returned to his seat with movements that proved he was well accustomed to Luna's gravity and sat next to the only other passenger in the capsule, a small, dapper man who wore gaudy knee breeches and stockings, tricorn hat, and frock coat.

"Fairly standard Forager lashup, Page," the big man reported distractedly, considering the problem.

Page sighed. "Do we wait for another time, then?"

"Nix. They might evade us again. We'll take them inside the lashup."

"*Inside?* How're we gonna do that, Shilly?"

Shilly rubbed his block of a jaw. "I think I've got a way. When we get to Hubble, call Jord at the High Movers' Stop. Tell him we'll meet him in one hour, and that we'll need some special arrangements."

CHAPTER 7

WONDERMENTS

"THE MAIN THING TO REMEMBER," ALACRITY CAUTIONED Floyt, "is that most of the unusual taboos in a lashup have to do with the air supply. Safeguarding the integrity of the seals and locks and hulls. *No* jokes about vacuum or leaks or anything like that."

"Alacrity, I don't *know* any jokes about air leaks." Floyt frowned as he tried to knot his floppy red-silk four-in-hand necktie properly. "Do you? Why in the world would anybody joke about such a thing?" He was more convinced than ever that all offworlders suffered from congenital mental disorders.

"Some of us do it to ease the tension. 'The air's always fresher on the other side of the hatch,' know what I mean? Oh, never mind! Just remember that that kind of talk's bad manners around here."

The Foragers had insisted on lending them festival clothes and Alacrity was examining himself, pleased with his image. He wore a shimmering, close-fitting shirt of spectraflex that rippled with color-shifts as he moved, its collar and shoulder seam raffishly agape. Along with it he wore metallic green tights and mantlet.

Floyt was resplendent in saffron yellow blouse with extended shoulders and sleeve billows, crimson tie, and brown taperslacks, along with his Inheritor's belt; Alacrity had insisted that a guest was perfectly safe, even from prying, in a lashup.

Guest quarters were the scavenged forward section of a *Virago*-class patrol craft from the old Solar Pact navy. Floyt had marveled at how the lashup was cobbled together with dome fitted to nacelle, pressure-quonset to hull, tunnel to warehouse. One missing panel in their quarters had been replaced with a big blister of stained glassplas, depicting a magnificent fleur-de-lis, out of some vessel's chapel.

The Earther, who'd avoided using *Mindframe*'s complicated and highly unorthodox-looking head, had immediately tackled their lunar lavatory and found the experience comfortable, sanitary, and simple. One of his major fears about space travel had been dispelled, contributing considerably to his good mood. Still, he said, "Alacrity, I'm telling you, I'd rather not have anything to do with this Sockwallet festival."

He saw the breakabout's sour look and amended, "I mean, Shipwreck, I don't want—"

"They're just showing us a little hospitality. You don't want to offend them, do you? Bad for the mission."

Alacrity had started playing Floyt's conditioned commitment to his mission against his natural aversion to non-Terrans. The breakabout had guessed shrewdly about the tack selected by the behavioral engineering team, and when he put things that way, Floyt found, the company of off-world mongrels didn't seem so detestable.

But Floyt hated feeling manipulated; Bear and Earthservice had done quite enough of that. "We're strangers to them. I don't see why they should care whether we enjoy ourselves here anyway," the Terran huffed.

"It's as much for the Sockwallets as for us. Foragers don't let many outsiders inside their lashups, you know. This gives them an excuse to whoop it up and show off their kids." He turned sideways and eyed the dressing-imager critically.

"Children? Why is that so important?"

"Makes them feel like part of the group." Alacrity adjusted his mantlet fastidiously. "Loved, appreciated. Common to a lot of cultures."

"Common in Terran cultures, once," Floyt mused, gazing through a thick bull's-eye porthole at the stark lunascape.

Gunny appeared at the lock just then. "Shipwreck! Delver! You're keeping people waiting, boys!"

Foragers let outsiders think them malodorous tramps. They proved differently to their guests. The Sockwallets turned out under the great inverted bowl of the main dome, gathered around their pylon. Toddlers to oldsters, they were scrubbed and groomed, scented and attired in every sort of finery. Floyt could now appreciate how beneficial it was, in a sealed environment like the lashup, to place heavy social emphasis on hygiene, filters and purifiers notwithstanding.

Since leaving Earth, he'd been subjected to a number of different scent-ambiances, *Mindframe* and Billingsgate Circus among them. But the lashup's was the most pleasant, with its suggestions of flowers and fresh breezes, open sky and summer rain. Floyt wondered how they did it.

The preadults there, in particular, were preening. Arrayed in the very best clothing they owned or could beg or borrow, they were doing their best to look formal and grown-up, even while they blushed or indulged in a bit of horseplay.

About a hundred people were already present, with more arriving all the time. The dome had been polarized a bit to cut the sun's glare. Tables and chairs, in mismatched variety, had been set out.

As Floyt watched, the Sockwallets rolled out kegs of Old Geyserfroth, the superlative pilsner that had been brewed on Luna since the First Breath. They uncrated noble, prismatic bottles of Gunga Din Gin brought with them from Raj, planet of their previous lashup. Assorted other beverages and concoctions appeared in squeeze bottles and decanters, demijohns and skins, and various punch bowls, some of which were big enough to wade in.

The light gravity helped the tables bear up under the prodigious weight of the smorgasbord set out. Despite Earth's isolationism, the moon had a comfortable, even thriving economy, being a tax haven, manufacturing center, trade nexus, and main intermediary for Terra. The Sockwallets had done well here, and this was their opportunity to indulge themselves and celebrate.

The Foragers fell to with unrestrained gusto. Self-appointed hosts and hostesses began pressing drinks of all types on their guests. Alacrity gratefully accepted a Geyserfroth, and Floyt was introduced to a formidable, fruity libation called "Fireman, Save My Child!" that was reputed to be an effective antiscorbutic. Gunny held a tall, moist tumbler filled to the brim with a lovely verdant drink he called a Kamikaze.

Music drifted through the dome; the chatter nearly matched it in volume. The Foragers switched from language to language without hesitation, though Terranglish seemed most popular. Gunny seated the guests of honor in hand-molded chairs at a long table near the pylon, then lowered himself into a mammoth seat of his own as the celebration picked up intensity all around them.

"How do you like the music?" Alacrity shouted to Floyt.

"I just hope no one asks me to dance. But it's—very sprightly," he conceded.

"Don't worry. They don't do much formal dancing. The Outfits move around too much; zero gee, heavy gee, and everything in between. Lots of Terran dances'd get you a concussion on Ceres, if you were silly enough to try 'em, or a broken leg on Mammon."

The Sockwallets were having a grand time nevertheless. Some played conventional instruments, sound synthesizers, and improvised noisemakers. Others used offworld devices Floyt couldn't identify. The lashup residents sang out wholeheartedly. Some of it sounded eerie, having been created for and in other atmospheres.

There was dancing of a sort, sidling and bouncing, jump-spinning and strutting, improvised in the light gravity. There was also a lot of drinking and joking and eating and merriment and more drinking.

Sockwallets were now fetching the visitors samples of this and that from the smorgasbord.

"Poached yabs," Alacrity called as Floyt poked at a mass of gelatin beryls, "from Aphrodite, where all the founding fathers were mothers."

They weren't bad. Floyt pointed to a basket of stuff that looked for all the world to be a pile of stir-fried lint. Alacrity shrugged, baffled.

"Cider floss, from Conniption," Gunny called, resolving the mystery. "Not a bad planet, as a matter of fact—practicing law for money there will earn you public impalement."

Some of Gunny's own vaunted Space and Thyme Ragout appeared, followed by shot glasses of a liquid called ratafee, then creamed tuft-scuttler roe, which Floyt thought resembled blobs of zinc ointment.

He tasted something that might very well have been cornbread stuffing, a dish he'd sampled in a history seminar. Marveling, he tried short ribs. *Protein still on the ossicle!* The sauce was sinfully good.

Floyt was amused by the Forager names, which had been handed down proudly since the strange culture had come into being in the First Breath. He met Scurry Clutchbuck and Honeytongue Wampum, Bigwig Swellbundle and Coaxer Reampocket.

The Sockwallets were cordial and folksy, touching in

their earnest efforts to make a good impression. Somewhere in the midst of greeting Itchpalms and Lustducats and Moneymoils, Hobart stopped pretending to be civil and actually began liking them.

The crowd swelled, filling the dome. Simoleanna Coup somehow ended up sitting next to Alacrity. She was quite striking in a snow-white, sequined sheath gown cut rather high on the hip, with matching cloche and high-heel shoes. She and the breakabout were engaged in exploratory conversation.

Gunny proposed toasts to the guests; toasts to the Outfit; to Luna and Earth; a safe trip for Alacrity and Floyt; peace; prosperity; and anyone anywhere who had ever screwed over a customs official in any way, shape, or form.

Alacrity and Sim nuzzled and whispered in each other's ears. Floyt found himself wondering dizzily if all this debauchery wouldn't prejudice Earthservice against him, and began thinking about how he could gracefully withdraw from the bash. Just then he realized that Gunny was talking to him.

"Yessir, Delver," the Forager averred, splashing a little Gunga Din and tonic, which fell with leisurely beauty. "The Third Breath will be the one, you'll see. Third time's the charm! Haven't we known that all along? No more dark ages!"

"Are you talking about the—whatsit—the Cooperative of Species?" It was an embryonic organization, Floyt knew; his orientation hadn't mentioned it in detail. He only recalled that it wasn't given much hope of enduring; his brain felt fuzzy.

Gunny had set sail on a stately voyage of discourse. "Naw, not that debating society! We're discussing the real item, human reciprocity—*lifeform* reciprocity—on an interstellar scale. Progress! Freedom! And this time it's gonna last."

The Sockwallets' boss looped a large arm around Floyt's

shoulders. "The word's gettin' around, you see." He began nodding to himself, blinking, breathing high-octane fumes on his guest. "To poor miserable beaten-down sods everywhere. The caste-imprisoned and the class-encysted. Worlds and worlds of 'em."

Floyt's brow furrowed. "*What* word, Gunny?"

The boss swept his glass through a gesture that took in the majority of Creation. "That! Opportunity! Get 'em to understand that the galaxy's accessible now and they fill in the rest! Revelation! Renown! A true and perfect love!"

"Damnation!" threw in a Forager who was passing by with eight liter-mugs of Old Geyserfroth in her fists. "Paradise!"

"Change," somebody laughed from the sidelines.

"Power!"

"Hope," Sim added quietly from her seat on Alacrity's lap. Alacrity said nothing, studying Floyt and listening, to decide whether he ought to divert the conversation.

"Maybe the secrets of the Precursh—cursh—Pre*curs*ors, damn it!" a tall redhead finally got out; the crowd whistled and cheered his success.

"Or the key to the universe!"

"Same thing!"

"A grand spree across Immensity!" Gunny trumpeted. "A chance to find out who they are and what they can do. And the word keeps getting around. No matter what the paranoid little local rulers do to suppress it—the single-system politburos, the phony popes, and planetary strongmen. The word gets out!"

"You mean, 'in'," Alacrity corrected mildly.

"How does the word get around, Gunny?" Floyt asked in a neutral voice. "Who gets it around?"

"Nobody." Gunny shrugged ponderously. "Anybody."

Sim flung her hand up in a graceful gesture. "Sometimes, Delver Rootnose, if it isn't too much trouble, *we* do." She,

Gunny, and the other Foragers laughed, but Alacrity didn't join in.

Floyt blushed, feeling that he was the butt of their joke. He'd heard enough; it all struck him as anti-Earthservice. More, a secret part of him found it too delirious to dwell upon.

He gathered himself to leave, whether it was rude or not. Gunny, shaking his head like a buffalo, said to no one in particular, "Got all interested in hearing m'self talk, there." His head cleared a bit; he slid a splendidly painted porcelain dish toward Floyt. "Almost forgot; here're your wonderments, Delver."

In the dish lay two delicacies that looked like folded pastries or turnovers, one with white icing and the other, orange. Floyt was halted in mid-rise.

"Wonderments?"

"Guest gifts," Alacrity clarified, making a long arm for one while holding onto Sim. She reached, stopped him when he would've taken the white one, and guided his hand to the other.

Floyt wavered, then took the remaining wonderment dubiously. Gunny showed him how to open it. Inside was a commemorative coin with the dates *April 12, 1961–April 12, 2461* and the inscription TERRA: 500 YEARS IN SPACE, circling a portrait of Yuri Gagarin.

Floyt gasped. A coin like that, struck in the bright noonday of the Second Breath—the gift was overwhelming.

"Safe landings, rig," Gunny bade.

"I—Gunny, I can't accept a thing like this."

"Um, that is, y'see, Delver"—Gunny's thick eyebrows danced—"I'm afraid it's not what you could really call *authentic*. Luna's lousy with ersatz souvenirs. But it's the thought that counts."

"The thought plus the markup," someone joked.

"Thank you all very much." Floyt rubbed his thumb

ACROSS TERRA: 500 YEARS IN SPACE. He was caught in a whirlpool of conflicting emotions.

Alacrity saw, and blustered, "Now, let me see what kind of karmic value the Sockwallets have me tabbed for, here." He made a big production of opening his cake, getting into a dramatic wrestling match, panting, "Nice and fresh, hah?" Foragers hooted and jeered him on.

In the end he drew out a long chain of fine gold links holding a heavy, ornate Christian cross. Floyt was willing to bet Balensa could've identified the metalworking style.

Alacrity's long fingers found a hidden release. Inside the cross was a sliver of extremely aged wood.

He stared at Sim. "You can't be serious."

"You're right. Some crosses came our way on Holy See. We got slivers of wood off a piece of pool cue in the wreckage over at the mass driver. I aged them myself."

Alacrity glanced around at his hosts. "I'm speechless, rigs, except—drinks all around!" The Sockwallets clapped and stamped their feet in the light gravity. The party was at full velocity; the dome shook with it. A group nearby was singing a song Floyt thought he recognized. The Foragers had reworked "Bless 'Em All" to extol their own life. Everyone joined in the chorus, Floyt included.

While the racket went on, Gunny motioned Floyt closer. "I've been meaning to ask you, if it's not too much trouble..."

He pulled a sheet from beneath his sweater. It was a yellowed piece of paper preserved in some sort of clear, flexible coating.

"It's from the real old days," the boss confided, a bit owl-eyed. "I couldn't puzzle it out, though, and I didn't want to just go showing it around."

The handwriting was a strange combination of old English script and the lovely, vanished Palmer method. Floyt had taught himself to read both in the course of his genealogical studies. He skimmed the paper. "Where did you get this, Gunny?"

"It came to us here on Luna; fella said a Forager gave it to an ancestor of his."

"It's in Ancient English, Gunny. It's from Shakespeare, *King Henry VI*, and it says:

> *My crown is in my heart, not on my head;*
> *Not deck'd with diamonds and Indian*
> > *stones,*
> *Nor to be seen: my crown is call'd content;*
> *A crown it is that seldom kings enjoy."*

Floyt handed it back, and Gunny said, "Thanks, Delver." No thumps or hand-pumping this time.

Clearing his throat, Gunny pounded the table. "Hey! HEY! SETTLE DOWN!" he bellowed into the resonant din. "It's about time Delver Rootnose and Shipwreck Mazuma met the pride of the Sockwallets!"

Uproarious Foragers calmed quicker than Floyt would've thought, clearing a space just behind the guests. Gunny swung his chair around to face it; Floyt and Alacrity did the same. Simoleanna removed her tongue from Alacrity's ear, sliding out of the way, and he lifted his hand from her thigh. The lights dimmed, except for those focused on the cleared area.

A thin, black-haired girl stepped forward, then slowly made her way across the floor. Her long slender feet, in slippers that reminded Floyt of opalescent toe shoes, scarcely touched down under her fractional weight. Her straight, shoulder-length hair was crowned by a slim, shining diadem.

She moved with conscious pride, chin held high, although it was clear that she was nervous. Sounds of approval and affection arose from the massed Foragers.

They began to hail her, calling her name; Sweetalk didn't

pause as she walked to where Gunny and the lashup's guests waited. Her elders called out compliments: how gifted Sweetalk was with painter's palette and long-range detector; how fair she was and how good a trader; how lucky they were to have her among them.

"Sweetalk, so helpful and patient!"

"With always a cheering word!"

Her face glowed.

She blushed deeply, though, being introduced to the outsiders. Floyt took his cue from Alacrity and stood, inclining his head to her. The Terran reflected on the amazing difference between the Sockwallets' camouflage and their real way of life. *How it must bind these people together*! he realized. Earthservice psychprop couldn't keep him from smiling at Sweetalk.

She went aside, to the open arms of her family. The Foragers' practice was not too different from some Terran customs of long ago, Floyt knew. *How was this lost?* he wondered.

A little boy, towheaded and blond, perhaps four years old, was approaching somewhat uncertainly. The visitors remained standing and waited.

"Boodle," one of the Foragers proclaimed. "Who reads and writes two languages now!"

"And can already play the bistal!" another pointed out.

"It doesn't mean they won't slap his landing gear if he gets out of line," Alacrity murmured to Floyt out of the side of his mouth. "But for right now, look at the kid swagger."

Boodle, giggling, broke protocol a little by clinging to Alacrity's boot-guarded knee with one hand, waving to his family with the other. The breakabout was nearly helpless with laughter. Someone half sang that Boodle was a joy to them all, but the boy showed no sign of dislodging himself. Floyt joined in the general guffawing.

"And this is Angle," a clear tenor warranted from one side. "Nearly an adult now!"

The boy Angle was gangling and copper-haired, freckled and pale. He wore a resplendent costume and was very grave, coming as close to marching as was possible on the Moon.

Alacrity had tousled Boodle's hair and gently shoved him off on his way. The breakabout was watching the child bounce happily toward the throng. Angle, pausing, looked to Floyt and bowed. Not knowing what else to do, Floyt returned the bow and automatically offered his hand. The Sockwallet Outfit let out a collective *Ah!*

Angle's face reflected surprise, but he responded at once. He and the Earther gripped one another's right forearms. The Foragers cheered and applauded the compliment Floyt had rendered, greeting Angle as an adult. They saluted the boy's new majority. Angle broke into an awkward grin, blushing furiously. Alacrity, too, traded grips with him.

More Forager youngsters came toward them. The adults hailed and praised. Loud declarations were made about the good fortune of the Sockwallet Outfit; these children were its hope and future. The celebration became more boisterous, in contrast to the lifeless, sun-drenched lunascape just outside.

Hobart Floyt had never had a better time in his life.

"In my opinion, the Sleep of the Just is probably a low-gravity one," Floyt informed Gunny Readyknob as the crowd moved toward the main dome once more.

Gunny chortled, body moving in wavelets. Alacrity had gained them entry, but the Earther had won an acceptance of his own.

The two were again dressed in their traveling clothes. Floyt felt better than he'd have expected after the revelry. He attributed part of that to Alacrity's having set their quarters' air supply for an increased oxygen content, and part to the pleasures of low-gravity sleep.

He felt there was more to it than that, though. Earthservice programming notwithstanding, Floyt was enjoying himself, albeit a little guiltily.

Children capered among the grown-ups. Festive clothing had been put away, but the holiday mood lingered. Angle, newly adult, strode along proudly with the holstered Captain's Sidearm slung from his shoulder. As an honor to the guests, the weapon had been under Gunny's personal keeping. He had delegated to Angle the task of carrying it and returning it to its owner in the airlock, as per ritual. The boy was almost bursting with delight.

Alacrity skate-skimmed along next to Simoleanna, and both were looking at each other wistfully, though holding hands was out of the question for two people bouncing in fractional gravity. As far as Floyt could recall, the break-about had been unable to slip away during the revelry, and had slept in the guest quarters. Still, the offworlder had been selected because he was resourceful, and the leers he was exchanging with Simoleanna were almost indecent.

The inner hatch was already swinging open; several men came through, wearing the deceptive fashions of the outer guards. They moved out of the way of the mob, to watch the leavetaking.

Most of the Outfit wouldn't be going to the platform, having other work to do. As the crowd neared the half-ajar inner hatch, Alacrity and Floyt stopped to say good-bye. At the sidelines, Shilly, dressed in the shabby clothes of a depot worker, readied himself.

His floppy, visored cap was pulled low; the heavy pistol tucked into his belt under his jacket pressed against his middle. He moved to a spot on the edge of the throng where a few stragglers—children—stood. He saw that Page and Jord were almost in position.

The husky assassin's nerves tingled with a pleasure beyond any he'd ever derived from sex, drugs, or any other stimulus. The tension and anticipation were something he savored completely and clearly in that moment. His broad hand closed on the grip of the handgun. Page and Jord would have second and third shots, respectively.

Floyt was being embraced by the Foragers' behemoth of a boss. Fitzhugh was talking to a few of the others, one woman's hand in his. Shilly made sure none of the adults were near, or looking his way. Then he slid the pistol out of his belt and raised it calmly, centering his sights on his target.

"Gun!" screamed Sweetalk, who'd been dawdling to one side, as she launched herself at his wrist. Lunar gravity helped; she sank her teeth into Shilly's wrist, wrapping her skinny legs around his arm, driving his gunhand around.

The energy bolt, passing within half a meter of Floyt's skull, coruscated and spattered off the inner hatch in a backwash of heat and molten metal. Sweetalk had driven the gun sideways rather than upward, with the single object of sparing the dome any damage. It had very nearly been a primal reflex; any threat to the lashup's artificial atmosphere must be eliminated, at any cost.

Shilly tore Sweetalk from his arm and hurled her aside, to thump against the dome with a dull impact. She lay still. But three more children, twin pubescent girls and a chubby boy, swarmed up onto him. The boy clung to the assassin's gun arm, biting down as hard as he could, drawing more blood, clubbing blindly with a free hand. One of the girls clamped an arm around the man's neck, scratching at his eyes, trying to bite off his ear. Her sister grabbed the remaining arm and a fistful of the outsider's hair, kicking and yanking.

Page, Shilly's dapper little partner, had produced his own gun, but couldn't spot the target. Jord, his nerve gone, began edging toward the airlock.

Alacrity had reacted to the first shot, throwing Floyt to the floor and covering the Earther with his own body. From where he sprawled, Floyt watched the violence with horrified fascination. Homing in like missiles in the lunar gravity, Foragers sprang at the big assassin, striking with hands and feet, grappling and snapping.

Abruptly, another hissing hum of gunfire sounded, and a shriek; Alacrity lifted his head to see Page go down under Gunny and several others, but one Forager had been shot.

Angle was trying to pull forth the Captain's Sidearm, but couldn't work the retaining-strap lock. He made his first adult decision.

"Shipwreck!"

Alacrity heard, and spotted him. Angle threw the gunbelt, a singular act of trust from a Forager inside his lashup.

Alacrity snagged it out of the air; in another moment he had the big handgun free. "Don't kill them!" he bellowed, wanting some answers to what was going on. But the Sockwallets weren't hearing that as they raised wordless, animal cries of hatred. He could hear the assassins' screams and the thudding blows. "I said, don't kill—"

Another shot blared. The breakabout whirled as clutching his leg, another Forager fell. A third intruder was poised as the inner hatch, its automatics activated by the gunfire, sealed shut, trapping him in the lashup. So much commotion and chaos surrounded the first two intruders that no other Foragers had noticed him yet.

Jord saw Alacrity spot him. He began to bring his weapon to bear, but the breakabout already had the Captain's Sidearm raised. He steadied it with both hands and squeezed the trigger.

The pistol's report filled the dome like an explosion. It had been developed for use against boardings, riots, or mutiny; by design, it emitted a terrific amount of visible light and sonic energy, for shock effect.

Jord's shoulder, head, and most of his upper right arm disappeared in a gush of incandescence. His remains were thrown against the hatch, to slide to the floor. Smoke drifted up, swirled and drawn by the circulation system; the odor of the exploded, burned flesh and bone made Floyt nauseous. The stench, and Alacrity's single, apocalyptic shot, drew the Foragers back from their fighting frenzy.

As the sounds of conflict died away, Alacrity hastily stooped to slide the Captain's Sidearm away from him; he didn't want to be attacked by mistake. Floyt was standing next to him by then, and Gunny and the others were trying to bring order. To the Earther, the eeriest thing was the utter silence of the children at that moment, their almost unnatural discipline.

He took one look at the gory wreckage that had been Shilly. The smell of his blood vied with that of the charred corpse of Jord. Shilly was eyeless, virtually faceless and formless. Alacrity was still staring toward the man he'd shot, eyes unfocused.

"No interrogations today," the breakabout mumbled.

"One of the oldest tactics on Earth," Floyt commented, regarding the gaping hole in the side of the shipping container.

The would-be murderers had entered the guarded tunnels inside a large, partially hollowed-out gypsum processor. It was appropriately packed and marked for delivery, with concealed audio and video pickups to let its occupants know when it was safe to emerge.

"But how did they know when we were coming to the lock?" Simoleanna puzzled, gazing at the life-support equipment within the processor.

"They were in commo with somebody monitoring the capsules, it looks like." Gunny's tone was flat, but the look on his face was sheer rage. None of the Foragers had been killed, thanks to the instant responses of the children. Four had been shot, two wounded seriously. Sweetalk had come into adulthood just behind Angle; her collarbone and right wrist had been broken in defense of the Sockwallet lashup.

There'd been at least one other accomplice, possibly

more. The guards at the platform had been disabled by stunblasts fired from behind. Whoever it was had held a capsule for escape but, perhaps failing to hear from the three assassins and losing nerve, had deserted his fellows.

Gunny rejected the idea of having the capsule intercepted. "Unlikely whoever it is will still be aboard. And we don't want the law in on this."

Floyt, who'd been worrying about an investigation making them miss their starship connection, asked, "But what about the bodies?"

The Forager boss gave a brief snort that wasn't humor. "What bodies?"

"Oh . . ."

"We owe you an awful lot," Alacrity said.

"Yes, you do," Gunny concurred. "See that you remember it; if you find out who's responsible, I'll expect to be informed."

"I promise."

Word was relayed from the platform that another capsule had arrived and was being held. Alacrity exchanged glances with Simoleanna, but there was no time, and there were no proper words for the moment.

"Get going," Gunny Readyknob ordered. "Starships don't wait."

CHAPTER 8

DIVERSIONS

AS THE CAPSULE SHOT TOWARD LUNAPORT, FLOYT adjusted the Inheritor's belt under his outer clothes and commented to Alacrity, "That was a very good shot. Er, it was, wasn't it?"

"Adequate, I guess." He rubbed the holster briefly. "First time I ever had to use it like that." Alacrity began rummaging in his warbag. "I scrounged something off Gunny before we left. Thought we might want it, after what happened."

He dug out a handgun, a modern reproduction of an archaic Webley .455 Mark VI revolver used in Great Britain before the space age. He opened the top-breaking pistol and showed Floyt the basics of its operation. The reproduction Webley was loaded with fat, soft, slow dumdum bullets, which were known, for reasons shrouded in antiquity, as "Chicago popcorn."

"Of *course* I know what 'popcorn' is," Alacrity snorted, when Floyt asked. "It's the ceremonial pastry you Earthers used to decorate the traditional Yule log," he finished smugly.

Floyt smiled to himself, but refrained from comment. In

view of the recent proof that they were in danger, he revised his attitude about weapons.

One hour later, the starship *Bruja* lifted out of Lunaport with Alacrity and Floyt safely inboard.

She was a general-cargo freighter out of Bolivar, and the two companions were the only ones to have availed themselves of her limited passenger space. The skipper was only too happy to alter course slightly for a stop in Epiphany's stellar system; arrangements made by Weir's executors included a voucher payable by the Bank of Spica, for first-class passage for Floyt.

Capitán Valdemar, sensing the pressure under which Earthservice reps were negotiating, had charged the top, all-inclusive fare listed on the fee schedules of luxury liners, plus a hefty course-deviation bonus. Earthservice auditors had wept at the amount of money being transferred, none accessible to them. Capitán Valdemar, notoriously grasping and tightfisted, had, under the circumstances, been content to allow Alacrity to deadhead on the voyage, since there was plenty of space available.

The *Bruja* was making ready for translight. At the Terran's insistence, the two had watched the liftoff on screens in the tiny passenger lounge. At Alacrity's, they were drinking blastoff cocktails, a tradition in many human-run spacecraft. The drink differed from vessel to vessel.

"I can't find any listing for Bolívar." Floyt frowned as he consulted a portable data bank provided by Earthservice.

"That thing's full of Earthservice errata-data," the breakabout replied. He took another swallow. "An awful lot of worlds changed their original colony names. I mean, who wants to live on a place called New Passaic?"

The purser/third mate refilled their goblets with more of the *Bruja's* blastoff cocktail, which was known as an *emboscado*. Like the rest of the all-male ship's complement, he wore a heavily adorned uniform of green leather jacket and tight britches, with red, ruff-collared blouse. He cued up

Wainwright's *Liftoff Overture* on the sound system. Alacrity was more partial to ditties like "High Movers Reel," or "Breakabouts' Waltz," but said nothing.

With differing attitudes, the three men watched Luna's crescent shrink behind them. The forward screen registered little change. Then there was a distinct rise in the sensation of activity within the compartment, something impossible to define but vividly felt.

"Breakers," Alacrity toasted solemnly, raising his goblet. Floyt held up his as well, and they clinked with the purser. An unprecedented feeling coursed through Floyt, like enormous velocity without movement, as the *Bruja*'s captain cut in the Breakers and the Hawking Effect generator set the craft thrumming. Then there was an over-the-top sensation, and the outboard screens went blank.

The purser left to attend to his duties. Floyt looked around the cramped compartment for a reader, drawing from his pocket one of the info chips given him by Supervisor Bear. It was labeled:

PROJECT SHEPHERD
MISSION BRIEFING FILE
EYES ONLY: HOBART FLOYT

"Are they serious?" Alacrity sniggered as he reached for it. "I have to see this."

Floyt held it away from him. "I'm sorry, Alacrity. This is classified Earthservice material."

"Ho, from here on in, you *are* the Earthservice. Or at least, that's the attitude a lot of people'll take. Aren't you going to feel a bit stupid arresting yourself for a security breach?" To his surprise, the breakabout felt an odd twinge even *joking* about that, perturbations from his conditioning.

"It's still a sensitive document, Alacrity."

"It's a coprolite, is what it is. You never handled a

sensitive document in your life, Ho, because Earthservice'd
never let you." He was leaning over the bar, ransacking.

He came up with a reader. Floyt decided that he had
little to gain by losing his temper with the breakabout, who
did seem to be doing his job. The Terran hesitantly handed
over the chip; Alacrity popped it into the machine.

He skimmed the projected data, chuckling, then began
reading. "'Citizen Floyt is enjoined and warned against
unnecessary exposure to or indulgence in offworld habits,
attitudes, customs, practices, turns of phrase, and/or other
aberrations. Individual is warned that failure to comply may
require postmission measures including, but not limited to,
conditioning, deconditioning, behavioral engineering, attitude modification, memory adjustment, sequestration, radical reorientation, and partial or total loss of Earthservice
privileges, rights, and prerogatives.'"

He looked around at Floyt. "You traded grips with that
kid Angle, back at the lashup. Think you ought to stick
your arm in a sterilizer?"

"That's not fair! You know, like it or not, they're going
to debrief me when I get home. It's nothing to joke about."

"I agree, but it's that or puke."

Floyt tried to grab the reader, but Alacrity pulled it out
of his reach and scanned on.

"Blah, blah, jibber-jabber—oho! 'Undue fraternization
with escort or other offworlders could prove prejudicial to
postmission disposition of this case.'"

"Alacrity, *that's enough*!"

The breakabout wasn't listening. The radiant yellow eyes
were slitted now. "They even talk about *contemplated* mis-
conduct." Floyt reached for the reader again, but the other
was much taller and longer of arm.

"Maybe you'd better start sedating yourself; wouldn't
want any impure thoughts."

Floyt lost patience. "I just want to complete this mission
with a minimum of trouble, Fitzhugh. Now, *give that back*!"

Though there'd been the reference to their common dilemma, it was more the tone of Floyt's voice that inadvertently triggered Alacrity's conditioning. The derisive smile vanished; Alacrity seemed paralyzed for a moment.

He suddenly felt contrite. Here was likable Hobart Floyt, coping as best he could with a predicament that was none of his fault, and he, Alacrity, was adding to the man's problems needlessly, acting like a delinquent.

"I-I'm sorry, Ho." A little benumbed, he slid the reader along the bar, back to Floyt. "That was out of line, I know."

But deep inside, something was shrilling, *How much of me did they get?* and was terrified.

It dawned on Floyt what had happened. "No, no harm done. Forget it, Alacrity."

The breakabout nodded absently, distracted and confused. Floyt tried to see the matter as an unfortunate but minor incident. *At least things will proceed more smoothly*, the Terran thought. *Or is that my own conditioning talking?*

Capitán Valdemar saw no reason to assign the deadheading Alacrity quarters alotted for paying passengers, even if there weren't any others. Since there was room in Floyt's cabin, they'd been billeted together.

As Floyt studied the glowing instructions etched by the entrance to the head, Alacrity dug into his warbag, tossing things onto the fold-down conform-bunk he'd chosen. There were long, heavy gauntlets, a few wads of clothing—mostly standard spacer's attire—and a personal kit. Strapped to the bag was a sheath, from which he drew a metallic-looking umbrella.

Alacrity sat and changed from the pathfinder boots into soft tabi with separate toes. Then he opened the front of his shipsuit so that the chain carrying his wonderment could be seen.

He rose and took up the umbrella. "I'm going to look around a bit. If you need me, use the intercom." He didn't

have to add that it would be a better idea all around for
them not to be pent up together just then.

The *Bruja* had been scheduled for a lunar call before
Weir's death, and made no changes in crew. It was pro
forma that all inloaded cargo had been carefully inspected.
Too, passage for Floyt and Alacrity had been negotiated in
strictest secrecy; Alacrity was therefore fairly sure that Floyt
would be safe in transit.

Such basics of shipboard life as hadn't been explained
by the purser were easy enough to find out about. Spangla-
terra was the *Bruja*'s official tongue, but there were few
breakabouts who didn't speak at least passable Terranglish.

"They won't mind you touring the ship if you feel like
it," Alacrity said. "The off-limits areas are all secured and
marked, like the power section and the Fuckup Factory."

"The *what*?"

"The bridge, the control room." Floyt nodded, still perus-
ing the instructions. Alacrity left.

It wasn't hard to find the ship's broker; most human or
mixed vessels had one, whether they were called that or
fixer, or fo'c'sle chaplin.

Gabriel was a well-fed little hornet of a man with reddish
hair and mustachios and quick gray eyes. He was obviously
doing well, having a tiny cabin to himself though he was
only a common crewman. He invited Alacrity in and asked
what he could do for him.

"Well, you can tell me what the ship's game is, just as
a point of origin. Poker? Wari?" Then Alacrity remembered
that the ship's homeport was Bolívar. "No, wait; dominoes,
right?"

"Monopoly. Do you play?"

Alacrity came up with his lucky playing token, a racy
little one-seater sky coupe. It was a real spacer's piece, with
freefall stickum on the bottom. "But I haven't got much
cash. What're the stakes?"

"Fifty ovals to get in, I'm afraid."

In due course Gabriel was looking the umbrella over with an experienced eye. "It's a Viceroy Imperial, from Outback," Alacrity told him. "Practically new."

Aside from footgear, an umbrella—or "gamp" or "brolly"—was often more useful than anything a breakabout took groundside, including guns and commo equipment. The Imperial was top of the line, rugged and extremely versatile.

Gabriel opened it, examining the ribs and gores, working the runner, checking tacks and joints. A brolly was also a parasol, walking stick, seat rest, and weapon. The Imperial was big enough to serve as an emergency shelter of sorts and had drop-down protective netting.

"Twenty's the best I can do," Gabriel pronounced mournfully. Alacrity played out the scene, hunching his shoulders at the proper moment so that Gabriel caught sight of the chain. Gabriel whistled when he opened the cross and saw the sliver of decayed wood. He wasn't fooled, but he knew there were always those who could be.

They finally agreed that it would be collateral—unless Alacrity lost—and the fifty changed hands. As Gabriel saw his customer to the door, an odd-looking little being bustled toward them along the passageway.

Evolution had given it shape, coloring, and texture that suggested to Alacrity a potato augmented by eyestalks, tentacles, and stubby podia.

The being was preceded by an incongruous aroma of powerful cologne.

The thing waved a bouquet of tentacles at Gabriel. "Ah, there you are, charmer of engines! Well met!"

"Hello there, Squeeb. Alacrity, meet technician-in-training Squeeb, from—" The name of the planet sounded as if Gabriel were clearing his throat.

"Or as you humans call it, Hyperbole," Squeeb put in brightly, speaking in a birdlike voice from an organ located at his top, in the center of all those eyes and tentacles. "Nice to meet you."

"Squeeb's the first of his people ever to go space traveling," Gabriel said.

"Hi-ho, for the life of a breakabout," Squeeb joked nervously. "Gabriel, the others invited me to join the game, but they forgot to tell me where it would be." Squeeb held up a membranous purse that clinked.

"Number four cargo lock," Gabriel told him. "Do you have a playing token?"

"Oh, the good-luck fetish; no. I was going to beg your council."

Gabriel held out a miniature wheelbarrow of some blue substance that looked like ivory. Squeeb's eyestalks gathered around it curiously.

"I can let you have this one for a very reasonable..." Gabriel began, then stopped. "Oh, here you go. Just make sure you bring it back." He dropped it into a curl of tentacle.

"I'm forever in the vastness of your largesse," Squeeb assured him, then scooted off.

Alacrity blew his breath out, shaking his head with pity. "Supper's on, hm?"

"Oof," Gabriel agreed. "They're going to skin him for sure. Too bad; he's a decent little troll."

"Except for his taste in after-shave."

Gabriel sniggered. "When he was assigned to a berth, he naturally thought to scent-mark his personal area. They almost cycled him out an airlock. So he started wearing Shore Leave to avoid offending anybody."

"I never saw a—Hyperbolarian?—before."

"I think Squeeb got stuck with the job of evaluating space travel for his people. All Hyperbolarians really care about is getting themselves an allocation of ground and having offspring."

"Limited living space?"

"Absolutely. The elders dole it out; when you've got

your personal domain, your 'ramazz,' you can start a family, but you can only have as many children as the ramazz can support. The more important you are, the more ramazz you get."

"And Squeeb?"

"*Nada*, zero. He's trying to resign himself to being a bachelor all his life."

"But how is he as an apprentice?" Alacrity wasn't at all sure he liked the idea of Squeeb fooling around in the chandelier guts of a Hawking Effect generator.

"Not bad at all. But he's worried about fitting in with the crew. He tries too hard."

"Do they ride him?"

"The usual. You know: sending him out after left-handed emery paper or a bag of dried squelch. That's why he's so happy they asked him to join the game. I don't think it'd bother him to lose all his money. He draws his pay through some kind of trade assistance program; I'm not sure he even *understands* money."

"He'll understand it if he loses it all."

"Six!" hissed Juan-Feng. "Chance! The Question Mark!"

Alacrity stoically hopped his sky coupe the six spaces and reached for a Chance card.

"The Capricious Curlicue of Cash," Juan-Feng barkered. "The Loony Loop of Luck. C'mon, show us the card, Fitzhugh! What's it say?"

"Sez, 'All Sino-Hispanic Players Kiss Your Ass.'" Alacrity glared.

Number four cargo airlock was a loud, humid den of banter, laughter, recreational substance abuse, and horseplay, but that drew some catcalls anyhow. Juan-Feng took it gracefully.

He toyed with the chain that held his union book around his neck, wrapping it around his finger. The tiny info wafer held his history as a spacer: disciplinary, medical, and technical details were all there. "Now I *know* you picked yourself a good card." He leered.

For answer, Alacrity buried the Chance card and, opening his playing till, began disbursing money around the circle. Even though it was early in the game, he was careful to let none of the others get a look at how much game currency he had or remind themselves what properties he'd bought.

Ortega, the dignified senior crewman who was acting as banker, silently registered the transaction on his master till. Everyone trusted him; he was also keeper for several of the ship's hand-throws, wherein crewmen pooled their money and took turns spending the jackpot groundside.

Ortega officiated without payment, for the prestige and respect involved. In the case of the game, someone had to make sure nobody smuggled in extra money.

"I always preferred dominoes anyhow," groused Alacrity, who'd lost quite a few gamebucks when the Chance card designated him Chairman of the Board. He'd been in Monopoly games where bluffing and side bets raised the ante, but this one was straight entry stakes, winner take all. It promised to be a long game.

A dozen men and Squeeb were present. The Hyperbolarian wasn't devoting much concentration to the game; he hunkered in his place, bouncing happily every now and then, the powerful aroma of his Shore Leave dissipated. His comprehension of the rules was vague, but he wasn't particularly worried about losing. He was doing his best to take part in the wisecracking and camaraderie.

"You sure the captain won't figure out something's going on?" Alacrity asked Juan-Feng. Only paying passengers were supposed to be able to carry on in *Bruja*, but covert rips were common on most ships where they were prohibited.

"Valdemar's too busy cooking the books, covering what he skims," was the answer.

Juan-Feng gloated over the money Alacrity had paid him, passing his benefactor a hip flask of knurled silver. Alacrity took a swig; his eyes popped and he fought for breath.

"*Zhopa s ruchkoi*, you scum! You got a prescription for this stuff?"

"Piquant, isn't it?" Juan-Feng took a long pull at the flask.

The board had been set up in one corner of the lock, the six players and the banker crowded around it. The set was a breakabout's model, and could have been used in freefall or on the bulkhead or ceiling.

Onlookers circulated between the game and the general mingling. Someone was playing torrid love songs sung in Spanglaterran by a woman with a pure and sultry voice. Drinking vessels clinked and sloshed. A fragment of conversation drifted to Alacrity, ". . . so we houdini'd out of there before you could say, 'Breakers, please!'"

"Who were you running from?" someone asked.

"Langstretch."

There were growls and guffaws. The Langstretch Detective Agency's network of operatives was more widespread than any government, and for the right money, Langstretch was relentless.

"Can I have your locker when they come and get you?" Juan-Feng called playfully.

"I heard the Spicans are thinking about sending another expedition to the Core," Abascal, who'd just come in, was saying. "It'll take years and years."

"It won't come back, anymore than the others," said Duarte, a lean, handsome youngster who held a beaker of effervescent red stuff. He sipped it, staring at the bulkhead. Listening with one ear, Alacrity was contemplating building a habitat dome on Ventnor.

"Why not?" someone objected. "The Heavysets do it all the time, and they do it a helluva lot faster."

"Heavysets also think going through the middle of a black

hole's a religious experience," Duarte shot back. "And they ain't about to teach us how they do it."

I've heard this conversation a thousand times, Alacrity thought. *Any second now, somebody's gonna bring up the Precursors.*

"The Precursors traveled faster than the Heavysets can," challenged the other crewman.

Duarte sneered, "The Precursors are long gone, brother, and nobody's ever gonna figure them out."

Juan-Feng landed on the Energy Syndicate and Alacrity collected his rent. Squeeb, swaying with the music, hadn't noticed Conklin's landing on one of his properties. Now Conklin rolled and moved, raising a middle finger to the Hyperbolarian. Squeeb wasn't in the least upset. Twittering, *"Salud!"* he merrily tried to return the gesture. It translated poorly in terms of tentacles.

Unexpectedly, Ortega commented, "I don't know that that's true—about the Precursors. I once saw the White Ship, saw them working on her. There's never been anything like her."

Alacrity gauged the responses around him. The White Ship had been conceived to solve the mysteries of the vanished Precursors. Thirty years abuilding, she was more legend than starship. She'd been designed, begun, halted, redesigned, fought over, and redesigned again. She'd been the subject of endless corporate and bureaucratic bloodletting and very nearly caused several wars. Her official name had been changed a number of times, but she remained the White Ship, unfinished.

"Hell with it," Duarte spat. "Me, I'd rather crew for some rich man in the next Regatta for the Purple."

"Or rich woman!"

"Especially a rich woman." Duarte grinned.

"That's not for you," Abascal scoffed. "Those high and mighty amateurs racing around in their little butterflies. That's not for a working spacer."

"But the money, old-timer," Duarte crooned. "And the good living. And the women, more beautiful even than a ship." A number of those present went along with that.

Squeeb happened to notice that Juan-Feng's token, a scotty dog with prominent tusks and a single horn, had landed on one of his properties. The crewman handed over the rent smugly. "I'll get it back soon anyway." He motioned to Squeeb's wheelbarrow, "You're bound to land on my real estate soon, Squeeb."

"Real estate?"

"Property. Land. Um..." Juan-Feng closed his eyes for a second, concentrating. "What d'you Hyperbolarians call it? Ramazz!"

The effect was amazing. Squeeb froze. "Ramazz?" He singled out one of his deeds with a tentacle tip. "You mean, this represents ramazz?"

"Of course! I explained the whole thing to you twice!"

"You did not," Squeeb contradicted crisply. "I was under the impression that this was some kind of Tarot game involving wagering for confections, and attended by sexual badinage." He held up one of the tiny habitat domes. "This, then, does not represent some sort of bonbon?"

"It's a *house* you dumb-ass legume!" Juan-Feng screamed. "You build it on your ramazz!"

The Hyperbolarian was trembling, eyeing his deeds. Alacrity remembered what Gabriel had said; how the Hyperbolarians' consuming drive in life was ramazz.

Suddenly, Squeeb scooped up the game box's lid, making minute examination of the rules with one eyestalk. Several more roamed the board, and the last two watched his tentacles take stock of his money and holdings. Before anybody could stop him, he delicately marked each deed with a minuscule dab of territorial scent. He was now shuddering and rippling.

"What're you doing?" Juan-Feng screeched. "Calm down or I'll turn a fire extinguisher on you!"

"Now then," Squeeb said in a precise tone. "It's my turn. I'm going to purchase two habitats. Also, we've been putting money in the Free Docking square that doesn't actually belong there; that must stop." He was turning the dice in his tentacles, getting the feel of them.

Alacrity curled his lip at Juan-Feng. "You had to go and open your big air scoop."

"All right, all right," Juan-Feng soothed, slipping the human players a wink. No doubt he figured they could gang up and squeeze the Hyperbolarian out of the game. Alacrity wasn't so sure about that, but he was pretty sure he knew what was making Squeeb shudder as the creature fondled his ramazz deeds and set out to acquire more.

Alacrity was pretty sure it was sexual rapture.

Floyt settled in, exploring the cabin and amusing himself with its various comfort, service, and environmental controls. The compartment was spacious, and if the accommodations weren't sumptuous by the standards of a passenger liner, they were more than comfortable to an Earthservice functionary.

Bruja's officers and crewmen had treated him with the distant civility due a groundling passenger whose fare had worked miracles for the balance sheet. The Earther found their odor strange, owing to the foods they'd eaten, the substances with which they'd come in contact; as strange as the Sockwallets' and yet very different.

If they were curious about his Inheritor's belt, they refrained from showing it.

The ship's atmosphere was odd to him too, duplicating that of the vessel's homeworld. Gravity was slightly heavier than Terran. Floyt's main objection was that the *Bruja* ran on the day-night cycle of Bolivar, which was slightly over thirty-three hours long.

But most services—including the passenger lounge bar and recreational facilities—were accessible during all five watches. He decided to keep to his accustomed twenty-four-hour day as well as he could. He also thought it would be wise to wait for a while before touring the ship; that way, he wouldn't cross paths with Alacrity. He addressed himself to the task of becoming familiar with that part of the briefing file dealing with Weir himself.

Shorn of the psychprop editorializing and sermonizing, the story of Caspahr Weir was the stuff of legend.

He'd been born into slavery in the household of a planetary subruler under the Grand Presidium. His parents died when he was still a boy; a baby sister, Tiajo, was his only kin.

As a boy, he'd been extremely fortunate to be selected as servant-playmate to his owner's grandson. He'd been educated and had even traveled a little. Weir showed nothing but loyalty to his owner and satisfaction with his lot in life until he reached the age of—Floyt used his new proteus to make the conversion—sixteen Terran years.

The file wasn't clear as to what happened then; Floyt couldn't make out whether that was a shortcoming of Earthservice's data-collection capability or simply due to an absence of information of any kind. What was certain was that Weir's playmate-master was murdered and Weir and Tiajo fled with certain unspecified data snippets.

Caspahr and his sister joined a failing underground movement. Within five Standard years, Weir turned it into a full-blown revolution. Within another two, he was effective ruler of the planet where he'd been born a slave. By the time he was thirty, he'd eradicated the Grand Presidium.

From there he went on to forge a realm of nineteen stellar systems, binding many of them to him with oaths of personal fealty. For all the shortcomings mentioned in the file—warfare, cronyism, stupendous problems with displaced persons, and the failure to achieve universal suffrage—Weir's rule had come as a very nearly divine deliverance to the former subjects of the Presidium.

Floyt took his meals in his cabin and began dipping cautiously into the *Bruja*'s data banks. He abandoned his twenty-four-hour regimen and napped when necessary. Eventually, satisfied that he'd absorbed all the data he could assimilate, he cleaned up, changed his clothes, and went to tour the vessel, even though there wasn't supposed to be much to see in transit.

He stepped into the passageway and almost put his foot on a spiny little mass like a hyperkinetic sea urchin. It burbled in fear and zipped out from under with blurring speed. To his relief, it didn't seem inclined to go for his jugular.

A passing crewman called, "Don't you worry, sir; that's only Bartleby."

"I beg your pardon?"

"Ship's cat." The fellow disappeared around a corner.

"Cat?" The oily thicket named Bartleby extended a snorkle of some kind, an extremity like a moist green drinking straw. It sniffed at Floyt, then retracted. Bartleby flowed up onto the bulkhead and wandered off down the passageway, leaving no trail or scent that Floyt could detect.

Floyt was undaunted in his journey of discovery. It occurred to him that Earthservice might even let him publish something on the experience if he hewed to psychprop guidelines. Consulting a map of the ship's layout that he'd transferred from his cabin's terminal to the proteus, he proceeded.

Floyt passed the vessel's sensory deprivation tank. He'd enjoyed sensedep on Earth, and found it restful. Still, he didn't care to float in darkness listening to his eyelids blink and all that while there was a starship to be seen.

He knew he could borrow an induction helmet and sample its artificial stimuli, but he wasn't sure that would be wise; after they'd disembarked from *Mindframe*, Alacrity had made very disparaging remarks about "skull-to-hull hookups."

Next along was the *Bruja*'s sensorium, a miniature multimedia theater. Its menu offered none of the perversions the psychprop officers had warned against; Floyt didn't know whether to be relieved or disappointed.

He ordered up a seat for one in the center of the modest compartment. Sitting, he selected a program, something called "Ball-Struggle."

He found himself surrounded by a shoving, struggling mass of shouting, sweating men in skimpy white loincloths. They laughed and roared and babbled in some offworld language.

He felt the breeze and the sun's heat, or something very like them; he seemed to smell dust and perspiration and incense. He couldn't help shying away from the pushing, heaving teams.

Rechecking the menu, he discovered he'd summoned up *Hakozaki-gu no Tama-seseri*, a ritual recorded at the rebuilt Hakozaki Shrine on Fukuoka, but originated in Terra's Japan.

The straining mob fought and grabbed at the prize ball, some sitting on their teammates' shoulders. From the sidelines, priests hosed water onto the melee.

Floyt was openmouthed. Earth had nothing like the sensorium, at least not for functionaries. He picked another sequence.

He hung in space, near the center of a globular star cluster, lost in brilliance shed by half a million distant suns . . .

Floyt mustered his self-control and canceled the sequence before and around him. A limitless, rust-colored plain, spread under a fey red sun, vanished. It took with it tens of thousands of hooded, chanting worshipers before their human sacrifice could be carried out at his feet.

He sat for a few moments, shaken. At last he returned to the passageway. When he'd meditated for some seconds on why the sensorium would never, never be allowed on Terra, he continued his wandering.

He came to an open hatch and peeked into an empty compartment. Crew quarters. He eyed the knickknacks and souvenirs, erotica, art, and pornography the breakabouts had picked up in their travels. Every item was secured against weightlessness or maneuver forces.

The sound of a nearby hatch made him yank back into the passageway. An outrageous being appeared, gurgling Terranglish, which he supposed to mean that it wasn't a colleague of Bartleby.

To his credit, Floyt stood his ground. His experience in the *Bruja* had been unnerving at times, but nothing, he'd decided, to excuse unreasoning panic.

"Oh, thank you! Thank you so much, Gabriel," the thing was gushing, "for the loan of your token." It held up a little doodad of some sort in one tentacle. In another, it clasped a bulging bag that clinked and swung heavily. A third embraced a Monopoly game; others caressed the deeds from the game—all of them.

"My pleasure, Squeeb," Gabriel said, following the Hyperbolarian out into the passageway from his cabin.

One of the eyestalks had caught sight of Floyt, but Squeeb's attention was still on the broker. "Do you think . . . that is, the token is doubtless an heirloom—"

"It's been in the family forever," Gabriel conceded.

"But I'd hoped you could see your way clear to . . . it's been so lucky for me—"

"Fifty ovals?" Gabriel suggested.

"Done!" The creature dipped into its sack and counted out the sum. Floyt did a quick conversion in his head and concluded that this Squeeb had had himself a streak of luck. Gabriel's smile couldn't have been any wider without injuring his face.

The two parted in mutual affection. The being waltzed happily in Floyt's direction. "Greetings upon you," it chirped. "Citizen Floyt, are you not?"

"I am."

"How do you do? I am Apprentice Squeeb, and this

Monopoly game is the craze that will soon grip all Hyperbole."

"Oh? Er, good." At least, he hoped it was.

"I must be off," Squeeb told him. "But you must promise to tell me about your Earth. Some of *Bruja*'s tapes gave me knowledge of its history. Observe!"

Squeeb shifted his various burdens and placed one tentacle reverently over the region of his heart. He then began to sing with great feeling.

> *"Oh, I wish I were in Disney,*
> *Away! Away!*
> *In Disneyland I'll take my stand,*
> *To live and die in Disney!*

—That's one of my favorites!"

Floyt coughed, "Yes, well, we'll have to talk about that sometime."

"Tickety-boo! Bye for now!" Squeeb sallied off to gloat over his ramazz and his entrepreneurial future.

"Citizen Floyt," Gabriel said, who'd watched the whole thing, "you're the man I've been looking for."

"I'm afraid that board games really aren't my strong suit."

"Mine either. I have something that might interest you, though."

The keepsakes in the crew quarters had aroused Floyt's acquisitive urges. He entered the broker's booth of a cabin and accepted a seat on the bunk while Gabriel perched on the desk. They were practically touching knees. It reminded Floyt of his hall closet study on Earth. "What did you want to show me?" he asked.

"This," answered Gabriel. He held an auto-styrette in his hand.

CHAPTER 9

TRANSPORTS OF DELIGHT

SOME INNER WATCHDOG THAT HAD BEEN ON GUARD SINCE the woman had ambushed him on Terra acted now.

Floyt pushed himself to one side almost instantly, lashing out with his feet. He made contact; Gabriel yelled as Floyt, unable to get past him, leaped on him, clutching the hand that held the injector. They lurched together for a few seconds, then tumbled into the passageway, falling to the deck.

"The captain has the power to marry you, y'know," Alacrity said, bending over them.

"He's crazy! *Chinga!*" Gabriel hollered, struggling to his feet.

"I—he—" the Earther floundered as Alacrity helped him up.

"C'mon," Alacrity cut him off, snatching up the styrette and glancing around to make sure they hadn't been seen. Floyt allowed himself to be crowded into the cabin again.

Gabriel was still boiling with oaths. "He should be locked up, that's what!"

Alacrity persuaded Gabriel to palm a hidden lock on his bunk. Noiselessly a huge tray slid out of concealment. Floyt gaped at niches holding expensive recording gear and other instruments, jewelry, phials and bottles of liquid, capsules and spansules and tablets, styrettes and inhalers. There were info slugs, costly proteuses, and false documentation.

Floyt saw that he'd interrupted a sales pitch, not a murder attempt. "I'm so sorry! Commerce never occurred to me."

"What's in the styrette?" Alacrity asked.

"A mnemonic drug." Gabriel looked to Floyt. "I mean, you're doing research, aren't you? That's why you're traveling, right? I thought you could use it." His anger had ebbed. "You made an honest mistake, I guess."

"You've got to be more careful around my associate here," Alacrity cautioned. "You're lucky I came along when I did." He slipped Floyt a wink.

As they made their way back to their cabin, Floyt noticed Alacrity's bleary eyes and surmised, "Monopoly?"

"Ever since I left you. I got cleaned out," he sighed. "People who enjoy a game are one thing; life forms who get sexual gratification out of it—"

"Maybe we can get your cross back from Gabriel. I assume that was your cross in his treasure trove."

"Yes. Well, Sim knew she was bankrolling me with it when she gave it to me."

Back in the cabin, Alacrity handed Floyt a fistful of data slugs. "I borrowed these for you. I figured you'd be through with that Earthservice manure pile you call a briefing file by now."

Floyt sorted through the little lozenges, activating their labels. Lurid graphics with an emphasis on passion, violence, and sensationalism popped into view.

"Caspahr Weir Versus the Transuranic Flame Goddesses of Death," he read from the first. And from the second, *"Caspahr Weir and the Invasion of the Time Maggots—* Alacrity, what in the world *are* these?"

"This title's my personal favorite." Alacrity singled one

out. *"Caspahr Weir Meets the Teleporting Pygmies from the Galactic Core."*

The books had all been written by, or at least published under the pseudonym of, Bombastico Herdman. "Weir was one of those characters nobody really knew much about," Alacrity explained, "even while he was making history. But a lot of people were curious, so somebody fictionalized him."

"Penny dreadfuls!" Floyt cried. "Dime novels; shilling shockers; pulps."

Now it was the breakabout's turn to look nonplussed. "Lofty examples of early Terran literature," Floyt clarified.

Communications on Earth were instantaneous, of course, or near enough as made no difference. But the fastest that information could travel among the stars was the speed of a messenger ship. Too, the use of modern recording equipment wasn't always feasible, for a staggering variety of reasons. There was also an incalculable amount going on, constantly, everywhere.

All of this had brought about a renewal of the human powers of description. It had revived as well certain of the earliest forms: tall tales, the traveler's narrative, legends, and folklore. And these books. Floyt recalled that the opening of the American West was as much invented on the spot as chronicled.

"The bos'n I borrowed them from said that this Bombastico guy doesn't write about Weir anymore. But I thought there might be something useful in with all the swash."

Floyt held the "penny dreadfuls"—that was how he thought of them—in his hand. "Thank you, Alacrity. I appreciate it."

Alacrity was fiddling with his Monopoly piece. "Look, I want to get this deal behind me, I admit that, but I want to do it the right way. I don't know if it's occurred to you, but there're things I'd prefer to be doing right now, too."

He thought for a moment before adding, "Things that are very important to me."

"I see."

"Capitán Váldemar's due to cut out the Breakers in about another couple hundred hours," Alacrity announced. Then he stretched out, silver and gray mane cradled on his interlaced fingers, face to the bulkhead. He was snoring softly within seconds.

Despite *Bruja*'s purification system, the air carried more than a hint of incense when the skipper conducted mass. Floyt came down with a slight case of what Alacrity referred to as the "flow-flows." The breakabout said, "It happens to everyone, sooner or later," and gave him one of the powerful nostrums that were common among travelers. Alacrity somehow managed to get back into a marathon Monopoly game, winning back a small measure of what he'd lost. Floyt read the books of Bombastico Herdman, delighting in their outrageous fabrications.

Time passed.

In the *Bruja*'s entertainment banks, the Terran discovered, among other things, recordings of long-ago Earth radio and television broadcasts, recaptured when humanity's expansion had outraced the speed of light. Floyt found them engrossing, if frequently incomprehensible. Fibber McGee's closet made him howl with delight, though, while original footage (that incredibly outdated word!) of early space exploration stirred him in spite of Earthservice indoctrination.

He discovered recordings of a contemporary series, an extremely popular program called "Doomsday." To his amazement, it concentrated solely on disasters of planetary dimensions. Worldwide deluges, complete social breakdown, and global quakes were among the things relentlessly catalogued and rated for destruction and misery.

When he mentioned it to Alacrity, the breakabout's voice

became brittle with animosity. "Yeah, if some poor bastard's home's been hit by an asteroid thirty kilometers wide, you can bet there'll be a ghoul from 'Doomsday' on the scene, sticking a pickup in his face and saying, 'How do you *feel* at this moment, sir?' Some places, they run that show all day and all night, the All-Doomsday Channel. Myself, I can't stomach it."

Neither could Floyt. He dismissed the program as a mental disorder.

He came to like the *Bruja*'s highly spiced food, and the flow-flows didn't recur. He spent hours staring at the Inheritor's belt and wondering what was to come. He had several bouts of homesickness, although his conditioning helped a little against that. In due course, Capitán Váldemar cut out the Breakers. The ship was in Epiphany's stellar system.

The *Bruja*'s PA system struck up "El Desembarque," as the two companions made their way to her main lock with their baggage. Except in the broad sense, the vessel wasn't anywhere near Epiphany. By law, outsystem craft were required to stop at Palladium, the system's heavily fortified third planet. When the pair passed the big viewport blister near the airlock, the Earther stopped dead. Alacrity nearly trod his heels before he, too, saw that the scene was worth a look.

Palladium was a glowing, red-gold, clouded-ball. But even more august were the aircraft lying close by the *Bruja*.

Outsystem traffic was confined to a tight holding area, with the majority of the planet's weaponry concentrated on it. But even that rigidly defined volume of space was so large that vessels were rarely within visual range of one another. However, Floyt and Alacrity could see no less than four gargantuan starships from where they stood.

The breakabout cursed softly. *Bruja* crewmen were crowding to get a look too. Three colossal dreadnaughts, like gleaming scarab beetles, floated more or less at rest, relative to the freighter. They were quilled and stubbled with weapons and the vibrissae of detection and commo gear. The ships struck Floyt as ominous and invulnerable.

The battlewagons were ranged around the fourth ship, though, and it was that one that really arrested the attention of the onlookers. At some six kilometers in length, she was an incredible Fabergé egg of a vessel, dwarfing the warships.

"That's the *King's Ransom*, Governor Redlock's flagship," Juan-Feng piped up. Floyt recalled that Redlock was Weir's grandnephew by his only marriage. Weir himself had died without issue. Redlock had served the old man as a military commander and political counselor since first coming into manhood. Weir had apparently been very fond of him.

"The other three are ships of the Severeemish Navy," Duarte added.

"It looks like some kind of standoff," Floyt said. He wondered in alarm if they'd wandered into the opening engagement of a war. From what his briefing file had said, the Severeemish were the most militaristic of the governments that had been obliged to acknowledge allegiance to Weir. They were also easily provoked, and since Weir's death, the Severeemish had been restive.

"No standoff," Ortega opined. "*King's Ransom* may look like a fat target, but from what I've heard, she could have three battlewagons for a light snack."

"Still, I wouldn't want to be within a couple of AUs if they started spitting at each other," Alacrity declared. "What're we doing here?"

"Orders from Palladium Control, right after we came out of Hawking. We're to transfer you directly to *King's Ransom*. It seems the governor's giving you a lift to Epiphany, personally."

Ortega grinned at their expressions. "Now, now, don't look so pale, my friends. Remember, they've declared High Truce, at least until Director Weir's will had been read."

There was no point in objecting; *Bruja* warped for the awesome flagship. Closer in, they could make out weaponry and other equipment among the vessel's overdone ornamental splendor. There were also environmental enclosures, immense ones, containing not just aeroponics and hydroponics, but parks, groves of trees, and what appeared to be open bodies of water. Then the *King's Ransom* filled the blister. Juan-Feng, nervous, urged the two passengers to the lock.

Freighter mated to flagship, and the lock cycled. The *Bruja*'s captain and his first mate arrived, distracting Floyt for a moment. He started when he saw the ranks of men waiting in the open lock.

"Celestials," someone murmured. "The governor's elite."

The Celestials were of a type, all taller than Alacrity, muscular, but lean and fit. They wore blue-black uniforms with embroidered nine-pointed silver stars on each shoulder. They were hard-eyed and looked quietly sure of themselves.

A Major of Celestials stepped forward, saluting precisely. "Governor Redlock and Queen Dorraine request the pleasure of the company of Citizen Floyt of Terra."

That, he'd addressed to Floyt, having seen the Inheritor's belt. The major carried an ornate, instrumented baton capped with a Winged Victory figurine. He passed the baton close to Floyt's belt. Neither of the two travelers saw any blinking lights or heard any buzzing, but the major appeared satisfied.

Turning to Alacrity, he went on, "And you, sir, are—"

"The name's Arturo Fernkiss," Alacrity said, adopting an alias by reflex.

The major did not quite smile. "I was about to say, Master Fitzhugh, that you are invited as well, of course."

Floyt was patting his pocket. "I have my identification here, somewhere..." He recalled that it was in the leg pouch, and began to go down on one knee to retrieve it.

"That won't be necessary, Citizen Floyt," the major said.

"If you'll be kind enough to let my men assist you with your baggage, I'll escort you both to His Excellency."

To Floyt, the total absence of other formalities involving documents and ID was shocking. That just didn't feel natural to a man who'd grown up under the Earthservice.

Two Celestials fell out to take the luggage. Valdemar nervously handed the Webley and the Captain's Sidearm to the major and about-faced. It seemed that the capitán couldn't get outsystem fast enough.

In seconds, Floyt and Alacrity were whisked into *King's Ransom* on a low, silent passageway tram. The ship's gravity matched that of Epiphany, so close to Terran as to make no difference, and slightly lighter than *Bruja*'s had been. The two watched as men and women wearing uniforms of Celestials, crew, officers, marines, strike wing, and civilian specialties passed in both directions. They had blurred glimpses into passageways and compartments, enough to know that the vessel was a posh little world, but a singularly well-defended one. The tram slid to a stop, and the Celestials once again formed up as honor guard.

A massive alloy plug of a hatch made a sound like a popping kiss and rolled aside. Alacrity and Floyt were ushered into a formal reception chamber four times the size of the *Bruja*'s number-one cargo hold. The major announced them.

Governor Redlock had been born on the wrong side of the blanket, but that hadn't kept him from winning a high place in Director Weir's realm. He was only a hand's breadth taller than Floyt, but sturdy as a stone monolith. His namesake topknot was bright scarlet peppered with gray. He was light complexioned, but had seen decades of weathering. He had a lumpy pug nose and shrewd blue-green eyes.

Redlock wore a dress uniform of Celestials and an Inheritor's belt, with only one other decoration: a crescent-shaped gorget with nine different sunburst designs picked out in

luminous jewels on black enamel. One design was that of
a binary star system. All of them were under his governance.

Just then his attention was elsewhere. "That's Redlock,"
Floyt murmured to Alacrity. "He has the High Justice."

"Well whatever you do, don't cross him," the breakabout
murmured back. "He could make us dead a lot faster than
anything you could put in a styrette."

Queen Dorraine of Agora, a planet settled early in the
human expansion to the stars, was taller than her husband.
Her skin was a creamy brown; her hair fell in a midnight
cascade, glossy, waist length, crowned with a diadem of
woven, radiant filaments. Redlock's wife was lissome, her
eyes a shining amber brown. Alacrity and Floyt found themselves staring at her superlative face.

Her gown swept the carpet and might have been cro-
cheted from minute beads of light the color of her eyes.
She too wore an Inheritor's belt. Floyt was especially taken
with her, having done some research on the Agoran royal
line.

A third party was there, a stately-looking man resembling
Dorraine in height and grace, skin and features. He was
clean-shaven, like the governor; his black hair showed some
gray.

"Welcome, Citizen Floyt, Master Fitzhugh!" Dorraine
bade in a melodious contralto. "I am Dorraine of Agora.
My husband, Governor Redlock; my father, First Councillor
Inst."

The governor barely acknowledged their presence; Inst
favored them with a polite inclination of the head. Even
Alacrity had the sense to bow. But the three nobles already
had returned their attention to a projection stage, where two
commoimages waited to continue an interrupted conversation.

"Severeemish," Floyt whispered from the corner of his
mouth.

"Ugly, aren't they?" Alacrity observed, studying the hologram. "Got themselves a *lifetime supply* of ugly, I'd say."

"As you can see, Minister Seven Wars, General Sortie-Wolf," Redlock was saying to the Severeemish, "other guests have arrived to accept our hospitality. We extend it to you as well."

The Severeemish scowled at the two travelers. Their race had branched away from mainstream humanity through genetic engineering and selective breeding. The minister and the general were some 210 centimeters tall, with hulking physiques and bull-like, corded necks bulging their uniform stocks. Their heads were long and seemed top-heavy, their leathery skin very ruddy. Severeemish, if these two were a fair sample, had dark, close-set eyes protected by thick ridges of bone. They had long brawny arms, and their powerful hands were equipped with nails like glittering daggers. They wore austere uniforms under garrick coats that emphasized their breadth. Severeemish hair was like white steel wool.

"We are not here as Inheritors," the minister said. "My son and I are here to see that our Observances and Usages are upheld. When Weir accepted the fealty of the Severeemish, he accepted that stipulation. The obligation falls to his successors."

"Why should we not travel in our own ships?" the general added. "What does it matter to us that you invite two vagabonds to voyage with you?"

Floyt made a wry face at that; Alacrity ground his teeth audibly. *Being used is becoming a way of life*, he reflected.

The first Severeemish went on, "There can be no—"

"Weir the Defender stipulated nothing about allowing Severeemish vessels of war to approach Epiphany, Minister," Redlock broke in. "And you and the general *are* Inheritors, no matter in what other capacity you come. Now: you may bring a retinue of reasonable size to Frostpile, of course.

You may travel there by shuttle if you choose, though my flagship will be far quicker and more comfortable."

His tone took on a calculated edge. "But no warships except our own go near Epiphany; that has always been the rule. If you wish to contest the point, perhaps you'd care to bring the *Ignipotent* alongside the *King's Ransom* and exchange broadsides."

The burly images stared at him for long seconds. Then the minister sneered. "This is a transparent effort to keep us from seeing to it Weir's Inheritors live by his word. But you will, in every particular, mark that well! The Usages of the Severeemish will be honored. My son and I will transfer inboard the *King's Ransom* immediately, along with our party."

Redlock would have spoken, but Dorraine took his hand and purred to the images, "We look forward to the pleasure of your company, Minister Seven Wars."

"And if you believe that . . ." Alacrity muttered to Floyt as the Severeemish evaporated.

Arms open, Dorraine floated toward her two guests like Beauty's own embodiment. "Inheritor Floyt, Master Fitzhugh! We were worried about you; you're the last to arrive."

They found themselves acting chivalrous, stuttering their thanks; she had that effect, they would learn, on almost everyone. Redlock's expression, though, indicated that they were more nuisance than guests. Floyt nevertheless found himself glad that their appearance had been of help to the queen. Alacrity was additionally glad that they wouldn't be stuck on one of the undoubtedly less luxurious military shuttles.

Inst descended to exchange pleasantries with the two, as cordial and well-spoken as his daughter.

But after a few minutes Redlock strode from the compartment, proclaiming brusquely, "We boost as soon as those two brutes are inboard. One hour to Epiphany. We'll shuttle down to Frostpile in the *Blue Pearl*."

* * *

Dorraine made exceedingly polite excuses and departed too, along with her father the First Councillor. Left to his own devices, Alacrity assaulted the comestibles dispenser right away in order to get a head start on the next several meals.

Floyt paced the cavernous compartment, studying its hangings, stellar charts, neorepresentational paintings, and furnishings, which looked as beautiful and fragile as Tiffany glass, but felt indestructible and immovable. A scandalously sybaritic head adjoined the compartment.

Neither man was surprised when they found that the hatch to the passageway had been secured from the outside.

Floyt tried to coax *Sheherazade* from the entertainment system, deeming it the appropriate background music for *King's Ransom*. But, unable to find the piece, he settled for some Dixieland. Alacrity had no objections.

Floyt located a control that opened the inner and outer armored panels and exposed a yawning convex of viewport. He got himself a snifter of brandy and ascended to the observation pulpit there.

Alacrity trailed along, bringing an outlandish sandwich and a mug resembling a cuspidor with a handle on it, rich brown foam running down its side. "So he's a governor and she's a queen, but he has the final say, Ho?"

Palladium dwindled behind them; as with *Mindframe* and *Bruja*, there was no sensation of movement as *King's Ransom* boosted for Epiphany.

"Dorraine is queen of Agora. But Agora is just one of the planets under Redlock's governance. You caught the nine-starburst designs? For the nine systems he rules?"

"Ung-hng," Alacrity responded from the depths of the cuspidor. Then, "But what're those goons so worked up about? The Severeemish? You're the one who's been doing all the research; c'mon, show off a little here."

Floyt had parts of the story from the briefing file, the

Bruja's info banks, and some of his own genealogical studies.

"The emigrants to Agora left Earth in a hibernation ship; this was right after the Solar Court outlawed generation ships."

Alacrity forced the food around in his mouth and cheeks in order to get out *"Outlawed?"*

"They deprived 'caretaker' descendants of their fundamental rights of choice. If we start digressing now, it'll take a lot more than an hour," Floyt said, peering forward in hopes of spying Epiphany.

Alacrity motioned him to continue, spilling bits of meat paste and vegetable and splatters of condiments. Floyt felt stately and sage, there in the lap of the universe. He inhaled the brandy and stared out into space.

"Well, the colonists had been thoroughly screened—and in those days, that meant exhaustively, including medical histories and heritages of the nth generation.

"But the biota on the planet they wanted to colonize, Agora, had a rude surprise for them: a whole new range of allergens that produced reactions in people who'd never had any before."

"The answer to that is just to keep on moving, rig," Alacrity managed around the last of his sandwich.

"Couldn't. They couldn't even hang in orbit at that point; a malfunction or something. Practically everyone was subject to severe allergic reactions, and the fatalities began at once. And because of the ship's malfunction, their medical resources were very limited."

Alacrity didn't have to be told what a disaster Floyt was talking about, and what a hellish situation it must've been as colonists were felled by acute asthma and rhinitis, anaphylaxis and the like. "But what about Dorraine?"

"It turned out that a few colonists and crew had no allergic reaction of any kind. All that screening had turned up people immune even to Agora's allergens; something to do with immunoglobulin production, I think."

And the thymus and dendritic cells, Alacrity suspected, but it was Floyt's show, and he waited to hear more.

"They were the only ones who were really functional, and they ended up keeping the colony from falling apart. They ran things."

"Under those circumstances, they probably had to do a lot of the scut work too," Alacrity put in.

"I don't doubt it. At any rate, soon there was a faction favoring an attempt to repair the ship and leave Agora. The colony split wide open, and the bailout faction left under the leadership of one Beltran Severeem."

Alacrity mouthed, *O-ho!*

Floyt nodded. "That's right, the founding fiend. Only, none of the immunes went along with him. And when he and his people got to the planet they'd picked, Desideratum (and they only made it by the skin of their teeth), they found out that nature or the Precursors had played a stupendous prank on them—the biota of Desideratum were derivatives or forerunners of those on Agora."

Alacrity blew his breath out silently. Floyt continued, "Severeem and his followers dug in and survived somehow because it was either that or die; the ship was finished."

"That's been known to work wonders for personnel motivation," Alacrity mused, gazing out at The Strewn.

"Meantime, back on Agora, Dorraine's ancestors naturally got to be in charge, and naturally interbred. It didn't cause too many problems, even though the gene pool was small; most of the undesirable recessives had been screened out of the colonists. Their children inherited immunity to Agora's allergens, and the immunity got to be synonymous with nobility."

"So her family's that intermarried, huh?"

"Most of the original blood's mixed now," Floyt replied. "Dorraine's the last of the purebred. And Inst, of course."

"Yeah, well, Redlock doesn't strike me as the type to give a damn whether his kids' noses run or not."

"Same here. Now, a few generations down the road, Agora got to the point where it could launch its own starships, one to Earth and one to Desideratum, with which there'd been very sporadic, garbled communication. Are you still with me?"

"Let 'er jet."

"The Severeemish were in rough shape, a warlike tribal society, most of its technology lost. They'd learned to cope with the allergens and IgE antibodies, using dilators and antihistamines, antishock agents and vaccines. Immunizing treatment had become part of their religion.

"The Agorans helped the Severeemish; the royal family's immunities practically had the Severeemish worshiping them."

"Oh yeah? Well if you ask me, those goons'd still probably kill somebody just to fill up a lull in the conversation."

Then: "So Dorraine's been the fair-haired princess to them. But Redlock—"

"No, no! I still haven't gotten to the part about the war."

"Listen, we haven't got all day, y'know." Halidome, Epiphany's star, had grown appreciably brighter and slid across the great shield of the viewport as they talked.

"*Tch!* Keep your dainties on, rig! Some bunch of ravaging Visigoths invaded Agora and took over when Dorraine was still a child. The whole royal family was killed, except for Inst and his daughter.

"He got her away in disguise, but they were rounded up and imprisoned. They spent years together in a succession of concentration camps on several planets, under assumed names."

"*Those* two?" Alacrity marveled. "They must be a lot harder than they look."

"I'd say so. Somehow they kept each other alive through starvation, forced labor, beatings, and liquidations. And, I suppose, when Dorraine was older...other things. Until one day when they woke up and the sky was full of Redlock's ships.

"Inst identified himself and proved his claim. The Agorans were still fiercely loyal to their constitutional monarchy. Since Inst had only been royal consort, he wasn't in the line of succession. Redlock set Dorraine on the throne and made Inst regent.

"Agora swore allegiance to Weir through Redlock. Dorraine's rule has been the most popular in about a hundred years and Agora's a bulwark of Weir's realm. Oh, and of course, Redlock married Dorraine."

"Of course. Do we get to the part about the Severeemish being a bunch of soreheads anytime soon?"

"Go piss in a socket! By that time the Severeemish were a confederacy of three planets, and they'd built themselves into a formidable military power. They saw their chance to do a little land grabbing in Agora's system during the Agoran subjugation, but it led to war once Redlock was on the scene."

"Good old Redlock. I heard something about this. The Severeemish fought Weir to a standstill, right?"

"I suppose that's fair enough to say, but it cost them terribly. They'd already sworn never to surrender. To save them face, they were allowed to vow fealty through Dorraine. They still remembered their debt to her ancestors."

"Their memories were set on SELECTIVE."

"Uh-huh. The Severeemish Confederacy became a sort of client state."

"Not bad. Economical."

"Weir's specialty. And in return, Weir promised to abide by their Observances and Usages, and all the protocols that go with them. It'll probably make his funeral quite a shindig."

"But why do they want trouble? At least, that's how *I* read them."

"They're nothing if not stiff-necked. I suppose they'd

love a chance to get out of their oath, now that they've rebuilt their military. But they're too scrupulous about their oaths to just renege on one. Too feudal, too militaristic; it would rock their whole social structure. So they're trying to provoke a rift."

They watched the starscape swing by. Alacrity discovered how to get the dispenser to cough up an extraordinary Epiphanian champagne; Floyt sampled it with delight. All too soon, by Floyt's reckoning, the major of Celestials appeared to show them to the flight deck, and the *Blue Pearl*.

CHAPTER 10

MIXERS

THE *BLUE PEARL* RESEMBLED EXACTLY THAT, A BALL SOME forty meters in diameter, made of smoky blue glass with a silvery reflectiveness to it.

The companions had long since stopped worrying about guns and luggage. The High Truce declared for Weir's funeral was all-encompassing. Celestials, looking like so many lethal orchestra conductors, waved weapons-detection wands around them before they boarded.

Power source and crew, detectors and weaponry and other machinery were tucked out of sight in the *Pearl's* bottom. There were terraced decks and lush foliage in well-anchored planters; there were deep carpets and a live string quartet of females dressed in classic black gowns and wearing bluish cultured pearls. There was a catering board tended by nubile young women. There were also handsome young men among the staff, but the breakabout only noticed the ones who were carrying drink trays.

"Oboy! D'you think a feature spread on this thing would go under 'Modern Spacecraft,' 'Opulent Lifestyles,' or

'Outdoor Living?'" He plucked a tangerinelike fruit from a tree and looked around in excitement.

"Relax, Fitzhugh," Floyt advised.

Dorraine and Redlock were present, in conversation with the two Severeemish. The queen had apparently achieved the incredible—she had charmed the minister and the general into something resembling civility. Redlock turned a warning eye toward the Terran and the breakabout.

"I don't think he's dying to get to know us right now, Ho."

"I'd say you made a good call. Come; I'll buy you a drink."

Lesser personages floated about, crew and civilians, and a number of Celestials, though no one but Dorraine and Redlock, Seven Wars and Sortie-Wolf and Floyt wore an Inheritor's belt.

Alacrity made elaborate overtures to the bartender, who bore it with the good grace necessary to her calling. But his wide, tawny eyes roved the *Blue Pearl*, weighing, assessing. He and Hobart joined the others in exclaiming as the craft moved off the flight deck and Epiphany loomed near.

The planet was mottled in greens, grays, and browns, aswirl with blue-white clouds. It rolled under them as the *Pearl* descended.

Alacrity noticed two more Severeemish off to one side. The bartender told him that these were Corporeals, members of a special corps of bodyguards and shock troops. The Corporeals and the lithe, dangerous Celestials eyed one another with relaxed, chilly calculation. The breakabout wasn't sure where he'd put his money if it came to a fight.

The flight to Epiphany took them on a long, curved course in order to show off some of the most spectacular scenery on the planet. Floyt found it extremely novel to hear conversation, laughter, and the glancing of bottles and drinking vessels as the *Blue Pearl* flashed along high over Epiphany.

They saw sheer, razorback mountains thick with undergrowth and cloud forests, enclosing inaccessible ripples of valley. They hurtled over swamps and tangled jungle, lava-lakes and geysers, snarled rivers, and an archipelago like a necklace out of heaven's lapidary. They gazed down on angry seas, and snow-crowned peaks that topped 14,000 meters. Floyt's determined loyalty to Terra's beauty was severely tested.

Frostpile was an assemblage of forms that shouldn't have coexisted in such harmony but did. The effect was one of a city of intagliated crystal. It rose in twisted spirals like unicorn horns, and turrets resembling rampant hooded cobras; towers that put Floyt in mind of toadstools; finials; fans; pinions. There were grand esplanades and arcing fountains.

Frostpile had projections like battering rams and subsections that might have been tethered dirigibles; spidery bridges and lacy miradors. All of it was flawlessly integrated, and there was an apparent weightlessness to it. There was a good deal of sky traffic: touring hansoms, troop carriers, patrolling air-cutters, a hover phaeton, and individuals in grav-harness.

Alacrity picked out fortifications, and plenty of them. Frostpile was one sugar candy that no one was going to swallow at a gulp.

The *Blue Pearl* landed on top of a central tower, its roof more than a quarter kilometer on each side. No sooner had the ship touched down than Weir household troops, the renowned Invincibles, formed up. Liveried servants and porter automata and under-seneschals swarmed forth.

Floyt and Alacrity, among the last to disembark, found themselves on an acre or so of midnight-black carpet worked in gold thread with the Weir coat of arms, whose most prominent device was a broken slave collar.

Dorraine, the governor, Inst, and the Severeemish were

the center of the attention of the massed household personnel, and the warm, tangy afternoon air was filled with martial music. Floyt saw that Alacrity was watching him expectantly. Then the Terran realized that the Inheritor's belt was their only credential. It made Floyt feel that much more estranged from Terra and resentful of Bear, if not Earthservice, conditioning or no. He tried to put it out of his mind; it could only mean trouble at his debriefing.

The breakabout guessed what was running through Floyt's mind. He patted the Earther's shoulder. "Just don't pick up any good habits, Ho, and you'll do fine."

An assistant under-seneschal found them and festooned their bags about an autoporter. At his invitation, they seated themselves on jumpseats that folded down from the machine's sides. The man instructed it, and the robot hummed off toward their quarters. Everyone else there ignored their departure.

The porter floated down a long ramp within the tower, the winding descent leading it into a side corridor. The place was built on a scale suitable to titans. Walls, floor, and ceilings were smooth and translucently bone-white. There was constant, bustling traffic.

They were halted once, at a junction checkpoint where Invincibles scanned for weapons. When they'd resumed their way, Floyt glanced out an observation deck window and saw that they were headed for one of the captive dirigibles.

The under-seneschal brought them to a suite on the upper sweep of the form, well away from the central structures of Frostpile. Its front door, a cluster of curved, overlapping surfaces, didn't simply swing or slide out of the way; to Floyt's astonishment, it *blossomed* open.

They stepped through into a spacious living-receiving room. Half the room lay under a broad shield of skylight that gave them an enviable view of Weir's stronghold. The suite was decorated in the sumptuous, excessive New Elegance style originated on Laissez Faire. The deep pile of the aqua-marine carpet brushed their ankles. From the lighting ten-drils drifting overhead to the floor's texture and temperature controls, the suite was obediently, indulgently, exhaustively luxurious.

Floyt wandered out into it, mesmerized by the beauties of form, space, light, and scent. Alacrity cut short the under-seneschal's explanation of the suite's environmental system, service, and commo arrangements, and the layout of Frost-pile.

Departing, the man told them, "There's an orientation program available from the communications terminal. It explains the behavioral constraints now in force." He left in haste; other, *important*, guests were to be seen to. The two visitors had barely begun sorting themselves out when the door flowered open again and a woman strode exuber-antly—very nearly *bounced*—into the suite.

She scarcely topped 150 centimeters, plump and round-cheeked with a halo of tight brown curls and cheery eyes the same color. Over a light blouse she wore a loose one-piece garment that reminded Floyt of rompers. Altogether, she put him in mind of a very animated child.

"Welcome to Riffraff Alley." She beamed at them. "I'm Sintilla."

Alacrity found himself grinning back at her while Floyt made the introductions. "Riffraff Alley?" the breakabout echoed.

"That's my name for it." She waved a hand to include the dirigible in general. "Old Grandam Tiajo stuck all of her least welcome guests out here."

"Weir's sister, right?" Alacrity asked. "Chief executrix and all that?"

Sintilla nodded.

"If this is exile, I'll endure it somehow," Floyt allowed.

Sintilla smiled again. "Oh, it's passable, but you should see how the gentry in the core districts live." She eyed the

Terran speculatively. "So, at last I get to meet the mystery man from Earth."

"What's that mean?" Alacrity pounced, natural and programmed suspicions flaring.

She scrunched her nose at him merrily. "I might as well confess right now: I'm a journalist. I'm here to cover the funeral rites, but there'd be plenty of interest in a story about a native Terran. A lot of people are curious about Hobart. But Tiajo isn't one of them; she's just plain piqued."

"At *me*?" Floyt cried. "Whatever for?"

"At her brother, too— except that she'd never admit it— for adding you to his will at the last minute without consulting her. That's why you two are here with the rest of us undesirables."

"Suits me," Alacrity huffed.

"At any rate, we're not interested in being interviewed, thank you," Floyt told her.

"Now, wait! There're things I can do for you too, y'know. I'm conversant with most of the who, what, and why around here."

"So?" Alacrity was attempting to adjust his proteus to Frostpile's system, without much luck.

"I can fill you in on things. For starters, you might as well not bother trying to patch into the commo systems with your own equipment."

Alacrity stopped fiddling. "What're they, all on-line encrypted?"

She shrugged. "Not my line of work. All I know is, if you want a comset that works, you have to use one of theirs. Accessors, proteuses, interfacers—they're not much use on Epiphany."

"That seems unduly restrictive," opined Floyt, who was once again beginning to miss his accessor, "even for security's sake."

"Anyway, that's something we would've found out for ourselves," Alacrity pointed out.

Sintilla gave him a look of clownish pity. "Yeah, and you can screen the protocol orientations, but that's just not the same as having a pal who knows the ropes, is it? Look, I don't want to grill you guys; I just want to see how things go for you here, same as for all the others."

In spite of the Earthservice warning against unnecessary fraternization, Floyt could see where knowledgeable advice might be of great help to his mission; even Alacrity seemed a bit out of his league in Frostpile.

"Very well," he said, surprised to find himself making decisions. Alacrity withheld any objection; her story would be easy enough to check out, and in any case, he had no intention of trusting her or anyone else. Besides, he was prone to sympathy for a fellow underdog.

"Jubilation!" she laughed, clapping her hands. "Did anybody offer to show you around Frostpile? No? Well then, I'll do it, unless you're too tired."

They were both restive from shipboard confinement. Sintilla summoned a corridor tram, and they were off, descending into the main part of the stronghold.

The corridors teemed with robotry and automata, Invincibles and other household members. The Weir guardsmen were a more heterogeneous group than Redlock's Celestials or the Corporeals of the Severeemish. A good many older men and women wore the heavily braided and decorated red and gold uniforms; Sintilla explained that many had been Invincibles all their adult lives. More than half were liberated slaves; all were unsparingly loyal to the Weir family.

Floyt was fascinated with the variety in dress and appearance of those traveling the corridors afoot and on trams. He saw one young woman in a glittering outfit like a matador's suit of lights; she looked like some sort of royalty.

"Food technician," Sintilla explained when he asked.

The journalist pointed out assorted places and things of interest or importance and filled them in on the history of the place. Originally, Tiajo had planned to select one of several high-flown names for the Weir seat of power. But during the construction, her brother had, with typical lack of reverence, taken to calling it Frostpile. The name had caught on, and to Tiajo's consternation, she had never been able to dislodge it.

"Is Weir laid out in state?" Alacrity asked. He had no idea what the local custom was.

"Uh-huh, in the family complex," Sintilla supplied. "But no outsiders will be permitted until the ending ceremony."

Three times Invincibles at security checkpoints flagged them down for quick, courteous but thorough detector searches. And, detectors swiveling, floating surveillance drones drifted along the corridors.

"What're they afraid of?" Alacrity wondered aloud.

"That somebody'll violate the High Truce," Sintilla said. "That's why Tiajo wouldn't let any of the Inheritors or guests bring along a big retinue or entourage. Only one or two companions apiece, like Hobart."

"Or the Severeemish, with those Corporeals," Floyt mulled.

"Don't the privileged classes miss their concubines and nannies and hiney wipers?" Alacrity wondered.

"Frostpile can provide any and all on request." Sintilla giggled. "Every one of .'em loyal to Tiajo."

"And so all the visitors are on a fairly equal footing, regardless of rank," Floyt realized.

The little journalist nodded. "There are plenty of grudges and feuds among the various parties. Everybody's salivating for his slice of the Weir fortune and realm, too. Not to mention the trouble you're bound to run into anytime a mixed crowd like this one gets together. It's a good idea *not* to discuss religion or politics."

"Or history or art," Alacrity added.

"Or sports or sexual credos," Floyt contributed. He wondered if the Invincibles were also keeping their eyes open for stray medical styrettes.

"Actually, the guards are trying to be very discreet about all this searching," Sintilla told them. "When the Daimyo of Shurutzu arrived, the Invincibles scanned his baggage and got a strong reading. Turned out he'd packed along a favorite biosynergic, um, 'marital aid.' Impressive, but not lethal. Anyway, wasn't there a flap about that! Now the guards are being more circumspect."

They arrived at the Hall of Remembrances and dismounted. The place was crammed with memorabilia collected during Weir's long, eventful life. Just within the entrance was the flying throne in which he'd been sitting when he'd died, out in the meadow beyond Frostpile. Rows of shining exhibition cases, display cabinets, and shelves were lined with weapons, trophies of war, and ceremonial artifacts and clothing.

The place was nearly a maze, with orientation supplied by floating holos and illuminated floor strips. With a jaunty stride, Sintilla led them into it, calling back, "This is one of my favorite places in Frostpile."

There were personal keepsakes and lavish gifts of state. The precious items—scepters, crowns and diadems, jeweled staffs and batons, and similar symbols of Weir's accumulated titles and ranks—were arrayed in special security cases, monitored by elaborate alarm systems and closely watched by sharp-eyed Invincibles.

Less grandiose items were shown as well. Among these was the original hard copy of the famous message from the Srillan admiral, Maska. Weir had attempted to expand into Srillan territories while the aardvarklike aliens were occupied elsewhere. Maska, then Srilla's youngest flag-rank officer, had somehow managed to bluff his other enemies and throw together a huge armada with which to confront Weir.

Maska had made it a point to broadcast his message in cleartext. Floyt now bent down to read the hard copy.

SIR:
UNLESS YOU AND YOUR FORCES WITHDRAW IMMEDIATELY
UPON RECEIPT OF THIS COMMUNICATION, I SHALL CER-
TAINLY KICK YOUR ASS ALL OVER SEVERAL CONSTELLA-
TIONS.

Weir had indeed withdrawn, one of his few reversals. He and Maska had later become friends. The Earther scowled at the reference to the beings who'd done so much damage to his homeworld.

"Dame Tiajo set all this up," Sintilla commented as they strolled along the glowing guidance strip on the floor. "The old man was never much for parading his accomplishments."

They stopped by another case. On black velvet rested a crude-looking little handgun. Alacrity could see at a glance that its primitive sights weren't very accurate. It lacked safety, trigger guard, and adjustment controls of any kind.

The placard next to it gleamed:

THE EMANCIPATOR PISTOL. THIS MASS-PRODUCED WEAPON
WAS AIRDROPPED IN GREAT NUMBERS THROUGHOUT THE
GRAND PRESIDIUM BY THE OPPOSITION LEAGUE INTELLI-
GENCE CORPS FOR USE BY REVOLUTIONARY GROUPS AND
SYMPATHIZERS. THIS PARTICULAR UNIT IS THAT FOUND BY
CASPAHR WEIR AT (STANDARD) AGE SIXTEEN YEARS.

"Never saw one before," Alacrity commented as they gazed down, faces reflected like ghosts in the crystal pane.

"The Opposition League seeded them on lots of planets, with instruction-beads. Weir found one early on."

Floyt listened to her then regarded the Emancipator dubiously. "It doesn't look very impressive."

"It was one-shot, short-range," the little woman answered.

"And with it, Weir made his first kill. See, the idea was, you found one on the ground someplace, stuck it in your shirt, and waited. It was for killing a sentry or whoever. Then you took *his* weapons and ammo and equipment.

"But those little gizmos are built to take it. You can recharge them from almost any energy source. The propulsion unit will shoot just about anything you can fit into the firing chamber: slugs, pebbles, pellets—practically anything."

As they moved on, Floyt inquired, "How is it that you know so much about the Emancipator?"

"Weir told me."

They halted. "You *knew* him?" Alacrity demanded. The peppy little extrovert in rompers didn't look like the type to hobnob with interstellar rulers.

"Sort of. He let me interview him, from time to time, the last few years. I'm the only correspondent who's been permitted to cover the funeral, didn't you know?" She winked merrily. "It was Weir's stated wish, so there wasn't much Tiajo could do about it except stick me out in Riffraff Alley."

"Who're you working for?" Alacrity asked tersely.

"Oh, I free-lance," she informed him brightly.

Floyt was listening with only half an ear, still thinking about the Emancipator. Of the vast number dropped, of the fraction of those found and the percentage of *those* actually used, only one had fallen into the hands of a Caspahr Weir. But that had been sufficient. The truth was more astounding than anything in the penny dreadfuls.

"What was he like, Weir?"

Sintilla turned to Floyt. Alacrity waited for the answer as she pondered for a moment. "Y'know, Hobart, damn it, I've never been able to answer that one in a few words. If at all. A very complex man who always made simplicity work for him. Lots of inner conflicts, but a great sense of humor. Everything they called him was at least a little bit true: savior and opportunist, ruthless and compassionate. See what I'm driving at?"

"I'll have to think about it."

Much of Frostpile was closed in preparation for the various devotional services and rites or off-limits for security reasons.

"Which is too bad," Sintilla remarked, "because the palace would actually remind you of a lively little community. There's the Frostpile All Volunteer Light Opera Company, and the Invincibles' joints, like the Hazardous Duty Rathskeller, sports clubs—"

"What about gambling?" Alacrity was quick to inquire, with an avaricious gleam in his eyes. "Cribbage? Two-ups? Marbles?"

She chuckled, "Uh-huh! Also dice, egg jousting, and, I suppose, pillow fights. But you might as well forget 'em; Tiajo doesn't want guests mingling with the hired help."

Alacrity's face fell.

Floyt tut-tutted. "Oh, cheer up; you can always cheat yourself at solitaire."

"It's not the same thing, Ho."

Sintilla, who appeared to be on familiar terms with many of the people in the place, led the two to a high tower shaped like a shark's fin. They found an empty exedra, and the woman showed no hesitation in ordering refreshments.

They looked out over the palace stronghold. Frostpile was being readied for many diverse activities. Complex, highly technical sporting apparatus was being tested; in an enormous open area, Invincibles and Celestials were drilling. In another—Floyt couldn't tell *what* was going on there.

"They're gearing up for the Hunt," Sintilla said.

"Hunt?" It was a sport long unpracticed on Earth. "Disgusting. I'm surprised anyone would have anything to do with it."

"Fine, because we're not going to," Alacrity put in. "Too many chances for, ah, mishaps."

"You'll be there if you want your inheritance, Hobart," Sintilla informed him. "Those Severeemish'll make sure of that; even Tiajo won't cross them."

The two wasted a few seconds in protestation, then Sintilla elaborated. When Weir had accepted the fealty of the Severeemish, he'd also accepted the obligation to live up to their Observances and the Usages thereof. Most of those involved what amounted to lip service. Others, like those surrounding the death of a liege lord, were different.

For the Inheritors, there must be proof of respect and custom, in the form of games, a Hunt, and the drinking of something called the Thorn Cup. If Weir's successors failed to keep to that, the Severeemish would have, by their lights, just cause to consider their obligations and fealty at an end.

"And Redlock and Tiajo can't afford that," Sintilla finished. "The Severeemish are too valuable as allies, and too dangerous as potential enemies. Hobart will have to participate or be disinherited."

"Dandy," Alacrity groaned. Down below, he could see preparations for the Hunt being made, where she'd pointed them out. Invincibles were inspecting weapons, portable shooting blinds, vehicles and aircraft of assorted types, and hunting beasts.

"Wait a minute, Sintilla," Floyt began.

"Why don't you call me Tilla? Most people do."

"Tilla, then. I have to *participate*. Does that mean I don't necessarily have to win anything? Or kill anything?"

She nodded perkily. "That's the way I understand it."

"Listen, that's not so bad, Alacrity." Certainly, it wasn't enough to interfere with his compelling urge to see his mission through.

Alacrity rubbed his chin. "What's this Thorn Cup?"

"Nothing, really. And there's the formal dinner tonight, but that's—"

"Nothing, really," Alacrity predicted. "How formal?"

"To tell you the truth, it's an overdone get-acquainted bash. They won't go in for speeches or anything, if that's what you're worried about. Or for lamentations and mourning, either; that's considered bad taste. And, of course, the residents of Riffraff Alley will probably be thoroughly snubbed. Anyway, we've got some time before then."

"For what, Tilla?" Floyt wondered.

"This." She pulled off her expensive little proteus and set it for sound recording, placing it on the table between them.

"Now, Hobart, what can you tell my readers about the decadent sexual practices of Old Terra?"

CHAPTER 11

HETERO DYNING

WHEN SINTILLA SHOWED UP AT THEIR SUITE TO COLLECT them for dinner, they were a little logy, having transferred from *Bruja*'s evening, via the short voyage inboard *King's Ransom*, to the early afternoon of Epiphany's twenty-hour day. A brief nap hadn't helped much.

Soon they had found themselves in early evening again. The suite door bloomed for them, and they went forth.

If Frostpile by day was an enchantment, by night it was very nearly overpowering. It glowed like gauzy daylight, sending rainbow rays dancing and patterning in the sky. Free-floating lightshapes—hoops and polygons, globes and spirals—roamed, throwing bright, colorful rays. Other illuminations flared throughout the place, things resembling gemstone candle flames, darting firewisps, and intricate whorls; some were stationary in nooks or sconces, while others gave the impression of being capriciously and joyously alive. The great corridors radiated a milky luminescence.

The bouyant little free-lancer literally took them in hand,

walking between the two as they entered the cyclopean dining hall.

The Inheritors were few, but there were hundreds of family friends, escorts, consorts, cohorts, representatives, acquaintances, and observers. As regarded attire, the gathering made the merriment at the Sockwallet lashup drab by comparison. It resembled a combination Mardi Gras, costume ball, and saturnalia, in dress if not in behavior.

Though many were no taller than he himself, Floyt was again impressed with the extreme height so common among non-Earthers. Even Alacrity was far from being a standout in that crowd.

One young couple apparently felt completely proper in the nude and depilated except for dramatized brows and lashes, and emitting glowing auras, he in red and she in blue. Alacrity suspected that the generators were hidden in their abundant jewelry.

A resident of Harvest Home lumbered by in his segmented, artificial carapace. A Königswold grandee swaggered past, bereft of his traditional weapons harness for the duration of the High Truce.

Thanks to the Earthservice psychprop planners, though, Floyt drew attention from all quarters. He wore white tie and black tails, batwing collar, dancing pumps, starched shirt, vest, and pearl studs. He also wore a watch chain, without a watch, but with his wonderment for a fob. His Inheritor's belt somehow managed not to look incongruous with his formal attire. Floyt couldn't have been more a figure out of legend if he'd worn the Regalia of Pharaoh.

Alacrity somehow felt proud when he saw all those O-shaped mouths aimed their way as he, Floyt, and Sintilla wound toward their table. The breakabout was wearing a dress shipsuit, a tight-fitting garment that made him look like a jetskate racer. Sintilla wore a riotously multicolored variation on her trademark rompers.

The hall was a looming, endless-seeming place warmed

by every manner of light effect: free-floating and circulating, reflected and directed. They were of all colors, ranging from muted to dazzling. Alacrity spotted drones sailing lazily overhead, roving inconspicuously.

Tables and seating, eating and drinking utensils, and place settings had been painstakingly arranged, individualized for the outlandish assortment of guests. Some tables floated; one, for the Overseer of Wayward, looked very much like a well-anchored trough. Around the room, stemware glittered and alloys shone; rich fabrics vouched for Tiajo's hospitality.

Gently luminescent seating holos hovered over the crowd, descending and rising in a stately cycle to indicate tables. Some of the tables had been constructed for nonhuman diners, a few of whom were in environmental containers of various types; their gathering at one particular table put Alacrity in mind of a space station with wildly different vessels moored around it.

Floyt noticed that, unlike the *Bruja* and the sealed habitats of Luna, Frostpile permitted smoking; a bewildering intermixture of fumes drifted to him. Just then he was approached by a portly man with a carefully tended white beard and an engaging smile. The man wore fine robes and a sort of surplice and an Inheritor's belt. He offered his hand, Earth style.

"Citizen Floyt? I've been looking forward to making your acquaintance, sir! Allow me to introduce m'self; Endwraithe, board member, Bank of Spica."

Alacrity was watching carefully. The Central Bank of Spica was the closest thing humanity had to a common banking house. Floyt's own travel voucher had been drawn against it, and its notes were the most reliable medium of exchange there was. And here was one of its senior officers buttonholing Functionary 3rd Class Hobart Floyt.

"This isn't the time or place for it, but I'd just like to talk to you at some point in the near future. The bank is

always interested in opportunities for proper placement of
its venture capital, or in discussing matters with a prospec-
tive major investor."

The Earther stammered a reply. The banker patted his
arm. "I'll be talking to you, m'boy." He departed through
the crowd.

Sintilla said, "Hobart, I don't know if you realize this,
but there're whole mercantile dynasties that'd cheerfully
sacrifice their firstborn for an offer like that."

"I haven't really felt normal since I climbed off that
bicycle," Floyt sighed. "Alacrity, what did you—"

But the breakabout wasn't listening. A woman was wend-
ing her way in their general direction. Sintilla followed
Alacrity's gaze and clucked disappointedly. "Is *that* your
taste? An ice sculptor's wet dream?"

She looked to be about Alacrity's age. Certainly she was
close to his height, slim-waisted, with ample breasts and
hips. Weighty ringlets of chalk-blond hair framed her face
and tumbled around athlete's shoulders.

She wore sandals of strung carnelian, their color matching her lips, and what looked like a strategic black fog,
which drifted in slow migration around her body without
ever quite making complete revelations. Her skin was a
taut, almost gleaming white with little flesh tone to it.

"Probably gene-engineered." Sintilla *humphed*.

Alacrity, eyeing the woman's wide, mobile mouth, discovered that his own lips had parted. It took him only an
instant to conclude that her high-cheekboned face was perfect.

"Don't you ever think about anything but your libido?"
Floyt reproved.

"I'm at that awkward stage: adulthood," Alacrity threw
back over his shoulder as he moved off to intercept her.

She took in the working spacer's outfit, the wide, oblique
eyes that might almost be an animal's, and the wavy, silver-
in-gray banner of hair. Her expression was all good-natured

weariness, *Oh, go ahead and try, then, if you really must.* All in the midst of his infatuation, he was irked.

Long-necked, she held her squarish chin low, so that her big hazel eyes gazed up at him through sooty lashes.

"Is she really?" Floyt asked Sintilla. "Gene-engineered, I mean."

The journalist shrugged. "That's one rumor. She's the Nonpareil, Dincrist's daughter." When she saw the Terran's blank look, she amplified, "Another Inheritor, a very important man in interstellar shipping. She's his only child."

Floyt plunged after his escort with a feeling of dread, drawing near just in time to hear him introduce himself.

"Good evening; my name is Alacrity," he said with a lopsided fleer. "I'm with the athletic certification board. When will it be convenient for me to try out your recreational equipment?" He was counting on the idiotic look to make it work.

Arriving at the breakabout's side, Floyt smothered a groan. But the Nonpareil burst out in a full-throated laugh, managing, "Well, the name fits you!"

"Fitzhugh is right. Oh, er, this is Hobart Floyt."

She saw the Inheritor's belt and took in the swank formal outfit as she extended her hand. "A pleasure."

Floyt took it, not sure what to do with it. Just then a man appeared at the Nonpareil's side. He was taller than Alacrity, very fit-looking in a patrician way, middle-aged, with hair the color of his daughter's. He had the handsome tan of a titled outdoorsman, though, and wore an Inheritor's belt over his stylish dalmatica. He looked apoplectic.

"Oh dear me," Sintilla said softly from where she'd brought up the rear behind Floyt.

The Terran inserted himself into the situation with a confidence he didn't feel.

"Ah, Citizen Dincrist and, ah, Nonpareil, good evening. I am Hobart Floyt, of Terra." Without turning aside, he told his companion, "Our table is *this* way, Alacrity."

Dincrist seemed puzzled by Floyt's origin and the matchless white tie and tails. He said, "Nice to have met you, sir. In the future, please be kind enough to remember that I am *Captain* Dincrist. Come, my dear."

She inclined her head to them, one white curl bobbing across her eye, making her look mischievous. Then the Nonpareil went off on her father's arm.

"Alacrity, you have all the subtlety of an equivalent mass of falling masonry."

"Just being sociable, Tilla."

"You should've ignored her, Alacrity," Floyt put in. "Our mission, remember?" He didn't see Sintilla's eyes shift from one to the other.

Alacrity sighed in the Nonpareil's wake. "There isn't that much conditioning in the entire galaxy, rig."

The journalist took him by the elbow. "Feeding time, Fitzhugh."

Sintilla had filled them in on those other least welcome mourners and Inheritors who infested Riffraff Alley. They began to show up as the trio was getting seated at a table set as far to one side as it was possible to be.

There was a woman known as Stare Skill, a naturalist and xenologist, wearing her belt. A sad-eyed, lean woman in her fifties, she was famous for her work among the native sapients of a planet humans called Ifurin, which lay within the late Weir's realm. She wore no makeup, and her hair was short, for easy tending. She was dressed in a simple frock and low-heeled, comfortable shoes.

She arrived with her traveling companion, a member of the species she'd spent most of her adult life studying. Most humans found their language extremely difficult to pronounce. Weir's task-force commander, upon making regrettably warlike first contact with them on their homeworld, had called them *Djinn*. The name had endured.

This one was typical of the breed. If a satyr had evolved

under more than one and a half gravities, developing the rolling gait and intermittent knuckles-walking of an ape, he might resemble a Djinn. This one was shorter than Sintilla while walking erect, and a good deal more so now. He was a being of enormous cross section, with amazing musculature bulging on his long arms and bandy legs. He had jaws like a rock crusher, and jutting tusks.

He had glittering black claws, projections on his horn-covered knuckles. There were also spiky prongs on knees, elbows, and shoulders. His broad, hard hooves had been shod in thick, resilient pads for the visit. He brachiated up into his chair effortlessly as Stare Skill seated herself.

Sintilla made the introductions. The Djinn's chosen Terranglish name was Brother Grimm.

"Good warrior's name, huh?" Alacrity commented, eyeing the creature.

"No," the Djinn replied. Turning to Floyt, he went on, "It's in honor of the two brothers from your planet. The writers."

"He adores their stories," Stare Skill supplied. With some exertion, Grimm convoluted his hideous face into what Floyt presumed to be a smile.

He asked the Terran anxiously, "Would you know any of their descendents, Citizen Earther? The brothers, I mean. You're the first Terran I've met."

Floyt's ingrained hostility toward nonhumans vied with amusement and a certain regret, as he replied that he did not. The Djinn's disappointment showed, in spite of his inhuman features. "A pity, a pity..."

Alacrity, chin on fist, elbow on the table, tried to recall when he'd seen such a soft heart in quite so scary an exterior. Sintilla smiled, crinkles appearing beside her eyes, nose, and mouth.

Servicers started bringing open-top globes of marinated Epiphany fruit and mixed nuts. Sintilla caught Floyt's hand, inveigling him, "Tell me more about good ol' Earth. Please? It's all grist for the mill."

Floyt politely disengaged himself. "We've already been thoroughly gristed, Tilla."

The last of their tablemates showed up. "William Risk, at your service. For the right money."

"Billy Risk?" Alacrity erupted, almost upsetting the table as he rose and extended his hand. "*Kid* Risk?"

William Risk nodded resignedly, clasping wrists with the breakabout. He was slight, almost emaciated, with smooth salt-and-pepper hair and goatee and eyes a deep brown-black. He was several centimeters shorter than Floyt, and had a lifelong tan and deeply lined face.

He wore a faded yellow uniform of some sort, with pleated sleeves and fringed epaulets, but without insignia or rank. He looked sleepy, but was nevertheless one of the deadliest things that walked, or so Sintilla had said. Alacrity had recognized the name at once when she'd first mentioned it.

Alacrity saw the way the old man reacted to the name he'd used as a triggerman; the breakabout let it drop, and resumed his seat. Kid Risk, mercenary and gentleman, bounty hunter and survivor of the Illyrian Vendetta, found his seat next to Stare Skill. He greeted Brother Grimm, Sintilla, and Stare Skill; the journalist and the Djinn replied, but the older woman put a chill in the air with her barely civil nod of the head.

Alacrity caught himself gawking, and stopped. "My name's Alacrity Fitzhugh. Y'know, I used to read all those books about you: *Kid Risk Stands Alone*, *Death Card for Billy Risk*."

Floyt realized that this was another figure out of the new penny dreadfuls. Risk gave Alacrity a pained smile. "Well, I'm sure a sharp young fella like you knows enough not to believe everything he reads."

"Oh. Sure, well, *naturally*," Alacrity recovered.

"Those books gave me more trouble than just about anything else that ever happened to me," Risk told the table at large. "But there's not a lot you can do to defend yourself once somebody starts writing about you."

"How d'you mean, Captain Risk?" Brother Grimm asked. "Are the stories lies?"

"Not altogether, but they sure don't hew too closely to the truth. No. What I meant was, people started to come after me, for this reason or that."

"No denial ever catches up with a rumor," Floyt put in. The old man inclined his head. Sintilla was staring down at the table.

"The books and real life sort of got mixed up too," Risk recalled softly, looking to Stare Skill. "I had some awfully wrong ideas about myself there for a while, when I started believing them." The xenologist refused to meet his gaze.

After a moment, the old man shunted aside some sad preoccupation. "And you'd be Mr. Floyt," he ventured, using the ancient form. "I never met an Earther before." He hooked a thumb in his Inheritor's belt.

"A common failing around here," Floyt observed.

Kid Risk chuckled. Floyt's head swam a bit. It was only hours since Captain Valdemar had cut out the Breakers, and he'd already been involved in encounters so incredible that he doubted anyone on Earth would credit the story. He looked at his tablemates and thought, a bit spitefully, of what his wife Balensa would have given to share his meal.

The sound system blared a processional, and the Grandam Tiajo entered, followed by a covey of attendants and hirelings. She was decked out in intricate formal robes and a cloak, a slender old woman with a mountainous hairdo and a baton that strobed softly with a maroon light. The crowd applauded.

She reached the table at the front of the long hall, so far away that they had to stand to see her. She wore an Inheritor's belt larger and more elaborate than the others.

Redlock and Dorraine were among those waiting to greet her. Alacrity gazed around and could spot no other table but theirs and his own where there was more than one belt. The highest and the lowest, he supposed.

Tiajo spoke into an invisible pickup. "Thank you, thank you, my friends and *guests*." Floyt could've sworn she said that directly downrange at the riffraff. The applause gradually died.

She resumed, "As you know, my dead brother wanted no sadness, no melancholy, after his passing. Thus there will be none; we rejoice in our coming together, and in his full life, as he did. I will tell you what Caspahr would have said, if he were here."

Necromancy in reverse; she's putting words into the mouth of the dead, Floyt mused.

"He would have said"—Tiajo threw her arms wide, holding her baton high—"*welcome!*" More applause sounded, polite and brief.

Slight anticlimax, Floyt thought, but she was a somewhat over-painted woman well aware of her mortality, and she no longer had her brother to lean upon. She hadn't done too badly.

Uprange, at her end of the room, Tiajo had the rulers of planets and starsystems, envoys from most of the human-ruled portion of the galaxy. Weir's death meant a reshuffling of power, territory, wealth, and authority in local space, but the nineteen-system realm was a place of growing strategic importance. At a table near Tiajo's sat Seven Wars and Sortie-Wolf, the two Severeemish representatives, watching everything closely.

"There will be games, and the Hunt," Tiajo announced. "And then the Thorn Cup, and my brother's last rite, followed by the Willreading."

Alacrity sighed unhappily.

"But for tonight, avail yourselves of the hospitality of Frostpile."

* * *

A celebration at Frostpile was something to experience, Floyt decided, as course after course came at him.

The food was delightful, strange, some of it undefinable; the Terran made it a point not to inquire too closely as to just what certain things were. He knew a guilty regret that he would never again taste anything like that food after he returned to Earth.

There seemed no limit to the quantity or variety of food and drink that *human* servicers would bring promptly. Alacrity attempted to order an intoxicant that they couldn't provide, and failed happily. Brother Grimm made the acquaintance of ice cream produced right in Frostpile's kitchens; no one objected when he passed up all other food to gorge himself on it, ingesting an astonishing amount in eight or ten flavors. Kid Risk asked Stare Skill to dance, when music began to play, but she refused. But it wasn't that she was being rude, Floyt saw; after so many years among her beloved Djinn, she'd simply lost the knack of mingling with her own species.

Sintilla had taken advantage of the general milling and socializing to go table-hopping, seeking more grist. Billy Risk was explaining to Alacrity the story behind Redlock's flagship, the *King's Ransom*. It had been just that—the ransom of the monarch of a minor world, whom the duke had captured. Among the terms of the peace treaty had been surrender of the ship, then known as the *Versailles*.

Floyt discovered that the journalist's vacant chair had been reoccupied, by one of two girls. The second was standing behind her. They were identical, two brunette sylphs who looked several years younger than Floyt's daughter. They wore enormous wrist orchids and apparel consisting mainly of a few big, crucially located spangles. The seated one began, "I'm Cosset, and this is my clone-twin, Dandle."

Floyt raised his eyes imploringly to the ceiling.

"Are you the Terran historian?" she went on. "We'd so very much like to ask you some questions! You see, we're researching our family tree."

Dandle nodded agreement, batting her eyelashes, tresses bobbing. Floyt found himself embroiled in a complicated attempt both to explain that he wasn't a scholar and to field their questions. They listened attentively, wide-eyed. He didn't notice that Alacrity had left the table until he became aware of a weird, nasal chanting-singing nearby.

"*Ning-ning-a-ning!* Oh, Lord Admiral Maska's the most alert of commanders! (Frequently stays wide-awake through most of the battle!) *A-ning!*" Of course, it was the breakabout.

He was confronting a Srillan, a humanoid, resembling a sleepy, shambling anteater rearing up on its hind legs. The alien's long-haired brown pelt gleamed with the russet highlights of age. He wore an Inheritor's belt and a leg pouch, needing nothing else. The two were engaged in one of the aliens' affable mockery duels.

"*Ning-ning!*" riposted the Srillan. "Alacrity Fitzhugh we know to be the greatest of lovers! (For those who prefer intercourse to a slow eight-count!) *A-ning-ning!*"

They had, it seemed, heard of one another.

Maska and Alacrity were doing the prancing shuffle of their game in a subdued way so as not to disturb chatting, circulating guests. They were drawing attention anyway.

Onlookers were laughing. Alacrity's chance encounter with Maska was a welcome chance for both to show off a bit. Their respective ranks, even their species, counted little.

Cosset and Dandle had stopped their chattering; the blood had drained from the Terran's face. He glared at the antics of a creature whose kind had laid waste so much of Earth.

Floyt waited for one or the other to lose his temper as the simpering and gibing went on. He was unaware that to do so was an almost unforgivable breach of manners, an utter defeat in which the victor often took shame as well.

The admiral cooed, "So seasoned a breakabout! (Quick, give him a cookie!) *A-ning! A-ning!*"

"Such a handsome-pelted fellow is this Maska! (Raises dust clouds when he walks—fetch the carpet beaters!) *Ning-a-ning!*"

Floyt didn't realize that he'd half stood. *"Alacrity!"*

The younger man was shocked by the Terran's expression of loathing; he almost tripped over his own feet. Admiral Maska stopped too, and caught the look. He, like most informed parties there, knew from which planet came the man with the wondrous cutaway and Inheritor's belt.

Alacrity looked back to Maska and nose-sang, "I laughed with all your pleasantries!"

"I thank you for your pleasantries!"

They chorused, "It's good fun to share pleasantries! *Ning-a-ning-ning!*" They slapped palms with one another pattycake style. Then Maska strolled away, effortlessly reassuming an urbane dignity. Alacrity wandered back to the table.

Everyone had conspicuously returned to their conversations. Stare Skill finally relented and let Kid Risk lead her out onto the dance floor. Alacrity, leaning down to pick up his drink, took advantage of a pause in the streaming details of the clone-twins' lineage.

"That war was over two hundred years ago, Ho," he said quietly, then backed away.

Floyt tried to ignore him, thinking, *Not for Terrans!* He therefore failed to notice that the breakabout was making his way toward the Nonpareil, who was momentarily unchaperoned.

"Hmm, you really *can* dance." The Nonpareil smiled, swaying in Alacrity's arms.

And he really could, not simply because he'd been taught and had practiced, but because he loved it, the bliss and dreamy elegance of it, and sharing it with a woman.

And in the case of the Nonpareil, it took one to know one.

There was still a proper distance between them, but her eyes closed as they glided. His opening line, earlier, had been a mere attention getter; this was a rite of courtship.

She was impressed by the fact that he didn't feel the need to talk, only to dance. They finished the rest of the number without another word. And the next. And the one after. The space separating them gradually vanished.

When the large, live orchestra paused, the pair parted just enough to talk comfortably. "May I call you 'The' for short?"

"My name to friends is Heart. I don't think I'm going to call you Al or Fitz. I like Alacrity better."

"Good. Then so do I."

Sintilla had returned to her seat, and the clone-twins had mercifully departed. The free-lancer was describing to Floyt one Inheritor she'd pointed out, a strikingly handsome young man whom she referred to as Sir John of Idyll.

He'd just passed by, slender and dark, dressed in peacock-bright regalia of metallic thread suggestive of armor. Sintilla followed him wistfully with her eyes.

The people who'd ruined John's family when he was a boy, driving his father to suicide, had been Weir's enemies as well. The Director had helped the vengeful John, setting up and funding a cover organization, a philanthropic foundation.

"Since the boy was heir to a title of knighthood, Weir decided that the cover name should be the Surge On Foundation. Get it? *Sir John!*"

Floyt had to admit that the audacious pun tickled him.

"The moguls fell all over each other trying to go swimming in the gravy. John ended up breaking them all; they'll be in prison for life," Sintilla added. They watched him making his way through the crowd. It chanced that Sir John passed the spot where Alacrity and Heart were dancing.

And Captain Dincrist, Heart's father, was bound straight in the couple's direction at flank speed.

"Brace for collision!" yelped Sintilla. Floyt scrambled out of his chair and hastened toward them with the free-lancer trailing. By the time they arrived, the shipping magnate was railing at the breakabout.

"I do not care to hear any more! I will *not* have you speaking to my daughter or otherwise pressing your attentions upon her. Have I finally made that clear enough for even *you* to understand, you *nonentity*?"

Alacrity had fingers tensed and extended, in fighting style, at his sides, the muscles of his neck standing out. The Nonpareil's cool self-possession had been shaken, but her father was ignoring her efforts to insert a good word.

Dincrist looked to be in flawless physical condition. He was also completely self-assured, less because of the High Truce than because few had dared challenge his will in years.

Floyt and Sintilla broke through a coalescing crowd just in time to hear Alacrity say, "Not unless I hear that from *her*."

Invincibles appeared, then Dame Tiajo stalked into view, with an abrupt parting of the crowd. The Severeemish, Seven Wars, and Sortie-Wolf, were observing attentively, no doubt waiting for a contravention of the High Truce and their Usages.

"The truce," Sintilla hissed, her fingers digging into Floyt's arm. "Alacrity mustn't break it! Tiajo would throw you both off Epiphany!"

Alacrity had his weight divided, riding the balls of his feet. The Terran drew a deep breath and interposed himself. He was apprehensive, and the threat to his mission and the inheritance had his conditioning shrieking at him. And he was still angry at Alacrity's friendly display with the Srillan, Maska.

"My daughter has nothing more to say to you," Dincrist was telling the breakabout. "Now get away from her this instant!"

Alacrity looked as if he was about to make a fight out of it. But Floyt thrust his face up close to his companion's and shouted, "You're ruining everything! Do you hear me? I want you to stop this right now!"

As everyone watched, Alacrity seemed to have a minor seizure. Doubt crept into Dincrist's expression. Heart saw her breezy, flirtatious dancing partner transformed into a bundle of restrained rage. His natural contrariness was locked in combat with the Earthservice conditioning.

They gazed on a frightening contest, seconds in duration, open to the world but between only Alacrity and himself. Quick, slight contortions changed his face, and tension locked his posture.

For a moment, it seemed that he would shatter like glass. Then it was over. Alacrity, the incandescent anger fled from him, turned and passed through the bystanders, heading for the table.

"See that you remember your place from now on," Dincrist called after the unheeding breakabout. He took the Nonpareil's arm and led her away. She looked in Alacrity's direction once or twice in a dazed way. The onlookers dispersed.

Sintilla and Floyt found Alacrity sitting in his place, staring fixedly at nothing. He made no sound; his fists were balled so tightly that they shook. The other guests nearby—including Brother Grimm—were pretending not to notice. Sintilla sat next to him, watching him worriedly.

The Terran was trying to decide what to say when a finger tapped his shoulder and a voice said, "Citizen Floyt?"

Sintilla could hardly believe the sudden sideways flicker

of Alacrity's glare, the breakabout making sure, even in his strange depression, that there was no threat to Floyt's safety.

There wasn't. It was Tiajo's own high seneschal. "The Grandam Tiajo desires that you join her in the chambers of her late brother, Director Weir."

CHAPTER 12

PHYSICAL EDUCATION

IN THAT PART OF FROSTPILE HOUSING THE WEIR FAMILY complex, radiant mists circulated overhead like ground fogs that preferred ceilings, or neon smokes. They flowed and swirled, glowing in sulfur-yellow or electric blue, cinnamon and phosphorescent sea-green.

Weir's personal chambers were spacious, but would not overawe anybody who'd already seen the rest of his home. Floyt took in details of the master bedroom and worried about Alacrity, who, following dutifully behind, was still silent. Whether he was plotting revenge on Dincrist and/or Floyt himself or had simply accepted a repellent situation, the Earther couldn't guess.

One wall and part of the ceiling had been adjusted for transparency. Floyt gazed up for a moment at Epiphany's larger moon, Guileless Giles, and its smaller companion, the Thieving Magpie, with its bright flecks and shadow shapes. The Strewn couldn't be seen, due to the luminosity of Frostpile itself.

Alacrity became aware of low, melodious background sounds. He glanced at the terrace. There he saw what looked like a churning, glimmering nebula hanging stationary in midair a meter off the mosaic floor.

It was a five-meter-high mass of phase portraits and whirling brume, eddies and hazy adumbrations. It gave off tonalities and a deep, nearly subsonic hum.

"That is a Causality Harp, Master Fitzhugh," he heard Dame Tiajo say. "It is rather like wind chimes."

Causality? Can she be serious? He boggled. At another time, the Causality Harp would've captured Alacrity's gaze and locked the breath in his chest, but not then, wronged and resentful as he felt.

Tiajo sat in a floating pillow-lounge to one side of Weir's enormous bed and its medical appurtenances. Invincibles were stationed around the room.

Dorraine was perched charmingly on one corner of a slab-bench with her father, First Councillor Inst, standing by her side. Redlock, hands clasped behind his back, was standing near a gargantuan black iron fireplace cast in the shape of a conch shell. In it, coffeewood logs burned, giving off a rich pungency.

The Earther stopped and made a half bow, not sure that the Earthservice would approve of obeisance to an off-worlder but sensing that some courtesy was in order—particularly in view of the looks he was getting from the old woman and the governor. Either through truculence or because no demonstration would be expected of him, Alacrity merely halted and stood.

With a sweep of her hand, Tiajo asked Floyt, "You are familiar with *that*?"

For the first time his gaze went to the Weir family tree, which filled the entire bowl of the room behind him, where Halidome's light would shine on it in the morning, and through it and the translucent wall in the evening. Floyt had to remind himself where he was and what he was about; otherwise, he'd have been lost in the immense grandeur of the tree's detailed mosaic.

It was wrought of exotic gemstones and nodes of vari-colored light, the most intricate and gorgeous thing he'd ever seen. He'd heard that it was linked to a data bank, but saw no peripherals. Weir had only undertaken research into his origins and construction of the tree in the final years of his life; Floyt wondered what it might have become if Weir had had more time.

He found his voice answering, "I know *of* it, ma'am. But this is the first time I've ever actually—"

"Of course, of course," she snapped. "That's what I meant. How could *you* ever have seen it before?" Her inflection rankled Floyt, but he was used to holding his peace in the presence of authority. He thought, *If I had the wealth to build it, my own tree would be a dozen times the size of this one, old woman!*

"What I wish to know is what information my brother drew from your"—she made a deprecating gesture with the baton she still carried, which now gave off a softer glow—"your pastime."

Floyt looked at the tree again, skimming, reading greedily. Grandam Tiajo did something with the baton; a pencil of light sprang from it, to touch a node in the tree at random. The node lit up, and a gentle female voice filled the chamber.

"Casimir Weir, born approximately 4-2-2806 Standard. Raised on Shaitan and captured during the Agate Incursion." There were projections of Shaitan, the armies and machines that had fought during the Incursion, and of Casimir himself, an intense young man in ill-fitting uniform. "Prisoner-of-war status commuted to—"

Tiajo cut it off, then set the baton aside, waiting for Floyt's reply.

"Some of my findings have been published offworld—off Terra, that is. Parts of it touched on the late Bloodthrone Autocracy, but there's only a little about that here. Some dealt with the imported genetic material used in the development of the ruling house of Valhalla. One monograph touched on the royalty of Agora; they were a very purebred line. And certain of Duke Redlock's ancestors."

Floyt didn't add that Earthservice had used that kind of research as another example of how Earth's descendants had abandoned her.

"But in the main, I would say, my work made it easier for offworlders to trace their Terran roots; to discover how they're linked to the Homeworld."

"And for that my brother included you in his will and brought you these many light-years?"

Floyt spread his hands. "I can't think of anything else, ma'am."

"*Hmph!* I suppose you're aware, citizen, that not even *I* know the nature of some of my brother's bequests? Have you any idea what he might have left you in his will?"

The question was somewhat improper, Floyt knew, but he had no intention of crossing this old harpy if he could avoid it. "None whatsoever. It came as a total surprise, believe me."

"Very well. Thank you for your time, young man."

He realized he'd been dismissed. He was headed for the door with a still-silent Alacrity at his heels when she called after him. "Oh, by the way, Master Fitzhugh."

They stopped and looked back. She said icily, "You will observe decorum henceforth, is that understood? The High Truce is not to be violated. Anyone who doesn't comport himself properly will suffer for it. The games, the Hunt, the Willreading, and the drinking of the Thorn Cup—they'll all be shown unfailing respect. That's my solemn promise on the matter."

"I understand, Dame Tiajo." Alacrity sounded enervated and resigned.

As they trudged off looking for a corridor tram, Floyt asked, "What's a Thorn Cup?"

* * *

"It's a custom of the Severeemish," Sintilla elucidated the next morning as they headed for the outdoor sportsfest. "And Weir had to abide by it. Now his heirs have to too, or the Severeemish'll consider their fealty and their treaty void."

"Which they're itching to do," Floyt recalled.

Sintilla nodded vigorously. "And they'd be awfully tough enemies, at a time when Redlock and Tiajo don't need any more." She pursed her lips in thought, then confessed, "I really can't blame the Severeemish too much, though; they've fought wars for Weir's realm ever since the original treaty. They guard almost a quarter of it against all comers."

"But the Thorn Cup?" Alacrity, bringing up the rear, persisted. He seemed to have forgotten or put aside the incident of the preceding evening; no one else made any mention of it. But Floyt wondered if the issue could really have been set aside so easily.

"The Severeemish upper-uppers take the blossom of a beaker plant and wind a rider vine on it," she told them. "And when it's time, they yank it up and drink a toast to the departed."

"Is that all?" Alacrity rapped. "What's all the commotion about?"

"Riders are a sort of parasite, Bright Eyes," Sintilla told him. "They mimic whatever plants they contact, so there's never any telling what you're getting into when you drink a Thorn Cup—especially since the Severeemish spend a lot of time breeding new herbs and teas and developing drugs and mucking about with pollens and molds in their gardens."

"Poison?" Alacrity frowned.

"Not anymore, the way I heard it. But allergic reactions, even anaphylaxis; in old-time Desideratum there were fatalities, but the doctors'll be standing right there for the Cup, and there're no toxins. The toast might be unpleasant, but all the Inheritors will have to drink—you too, Hobart."

They'd come out onto the largest of the areas set aside

for the day's activities. Not yet adapted to Epiphany's day-
night cycle, the Terran stared about tiredly. Alacrity had
already adjusted.

Whether or not Dame Tiajo felt the Severeemish Observances a proper tribute to her late brother, she had no intention of giving provocation. By her decree, therefore, a spirited
gymkhana was in progress. The meteorological engineers
had provided a perfect day of cloudless, yellow-blue sky
and light, warm breezes. Frostpile was decked out grandly
with all sorts of banners and flags; Severeemish weren't
much for mourning.

Though Floyt still wore his Inheritor's belt, he'd selected
what he'd hoped would be an inconspicuous outfit from
among those offered him. He wore a loose sweatsuit and
thick-soled running shoes, both in muted brown. The day's
Sintillan rompers were very sporty. Alacrity had on a pair
of exercise shorts and light track shoes.

Before them lay buzzball tanks, track and field events,
and an archery range. And Frostpile's staff had provided
for everything else from weightlifting to jet-luge racing,
farracko to volleyball. To ensure that appearances were
maintained, many members of the household had been
pressed into service as participants.

There were variable-gee gymnastics, martial arts com-
petitions, and a battle-paddle tournament. Overhead, airbikes, gossamer combinations of muscle-powered aircraft
and sailplane, circled and swooped, their crews pedaling
furiously. They drew Floyt's rapt gaze every now and again,
and the others would wait for him to catch up.

The three passed trampolines, rings, parallel bars, and
balance beams. Trapeze enthusiasts flew and swung above
them. A heated, competition-size swimming pool had been
set up. Those who were so inclined could try their skill at
ring-toss or duckjack. Tiajo had drawn the line at diversions
like fangster-baiting and slash-dodge, however; the Sever-

eemish hadn't pressed the point, much as they adored sports involving danger, injury, and bloodshed.

A man approached Floyt. Remembering the triggermen at the Sockwallet lashup, Alacrity was watchful.

"Citizen Floyt? Hello, I'm the Presbyter Kuss, Church of the Universal Light."

The presbyter was about Floyt's age. He wore his plentiful brown locks in a windswept hairstyle and had a Vandyke beard. He was dressed in copper-colored shorts, running soleskins, and an Inheritor's belt.

When Sintilla had pointed the man out the night before, he'd looked more the churchman, arrayed in a gilt cassock and filigreed pectoral with its gem-set Tudor flower, the symbol of his faith. Now, beaded with perspiration, a towel around his shoulders, he was the picture of rugged good health.

"How do you do, Presbyter?" Floyt accepted the proferred grip.

"Oh, please, call me Kuss." The cleric grinned. "Look, I don't want to distract you from the, er, Observance here, but I'd like to get a few minutes of your time, if you can spare them, in the near future. I'd just like to fill you in on what the church has been doing—sort of between us Inheritors, if you see what I mean."

"Oh. I—I suppose so," answered Floyt, who shared the common, automatic deference toward clergy.

"Thank you, friend!" Presbyter Kuss dipped his head to the trio, passing his spread-fingered hand through the air in a kind of benediction. Then he jogged briskly on his way.

"Wants to get you alone for a little chat, hm?" Alacrity pondered. "Now why would that be, d'you suppose?"

"The Church of the Universal Light is very political," Sintilla supplied. "Weir secretly gave them money and assistance—so the rumors ran. He never actually confirmed it. The Universals worked against his enemies in a number of places, though."

"What would that have to do with me?"

"Nobody knows what your inheritance is, Ho," Alacrity reminded him. "With Weir gone, Kuss probably wants to make sure the gravy boat doesn't set sail."

"He's going to be disappointed if—" Floyt began, about to mention Resources Reclamation, forgetting that Sintilla was standing there.

"Anyway, he's not getting you off alone for some one-on-one conversion," Alacrity broke in hurriedly.

"That's fine with me."

"It's this Hunt that's still got me vapored," the breakabout continued.

"Why?" Sintilla asked.

"I don't like sport hunting, just for starters. But mainly, the idea of all those people stumbling around with all those guns has me skittish." Floyt voiced agreement; Sintilla looked at them uncomprehendingly.

They didn't elaborate, continuing their way instead. At least Inheritors weren't actually *required* to perform any formal acts of athletics. The three tossed a few tuck-sticks at targets and tried their skill on the jounce pads. All the while, Sintilla gently, genially pumped the companions for more information about their backgrounds. Alacrity finally asked why she was so interested.

"I'm planning to write a feature about this whole whoop-up, remember? You two are part of the story. I'm just earning a living, boys."

"Well earn it someplace else; we're bystanders," Alacrity shot back.

"Sorry, but that's not the way my readers would see it," she answered.

They came to a spot where Stare Skill and Brother Grimm had been accosted by the two Severeemish bodyguards, the Corporeals.

The woman had made little pretense of dressing for the day's nominal purpose, wearing a loose shift and thongs.

The Djinn stood at her elbow and stared daggers at the Corporeals.

Up close, the guards were particularly impressive, towering over the woman and the humanoid. Their crimson mouths and tongues made a startling contrast with their putty-gray skin; their muscles bulged. One of them was addressing Stare Skill.

"But you do not even put on the *appearance* of participating in the games." Seeing the approaching trio, he indicated them. "At least these ones make some effort to be part of things, feeble as those are."

"Just leave us out of it, Bulk Shipment," Alacrity said.

The other Corporeal toed a heavy barbell. "Why don't you show your sincerity and exercise with this, old female?" They chuckled coarsely.

That apparently offended Brother Grimm. "She cannot," he snarled at the Corporeals. "The equipment is broken—"

Waddling over to the barbell, he hoisted it easily. Showing his fearsome teeth, hands trembling, the heavy-gee native bent the bar across his knee.

"—as you can both plainly see," he finished, tossing it aside.

If anything happens, I want him on our side, Alacrity decided at once.

Sintilla drew Stare Skill and Grimm away, leaving the Corporeals to contemplate the mangled barbell.

"It seems that Seven Wars and Sortie-Wolf are so eager for an unfortunate occurrence that they've decided to create one if necessary," Stare Skill commented.

"If so, you'd have a difficult time proving it," Floyt pointed out.

"The situation here is so very peculiar," Brother Grimm declared, once more the mild-mannered companion. "It reminds me of the story of the wolf and the fox..."

While the Djinn drew his parallel, they made their way

to the buzzball tanks. There were three, of which only one was in operation. The tanks' controls and those of other equipment nearby were linked to a games computer, a field unit. Close by the unit was an area for maintaining mitts, helmets, and other protective and playing gear. Tools, tubes of adhesive, and bottles of spray insulation littered the place, along with odds and ends of padding and webbing.

The five stopped by the first tank, inside which Admiral Maska was playing against Dincrist. Floyt stared, intrigued. It was the first such game he'd ever seen. He felt bad about what had happened the previous evening, and did his best to keep his aversion to aliens from coming to the fore.

Maska was a strong competitor. He and Dincrist bounced off the walls, ceiling, and floor of the tank, turning in midair as the gravity field was rotated, tumbling and landing neatly, rebounding from the resilient, transparent panes. They hurled and batted with their bulky, insulated mitts, throwing the charged, cracking white ball of energy at the black scoring ring. The ring disappeared from the center of a wall or other surface, to reappear elsewhere, whenever the gravity shifted. The two wore safety helmets and assorted pads.

The tank's field was set at one-quarter gee. Srillan gravity was close enough to Standard that neither player had an advantage in that respect. Dincrist, smiling and tanned, wearing white shorts, his silver hair waving and flashing, was the image of the aristocratic sportsman. He was also a pretty good buzzball player.

Alacrity had found out a little more about the man and his daughter. For one thing, Dincrist's claim to the rank of captain was based on a mere two voyages made as figurehead commander of one of his family's luxury cruise ships while a real skipper actually ran things. Alacrity himself had considerably more command time than that, if in vessels of less prestige.

The Nonpareil had been raised in a protective, almost cloistered atmosphere until her mother's death. An only child, she now supervised the running of her father's numerous large homes, acted as hostess, and aided Dincrist in the family business. Dincrist's company and Weir had had many dealings over the years, and it was said that in recent years the Director had sometimes solicited Dincrist's advice.

Now Dincrist pressed hard for a final goal, the score standing at eight-all, the winning point available to either player. Random changes generated by the field unit kept both contenders cautious. Dincrist propelled himself upward and hurled the spitting, glowing sphere with one mitted hand, just as the gravity shifted.

The floor under him became a wall. He spun, to land well, while Maska made the change with an agile hop. The buzzball arced from its intended course, its ballistics changed by the gee shift. The target circle had moved to the center of what had been the ceiling but was now, to those inside the tank, a wall. To those watching from outside, it was still the ceiling, and the players were standing on the wall, the soles of their shoes presented to the onlookers. Maska leapt and caught the buzzball.

Dincrist moved for a blocking jump, but the Srillan kicked off a wall and changed directions. He hurled with both mitts, overhand.

Somehow, Dincrist was suddenly there, canny as an old pro. He caught the flaring globe in midair, coming dangerously close to receiving a painful shock from the scoring ring. Then he whirled, with impetus built up on his leap, released the energy ball neatly, and scored.

The stroboscopic scoreboard flashed Dincrist's victory. Maska relaxed languidly. The gravity gently returned to normal, drawing the contestants to the true floor. Sideliners entered the tank to hand Dincrist a towel and Maska a scent cloth, congratulating both on a good game. Several tried to claim a match against the winner.

Alacrity saw the Nonpareil standing nearby, taking it all

in proudly. She wore a daringly cut exercise maillot of clinging, glistening opalescent fabric.

"He's good," the breakabout conceded.

She didn't look aside at him, but seemed to have known all along that he was there. "Yes. He seldom loses."

There was an edgy silence. Alacrity couldn't for the life of him figure out what to say next. She spoke first.

"I shouldn't be talking to you, or listening either."

"Wait now, just because I got off on the wrong foot with your father doesn't mean that I—"

"There's no changing it." She met his stare now, big hazel eyes searching luminous yellow ones. "I mean that. Now, you were fun to dance and flirt with, but that's not worth seeing you get hurt—and you would be. My father is successful in a business that can be very rough. He's used to having his way."

"Why don't you let me worry about that, Heart?"

"*Tch!* Do you really think you're the first one to give me that he-man line? You're just not worth it, get me?"

"In that case, why should you care?"

"Because I don't want to see anybody hurt! I couldn't stand that again, don't you understand? *Not again!* I'm not asking you, Alacrity; I'm telling you."

She turned her back on him, but he wasn't through. "Not good enough, Heart. The martyr act's very dramatic, but you're not in any danger of pain. I think you enjoy this. You make it easy on yourself, and the hell with anybody else, and we both fucking well know it."

He put a hand on her shoulder, to force her to face him. She resisted. Just then Dincrist grabbed Alacrity's arm and spun him around roughly. "I warned you."

"*I* spoke to *him*," Heart blurted. Her father glared at her for a moment.

Admiral Maska came up and attempted to take Dincrist's elbow. "I believe I owe you a victory glass, sir." Dincrist didn't budge.

Floyt, who'd been dancing adroitly around Sintilla's questions, noticed what was going on. So did the free-lancer, her mouth popping open as the older man said, "This is your final warning to stay away from me and my daughter."

"Sure, skipper—unless you'd care to play a little buzz-ball, that is."

Dincrist's face broke into a feral smile. "Indeed? Why, yes. I think you're right. Just the thing." He began fastening his mitts back on.

The Nonpareil said, "Alacrity, *no!*"

"Alacrity, *yes!*" he parried merrily.

"You're both insane!" she flared, and strode away.

Floyt reached the breakabout's side. "Alacrity, I told you, this sort of thing isn't—"

"This sort of thing isn't 'this sort of thing,' Ho. It's just a friendly little frolic. Doesn't have anything to do with our agreement, read me?"

Floyt saw that, short of invoking the conditioning again, he couldn't stop things. He remembered how that had felt the previous evening and, too, what his own reaction had been when Arlo Mote tried to blind him with boxing-glove eyelets. Moreover, a buzzball contest could be monitored, and stopped short of serious injury.

"Ah, go ahead then, if you must. Get it out of your system," he muttered, stepping aside in disgust, almost bumping into Maska.

Alacrity was fastening on a helmet as he eyed a selection of mitts. A considerable crowd had gathered, and more were converging from other parts of the field every moment.

"I don't know that this is such a wise idea, truly, Citizen Floyt," the Srillan said quietly, ignored by everybody but the Terran. While Floyt agreed, he was incapable of doing anything but hastily moving away from the alien.

The crowd watched the two players donning mitts, pads, and headgear. Maska, seeing the revulsion on Floyt's face, was silently rueful.

The contestants entered the tank, stretching and flexing arms and legs, wringing out their muscles. Alacrity bent at the waist to touch the floor of the tank with the palms of his flexible, reinforced mitts. Dincrist did slow deep knee-bends. They ignored each other.

As they tugged and settled their pads, the first warning sounded. They went into crouching ready positions. From the ejector port a white glow began to emerge, the buzzball building its matrix. The target ring appeared. The buzzball shot into the tank while the second warning was still sounding.

Dincrist, winner of the previous match, leapt to meet it. It was an easy catch-and-land, since the random gravity-changing mechanism hadn't, in its computerized wisdom, seen fit to alter things yet. Dincrist whirled and bounced, then threw.

But with the ball in mid-arc, gravity shifted. It seemed to the players that the world flip-flopped. The scoring circle had vanished. The buzzball struck a blank wall.

While Dincrist was the superior player, Alacrity had spacer's reflexes and was not tired. The breakabout bounced under the tycoon, off the erstwhile floor, to take the orb on its rebound. Pirouetting expertly, he whipped the popping energy ball at the black circle, so close that he singed the hairs on his arm. He made the first point of the match.

Alacrity pushed off the wall-now-floor smugly. Outside the tank, one or two of the onlookers applauded the goal, but Alacrity could hear nothing. From his point of view, they were all standing out horizontally from a verticle grass surface. It gave him an unaccustomed sense of vertigo. Sintilla, holding money aloft in one hand, was apparently trying to make a wager.

Floyt was watching stoically. The breakabout couldn't see Heart, but he caught sight of Seven Wars and Sortie-Wolf.

Dincrist payed no attention to those outside. He waited,

breathing easily but deeply, poker-faced but plainly angry. Alacrity punched his heavy gloves together and smirked.

The sputtering, buzzing little sphere whizzed again. This time Alacrity grabbed it—almost. The gravity changed again; Dincrist's padded shoulder slammed into him just as he was stretched full length, leaping and reaching. The breakabout flew sideways, the wind nearly knocked from him, going *oomph*!

Dincrist reached, cupped, threw, and scored.

Alacrity picked himself up, now standing on the tank's ceiling. Dincrist the sportsman was oblivious to him, bouncing a little on the balls of his feet. The gathered audience no longer mattered.

The charged orb took form again. Alacrity took a running leap, high up, to rebound off the wall. It was a gamble. If the gravity failed to shift, or didn't shift in such a way as to make his move useful, Dincrist would take another point and Alacrity might put himself into ignominy or a medical ward. But he figured the change he was banking for was due. And he was angry.

He was also lucky.

His move had been against eight-to-one odds, but had paid off. Gravity swung the two around again. Dincrist missed a leap, skidding even at one-fourth his normal weight and in skid-resistant shoes. Alacrity's momentum gave him a good bank off a wall that was on its way to being a floor. From the outside, they looked like they were floating around; to the players, the tank was rotating about them.

Alacrity scored. Dincrist checked him again, this time slightly after his release, padded elbow to unprotected rib cage. There'd been enough of an interval that it seemed intended, but this was a pickup game, and the niceties of tournament play didn't count for much.

They waited, panting, not meeting one another's gaze, as the warning signal heralded another buzzball.

Floyt, surveying the scene, saw that Dame Tiajo had

arrived, followed by a covey of attendants and a number of Invincibles. The Earther hoped his companion would spot her; she would certainly notice any transgressions.

Presbyter Kuss was in the throng too, and First Councillor Inst. Except for Tiajo, just about everyone there was engaged in egalitarian jostling and jockeying for a better view of the match.

The players were on the move once more. Pretext had been dropped, Floyt noted with dismay; they were playing for blood. The buzzball flew like a sizzling meteor.

Alacrity caught Dincrist just right with his hip, but the older man spun away deftly, letting his whirling, padded elbow catch the breakabout. They both sprawled, Alacrity spitting blood in a scarlet mist. Then they had to scramble out of the way as the sparking buzzball bounced off the floor, zinging off on a new course.

The gravity altered once more. They fell toward the wall. Dincrist sought to extricate himself from the tangle of arms and legs by thrusting Alacrity downward, climbing over him in free-fall. Alacrity tucked in his head and pushed off with his feet, sending the other tumbling.

The buzzball, coruscating off the ceiling—now their wall—struck Dincrist on his unprotected bicep; he yelped in pain at the ball's jolting charge. Yet, for that moment, the buzzball was inert. Dincrist had the presence of mind to seize it. A second later, it glowed again as he sprang at the scoring circle. Outside, Floyt saw Tiajo snapping some indignant comment to an aide, no doubt on the thuggishness of the exchange.

All at once gravity reversed its dictates. This time, though, rather than gradually shifting or rotating, it simply increased. Both men were slammed against what had been one wall of the tank. Dincrist lost the ball, which fell away in a plume of light.

As abruptly as that had happened, the field altered again. The two plummeted back the way they'd come. It was clear that the tank's gravity was no longer at one-quarter gee, having increased.

"This is too dangerous," Floyt burst out. It wasn't his idea of a game, or even a sane way to fight.

"Something's wrong!" Heart cried. "The machinery's berserking! They'll be killed!"

She was right. The opponents were being rattled around like dice in a cup. The gee field was increasing in strength. If it went all the way up to Standard, both would be seriously injured at least, possibly killed.

Without warning, there was a new hazard. The buzzball, now zigzagging madly, shed lightning when it struck the walls. Its shock-level had been raised to one that could wound, perhaps kill.

Tiajo commanded that the match be halted. Alacrity and Dincrist frantically pressed the emergency-stop buttons on their mitts—to no avail. The buzzball continued its violent discharges and careening, while the players were hurled and dropped, then hurled again.

Redlock had appeared and was tugging at the manual release to the tank door, accomplishing nothing. The game's computer had overridden it, sealing the players inside. The Nonpareil hammered at the tank with her fists, screaming as her snowy curls whipped her face.

"Shut down the field unit!" Sortie-Wolf hollered in a parade-ground voice. Floyt joined the others who sprinted off toward it.

Endwraithe, the Spican banker, was first to reach the machine, only to discover that its protective panel was closed and that he couldn't open the latch; its mechanism was covered with a mass of epoxy from the repair benches, stuff that solidified to metallic hardness almost instantly.

Floyt, arriving on Endwraithe's heels, tried to help him, using every bit of strength, wrenching muscles, and tearing loose fingernails. It was hopeless. Into the Earther's mind flashed the image of Brother Grimm bending the barbell.

He shouted for Djinn, but Grimm, among others, was still attempting fruitlessly to get the tank door open.

Floyt started off to get the Djinn, even though it seemed a doomed effort. If the tank's gravity increased much more, those inside would be dashed to death before anyone could gain access to the controls.

Just at that moment Sintilla approached, yanking an Invincible officer along with her, tugging at his harness. Queen Dorraine was right behind. Taking in the situation at a glance, Tilla ordered, "Use your gun! Shoot the computer!"

The lieutenant was a loyal and courageous man, but only recently commissioned and not an individual of great personal initiative. Invincible officers were the only ones there who carried firearms, and the officer corps had been admonished by Grandam Tiajo in person to draw their weapons *only* in the event that some other person was using deadly force. She hadn't foreseen this eventuality, but one violated the orders of the grandam at the risk of general court-martial.

While the lieutenant was struggling toward a decision, Dorraine acted. She snatched the Invincible's pistol, a Nova Special, a cannon of a weapon, in a class with the Captain's Sidearm.

"You! Out of my way!"

Floyt and the banker needed no second invitation; they both dived for cover. Holding the Special cup-in-saucer fashion, the Agoran fired into the game's computer with one spectacular, sustained shot.

Smoke and brilliant eruptions, detonations and molten metal flew outward from the unit. Onlookers yelled in shock and fright. In the midst of the storm of scorching heat and flying debris, Dorraine cooly stood her ground and let the machine have it again.

Alacrity and Dincrist were sliding up a wall toward the ceiling when the field cut out. Luckily they hadn't gone far.

The artificial gravity yielded to the natural; they were abruptly headed for the floor at full gee.

They hit at the same instant and lay stunned, a meter or so apart. Alacrity levered himself up off his stomach so that he could see the scoreboard which, for some reason, still worked. The score was still tied.

"Son . . . of . . . a . . . *bitch!*" he ground out.

Household physicians entered the tank and examined the players on the spot, scanning with instruments, probing and poking. Both men denied that there was anything wrong with them. Aside from cuts, sprains, and strains, and what promised to be a bumper crop of bruises, they were correct. They'd been padded and protected for buzzball, and that had saved them because the gravity hadn't climbed all the way to Standard.

Heart knelt by her father's side, avoiding Alacrity's eyes. The two men traded a dirty look, but their grudge had been set aside for the time being.

"A miracle they weren't crippled or killed," pronounced the Presbyter Kuss.

"Never mind that now," Tiajo said. She'd summoned her Chief of Staff for Security, a colonel with many years in grade, who now wore a worried look on her face. She promised to brief Tiajo shortly on what she and her people could discover from the game computer's remains. Alacrity could tell at a glance that that wouldn't be much. There'd been only one security drone drifting in the vicinity of the tanks during the game, and it had been aimed the wrong way.

So, while it was manifest that there'd been sabotage, there was no telling who'd violated the High Truce or why. Defense Minister Seven Wars and Theater General Sortie-Wolf therefore had little ground for complaint to Dame Tiajo.

Both Alacrity and Dincrist were ambulatory but required observation. To avoid further friction, the physicians elected to divide into teams and attend each man in his quarters. That met with no objection, and both were floated away on hover-gurneys.

"Let the Observances continue," Tiajo bade as they drifted off. Guests took up their diversions again, but the general attitude seemed to be that the day's high point had passed.

Sintilla accompanied Floyt back to Riffraff Alley, standing at his elbow as he coded open the suite door. It seemed only polite to invite her in.

Alacrity was sitting up on the gurney, in good spirits. He held the remote control unit for the suite's commo terminal. As Sintilla and Floyt entered, he casually chucked it aside.

The only altercation came when the breakabout refused a sedative. The doctors were thorough and competent, but as serving physicians to the redoubtable Tiajo, less prone than many members of their profession to insist on having their way.

Sintilla kept up a bubbly stream of prattle, gossip, and innuendo. The doctors, finishing, left Alacrity some medication and the advice that he rest. When they'd gone, Sintilla said, "There were so many people gathered around the tank, any one of them could've rigged the buzzball computer."

"Including you, Tilla?" Alacrity asked softly.

"*Huh?* Oh, I see. Yeah, I guess I'm a suspect too. Except why would I want to hurt you?"

"If I got killed or injured, that'd make it a lot easier to get at Ho."

Floyt protested, "Then why would Tilla practically drag that Invincible over to the control panel by his ankle?"

Alacrity colored with embarrassment. "I didn't know about that. Sorry, Tilla."

She made a mischievous moue. "You're just doing your job, high mover."

Alacrity snorted. "Besides, who says the whole thing wasn't about Dincrist?"

"Dincrist?"

"Uh-huh. You should've heard him carrying on in that tank when we hit the heavy weather. I think he assumed somebody was out to get *him*, not me. One thing's for sure: *he* didn't have anything to do with it. And from what they tell me, he's got a lot more people who don't like him any more than I do."

Someone signaled at the door repeatedly, and kept it up. Rather than answer, Floyt, cautious now, activated the corridor pickup. It was Heart.

Aware that she was under surveillance, she bristled. "Damn your eyes, Fitzhugh! Open this door!"

"Speaking of suspects," Sintilla half sang.

"She does sound a tad hostile," Floyt agreed, surprised by the Nonpareil's pique.

Alacrity was neither surprised nor put off. "Let her in please, Ho."

Incensed, Heart stormed into the room. She'd changed from the maillot to a demure househabit that covered wrists and feet, its cowl thrown back to expose snowy curls.

"You really work at being a spoiled child, don't you?" she seethed at Alacrity. "I'd have thought you'd be more considerate, Inheritor Floyt."

"Wait! Calm down!" Floyt implored. "What's this all about?"

"You weren't in on it? The commo answering message?"

Before the breakabout could grab it, Sintilla pounced on the remote he'd been playing with when she and Floyt arrived.

"The terminal's set to refuse incoming calls." Sintilla manipulated the remote, and the terminal's answering device began to play lush ballroom music into the sound system. It was the same music Alacrity and Heart had danced to the evening before. After a few moments, the breakabout's solicitous voice announced, "Alacrity Fitzhugh has succumbed to acute indifference. Refunds available on unused portion with proof of purchase." The music continued until Sintilla shut the system off.

"Oh, Alacrity, how could you?" Sintilla asked.

"Arrested adolescence!" the Nonpareil fumed.

"How was I to know you'd mind?" was his innocent rejoinder.

Her eyes blazed at him. "I came over here to tell you what a spiteful thing that was to do. And I have something else to say to you while I'm at it."

Sintilla jumped to her feet, slapping her thighs. "Well, come on, Hobart. I'll take you up on that backgammon game."

"I beg your—oh! Yes. That'd be fine, Tilla." Floyt rose. Opting to leave Heart and the breakabout on their own tripped no conditioning alarms in the Earther. He was getting accustomed to the fact that he was no longer acting in strict accordance with either his upbringing or the dictates of the Earthservice. It didn't make him feel as bad as he'd have expected.

Alacrity made no objection to their going. When they'd left, he waited and watched Heart, wide topaz eyes boring into hazel ones.

"You can turn off the headlights, Fitzhugh. They won't do you any good."

"That what you came here to tell me?"

"I came to tell you that you're not being funny at all, just petulant. When you talk about not caring about how others feel, it wouldn't hurt to take a look at yourself first. And now that I've had my say, I'm leaving."

He jumped from the gurney, stabbing at the remote in mid-vector, moving to block her way at the door. The dance music came up again. He got his arms around her, and her perfume and the feel of her made it difficult for him to think straight.

She pushed at him to free herself. "Get away from me!"

"You came to tell me I was wrong about you. Well, didn't you?"

"Yes!" But she'd stopped struggling to separate herself from him. "I hate you for what you think of me. I *can* care for someone, but . . . you don't understand what could happen."

"'What could happen' is my bill of fare these days." He still held her, but gently. "You're not going to get me to say, 'I understand; be careful.'" He began moving with the music, fingers interlocked at the small of her back.

"Alacrity, you're not being fair. Let me go."

"No."

"Why?"

"I'm afraid you wouldn't come back."

He tilted his head, leaning toward her. Their first kiss was light, barely a meeting of lips, but lasting and sure. She yielded; the dance resumed. She buried her fingers in the heavy gray-and-silver mane that grew down into the channel of his spine, head to his cheek. He held her to him and drew the fabric off her shoulder to kiss it longingly.

The bannered glory of Frostpile filled the sweep of the skylight bowl; Halidome's rays picked out every particle in the air of the room, but they were oblivious to it all. The dance paused, and they kissed one another for minutes, lips and face, shoulders and throat, where each felt the other's racing pulse.

Both were breathing quickly. They were impassioned but unhurried. Her fingers dug into the muscles of his back; she wound a fistful of his hair, keeping his mouth locked to hers. Alacrity bared both her shoulders and kissed the pale swell of her bosom until she moaned, clasping his head to her. When he drew her toward his bed she went eagerly.

* * *

Later they lay together naked and warm in the Halidome light streaming down through the skylight, legs intertwined and arms around each other.

She said, "Alacrity, you have to promise me this won't lead to more trouble."

"That's all right with me. What's your father got against me anyway?"

"You're a breakabout. When he was younger, serving out his apprenticeship aboard family vessels, the high movers always gave him such a difficult time. He still carries the resentment around in him, even though he buys and sells fleets now."

Alacrity knew that breakabouts could be cruel in their hazing and harassing. He wouldn't have been surprised, though, to find out that Dincrist had brought a lot of trouble down on himself.

"Won't he go into launch mode when he finds out you're here?"

"He's sleeping; the doctor gave him a sedative. I'll be back when he wakes up." She pillowed her head on her arm and looked him in the eye. "There's something else; you don't have to answer if you don't want to."

"You mean am I using birth control? Yes."

She poked him one in the ribs.

"All right, what?" He began trailing the backs of his fingertips up and down her body slowly and lightly.

"Well, Hobart—mmm, that feels nice—Hobart's a sweet man, but sometimes it seems as though he's got some sort of hold on you."

"No, nothing like that," the conditioning and his own pride made him reply.

"Good, because I like him." She squirmed a little under his delicate teasing, laughing. "Stop, or I'll go into seizures!"

He leaned over her. "I'll go with you."

CHAPTER 13

TARGETS OF OPPORTUNITY

THE NEXT MORNING ALACRITY AND FLOYT WENT FORTH just after Halidome rose, as preparations for the Hunt reached their climax.

Floyt wore brown bush fatigues and Alacrity an old, comfortable gray groundside coverall, along with his pathfinder boots and a big, cobalt-colored kerchief knotted around his neck. The kerchief, like the brolly he carried slung from his shoulder, was a simple, versatile, and durable piece of gear with any number of survival uses.

Since both men had been opposed to Sintilla's accompanying them, she'd elected to sleep in and cover the event in a more leisurely and comfortable fashion.

The two arrived at one of Frostpile's expansive outer yards to find a scene of near-chaos.

All around stood Inheritors and others who planned to do their hunting from the luxury and safety of air and land craft, many of them organizing themselves into parties, in both the celebratory and sporting sense of the word. The hunting areas set aside for these groups had been carefully marked on the ground, so that airborne gunners wouldn't shoot those afoot or on animals. No pedal-powered airbikes were aloft this morning; the turbulence caused by the hunters' low-flying sporters made the flimsy craft too hazardous.

Some would-be hunters insisted they'd stalk on foot. Others demanded that shooting blinds be set up for them. A few stubbornly refused to hunt other than from animal back. Many individuals and parties demanded to be dropped into selected areas; others had decided to ride as far as possible on the ground and hike from there.

And apparently every one of the high-ranking visitors was used to having his or her way. Tiajo's staff members were dashing about with maps and navigational computers, intertial trackers, satellite-linked locaters, and much-emended lists, trying feverishly to accommodate everyone. The parties would be dispersed across much of Epiphany, though Alacrity had noticed that a small southern continent was being kept clear of visitors.

Floyt and Alacrity came upon some horses and inspected them curiously. Most resembled their forebears, terrestrial thoroughbreds, hunters, and jumpers, but several were peculiar strains bred in alien environments.

One such, with spiderishly long legs, and three-toed hooves like a prehistoric hipparion's, caracoled nearby. Beyond it stood a thickset colossus far larger than any percheron; as it reared a little, its lips pulled back to reveal the dentition of an omnivore.

Most of the mounts wore shin and hind ankle boots and had hooves cupped in protective bells.

A scattering of nonterrestrial riding animals was also visible, among them a creature resembling a millipede bearing a triple saddle and a slothlike beast whose face put Floyt in mind of Admiral Maska.

Most of the mounts had been supplied by Frostpile, but some wealthy guests had brought favorites with them from other star systems, making Floyt blaspheme at the thought of the cost.

Dressed in camouflage battle suits, the Severeemish envoys stood by, surveying the proceedings. Floyt suspected they were savoring the discord their Observance was causing at Frostpile.

Sortie-Wolf gave the two a friendly wave. "Poorly coordinated bedlam, wouldn't you say?"

"Then why don't you let them call it off?" Alacrity proposed as he and the Terran paused. "We could all go back to bed and get up again at noon for another breakfast."

Seven Wars barked laughter. "The obsequies, you know, the obsequies. Weir the Defender must be honored as befits a Severeemish lord, or our customs will have been flouted."

"Some honor," Alacrity sneered at the Babel.

"Ah, well, it will have to do."

"Citizen Floyt," the general said, "at some point I'd like to have a few moments of your time. I think insights are to be gained by soliciting an Earther's point of view. It bears remembering that Terra was origin world to *Homo severeem* as well as *Homo sapiens.*"

"Oh. Well, of course I'd be happy to sit down with you when time permits."

Maybe with about twenty, thirty Invincibles standing around, Muscles! Alacrity thought.

"Splendid. I've always wanted to trace my gene-heritage, both natural and augmentative. Your avocation is fascinating." Sortie-Wolf and his father waved good-naturedly and walked off to inspect some of the riding animals.

"Ho, you'll probably find them cross-indexed under 'Mutants, Ugly, Bloodthirsty, and Warlike.'"

"Still, the general was loud enough in suggesting a way to save you yesterday."

"That might mean he's shrewd, but it doesn't mean he's innocent." They resumed their way. "You know, I didn't realize what a stir you were going to cause with this genealogy stuff."

"To be frank, it surprised me too. I was taught that

offworlders didn't care about their ancestral background."
Something occurred to him. "Maybe when we get back to
Earth I can help you look into yours."

"Forget it." He knew at once that he'd overreacted. "What
I meant was, thanks anyway, Ho, but do me a favor and
don't. Don't even enter my name."

Floyt nodded, saying nothing. *Just when I thought I was
getting to know him.*

They came to one of an assortment of outfitters' mar-
quees, where a noisy disagreement was going on. A rather
attractive woman of middle age, smartly turned out in riding
pinks, her face carefully painted in a butterfly pattern, was
harassing an assistant armorer.

"Why, back home I'd have you flayed! I paid five thousand ovals for that rifle! Now, go fetch it for me this second!"

The servant answered calmly. "All guests' personal
weapons are being held offworld, Esteemed One, to insure
the High Truce. But we have many others from which you
are invited to choose." He held up a short, sleek energy
carbine with saddle-scabbard ring. Floyt noticed that it had
a strange fitting under the forestock.

"You imbecile!" she gritted, raising a sting-crop. "What
good is a weapon if anyone could own it?" She swatted the
carbine aside and strode away, swearing.

"Open season on armorers?" Floyt asked.

The man shrugged. "It's been like that all morning. One
young idiot demanded we return his poisoned throwing daggers; wanted to go hunting *fangsters*! Imagine? And the
Daimyo expected us to hand over an air-skiff mounted with
hammergun pods."

"Close airstrikes as a wildlife management technique,"
reflected Alacrity. "Very original."

"Alacrity, can't we just go sit this out in whatever passes
for a dungeon?"

Alacrity laughed. "Only if you don't want to be an Inheritor, Ho. But it'll be all right. See the guns? Every one is fitted with a governor—in the case of Madame Merde's carbine, the boojum detector under the forestock. Each hunter and staff member, gillie, and pilot will be wearing a functioning ID band. None of these weapons will be mistakenly—or even purposely—fired at us."

"But are they foolproof?"

"Supposed to be foolproof and tamperproof, Ho. We're gonna be careful just the same. I made some special arrangements yesterday evening."

Floyt thought about making a crack, but restrained himself. Alacrity had left a request for equipment, supplies, weapons, and an air vehicle. As the breakabout receipted for the ID bands and weapons, Floyt said, "I thought we weren't going to hunt? And these wouldn't be any good for defense; everybody else will be wearing bands too."

Alacrity was accepting two big-game rifles and a pair of handguns. "Well, there're always warning shots. And signal shots. And shots to scare away things that we don't want to kill but don't want to be eaten by either. Epiphany's only lightly settled; there're some mean specimens wandering around out there."

Other hunters were selecting all manner of artillery. One lovely, delicate young debutante picked out a terrifically powerful Forbes Annihilator that, to Floyt, resembled a neck-slung holorecorder of unusual size. Alacrity shook his head disbelievingly. The promised blastathon would be the lowest kind of lamebrained excuse for hunting: halfwits blowing holes through or setting fire to everything in sight except one another, which was, now that he thought about it, too bad. If the Severeemish truly wanted trouble on Epiphany, insisting on the Hunt had been an astute move.

They came to where Stare Skill, Kid Risk, and Brother Grimm were checking over the mound of equipment the outfitters had assigned them. The Djinn and the old mercenary seemed amiable enough, but the xenologist looked disconcerted and avoided meeting their gazes.

"So you three have thrown in together?" Alacrity asked as they compared notes.

"Yes, to—what's the term?—'lie doggo,'" Brother Grimm replied with his frightening smile. "So much is brewing around here that it reminds me of the story of the louse and the flea."

Alacrity resisted the temptation to ask why. Floyt decided that no matter who kissed the Djinn, or how much, there was no hope of his ever becoming a handsome prince.

Risk looked amused. "These two were kind enough to agree to look after an old good-for-nothing like me. Restores your faith in human nature."

Brother Grimm emitted strange, popping laughter as he picked up all their gear with no perceptible difficulty. "Such diplomacy, William! Such humility!"

Ill at ease, Stare Skill said curtly, "It's time we were on our way."

Floyt and Alacrity watched the trio move off in the direction of the ground vehicles. "Why should *they* be nervous?" Floyt wondered.

"Stare Skill and Brother Grimm are probably thinking that the Djinn's homeworld has a lot of strategic and economic importance, aside from happening to be the place where they live. Billy Risk must've piled up so many grudges and vendettas that by now he does it by instinct. But don't believe that garble of his about who's looking after who."

They started off again. "Stare Skill isn't showing much gratitude, though," Alacrity commented.

"Tilla told me that Kid Risk loved her and left her, a long time ago. Do you think she'll let him make amends—? Hey, what's the frown for, Alacrity?"

"I was just calculating how the three of them might react if they thought Weir bequeathed somebody sovereignty over—what's the Djinn's planet? Ifurin."

"Me, for example?"

"Yeah. Those brothers wrote some pretty gory fairy tales, didn't they?"

After staring around for a few minutes the two were directed to the landing area by a bemused Invincible. As they crossed the tumult of the mustering place, things seemed to have grown even more confused than before. "I talked to a few people around Frostpile," Alacrity confided, "then I reserved us a spot several hundred kilometers from here, far away from where anybody else ought to be."

"Why not stay in one of the base camps?"

"That might be playing into somebody's hands. Besides, Tiajo and the Severeemish will be nosing around. Seven Wars would like as not make us go hunting with them."

Many of the mounted hunters, astride saddles and perched in howdahs and riding bareback, were having more than a little trouble controlling their animals.

Alacrity nudged Floyt. "Look at Dincrist!"

The shipping magnate was talking with several friends, but Heart wasn't in the group. She'd told Alacrity the previous day, before going back to her suite, that she didn't share her father's passion for the hunt. Dincrist looked fully recovered from the buzzball game, but nervous. His hand stayed close to the holstered pistol at his waist.

Nearby, a particularly repulsive creature squatted on two sets of rear legs, following Dincrist with black, bulging eyes, growling and whining. Its mouth was crowded with serried rows of white, inward-curving teeth.

"Tame Gresham's beast," Alacrity muttered. "They use 'em for hunting humans as well as animals. I never did like those things."

The predator from Gresham's World swung its ugly head at the two and made a gurgling sound. Dincrist glanced their way, then continued scanning the yard uneasily.

"He's shakier than we are," Alacrity said. "I guess he's decided it was him somebody was trying to scramble in the tank." He opened his mouth to yell a comment, but Floyt stopped him.

"It would only make things harder on Heart, Alacrity."

The breakabout stared at him. "Thanks, Ho. You're right."

They passed on to where a caged animal huddled wretchedly in one corner of its confinement, quivering. It put the Terran in mind of a green, six-limbed homunculus. "This can't be an attack beast too?"

A gillie overheard them. "Now, that's a woodsprite." He gestured toward Dincrist's party. "They're riding after hedge devils today, and tomorrow, this little sprout. Too bad. They say there aren't many left." He went about his work.

Floyt squatted down, reaching into a cargo pocket of his bush fatigues. The woodsprite edged foward, sniffing. The Terran extended a piece of fruit he'd saved from breakfast. Nostrils flaring, the thing took the human's scent and moved closer timidly. Floyt tossed it the fruit. The creature caught it with one limb and devoured it as though famished.

"Alacrity, isn't there something we can—"

"Nothing!"

Resigned, the Terran fell in beside his companion and resumed their walk to the takeoff point, where vehicles of all types, crammed with every sort of outdoor equipment, were parked or grounded at assorted angles.

The craft Alacrity had reserved was a large, ungainly sky barouche that had seen better days. It bore the Weir crest and was laden with all manner of camping and survival gear.

"But Alacrity, do we really need all this junk?" Floyt gestured to the crest. "Not to mention the flying bull's-eye?"

Alacrity reassured him with a wink. He looked around to satisfy himself that they weren't being watched. The gillies and other staff members were too harried to be doing much spying. Those hunters who weren't occupied with difficulties and complications of their own were partaking of a prehunt snack and a bit of cheer as waiters circulated among them with trays.

Alacrity began to sort through the cargo, selecting a few items: a case of rations, a compact field generator, a two-man bubble shelter, and sleeping cocoons.

A young assistant motor-stable overseer came hurrying up to him. "I see you've got everything set, Reef," Alacrity said.

The young man nodded energetically. "You bet, Alacrity." He patted the barouche.

"Good." Looking around, Alacrity pointed to a row of surface skimmers. "Now, which of those is free?"

Reef's eyebrows knit. "Uh, all of 'em. They're mostly for local sightseeing."

"Well, which one's the best of the lot?"

Reef indicated an almost-new skimmer, fully charged. Alacrity leaned the rifles against it and began stowing the gear he'd selected. Floyt snorted with laughter.

The skimmer was an open vehicle with a fairing, two low-slung tandem seats, and a small luggage well between the rear seat and the tiny engine. A safety helmet sat astride each seat's control pommel. A navigation-commo unit bulged its nose. To Floyt's way of thinking, the ground skimmer couldn't have looked much more like a bobsled without being one.

"But, but what about the barouche?" the perplexed Reef asked.

Alacrity paused. "After we're gone, take it back to the motor stable and dismount the control stem or something. Then keep your lip sealed. But make sure nobody uses it, read me? Good. Here."

He surreptitiously passed Reef a Spican bank note. The assistant overseer palmed it and took an unhurried leave.

"Why shouldn't anyone else use the barouche, Alacrity? Wouldn't that help confuse anybody who was looking for us?"

Alacrity reached for a medical kit. "Yeah, but somebody might catch a missile or something that's meant for us. Not very likely, I admit, but there's always the chance."

They loaded a few more items, and Alacrity made fast the cargo. Floyt, watching, inquired, "I suppose the destination changes too?"

"Very good. Yup, I have a spot all picked out. We'll stay hidden until these social retards are through trying to vaporize local fauna, then come back as early as we can without giving Seven Wars grounds for complaint. Say, tomorrow mid-morning."

"Staying out of everyone's way is fine with me, Alacrity."

"Great. Want a helmet? I don't much favor them in a puny rig like this."

Floyt took one anyway. "I always say, don't wear a helmet if you haven't got anything to protect."

Alacrity got into the front seat, securing his weapons in their clips and buckling his safety harness. Floyt did the same, then tightened the helmet's chin strap and lowered the visor. The breakabout pulled on a pair of goggles.

Alacrity took the steering grips and toed the accelerator. The skimmer rose two meters into the air—very nearly its ceiling—and glided away slowly and silently.

It was pleasant to have the wind in his face again, Floyt thought as he leaned around Alacrity to watch. It was pleasant to leave his troubles behind.

Floyt was awakened by a cry of haunting, luminous, and mournful beauty, a sustained trill rippling down from the sky.

The Terran hiked himself around as quietly as he could in his sleeping cocoon, inchwormed, and poked his head through the yielding film that was the door of the shelter. He moved gently, not because he was alarmed or afraid, but because he knew instinctively that whatever had made that heartbreakingly beautiful sound would be timid, easily frightened away.

The little security field generator, attached to the edge of the shelter, hummed almost inaudibly. It was rated for most Epiphanian areas; anything with even a vestige of a nervous system would be repelled by the invisible barrier protecting the shelter. The area looked clear. Floyt flicked off the generator, the better to listen.

They had pitched camp atop a hill. Floyt, seeing the vegetation around it, recalled some of the names: snareweed and coronet shrubs, spark-nettles and culverin vines. There were lacy, translucent ice trees and patches of ribbon grass, blossoms and leaves, spores and undergrowth in startling colors, shapes and profusion. He couldn't spot the crier, though.

The wonderful sound came again. Floyt caught a flash out over the small valley below him, of something that made his breath catch in his throat. It was gorgeous, polychrome, blazing in a way that resembled metal one moment, stained glass the next.

It had two sets of wings like spun gauze and a wide, diaphanous tail. It soared unhurriedly and with consummate ease, just below the dawn line, calling like a lost soul and making the hair on Floyt's neck and arms stand up. His skin showed gooseflesh.

The bird thing tilted with supreme grace and slid in the direction of the hilltop camp, fragile and radiant. It trilled again. Floyt could hear no other sound, as though the whole planet were listening to the cries. They echoed and hung in the air for what seemed a very long time. The creature glided closer; the Terran reached out to awaken Alacrity so that he wouldn't miss it.

Then he saw that the breakabout was also awake and had been listening too. Now Alacrity rolled onto his stomach and edged into the doorway, careful to make no sound or sudden move. The glorious flyer banked again, its long wings a blur. It climbed above the dawn line and into the morning sunlight.

Yellow-red rays seemed to spray off it in a rainbow, brilliant and breathtaking, making them gasp. It wheeled; multicolored waves shimmered from it. Then it dove like a fiery meteor.

Floyt felt peaceful and content for the first time since the celebration at the Sockwallet lashup. Alacrity felt untroubled for a change; there were worse places to be than the unspoiled wilds of Epiphany, beneath this aerial dance.

Then a bolt of light brighter than the sun lanced up from below. It caught the flyer squarely in a harsh, explosive fireball. The shimmering rainbow flew apart; the creature crumpled to ash. With a last trill of infinite loss it fell, smoking.

They watched, stunned. Floyt cried his anguish as the two wriggled free of cocoons and shelter. Alacrity reached for the vision enhancers and held them up to his eyes. He scanned quickly, searching the area from which the shot had come. He spotted the hunting party almost at once, at the far end of the valley, picking its way through the scrub. Alacrity directed Floyt's attention that way with his free hand, as the enhancers, monitoring the breakabout's eyes, brought the focus into sharp clarity.

Dincrist was riding at the head of the party, rifle aloft, spurring his horse, laughing triumphantly, white hair gleaming. The Presbyter Kuss was behind him, among others. The hunting beast from Gresham's World loped ahead of the group, sniffing the ground, obviously on a scent. It set up a raucous howling, leaping and circling.

The bird thing had fallen into the river that wound through the valley and was being washed swiftly downstream. Dincrist made an impatient gesture, dismissing it; the kill had only been a moment's idle diversion.

"You unutterable shitheel," Alacrity muttered, keeping

the enhancer fixed on Heart's father, wishing for a second that his rifle wasn't safetied. "You gutless, soulless—"

Floyt was yanking his arm, saying, "Alacrity, *look*!" He pulled the vision enhancers down forcefully. Alacrity forgot his irritation at the Earther when he saw the little woodsprite, panting and spent, at the edge of their camp. It was injured, bleeding dark blood from a middle limb. As it had in its cage, it extended its snout at them, trembling, taking their scent.

"It found us," Floyt said excitedly. "It followed our scent."

"Well . . . possibly," Alacrity admitted dubiously. They'd spent a lot of time traveling at virtual ground level; if the woodsprite had been released early enough and was good enough at following airborne scents, it might have come after them on purpose, but that presumed an awful lot.

The Terran was approaching it with a bit of food. "Hey wait," the breakabout objected. "For all we know, that thing spits AP missiles."

Floyt had never had a pet of his own, of course, but he'd always felt a kinship for the timid little creatures in the childrens' petting zoos and school and lab menageries. He offered the woodsprite a crumb of ration, making chucking, clicking sounds. The thing sniffed him again, then reached out with three of its nimble little paws to snatch the food. It ate hungrily, watching them both, looking ready to bolt.

"Well, I'll be damned," Alacrity said. "Maybe he was somebody's pet before Dincrist got his hooks in him, Ho."

Floyt came up with another ration fragment. This time the woodsprite didn't retreat after taking it, but let him stroke its head softly. It made a gurgling, cooing sound of its own. Floyt heard noises behind him and turned his head—slowly, no sudden movements—to see Alacrity folding their cocoons while the shelter collapsed and contracted itself. "What are you doing?"

The breakabout paused. "Dincrist's hound is on the scent.

We can either hand over your pal there or give those morons a chase they'll never forget."

Floyt knew he should be objecting. While there was nothing *directly* prejudicial to their mission in what Alacrity had in mind, neither was there anything remotely advantageous about it. But the breakabout had apparently been right when he'd mentioned that three days' conditioning wasn't nearly enough for a complete behavioral reprogramming. Old attitudes and responses were likely to resurface if sufficiently evoked and unopposed by specific conditioning.

Instead of objecting, Floyt held out his arms to the little animal, knelt before it, cooed, then said, "All right there, Short and Desperate, what's it going to be?"

The woodsprite studied him for a long moment, then climbed into his arms. As he stowed their guns, Alacrity said, "Here, take my spare shirt. Rub him down carefully, and daub at the blood; we want to leave a strong trail."

Floyt did so gingerly. The woodsprite's smell was thick and musky, but not unpleasant. The creature endured the treatment.

"If you can find anything like a scent gland or sebaceous glands, Ho, give 'em a once-over. But don't get nipped."

Floyt lowered himself into his skimmer seat slowly. His companion reached down to buckle his safety harness for him, loosely and with surprising gentleness, so as not to alarm their passenger. Then Alacrity hopped into his own seat and brought the near-soundless little engine to life. He hovered, barely clear of the ground. The woodsprite pressed closer to Floyt.

"Alacrity, should I drag your shirt along the ground?"

"Uh, not if it'll leave marks. I'll slow down when we pass rocks or grass and you can take a swipe. But don't snag any thorns or bushes. If we leave cloth behind, they'll know something's up."

Following a narrow game trail, Alacrity eased down the

slope in the direction the little woodsprite had come from, backtrailing to keep the mounted hunters from spotting any remnants of the camp—though he doubted they'd left many. He spotted a track left by the woodsprite and veered over it. Floyt plied the shirt, and they headed downslope, leaving a fresh trail that would divert Dincrist's hunting animal.

"That Gresham's beast can probably follow a fresh airscent as easily as a ground spoor," Alacrity told Floyt over his shoulder.

As they cut across a low field, building a lead, careful to keep terrain features and trees between the skimmer and the hunters, Floyt carefully wafted the shirt over rainbow grass. Alacrity, having picked out part of his course from the hilltop, crested another rise, then took on the merest bit of altitude and began to set the hunters a merciless trail. He swooped under fallen logs and over rocks, squeaked between clumps of vile-smelling rogue ferns and across patches of snareweed.

Then it was over a shallow streamlet and a mudflat too soft and watery to retain small-game tracks. Trying to stifle the sound, Alacrity laughed louder each time he put some new obstacle behind them.

After drifting over a bed of tear blossoms, he rose and pulled to a halt in the shelter of an upthrust rock. "We don't want to outdistance them by too much. I *have* to see this."

They crept to the edge of the jumble and looked back the way they'd come, the woodsprite apparently content to wait in the skimmer. As the riders were still negotiating the rogue ferns, their animals balking at the stench, Baroness Myers inadvertently jostled the Presbyter Kuss, and the clergyman took a header into the ferns. At the same time, Chief Operating Officer Gloria "Kiki" Bernath of Amalgamated Mining was in midstream, spitting water and wading one way while her horse went in the other.

Dincrist's mount became mired as he tried to skirt the mud, so he was afoot, in it up to mid-shins, floundering and trying to extricate the animal. There was a great deal of wild gesticulation.

But mud-covered, foaming, and frenzied with the chase, the Gresham's beast was screaming its hunting cry while it raced along halfway between prey and pack. The Terran and the breakabout realized that, much as they were enjoying themselves, they couldn't stay where they were forever. "What do we do now, Alacrity?"

"Um. We can't just let the hitchhiker go; they'd pick up his trail again."

That hadn't occurred to Floyt. "So?"

"Let's take him to Redlock's camp. It's only a couple of kilometers from here. That's why I picked this spot."

"Redlock?"

"Well, the prey, there, is fair game, isn't he? And we've got him, don't we? So, we claim him and let him go later. What can anybody say?"

There didn't seem to be an acceptable alternative. The hunting party was beginning to move again. Apparently trained not to leave him too far behind, the Gresham's beast had circled around to wait for its master.

"All right," Floyt said. Off they went, careful to leave no tracks but leaving a trail through the worst parts of the area. Their only regret was for the horses that were going to have to follow it; for the hunters and the vicious Gresham's beast they felt no pity. Floyt found himself joining Alacrity in laughter; their ruse might be an irresponsible act of applied lunacy, but it was fun.

They discovered that the area wasn't completely devoid of big game when, rounding the bend in a dry wash, they found themselves headed directly for a granite ox, who had until that moment been enjoying a sand bath. Alacrity hit the accelerator and cut around it before the huge, armored behemoth could swipe at them with its wicked horns. Floyt looked back over his shoulder to see the bulky herbivore trotting away, and was glad that it wouldn't be around when the trigger-happy hunters reached the scene. He took up leaving the scent trail once again.

From time to time the two found a safe vantage point from which to gaze back at their pursuit with the vision enhancers. Several hunters had dropped out, either from exhaustion or injuries. Floyt spied Kiki Bernath sitting on the ground, nursing her ankle as her horse disappeared toward the skyline. It did the Earther's heart good.

And in time, through a serpentine course, never letting the hunting pack get too far behind but never letting it catch up too closely either, the two gleefully skimmed to the big, busy hunting camp of Governor Redlock. At Alacrity's instruction, Floyt tucked the scent shirt out of sight. The woodsprite had been safely concealed under the cargo cover, although it had been nervous.

Alacrity pulled to a stop in the center of the camp. It seemed that most of the guests were still out potting away. There were cages, preservation containers, and hooks for the keeping of game live or dead, whole or eviscerated. The stench of burnt game defiled the air; most of the slaughterment would go to waste.

A fourth choice was also available. Gillies were feeding some game into a large machine that had been airlifted out from Frostpile as a conspicuous show of hospitality, wealth, and power.

"Taxidermic robot," Alacrity commented as they unbuckled and dismounted to await the fun. "Rich people's toy." Dead wildlife was fed into it at one end, to be processed by the most rapid, modern computerized systems available, emerging a short while later, stuffed and mounted, at the other end.

Floyt looked around. No one seemed to have taken much notice of their arrival. Gillies and servitors were moving back and forth, attending to their tasks; a few hunters were scattered about, swapping lies. No other tracking animals were nearby, though Alacrity suspected that all the dead game in the area would confuse anything but the determined Gresham's beast anyhow.

"Shouldn't we claim the woodsprite now, Alacrity?"

"Don't you want to see Dincrist's face when we pull that whatsit out of the cargo boot?"

"But when Dincrist gets close to camp, he'll know something's up. He might even give up the chase." Floyt couldn't see any sign of an approaching horseman.

"Without finding out what's going on here? Not a chance." Alacrity was looking around, on the off chance that the Nonpareil was at Redlock's camp, but she was nowhere to be seen.

So they leaned casually on the skimmer, Floyt whistling nervously, the breakabout humming a half-remembered tune, until Dincrist, the only hunter left in the chase, pounded into sight on a horse ready to drop. His Gresham's beast preceded him, confronting the Terran and the breakabout with a slavering snarl.

Dincrist dismounted, and the two companions had trouble deciding which was frothing worst: man, horse, or tracking animal. "Fitzhugh, I'll have you dismembered for this! What have you done?"

"We gave you a little riding lesson, is all," Alacrity replied airily. Floyt, remembering the senseless slaughter of the magnificent flyer, laughed spitefully.

Furious beyond words, Dincrist reacted more violently than they'd foreseen, and the entourage members and subordinates who would ordinarily have restrained him weren't around to intervene. He lunged at the breakabout, swinging his nerve-fire riding crop. The sting-crop hummed wickedly; its lash cut Alacrity's cheek. The younger man froze in shock for a moment.

Floyt yelped and moved to separate them or something; he wasn't sure what. The peacemaking didn't get far. The Gresham's beast drove him away from its master by baring rank upon rank of tine-teeth. When he moved toward the skimmer and its guns, the thing tensed to leap; it smelled the woodsprite on him and knew he was an enemy. The only reason it hadn't savaged Floyt or Alacrity was that it hadn't been commanded to.

Meanwhile, Alacrity had made a few decisions of his own, the most important one being that he wasn't going to be hit again. He blocked the crop's second swing, meeting the edge of Dincrist's wrist with the back of his own. Their free hands locked. People were yelling in the background, but Alacrity couldn't take time to listen.

Dincrist, bearing down, was more concerned with the leverage of arms and torsos; Alacrity relaxed sinuously, sliding in as though he were boneless, and took the shipping magnate's legs out from under him in a quick foot-sweep.

But Dincrist, sportsman and athlete, was fast and strong, even discounting his age. He landed well and almost gave Alacrity a knee in the groin as the breakabout pounced on him. They rolled, battling wildly, back and forth over the field-tamped campground.

The Gresham's beast had driven Floyt back up against the bulk of the processor, where his clutching hand found a gillie's wooden staff. Floyt took it and whirled it out before him horizontally just as the creature sprang at his throat. Its jaws clamped on the thick staff, splintering the wood, and locked there.

Alacrity had the satisfaction of connecting solidly with Dincrist's mouth, knocking the carefully kept silver hair askew, seeing blood flow. The tanned gentility faded; Dincrist howled as he buffeted and struck at Alacrity with fist and crop, like a child in a tantrum. The opponents hammered at one another.

At the same time, the Gresham's beast, its forelegs clear of the ground, growled, yanked, and tugged Floyt this way and that. Floyt could only feel thankful in a horrified way that the beast's reflex was to hang on to the staff rather than release and try for a new hold. Still, he could barely keep his grip, and the thing was slowly biting the staff in two, its reeking, steamy breath making him gag.

Floyt's clumsy, intermittent kicks to the horror's underside seemed not to bother it in the least. If it disarmed him, it would certainly either maim him or turn on Alacrity to help its master. The staff began to splinter, and the Gresham's beast screamed, sensing victory.

Alacrity heard it just as he put the sole of his boot squarely into Dincrist's stomach. The older man's breath whooped from him, and he rolled away, groaning. The breakabout surged to his feet and tore Dincrist's crop away from him, twisting its control to maximum. He rammed it into the Gresham's beast's ribs just as it bit through the staff.

A charge of nerve-fire went through it, and the creature bounded aside in a paroxysm, away from the pain—directly into the feeding hopper of the taxidermic robot. Its long tail was held fast, for the moment, by the idling feeder mechanism, and scrabbling to free itself, it almost snapped Floyt's foot off in a near-miss.

The Earthman, with a feeling of surreal calm, slapped down the control bar.

"No!" Dincrist shouted from where he lay. But the machine sucked the Gresham's beast, its bulging, hate-filled eyes fixed on Floyt, out of sight and began making grisly sounds.

The shipping tycoon was on his feet, but Alacrity still had the crop, and others had run to find out what was going on, among them the two Severeemish envoys and an enraged Redlock. The governor saw that they were going to clash again. He stepped between them and, shorter than either by half a head and more, shoved them stumbling away from him in either direction. From the anger like a black hood above his eyes, it was apparent that he was in no mood to be provoked. Both opponents quieted.

"Ah, yes," Theater General Sortie-Wolf hissed unpleasantly. "The High Truce."

He couldn't be enjoying this more if you tickled him, Floyt thought.

"This bacterium is responsible for breaking the Truce," Dincrist managed, calmer now, just as Admiral Maska arrived to see what was going on.

"I got hit first; I hit back," Alacrity spat. His conditioning was now twisting his gut, as was Floyt's; they realized their peril.

Just then the clatter of the taxidermic robot drew everyone's attention. Their eyes went to the delivery platform of the processor.

With the others distracted, Floyt backed to the surface skimmer, where the woodsprite still cowered in hiding. He had no intention of seeing it fed into the machine.

Out onto the delivery platform slid the Gresham's beast, beautifully stuffed and mounted, in a very realistic pose. Its hide was clean, its teeth sparkled, and its glassy eyes were filled with hatred.

"Well," Alacrity proclaimed loudly, "you've gotta admit the effect's really lifelike. He's gonna look great in the trophy room."

Only Redlock's presence saved him from another attempt on his life.

CHAPTER 14

SATISFACTION GUARANTEED

DAME TIAJO WASN'T IN THE LEAST AMUSED.

Alacrity quickly lost his smile when the matter was taken before her, immediately upon the return to Frostpile. Floyt was quite frankly intimidated, belaboring himself, *How could we have gotten ourselves into so much trouble in so short a time?*

"Do you know what you've done, you foolish men?" The old woman's rouged face was quivering, her eyes searing them. Dincrist could no more meet her gaze than could Alacrity and Floyt.

Redlock stood near, having delivered an unbiased summation of what he knew of the incident. But the essential part, the question of who had provoked whom, and where the guilt lay, was still unclear.

Dorraine was present with her father, First Councillor Inst. Seven Wars and Sortie-Wolf were on hand, intent on seeing the Severeemish Usages observed to the letter. Admiral Maska was in attendance as well.

"You've broken the High Truce, that's what you've done, you foolish little men!" Tiajo added.

"I'm 197 centimeters," Alacrity muttered, studying the floor.

"Shut *up!*" Floyt and Tiajo both bellowed at him at the same moment, shocking one another. Floyt turned deathly pale, eyes screwed shut. Inst and Redlock exchanged the smallest grin; Dorraine hid her smile.

"You may discount the height of you that extends above your ankles, Master Fitzhugh," the grandam continued, tight-lipped. "For that is where I shall cut you off." Alacrity swallowed. "Someone is going to pay for what happened this morning. Now, it all seems to revolve around who struck the first blow. That would seem to be you, Captain Dincrist."

"But . . . Dame Tiajo, these runagates interfered with my rightful pursuit of my prey. That is, my *party's* prey; we'd been chasing it for over an hour."

"And that is provocation under the Usages of the Hunt," Minister Seven Wars contributed. "The Earther and his escort are clearly implicated."

"Yes, so long as the woodsprite was sole prey," Sortie-Wolf added. "One cannot pursue more than one prey and have exclusive right of pursuit." He looked at the disputants slyly.

"But he *had* two!" Floyt burst out. "Captain Dincrist shot down this—this bird, flying creature. We saw it."

"I bet we'd have trouble getting his friends' testimony on that one, though," Alacrity put in, addressing Tiajo.

"Where is the creature in question, the woodsprite?" Tiajo inquired.

"It escaped," Floyt announced, deadpan. In truth, the woodsprite *had* raced for the tree line, all elbows, rear end, and sole pads—escaping.

"The bone of contention has departed, eh?" Tiajo eyed Floyt, evaluating him in a new light, choosing not to contest his story. "Then, what does all this matter? Mutual apologies seem in order."

"Alas, no, Dame Tiajo," Seven Wars intoned. "That would violate the Severeemish Usages. There has been an infraction against the High Truce. This cannot be tolerated." Alacrity, paling, thought, *War!*

"But it's all so hopelessly muddled," Dorraine said. "Surely the Severeemish don't approve of punishing the innocent along with the guilty."

"Indeed. It is muddled beyond any solution save one," Seven Wars shot back. "A death duel will settle it."

Floyt felt a sudden need to sit down. Dorraine gasped. Inst exploded, "You can't be serious!" Maska watched without comment, and Dincrist's mouth was a silent O. Alacrity reflected that if the Severeemish weren't the ones who'd tried to eliminate Dincrist and/or himself in the buzzball tank, they were doing somebody an awfully big favor, whether they knew it or not.

"Absolutely not," Tiajo decreed. "The pitting of human beings against one another in that way was stopped when we threw down the Presidium. I will not permit it."

"You would accept our fealty and then mock our Observances?" Sortie-Wolf demanded hotly. Redlock looked at Alacrity as if he'd taken just about enough. But before the governor could speak, First Councillor Inst intervened.

"Wait! I see an alternative under your own Usages."

They all turned to him. The mahogany face was regal and composed, the voice deep and precise. "Your own histories speak of the Severeemish Lords Requiter and Paladin, who had a muddled dispute between them. If memory serves, the elders gave them permission to settle it with a contest short of a death duel."

Dorraine took her father's arm and kissed him. They all watched the two envoys expectantly.

"Ah, yes," Sortie-Wolf said, "but those circumstances were quite extraordinary."

"So are these."

"Are we to be bent to every little Severeemish dot and

dash?" Tiajo thundered. "Here we have a compromise within your Usages. Or have you come here *looking* for war?"

"Requiter and Paladin sailed one-man barbaustoes in a race through Slaughter Strait," Sortie-Wolf snapped. "As dangerous as a duel. What will you have? More tank-hopping? More ball-hitting? *Pah!*"

Tension gave the chamber a lightning feel. Floyt, like everyone else, was thinking desperately. Then, what seemed like a marvelous solution lit up his brain.

"*Airbikes!*" he shouted triumphantly.

"Do you guys realize how much money's riding on this race?" Sintilla was beside herself with excitement. "Spican bank notes, ovals, ducats, currency bangles—they're betting a fortune, everybody in Frostpile."

That stopped Alacrity. Maybe it would be more profitable to *throw* the . . . But his conditioning made him half dizzy at the unformed thought, because Dame Tiajo had vowed that, as executrix, she would penalize the airbike race's losers, by which she meant Floyt as well as the breakabout. The race would be run with two-man airbikes, at the insistence of the Severeemish, since Floyt was a part of the altercation.

And *that* meant that to lose was to jeopardize the inheritance that had brought them all the way from Terra. So Alacrity banished from his mind thoughts of anything except winning.

"Where's *your* cash riding, Tilla?" he snarled at her as he fit the sweatband down over his forehead.

"On you guys, of course. They're giving the most fantastic odds against you!"

"Will you quit being so damn happy about it?"

The roof that served as Frostpile's airbike hangar and takeoff station had become so crowded with bettors and other celebrants that Tiajo had been obliged to have it cleared, ordering all but a select few to remove themselves and find observation points elsewhere. Nearby roofs were filling up with laughing, shouting, drinking, boisterous people who were perfectly aware of the possibility of death or injury resulting from the race, and not in the least depressed about it.

Many of the men and some of the women were wearing copies of or fanciful variations on Floyt's cutaway, whipped up for them by Frostpile's resident designers and couturiers. Given the wealth and influence enjoyed by most of the guests, all signs pointed to Floyt's having started a far-reaching fashion craze.

"I'm still having a hard time believing you suggested this," Alacrity told Floyt. "You've never even *been* in one of these kites."

"But you have," Floyt reminded him patiently, for something like the twentieth time, as he pulled on lightweight biking shoes. "Alacrity, you and Dincrist and the others have dabbled in airbiking, but I am a *cyclist*."

He stood up. Though the shoes were already broken in, he'd put patches of skinsheath on his feet for protection. "I don't know much about star travel or guns and all that, but I'm very good at what's important now. You'll see!"

Has he changed, Alacrity wondered, *or am I just seeing him more clearly*?

The Terran looked again at *Thistle*, their airbike. She was a muscle-powered craft made of transparent metalar of quarter-mil thickness. She had a long pusher propeller and extremely lengthy shoulder-mounted wings that gave her good lift and soaring characteristics. *Thistle* also had a canard, a small steering wing, set at the end of a pole extending from her nose. Floyt thought the orange dawnlight streaming through her made *Thistle* a creation of unsurpassed beauty.

Floyt was glad that both competing bikes were conventional uprights; he had little experience with recumbents. It seemed that the Union Cyclist Internationale had banned the use of recumbents in official racing in 1938, Terran

reckoning, and a peculiar snobbism had kept offworld par-
venus from popularizing them in airbiking.

"I wish we could get going," Alacrity said, shivering.

"Yes. I'm cold too."

"It's not that, Ho. Halidome's going to rise soon. You
won't believe how hot it's gonna get inside that thing. Drink
all the liquids you can."

"But the weight—"

"You'll lose it double-'stat once we're airborne."

Floyt, an experienced racer, needed no further urging.
He swigged from a bottle of fortified fruit juice and bit into
another carbohydrate bar. Alacrity had two of the ground
crew give *Thistle* one more quick going-over with their
evaporators, to cut down on the weight of condensation
she'd have to carry aloft.

Over by *Feather*, the biplane airbike selected by Dincrist
and his partner, the Presbyter Kuss, some last-minute adjust-
ments were being made. *Feather*, like *Thistle*, was framed
with incredibly strong, light tubing and had fiber-cable control lines. Alacrity had chosen a monoplane over a biplane
because, even though the other was the more rugged design,
Thistle had an edge in maneuverability. He was even more
opposed to less conventional designs, like the flying wing
with a pedaling nacelle at both ends.

While Alacrity ran a last check on the tiny commo button
clipped to his wrist sweatband, Floyt looked over the pedaling assembly. He was once more amazed at the lightness
and strength of the exotic composite materials used. He
dearly wished to try an equally advanced bicycle—to take
one back to Earth, if it were possible. Surely that wouldn't
be too much to ask of Earthservice?

He turned his attention to the single landing wheel, and
the emergency snare mounted along the airbike's underbelly. It was a flat envelope of adhesive ribbons like those
of the snarley-ball thrown at Alacrity back at Machu Picchu.
Alacrity and the crew chief had pronounced themselves

satisfied with it; Floyt, eyeing the insubstantial stuff of the
packet, wasn't so confident.

First Councillor Inst stumped over to *Feather* in the metal
exoskeleton of an antigrav-harness. The Severeemish had
been opposed to any kind of safety escort for the two racers;
there'd been none in Slaughter Strait. But Tiajo insisted;
the route of the race, agreed upon after considerable wran-
gling, was over some rough and dangerous country. Argu-
ments for a shorter, safer course and more escort flyers had
been met by Sortie-Wolf's accusation that Tiajo was trying
to turn a grudge match into a dilettantes' outing.

So one escort was a compromise. Several nominees had
been discussed, including Redlock and Maska, along with
some of Dincrist's cronies. For various reasons, Alacrity or
Dincrist had objections to almost all. In the end they'd
settled on Inst, somewhat at Tiajo's urging. At least it stood
in his favor that he'd averted a death duel, or a war, by
dredging up a bit of Severeemish history.

By the time final arrangements—choice of routes, airbikes, escort, and so on—had been made, it was late in the
evening, but Alacrity demanded the opportunity for a test
flight, to check the lay of the land and the aircraft. The
Severeemish had told him, with vast amusement, to go right
ahead, since he had all night for the project. He'd made an
answer not suitable in polite company and dropped the idea.

Inst's exoskeleton was mounted with a small, powerful
winch whose cable ended in a snap-hook. He could make
fast to hoisting hooks located at the tops of the airbike
fuselages to prevent a crash—perhaps. Of course, he couldn't
save both at once. That, too, seemed to tickle the minister
and the general.

Inst also wore a medical kit and long-range communi-
cator. A pair of vision enhancers, flipped up, rode his brow.
Clipped to the power pack on his back was a blaster.

Alacrity had been very dubious about that last, but anyone on the ground out in the wilds was liable to run into

large, vicious things that were hungry and prepared to do something about it.

Crew people gingerly lifted *Feather* to fit her into her launch slot. Dincrist, Kuss, and a few followers came after. The tycoon's choice of the presbyter as partner made sense; the athletic clergyman had airbiking experience. And, he'd been one of those unhorsed and humiliated during the woodsprite prank. Jaw set and eyes narrowed, he now looked disinclined to discuss matters of the spirit with Floyt or anyone else.

More crew took up *Thistle* now. *Feather* would launch from station number one, *Thistle* from number five, in order to minimize the chances of friction between the two teams.

Tiajo sat near the hangar, with Dorraine, Redlock, Inst, and the two Severeemish. "I'm going to make sure the rules're clear," Alacrity said and ambled off in their direction. Admiral Maska intercepted him.

"I just wanted to wish you and Hobart well," the sleepy-eyed Srillan said. "I hope the Strange Attractors favor you."

"Strange Attractors?" Alacrity had heard the term somewhere, but couldn't recall its meaning.

"Antiquated terminology. It's come to represent the hidden forces holding sway over chaotic dynamics—you know: air turbulence, electrical potential across cell membranes, and so forth."

"Oh. Right. Well, we could definitely use 'em on our side. And an engine; I wouldn't mind one of those, either."

Maska snuffled laughter and added, "When a system is no longer deterministic, Strange Attractors are at work. Good luck, Alacrity."

"Thank you, Maska." He watched the admiral walk away.

Floyt and Sintilla made their way to launch slot five. At number one, Dincrist and Kuss had stripped down and were doing loosening-up exercises. Floyt shed his heavy coat; Sintilla held it for him as he too warmed up in the chilly air. The light of Halidome was just touching the uppermost reaches of Frostpile, turning it to orange-red intaglio. *Feather*'s team began boarding, moving gently and carefully.

The Terran glanced around and saw that Alacrity still stood near the nobles, but he appeared to be on the periphery of things. Redlock was erect in the manner of an ancient Prussian, Dorraine on his arm. She seemed to be addressing Seven Wars formally. After a brief exchange, the minister gave the queen a courteous bow; she returned it with a grateful nod of the head.

Floyt had stopped exercising and was watching Inst, who'd listened to the conversation with a certain tension on his face and glanced at Alacrity several times. The breakabout hadn't noticed.

At length, Alacrity got Tiajo's attention and began to speak. The grandam rolled her eyes to the sky, then barked something at him. Alacrity spread his hands, hunched his head down between his shoulders, and turned toward the launch stations.

As he walked, though, Heart appeared, stopping him. Dincrist, slowly pedaling to test his ship, was in no position to take notice.

She was stunning in an outfit all of red suede and heel-length hooded, crimson fur. She took his hand, squeezing it emphatically, and said something. Then she threw her arms around him, kissed him fleetingly but very hard, and was gone before he could reply.

He was still dazed when he arrived at the launch slot.

"I don't think he needs to do any warmups."

"There's no time anyway, Sintilla," Floyt replied.

Alacrity broke his distraction. He doffed his coat, and he and Floyt handed their proteuses over to Sintilla, every gram of weight being important in airbike racing. Besides, the instruments would only get in the way or be damaged. That left them in sweatbands, shorts, light helmets, and cycling shoes.

They boarded, Floyt taking the rear seat, which position

was still known, after centuries, as the stoker. Sintilla looked them over, then announced cheerfully, "I just *know* you two are going to make me rich!" She stepped back as a crew chief sealed them into the fuselage with a thermowand.

They were seated on long, narrow saddles, Floyt directly behind Alacrity. They began fitting the cleats of their shoes into the pedal impressions and adjusting toe clips and straps.

"Nice sendoff you got there," Floyt commented casually, his own voice sounding strange to him in the close fuselage. It was narrow, not much longer than the pedal frame, but high enough for them to sit erect.

Alacrity looked back over his shoulder at the Terran's innocent expression for a moment, then went back to settling in. "She told me she hopes we win," he said quietly.

Alacrity fit his shoulders into the brackets he'd have to use in order to pedal effectively; his hands held the control grips. Movements of the grips' stem also controlled movement of *Thistle*, so that it couldn't be used for leverage. On the control yoke were a crude altimeter, airspeed indicator, horizon indicator, and compass. Floyt was provided simple downswept Maes-type handlebars, which was fine with him.

Since airmasks weren't needed yet, they let them dangle around their necks. Floyt found that his saddle was soft and not slick, which pleased him in view of the sweating he expected to be doing very shortly.

Alacrity was still testing his controls. Floyt asked, "What was Dorraine saying to Seven Wars?"

"What? Oh, something or other about that Thorn Cup thing we're all supposed to drink tonight before the Will-reading. She can't take part in the ceremony. There goes Inst."

Manipulating the controls on his chest panel, Inst, standing almost upright, shot away into the sky at high speed.

"Why couldn't Dorraine drink from the Cup?" Floyt persisted. "Don't the Severeemish expect it?"

"Huh? Ho, for Fate's sake! Would you mind thinking

about the race? If we lose, you can count on old Tiajo to yang us *good*!"

Undoubtedly true, but Floyt had no intention of losing the race. The two began a slow cadence, pedaling at a leisurely twenty rpm, bringing the propeller up to an idle.

Floyt's inquisitive bent made him plow on. "I'm just curious, Alacrity. If you can't remember what Dorraine said, you should just say so, not bite a man's head off."

"Remember? Of course I remember! Uh, there's some sort of rule or stricture, from way back in her ancestors' time. Something or other about, 'Comfort those in sorrow, but look to the life hereafter, and do not drink the bitter dregs of grief.' Or something. Now will you let me alone and concentrate on the race?"

But that's not right! Floyt thought to himself. He knew something about the royal family of Agora; that was part of the material he'd become familiar with while researching the monograph that had come to Weir's attention.

He reached back in memory as the prop spun faster and he watched the muscles tense in the breakabout's back. The stricture ran on the order of, "Comfort those in sorrow, and, looking to the life hereafter, sweeten the bitter dregs of grief."

An obscure stricture, yet certainly not one that Dorraine should have gotten so wrong. But why should she—"

"Hang on!" Alacrity warned. Tiajo's hand was on the release. Floyt put thought from his mind and abandoned himself to pedaling. Their cadence rose to over ninety rpm, the prop's slightly higher. *Thistle* vibrated as though eager. Tiajo pressed the release. *Thistle* and *Feather* slid down their launch slots.

And Floyt found himself flying.

True airbike racing had begun as a sport wherein contestants began from a standing start at ground level and, by dint of soaring techniques and Homeric pedaling, covered a certain distance and reached a specified altitude, usually in a race to a higher landing spot.

But the sport's popularity grew beyond the elite band of dedicated masochists who were actually capable of such a feat; there were those who wanted to know how it felt to be a "real" airbike racer. The launch slots were born.

Floyt was gratified that the race wasn't the real thing. He doubted he and the breakabout would ever have gotten above ground-effect altitude.

As it was, they soared in the orange-red light of Epiphany's dawn, the planet's strange, enchanted landscape rolling by beneath the transparent undercarriage. Floyt was ecstatic, for all the fact that *Thistle* was a slow and wallowing bird.

The pedals spun and the chain whirred softly. The propeller sang. Both men breathed easily, and the dawn air was still. There was no other sound.

"Stay centered and let me do the balancing," Alacrity repeated. Floyt calmly chalked it up to anxiety. "Pedal!" the breakabout said. And Hobart Floyt did.

Alacrity tilted the canard and worked the other control surfaces. *Thistle* swung around toward the race course, *Feather* off her left wingtip by no more than ten meters.

There'd been some lack of agreement on the gearing to be used. Floyt had opined that gearing too high and pedaling too slowly would be bad, needlessly fatiguing, as in bicycling. Alacrity had insisted that, in airbiking, pedaling slowly-hard and pedaling quickly-easily were equivalent. Still, he'd given in and geared *Thistle* to suit Floyt.

"That's it! Keep it up!" Alacrity called back. Floyt smiled to himself. The two craft began the route, as marked, at something like twenty-five kph. Floyt didn't look about for Inst; he would be far to one side, pacing them and staying well clear. Even the most minute turbulence could have detrimental effects on the flimsy aircraft. For that reason, all aircraft in the region had been grounded for the duration of the race.

They passed over the first of the beacons set out by Weir staff members during the night, after the compromise route had been hammered out. Floyt caught a movement out of the corner of his eye. *Feather* was nearby. Dincrist and Kuss hunched over their handlebars, pedaling furiously, their propeller a blur. *Feather* pulled slightly ahead of *Thistle*.

Alacrity sought to increase the pace, shouting, "Don't watch them; I'll take care of that! Just pedal!"

"That's only a surge, Alacrity. It won't last long. Let them have the lead for now."

Alacrity thought that over as he pedaled, then complied. He held the pace, guiding them with skillful economy, loath to give up altitude for speed, since it might cost them dearly later on. Both broke into a light sweat.

Alacrity took a moment to spot First Councillor Inst, some distance starboard, aft, and below, cruising along in a standing position. The man really knew how to handle a grav-harness. He'd carefully taken up position so as to create no turbulence for the racers. Just then he was speaking into his commo headset.

Leery of the crosswinds at higher altitudes, the airbikes began the descent into a deep, winding, heavily forested river valley. Neither pilot spent much time searching for updrafts—risers. It was too wasteful of energy, altitude, and speed. Glancing back under his armpit, Floyt watched the first marker beacon disappear behind them.

They were sweating freely. The nacelle had grown hot and reeked of their perspiration. Floyt understood how such a cockpit had come to be referred to as a "nay-smell." Moisture began to fog the fuselage. They were buffeted by air currents; Alacrity fought the turbulence as they both pedaled harder. *Feather* was in the same dilemma.

Floyt pedaled more effectively than Alacrity; his cardiovascular and respiratory systems were more attuned to the work, and his muscles as well. Inst moved up close, one hand on the controls on his chest panel, the other holding the winch hook ready. The jagged tops of ice trees were floating past just beneath the undercarriage. But suddenly both ships hit an updraft, gaining a miraculous two and a half meters. Inst backed off.

"This is . . . a stupid sport," Alacrity panted. Floyt saved his breath. They were still thirty kilometers or so from Icarus Point, the finish line. After the forest would be an area dotted with thermal vents, where they could take on plenty of altitude if Alacrity could avoid getting a wing melted. Then, a salt-marsh delta, after which came Icarus Point. They had to husband their strength.

The light of the star Halidome was working its way down the valley walls. *Thistle*'s interior was like a steam bath, and her crew was losing moisture at an astounding rate. A tubular two-liter water blivet was mounted along the nacelle ceiling; Alacrity pulled down the extendable hose, took a sip without slowing, and passed it back. Floyt allowed himself a deep drink and let the hose snap back up into place.

They were pedaling at a cadence of ninety-five rpm. Alacrity seemed to be having trouble with the controls. Floyt asked what was wrong.

"Dincrist. Hitting his turbulence."

Floyt hadn't considered that problem. "Then we're going to have to pass him. Ready?" He pulled on his airmask, a simple arrangement connected by an overhead tube to a small air intake in *Thistle*'s nose.

"*Hey!*" Alacrity yelped. Floyt was already hard at work, pressing down with the ball of one foot, hauling up against his toe clip with the other. He was exerting himself at a near-maximum, *happy*. He whooped through his mask. Alacrity did his best to hold up his end.

Cadence climbed to one hundred. One hundred three. One hundred five. Alacrity felt a red-hot ice pick of pain in his right calf and didn't care, because *Thistle* was coming abreast of *Feather*, despite the frantic efforts of Dincrist and the Presbyter Kuss to hold their lead.

"See if you can pull in front of them," Floyt proposed in a muffled voice. "I've got my shorts lowered."

Alacrity didn't have the breath to find out if Floyt was serious; they both bore down.

Thistle drew into the lead and even gained a meter and a half of altitude, bringing them into the splendor of Halidome's sunlight. Alacrity gave a breathless cheer.

Floyt felt immortal. He pedaled on.

The valley broadened, and tributary valleys brought in runoff. Air currents here were much more active, but the airbikes hit no headwinds, and Alacrity was an excellent pilot. He eased up the strain on his right leg, working mostly with his left.

But the pedals seemed harder to work. He gave them a sudden burst of energy, but they resisted him. "Ho, are you okay?"

"Yes. Are you tired? I think I can handle things if you want to rest a bit."

"No, no. I thought *you* were causing the drag."

The crank axles moved as if they were in thickening glue. Floyt gave it everything he had. Things seemed to be going well for a moment, then the pedals again started to feel as if they were seizing up.

"Ho, it's not us," Alacrity called from the front saddle.

"I know," the Terran answered. "The pedals? Propeller?"

"Dunno. We can't stop to . . . look at 'em right now."

Thistle was losing way. *Feather* drew abreast, then passed her, Dincrist sneering at them.

"Alacrity, do you think—"

"What else? That *lowlife*!" Alacrity, winded, spared a few curses for the tycoon. Floyt suspected that the breakabout's anger had little to do with the Earthservice conditioning. This was a *race*.

The Terran pulled down his mask and leaned over to peer more closely at the power train. A new odor had begun to drift up from it, cutting through the sweat-fog.

"Alacrity, what's that I smell?"

The breakabout, pumping away madly, thighs and calves aching, perspiration blinding him, caught the odor.

"They gummed us up somehow!" He was fighting the turbulence of *Feather*'s backwash. "Something that . . . took a while to start working!"

Floyt wondered if someone other than Dincrist was responsible for the sabotage. Maska? Tiajo herself?

"Here comes Inst," Alacrity cried.

The First Councillor had altered his exoskeletal posture, skimming over to them like a swimmer. He held the winch hook in his hand. He spoke into his headset mike, but nothing was coming over Alacrity's commo button.

"Sweat must've gotten to it," the breakabout decided. He explained it to Inst with gestures. Dorraine's father gestured with his hook to the hoisting hook atop *Thistle* and looked at them questioningly.

Alacrity, spent, said, "What d'you think, Ho?"

The airbike was in a near-stall, and the pedals gave more resistance with each rotation. The ice trees waited below. "Maybe Tiajo will show us a little mercy, Alacrity. Or maybe we can prove sabotage."

"Yeah, that's true. You're right." Alacrity gestured, and Inst floated overhead to latch on. *Feather* was rounding a turn far ahead.

Thistle suddenly lurched up and forward, her wingtips bending down as Inst's grav-harness, set at maximum, took up her weight. Alacrity and Floyt relaxed from their exertions, morosely watching the forest fall away below.

"I've never had a race end like this," Floyt remarked dully.

"Sorry, Ho. We'd have won. You *had* it won for us."

"Thanks, Alacrity."

Inst banked them from the main valley into a side one, taking on more altitude. *Shortcut*, Alacrity registered absently, automatically piloting the airbike so as to make Inst's task simpler. At the speed the First Councillor was maintaining, they'd be back to Frostpile in no time. He started to think of schemes, pleas, emergency measures, and possible escape dodges.

But a short time later, Floyt interrupted his thoughts. "Alacrity, something's not right. Look at Halidome."

"What, stellar flares?" Even if Epiphany's sun were going nova, that wouldn't add much to their already catastrophic misfortune.

"No, no. I mean the direction. Inst is taking us *away* from Frostpile."

A little late, all of Alacrity's alarms went off. No wonder the commo button wasn't working; Inst had either sabotaged it or jammed its transmissions.

"He's behind it, isn't he?" the Terran asked in a composed voice.

"He's one of 'em, anyway."

"What do we do now?"

"I could release our hook, but he'd catch us in no time. He could either burn off our wings or force us down, hard." He scanned below; the land had opened up, and there were breaks in the forest. He saw a few places where he might be able to set *Thistle* down. The airbike required only a very short landing strip, and he had the emergency snare with its adhesive ribbons.

"I've got an idea, Ho."

"Don't bother telling me it's dangerous. I like it, whatever it is."

A few moments later, First Councillor Inst suddenly found himself shooting upward as *Thistle* released from his line. He regained control quickly, reeling in his cable and zooming down in pursuit.

The airbike didn't appear to be trying to escape him. Indeed, Alacrity was apparently fighting hard with his controls. With no propeller power and no updrafts, *Thistle* had a rather unfortunate sink rate. Inst neatly matched speeds, but the hoisting hook at the top of the fuselage remained in the open position. He couldn't reattach.

He deftly circled around for a look. Alacrity was out of his shoulder braces, trying to pilot and at the same time help Floyt with the hook release.

They noticed him. Alacrity hollered, "The hook's stuck open! It's broken!"

Suspicious, he came nearer. He'd never heard of such a thing, but then he hadn't dealt with airbikes very much. "Let me see! Get your hands away from it!" The tone in his voice brooked no disobedience; they were at his mercy. Steadying the ship with one hand, Inst pressed closer to the fuselage.

Alacrity nodded; Floyt eased back down, taking his hands from the hoist hook. It sprang closed, perfectly functional.

Inst's face was still clouding in anger when Alacrity, feet on the controls, whipped one shoulder brace out of its socket and rammed its open end through the fuselage at the First Councillor.

Most of the man's vital points were protected by the exoskeleton, helmet, vision enhancers, and commo headset, and so Alacrity aimed for his throat. But air currents and the minor perturbations of airbike and grav-harness made him miss. The tube plunged directly into the control panel on Inst's chest.

The tube was thin, to save on weight; its rim bit through the cover and into the mechanism's vitals, but crumpled. Violent energy eruptions spat and writhed; it was fortunate for Alacrity that the brace was made of a nonconducting composite.

At the same moment, Floyt punched his fist through the thin metalar, groping for Inst's blaster.

In a split second, Inst went one way—the exoskeleton reacting to his convulsion of surprise and the damage to it—and *Thistle* plummeted in the other, not a craft to be kept in trim for long under such circumstances.

Floyt, who hadn't managed to snag the pistol, now gripped his handlebar with one hand and tried to keep Alacrity in his saddle with the other, as the breakabout attempted to bring the ship under control. It may be that Floyt's toe clips and straps were the edge that saved them. Alacrity somehow righted *Thistle* long enough to get one shoulder into the remaining brace and toes into their clips.

"Pedal for your damn life, Ho!"

Whatever had been done to their power train, Floyt thought it had been alleviated, in some measure, by the train's respite while the airbike had been towed by grav-harness. Either that, or Floyt's fear and desperation had allowed him to tap hidden reservoirs of strength. He was up, getting the pedals spinning, pulling so hard that he bent the handlebars upward.

Slowly the prop began to pick up speed, though Alacrity held the dive and *Thistle*'s wings threatened to snap off. Wind streamed through the holes they'd made in the fuselage, causing drag, widening them.

All at once, Inst was coming at them again. Alacrity regretted that the ambush hadn't worked. Still, it hadn't been a complete failure; the panel was smoking, and Inst's erratic flight indicated serious damage to it.

It was plain that he could no longer tow them. They waited for him to incinerate them, or burn the wings off. Instead, listing badly, he seized the end of the starboard wing and rocked it. *Thistle* wobbled and shuddered; the two heard the wing joints creak. Inst could quite easily rip it off.

They got the message. Alacrity let Inst put him into a bank—gentle, but sharp by airbike standards.

On the new course, Alacrity said, "Wherever he wants us to go, it won't be healthy." He dipped the canard, and the airbike went into what was for her a maximum dive. "Get ready to give it everything you've got, Ho."

"The cranksets are seizing up again, Alacrity."

Inst wavered closer, hollering, "Don't force me to hurt you, Fitzhugh!" He gave the wingtip an emphatic slap. Alacrity held the dive. Inst began pushing upward on the underside of the starboard wing. Alacrity rolled away left. The entire airframe groaned and vibrated.

As the breakabout had hoped, Inst came at them again, clumsily, in his damaged suit. The Alacrity pulled up, hitting the wing spoilers, air-braking to a full stall. Inst overshot. In an insane, almost slow-motion maneuver, Alacrity had the First Counsillor below the fuselage. He hit the emergency landing switch.

The deployment surge blew apart the envelope along *Thistle*'s underbelly. Adhesive landing ribbons sprang out in all directions, many of them hitting Inst, entangling him like a bug.

He flailed, trapping himself further. He could no longer manipulate his chest controls. His erratic movements yanked and pulled at the airbike; its airframe began to come apart.

Thinking, *We should've let him take us, I guess,* Alacrity fought to keep the ship on something like an even keel. There was no selecting a spot; they would come down where they would.

Epiphany spun at them. Inst's thrashings pulled them every which way. Floyt braced himself against his handlebars and watched the First Councillor's desperate expression until a snapping of exotic materials announced the tearing loose of the starboard wing.

CHAPTER 15

THE GAME'S AFOOT

FLOYT YOWLED, AND ALACRITY OFFERED HIS SOUL TO THE
Infinite on very easy terms.

An instant later the breakabout realized they weren't quite
falling and saw why. Inst was held fast to the starboard side
of the undercarriage, providing just enough lift to keep
Thistle from simply dropping like guano. As it was, they
spiraled in.

For one mad, frozen instant, Floyt was looking into Inst's
eyes through the fuselage. Dorraine's father was hollering
into his commo headset, but in his face there was only
surrender.

They bashed down on rocky ground, halfway up the side
of the valley, the canard hitting first. Its pole snapped in
two and was driven back, passing through the water blivet
and out the top of the ship. Water showered over them as
Thistle slammed down.

Inst impacted with a ghastly crump of metal, rock, flesh,
and bone. He managed something halfway between a scream
and a groan, cut short almost as soon as it began. The airbike
bounced, jarring, the pedaling frame bending and buckling.

239

Thistle's nose hit as Inst's exoskeleton jarred up against the undercarriage, jolting Floyt and Alacrity from their saddles, slamming both riders forward. With the handlebars to hang on to, Floyt fared better than the breakabout. He felt his shoulders wrench and his left hip jolt against the handlebar as he narrowly missed dashing his crotch against its stem. His feet burst from toe clips and straps. He couldn't stop his face from grazing off Alacrity's lower back.

Alacrity broke the control stem off and bent his remaining shoulder brace, his feet leaving his pedals. His head bashed through the metalar before him, millimeters to the left of the slender hag-oak sapling that stopped the airbike.

Meteorlike specks of light whirled before Floyt. The Earther felt warm, sticky blood on his face, and he heard himself groaning and panting raggedly. The breakabout sounded even worse. Wiping at the blood, Floyt hissed then sobbed in pain and realized dazedly that his nose was broken. He looked down to see that *Thistle*'s ruin—and one of his feet—rested on the torn remains of Inst and his demolished grav-harness.

Floyt turned his eyes away and, insulated from nausea by shock, got out, "How badly . . . are you hurt, Alacrity?"

The breakabout was trying weakly to extricate himself, to little effect. "I think . . . I think I broke a rib or two." He grimaced. "And it feels like my leg's bleeding. You hurting anywhere?"

"Everywhere. Don't move."

Floyt managed to hunch forward and did his best to check his companion. Alacrity swore through clenched teeth as Floyt probed gently. The breakabout was resting on a jumble of wreckage, including the control stem and the bentback hag-oak sapling.

"I think you're right," the Terran told him. "I don't think you should be moved."

"But I . . . hate the view here, Hobart."

"Stop talking. Somebody's bound to come looking for us."

"Ho, we're kilometers off the racecourse, remember?"

"Yes, but Inst was using his headset before the crash. There might be aid any time now."

Alacrity stopped panting and said urgently, "Get Inst's gun. Hurry!"

"But Alacrity—"

"I said get it! Inst was headed someplace in particular. That means he had somebody waiting for him, and that's who he was calling. Now will you get his blaster?"

"It's no good, Alacrity. I saw him drop it after you snared him. I guess he was going to try to burn himself free, but he lost his grip on it when *Thistle* yanked him around."

"Then we *really* can't stay here." Alacrity began to stir weakly. "Besides Inst's little helpers, there'll be things around here sniffing after the blood. And we're a lot lower on the food chain than we were a little while ago."

In the end, Floyt simply tore away most of what was left of the airframe. It came away easily, but the task was still difficult for Floyt in his woozy condition. He got a shoulder under Alacrity's good side, his right, and did his best to move him delicately. Alacrity yipped with pain anyway. To make things even worse, they were compelled to step on Inst to get clear of the wreckage.

Floyt set Alacrity down and went back to check the jellied corpse of their attacker. Floyt had never seen a human being in anything like this condition. It looked unreal, something phonied up for a museum exhibit. There wasn't much of Inst left intact except that awful, staring face. The exoskeleton was in pieces, the commo headset destroyed. Floyt had to pause twice in his search to retch.

The instruments mounted on *Thistle*'s control stem had been reduced to chaff, and the medikit had virtually exploded on impact, but the Earther scavenged some tension bandages, an irrigation cannister, and a coagulant aerosol. There was also a packet of styrettes of various kinds; for an instant he recalled the fight in the corridor on Earth, a lifetime ago.

He sat for a moment, numbly wiping from his hands what he could of the blood. Alacrity groaned, "I just can't figure this out. I mean, *Inst. Why?*"

Floyt barely heard him at first. He could only think of how much wild country lay around them. He was wrestling sluggishly with the many unknowns bearing on their death or survival. How quickly would it be realized that Inst and *Thistle* were missing? How large a search would be mounted, and with what vehicles? What could the two expect in the way of weather, predators, complications from their injuries, and exposure?

And Inst's hypothetical cohorts were another factor entirely.

But gradually Alacrity's question penetrated. Inst. Something about him had set Floyt to thinking back at Frostpile. He shook his head, finding it difficult to string two thoughts together.

Alacrity hummed loudly, briefly, in pain. Then he nose-sang, "*Ning-a-ning!* Nice flying, Alacrity! (A shame about the landing!) *A-ning!*"

Floyt snorted laughter and blood. "Let me see—isn't one of the first survival rules to stay with the downed aircraft?"

"Varies with the circumstances. In this case, there's not much aircraft to stay *with*."

"So what do we do, Alacrity?"

"Crash dieting combined with a program of rigorous exercise: walking."

They both squinted at Halidome, calculating direction. The Terran was surprised to see that it was still early morning. Floyt began to clean himself up as best he could with the medical supplies. He wiped the blood from his face and stopped the bleeding of his swollen and swelling nose. Even the light pressure of the irrigation spray and coagulant mist made his eyes tear. Then he cleaned and closed Alacrity's injury.

"Nice break you've got there," Alacrity commented admiringly. "You're going to have a real bump in your graph."

"It's like trying to see around the back of a hoverbus. Shall I bandage your ribs?"

"They don't bind cracked ribs anymore, Ho. What's the Earthservice teach you people?"

"The wisdom of traveling by ground conveyance. Uh, what about Inst's body? Should we bury it, do you think?"

"For all we know, on Agora they save their corpses under bell jars. You feel like digging a grave with your hands? Or collecting rocks for a cairn? Or just bundling his leftovers along with us? . . . Didn't think so."

"But how are we going to prove what happened?"

Alacrity considered that. "Nice catch. We'll just have to do it some other way." They heard a distant sound, something between a predatory scream and a siren.

"Because," Alacrity went on, "if we wait around much longer, we'll end up with two one-way tickets on the Alimentary Local."

The Terran assisted the wincing breakabout to his feet. Small, six-winged flyers were already circling overhead. After a few steps, Alacrity said, "It's not too bad. I think I can make it." He squinted off in their intended direction.

Floyt felt a bit woozy. Alacrity was swaying a little. There was no way for them to know if they had infections, concussions, or internal injuries, and little or nothing they could do about them anyway. Floyt carefully set the tip of a styrette to his shoulder and gave himself an intramuscular injection of stimulant. Alacrity made no objection when the Terran did the same for him.

"We'll have to travel downwind as much as we can," the younger man said. "We can try to have a tree within running distance, but we'd better steer clear of heavy undergrowth except in a real emergency."

He sighed. They knew only the barest minimum about Epiphany's wildlife. It looked like an easy day for getting killed. *Thistle*'s frame was useless, so Floyt laboriously broke two branches off a fallen supplejack tree for use as staffs and weapons.

Alacrity pointed toward where he thought Frostpile was. "Helluva slog. I wish we had something tougher than cycling shoes." He thought longingly of his ranger boots. "Have you done much hiking?"

"A bit. Would you care to hear a marching song?"

"I don't know if I'm up to it."

"How about a trudging song?" As they started, he began through his inflated, livid mask of a face:

> *"Oh, I've got a mule and her name is Sal,*
> *Fifteen years on the Erie Canal . . ."*

He was soon too short of breath to sing. They hadn't gone very far before the predator appeared.

They'd begun by walking fifty paces, then resting. Both felt better, if a little drifty, as they began moving and the injections took hold. They increased the quota to one hundred paces.

Floyt spied a patch of spore bulbs like those he'd seen some of the gillies using to check wind direction. He tugged one free and punched a small hole in it. As the pair slowly descended toward the stream running through the valley, he occasionally squirted a smoky stream of spores into the air, watching its drift.

At first they intended to ford the tributary and walk the easier bank back to the river and the race course, but even from a distance they could see that the green, silty water crashed and foamed off the rocks in its watercourse, rushing headlong, practically a river in its own right.

They halted on the slope, searching for a spot to cross. "The shape we're in, that stuff'll knock us over as soon as we're in above our arches," Alacrity said as he surveyed the many spots where green water became white. "And it doesn't look like it gets any better downstream."

"Well, upstream's the wrong direction altogether, Alacrity. And at least if we stay on this side and follow the—"

He was cut off short as a hair-raising scream resounded from the ridge above them. They looked upslope as something slinked from the undergrowth and reached the airbike wreckage in one fluid motion. Floyt's fleeting impression was of a mottled blur of flailing, whipping tentacles, slender, muscular legs and body, and wide jaws—three of them—surrounding a circular mouth with a long, curling, bifurcated tongue and rows of spiky teeth.

The creature seized Inst's remains at once, flinging aside a few scraps of *Thistle*. It fed loudly, gnawing and lapping, snapping and crushing bones and sucking the marrow, its tentacles stuffing its mouth with incredible speed.

"Fangster!" Alacrity yelled. "Must've smelled all the carrion from the hunt." Usually the creatures kept to the high mountains. "Reef said those things are always hungry. We've got to get out of here. What's left of Inst sure isn't going to keep it busy for long."

The fangster was holding up an unidentifiable part of the First Councillor with some of its whiplashing tentacles, spreading and slitting it with others in a gruesome parody of dissection, stripping away flesh with its jaws and tongue. It was gorging on every available morsel.

No tree worthy of the name was within reach, so they started to stumble downslope and downstream, trying to get to open ground. Soon the fangster was making occasional screams again.

"Sounds like he's getting ready for the main course," Alacrity grunted. The pain in his side kept him in an agonized crouch as he trotted. The two descended to the tumbling stream at breakneck pace, barely saving themselves, time after time, with their staffs. They dislodged stones and soil and raised dust, slipping and skidding, risking a fall or a fractured ankle. They were lashed and scraped by undergrowth.

The fangster's cries were much nearer as they broke through to a bank of stones in all colors, most of them rounded and smooth. But no boulder was big enough to offer refuge. The water crashed and slammed against the rocks, throwing up a constant drizzle.

"There's no way we'll outrun it," Alacrity admitted. "We'll have to try to drive it off, and hope that Inst took the edge off its appetite." He squatted, laying his staff aside, and palmed a rock, weighing it in his hand.

Floyt doubted their ability to deal with a fangster using sticks and stones at the best of times, much less in their current condition. "What about fording?"

Alacrity gazed at the roiling water again. "We'd get knocked over and get our brains mashed. Maybe as a last resort."

"No, look." Floyt quickly selected a disc of rock. He lifted it with a grunt, offering it to the breakabout. "Take it! It'll help you keep your footing!"

Alacrity was about to object when the fangster's hunting cry changed his mind. He dropped the throwing rock and hollered in agony as Floyt made the transfer. The breakabout tried to bear as much of the ballast's weight as possible with his left arm, on his uninjured side. Still, it was a moment-to-moment battle not to give in to the torment and drop his burden.

Floyt had seized a blocky stone. Now they eased into the water, trying to steady one another as much as they could. It was paralyzingly cold, a snow-fed stream.

Their cycling shoes gave them only marginal purchase on the sluiced rocks of the streambed, and the rushing current hit their upper bodies like an avalanche. Clutching their weights, buffeted and pounded, they struggled in deeper, and deeper still, wondering if they'd freeze before they made it across.

Alacrity took a misstep and nearly went under. The Earther, trying to keep one eye on his companion, was nearly drawn into a whirlpool, then turned his ankle, but managed to hobble on. Alacrity somehow contrived to hang on to his boulder with the arm on his good side and use the other to pull Floyt through, though the torment of it brought a shriek from him.

Swirling at waist level, the water kept them tilting and wavering, fighting desperately for balance, warring for each step. They heard a snarling wail behind them—the fangster at the bank. They didn't dare turn to look. A denizen of the peaks, the thing had struck Alacrity as being almost spindly. He hoped that meant it had no stomach for a swift, cold bath.

Floyt stepped into another hole and went under, floundering and dropping his ballast. Alacrity released his own and lurched for the Earther. They were spun like leaves, and both expected to be pounded to shreds. But fickle waters spun and bucked them toward the far bank, and Floyt was able to grab a large rock sticking above the foam. Alacrity felt his feet touch bottom. In moments they were dragging one another onto dry land.

They collapsed, blue-lipped, exhausted, and shivering uncontrollably, teeth chattering. On the far side of the stream the fangster scuttled back and forth, watching them with eyes like green flames, whining and spitting at them, the quills of its tail standing out stiffly. Nevertheless, it made no effort to test the water temperature.

"However in creation did you think of using ballast?" Alacrity asked when he could talk again.

"I read about it. In *Skagway Scanlon, King of the Klondike*."

"Penny dreadful?"

"Dime novel." Floyt considered the raging, frustrated fangster. "In Skagway's case it was a Kodiak bear, of course."

"I have to start doing more reading. I really do."

At that moment a sound drew their gaze to the head of the valley. Two lean, heavily armed air cutters were bearing down on them while a third flew high cover. The fangster snarled defiance at them, then slid away into the brush.

"How do we know they're real?" Floyt remembered that Inst probably had confederates somewhere out in the Epiphanian wilds.

"Doesn't matter who they are," Alacrity chattered. "They've got us. I'm not so sure who I'd prefer anyway."

Floyt stopped shivering for a moment. "What do you mean?"

"We killed Inst, remember? Or at least got him killed."

Floyt went back to shivering.

The Invincible rescue team that piled out of the cutters turned out to be the authentic item, though. Paramedics treated them while guards established a perimeter and the major in charge of the detail questioned them. His expression became increasingly grim as he listened. He dispatched one of the grounded cutters to search for Inst's remains. As soon as the two survivors had been seen to, they were hustled aboard the remaining cutter under close guard.

On the way back to Frostpile, one of the paramedics asked Floyt if he'd mind answering a few questions about Earth. She was doing research in her spare time, hoping to draw up a family tree.

CHAPTER 16

RELATIVE VALUES

"DEATH," REDLOCK RULED LESS THAN AN HOUR LATER IN Dame Tiajo's chambers. Several of the surveillance drones that were floating near the ceiling dipped closer, prepared to carry out his will on the spot.

Thistle's wreckage and the remains of Inst and his harness—what little there was—had been found and brought along as evidence. Mercifully, none of it had been trotted out. The only other significant delay had been for a brusque cleanup, not for the sake of the two survivors but to avoid offending Epiphany's nobles. After a rather cursory bioscan, the medics had decided that the companions didn't require immediate attention. Surrounded by Celestials and Invincibles, they'd found themselves before an impromptu board of inquiry. It was an hour to noon.

"Death for both of them," Redlock reiterated. Ignoring the obedient drones, he held out his hand to one of the Invincible officers. The man looked questioningly at Tiajo, hand on his sidearm.

"For defending ourselves?" Floyt asked quietly, his voice

sounding strange to him, coming as it did through his swollen face and broken nose. Both his eyes were blackening.

"For murder!" Redlock shot a quick look at his wife. Dorraine was still off to one side, not weeping but eyes downcast, as if no one else were there. Near her, at the vast viewpane that showed much of Frostpile, Maska stood, a calming presence even though he said nothing but only watched, sad-eyed.

The Severeemish were there, almost at attention. If they were inclined to gloat, Floyt noted, they didn't dare show it.

"That's for you to decide, isn't it?" Alacrity asked the grandam. Tiajo, seated, was plainly trying to collect her thoughts and composure. It was clear that, while she seldom crossed wills with Redlock and held a great deal of affection for him, she had her reservations on this subject.

"Defended yourselves? Against *Inst*?" Redlock's scarred cheek tugged with amusement. "A lie, right on the face of it. Why would he threaten two lowlies like you?"

Alacrity was caught up in the same question; he hadn't figured it out himself. But Hobart Floyt replied evenly, "Governor Redlock, you'll have to ask your wife that question." The breakabout's mouth fell open.

Redlock's face went bloodless; he made to take the Invincible's gun, permission or no. But a sound escaped the queen of Agora, of resignation and despair, but not a sob—Floyt couldn't picture her ever crying.

"If you don't speak up, Highness," the Terran went on, "you'll forfeit my life and Alacrity's too." Dangers and fear and hardship had put an unswerving candor into him. Alacrity could see his companion tremble, but his voice didn't.

Redlock was listening again; Floyt's accusation had hit some target.

"Did . . . did my father really try to *kill* you?" she asked at last. The stately carriage was now slumped, the superlative features infinitely sad. Redlock stood rooted and mute.

"I don't believe so. He could've done that easily," Floyt said into the silence. "But he meant to keep us from getting back to Frostpile. It would have been enough to force us down where subordinates were waiting, wouldn't it? Until the Willreading and the Thorn Cup were over?" He didn't sound accusatory; he was gentle, consoling. "No, I don't believe he would have killed us under any circumstances."

Dorraine squared her shoulders and turned to Floyt, clear-eyed, with the barest smile of gratitude. "Thank you."

"But . . . why?" Tiajo asked. No one could remember her ever having been so subdued. She adored Dorraine almost as much as she did Redlock.

The queen assembled her courage. Just as Floyt was about to answer for her, to spare her, she spoke. "I'm not . . . I wasn't his daughter. Not the daughter of his body." Her chin came up. "But the daughter of his heart. And he was the only father I ever knew. We loved each other very much."

Redlock's hands were dangling at his sides now. He moved to his wife, and Alacrity silently let out his breath. Dorraine threw herself into Redlock's arms. "What will happen now?" she asked, looking at the envoys.

The complex system of allegiances and fealties sworn by the Severeemish, in part through the queen of Agora, had been couched in terms of blood and lineage. Now it seemed that they were null and void.

"We kept the secret for a very long time," Dorraine began slowly. Seven Wars and Sortie-Wolf listened, unblinking. "We kept it from . . . from everyone. Inst—my father, if you will indulge me—"

"I don't care," Redlock broke in. He told the towering Severeemish, "She's my wife, queen of Agora. That's the way it'll remain."

Peace and war hung in the balance. But unexpectedly, Theater General Sortie-Wolf inquired gently, "May we know the circumstances?"

"He found me during the fourth year of the Turmoils, after his . . . after Dorraine died in a concentration camp on Rawbone. Without Dorraine, there'd be no succession. He and Dorraine hadn't been recognized by anyone for their real selves; you know that. He chose me because I looked like Dorraine. I was the right age too."

She glanced out the viewpane at Frostpile. "I don't remember much about my own family, except that I was separated from them."

The dark eyes flashed at Redlock again. "I'd been alone for a long time. I don't know how many camps I'd been in. I don't know why I wasn't liquidated. Inst took care of me and taught me what I had to do."

"You were an apt pupil," Seven Wars commented.

"And then one day the warships came." She squeezed Redlock's hand. "And we were liberated. Then you put me on the throne, my only love. Everything was chaos, back then. Inst altered records and identification data. He destroyed or altered files, family holoportraits, and all the rest. He made me Dorraine in every particular."

"Except one," Floyt maintained. "You didn't have the allergen immunity."

She nodded slowly. "I took treatments in secret over the years. Nothing on Agora could have betrayed me. But no one can be immunized to every allergen."

"The Thorn Cup!" Alacrity blurted. Everyone saw it now. Mimicking flora from Severeemish worlds, it would very likely incorporate an allergen or toxin with which her immunizations couldn't cope. The woman they all still thought of as Dorraine would have run the risk of exposure if she'd agreed to accept the Cup.

"But there was that old family stricture. The idea of using it came to my father when Director Weir took a turn for the worse. And so I could avoid the Cup after all." She sounded bewildered. "And so it still doesn't make sense. Why should he need to have you out of the way, Hobart Floyt?"

"Your father modified the wording of the stricture," he said quietly. "If he didn't tell you that, it was probably to keep from burdening you. And you told it to your husband and Dame Tiajo in good faith. Then Inst discovered that I'd been included in the will at the last moment."

Alacrity thought of the conversation just before the air-bike launch; Inst had heard Dorraine misquote the stricture in Alacrity's presence, and that probably deepened the First Councillor's resolve. Of course, by then the plan to get Hobart Floyt, amateur historian and genealogist, out of the way must already have been made. With the Severeemish looking for any excuse to revoke their fealty, it had been an absolute necessity.

It had only taken a bit of luck and a certain amount of guidance on Inst's part to bring about an opportunity to put Floyt out of the picture—Inst, who'd forestalled a duel with mention of a race; Inst, who'd spoken out so strongly for reason and prudence, making sure that Tiajo would favor him and the contestants compromise on him as race escort.

"Your father could've killed us, easy as could be, Dorraine," Alacrity said. "But he didn't. He didn't even try."

"All that is well and good," Defense Minister Seven Wars conceded. "But it is clear that a lie has been foisted off on the Severeemish." He was now at rigid attention, addressing the queen. "Weir had us swear fealty to the daughter of Inst, a woman of royal blood. With all deference, madam, you are not that woman."

Floyt and Alacrity braced themselves; the room was still. In moments word could leap forth faster than light, and war would dismantle Weir's lifework.

"Of course, she *does* rule Agora," Sortie-Wolf pointed out, to end the silence. He turned to Seven Wars. "Father, do you think that part of the oath might apply? A mere technicality, of course..."

"Of course," concurred Seven Wars, fingering his chin

with steel-hard nails. "And another: Inst referred to her as his daughter, not just once, but on many occasions. Not a formal adoption proceeding, perhaps, but a strong point of usage."

There were puzzled glances and knotted brows all around the chamber. Seven Wars and Sortie-Wolf were enjoying themselves enormously.

"Sophistry, perhaps," the son warned.

"But the sort our lawgivers dearly love to haggle over," the father averred.

"And just what are you both driving at?" Tiajo demanded.

They gazed at her innocently. "Why, that there must be a reappraisal of the Severeemish oath of fealty."

"You know that I'll never let you break away from the Domain," Redlock said.

"Oh? And do you think you can defeat the Severeemish a second time? We are stronger now than ever."

Redlock would've spoken to that, but Tiajo got there first. "You haven't answered my question. Why this talk of lawgivers and technicalities? And reappraisals?"

Sortie-Wolf smiled ferociously. "The Severeemish *have* grown stronger since coming into your sphere. And prospered as well. Why should we wish to break away? We've fought for you, and fought well; that was our promise. But now it's time for fealty to end, to be replaced by a true alliance between free and equal participants."

Seven Wars produced a data capsule. "Our lawgivers have devoted some thought to the issue. Recent developments"—he nodded to Dorraine—"seem to make this an appropriate time to present their exegesis."

Just happened to have it along, hmm? Alacrity scoffed to himself.

The minister gave the capsule to Tiajo while Floyt thought, *When, in the course of Severeemish events . . .*

"You were waiting for something like this!" Alacrity exclaimed. These stiff-necked, legalistic, surprisingly loyal people plainly would never dream of asking that an oath be dissolved without some grounds.

"Boy, have *we* been used." Floyt shook his head in disbelief.

"Ah, not altogether," Sortie-Wolf replied. "You managed to bring a great measure of trouble upon yourselves." To Tiajo he said, "Please consider carefully what we have said. We would be steadfast and faithful friends. You know the worth of the Severeemish word."

The old woman nodded, lips pursed in thought. "I've never had cause to doubt it." Her eyes moved to Alacrity and Floyt. "The memorial ceremony will begin in a few hours. Go and prepare, both of you. And see that you mention nothing that's happened here, or I'll show you how difficult life can be."

"Hey, but what about—" was all Alacrity got out. By now, all Tiajo had to do was beetle her brows, and he shut up. As the two made a fast exit, Floyt noticed that Seven Wars and Sortie-Wolf were bowing low before Dorraine, rendering formal condolences for the loss of Inst. He hoped that was a good sign.

CHAPTER 17

BEYOND THE DREAMS OF AVARICE

THE HOUSEHOLD PHYSICIANS WHO TREATED THEM WERE
the same ones who'd seen to Alacrity after the buzzball
game; the doctors allowed as how they were beginning to
feel right at home in the suite. As Sintilla gamely attempted
to pry information out of them, Floyt reflected on what
unfortunate shape he and Alacrity would have been in after
only a few short days if not for the excellence of Frostpile's
medical care.

The breakabout interrupted his treatment periodically for
attempts to contact Heart. The result was always the same:
the communications terminal in the suite of rooms shared
by the Nonpareil and her father had been set to refuse all
incoming calls.

"I'm going over there," Alacrity announced at last, struggling to rise.

"No!" Sintilla warned.

"*Hell*, no!" Floyt seconded. "Tiajo's mad enough as it
is. We don't need any more trouble today, Alacrity!" The
breakabout let a doctor push him back down onto his bed.

"What *is* the grandam so angry about?" Sintilla pressed.

"Would you two lugs have the decency to play fair? Haven't I always let you in on the dirt around here? Now, I know that you didn't finish the race, and Inst had an accident or something, but I can't get one straight answer out of anybody. How'm I supposed to make a living, fellas?"

"Have you considered a career in commoscreen canvassing?" Alacrity inquired sweetly.

She made an obscene gesture at him.

"We truly aren't at liberty to tell you, Tilla," Floyt said gravely. "It wouldn't be fair to ... someone who deserves better. But it will all come out soon, I expect; then we'll tell you everything we can, I promise you."

"You better," she grumbled, rising and moving for the door. "I'm still counting on you guys to make me rich."

Exhaustion and the effects of their medical treatment combined to make them sleep the afternoon away. As a result, they had to rush in order to make Weir's funeral on time.

They'd put aside their own clothing for the flowing, togalike robes required by the ceremony, and soft tabi that eased their abused feet. Floyt had resumed his Inheritor's belt.

Since they were about to penetrate one of Frostpile's inner most sanctums, they were routed to a new checkpoint and scanned with weapons detectors and telltales. As they were boarding a special corridor tram on which Endwraithe, the Spican banker, was already seated, they heard a commotion behind them.

"Good luck, boys! I'll see you later!" Sintilla, her way blocked by an Invincible, was waving to them.

The tram was starting to move. "We'll tell you all about it!" Alacrity called to her. Endwraithe was lost in thought. The two fell silent for the duration of the ride.

Following a complex path, the tram gradually wound its way to the highest point in Frostpile, the top of a spire that spiraled like a unicorn's horn. They passed guards and patrols, hovering drones and surveillance pickups, and still more weapons detectors and monitoring emplacements.

At the spire's summit was a spacious mirador, within it a formal garden. All three disembarked from the tram. An Invincible officer and his squad, in dashing, resplendent dress uniforms, scanned them yet again. They were then admitted.

Only those who wore the Inheritor's belt and their invited companions were present, fewer than thirty in all. The many bequests and legacies going to groups and organizations would be taken care of later; the staff and household, along with certain other subordinates, would receive their recognition separately. But all those mentioned by name in the great man's last will and testament were present. It came to Floyt then what company he was keeping.

All wore robes, and Inheritors their belts. Stare Skill was there with Brother Grimm; Kid Risk, Sir John, and Dincrist had all come without escort, and spoke together now. Endwraithe went to join them. Alacrity restrained himself from confronting Heart's father; it could only hurt his own situation and threaten Floyt's.

Admiral Maska was standing by himself. The stoop-shouldered Srillan twitched his long snout and made a solemn, shallow bow of greeting to the two. Tiajo, Redlock, and Dorraine were near the center of the garden, conversing quietly with the Severeemish.

The governor saw them and walked over. "The forensic team examined the clothing Inst wore at the sportsfest. They found traces of the epoxy that was used to seal the game's computer," he confided.

"Careless," Alacrity commented cooly. "It was probably a spur-of-the-moment thing." He hoped everybody was properly impressed by and grateful for his clement attitude.

"We also found out that he'd procured an ampule of an Agoran virus some time back," Redlock said. "Nothing lethal, but it would've immobilized an unprotected person for quite a while."

"That's probably what your little playmate on Earth was trying to get you to sample, Ho," Alacrity concluded.

"I suppose if you insist on an investigation, my wife would accommodate you," Redlock informed them, jaw set.

"No. No need for that," Floyt assured him. Alacrity withheld his own opinion. Redlock looked relieved.

A deep tone sounded through the garden. Halidome was gone, and a gorgeous red dusk had settled.

"If you wish to pay last respects, you've only a little time," the governor told them. He bowed, then went to rejoin his wife.

On a crystal bier near the center of the garden reposed the body of the Defender, Director Caspahr Weir, under the blue-white aura of a preservation field. The bier rested on a piece of apparatus strange to both of them, though Alacrity saw it was some sort of projector.

They had their first glimpse of the man whose actions had thrown them together and drawn them across the light-years. He was unremarkable, even in the uniform of a supreme commander. He wore only one decoration, a medallion with nineteen jeweled starbursts on it.

He was small, a good deal shorter than Floyt, and lean into the bargain. He'd accepted natural aging; his face was networked with lines of care and years. The hairs on his head were white, few, and threadlike. His hands, clasped across his middle, were in embroidered military gauntlets, but their gnarled frailty could still be seen.

"He looks so tired," was what Floyt found himself saying. "So very *used up*. Doesn't he, Alacrity?"

Alacrity agreed. He bade the old man in a murmur, "Sleep well, old-timer."

"And thanks," Floyt blurted.

Alacrity turned to him. "Thanks for what, Ho?"

Floyt shrugged, trying to pin it down for himself. For

being compelled to leave his homeworld, practically thrown out? For being placed in lethal danger? For an inheritance that was still an enigma? But there'd been star travel, too, and the Sockwallet Outfit; the grandeur of Frostpile and the exhilaration when *Thistle* showed her prop to *Feather*.

"For everything," Floyt decided.

Another of the deep tones echoed through Frostpile. Minister Seven Wars moved to a large, hand-carved planter in the center of the garden. Its decorations were the grotesque battle symbols and gargoyle masks of the Severeemish. Seven Wars began working at the base of the Thorn Cup.

In keeping with the Usages, the Cup was one of those nurtured in the innermost courts at the Holy Bastion on Desideratum, which was also called Severeem Prime. It had begun life as a beautiful beaker plant, with scalloped, bell-shaped blossom upturned, veined and tinted with every color imaginable.

It had been wound with a rider vine. The parasitic vine had become one with the beaker plant and had begun feeding off and ingeniously mimicking other plants, seeds, and spores it contacted.

Once the Severeemish had drunk the Thorn Cup as a test of sincere grief and bravery, and the worthiness to inherit or succeed. The Cup had often been lethal. Nowadays, drinking a Thorn Cup entailed only a certain unpleasantness. But the gardens of the Severeemish were always abundant with the herbs and flowers, molds and other vegetation they bred; an individual's reaction to any particular Thorn Cup was unpredictable.

Seven Wars parted the beaker plant's stem and the rider vine wrapped round it with fingers like metal talons. He ignored the dappling and bright warning colorations, and the triangular, oily blue leaves imitative of a keepaway.

From the vine dangled small pods containing spores copied by the rider from cloudscrub. Wheeze-moss clung to it too, and ersatz chokeberries. Sortie-Wolf handed his father a large, highly polished flask made from a jet-black tusk and crowned with a cuspstone cap and stopper of translucent beige. Even though the flask and its contents had been minutely examined, a detector drone, like a miniature mantaray, closed in overhead, aromatics sampler and optical surveillance pickup extended. The Severeemish were neither surprised nor offended; their hierarchy, too, had its intrigues and assassins.

Seven Wars held the flowering chalice without concern, unmindful of contact with the molds and leaves. He charged it with a full measure of syrupy green liquid. The minister raised the Cup to Weir and, as pourer, took the first sip.

The rest of the Inheritors were gathering around. Seven Wars held the Cup out to Tiajo, ignoring the oily blue keepaway leaves that brushed his knuckles and the back of his leathery paw.

The old woman took it carefully and held it in trembling hands. She raised the vessel to her late brother, then sipped. She sneezed and spilled a few drops as she moved it away from herself.

Redlock was quick to take the Cup from her as Tiajo sneezed again and her eyes brimmed over. But Floyt saw that they weren't simply allergy tears; her shoulders shook, and Redlock motioned aside for the moment a physician who would have offered her an eye-mist dispenser.

Redlock's breath rasped a little as he lifted the Cup to Weir; his skin wasn't as thick or leathery as that of a Severeemish; the keepaways immediately raised white welts. Dorraine was still off to one side, watching. Maska held out his hand; the governor passed the Cup to the admiral.

Maska's sensitive snout began to sniffle and run, and he too sneezed. His Srillan physiology was sufficiently like a human's that his eyes began to water and swell shut.

Dincrist, whose turn was next, held the Cup with elaborate wariness and a distinct lack of reverence. He took a deep breath and held it while he stole a quick sip. It was an ignominious performance, and Floyt thought he detected scorn on Tiajo's face between sneezes, but Dincrist showed no adverse effects.

The Cup continued its round. Household physicians moved in to attend those who'd already drunk. Two showed signs of anaphylaxis, requiring antishock and adrenaline injections. Hives were treated, and abrupt lymphatic swelling, agonizingly itchy eyes, and nasal passages were soothed and sneezing stopped.

Stare Skill's draught had her short of breath, the air making noise in her chest. Brother Grimm helped insure that the Cup didn't fall; no one took exception. Stare Skill finished the ritual, and Seven Wars refilled the chalice. Grimm supported Stare Skill as the xenologist inhaled a dilator-decongestant-antihistamine. The Observance went on.

When the Cup reached Floyt, all eyes were still with it as Dorraine was the only other Inheritor who had yet to drink. With a mental shrug, Floyt took the Cup in both hands and raised it to the funeral bier and its burden. The draught was bitter and sour and thick, but somehow invigorating, quickening.

Dorraine walked to Floyt, taking the Cup without caution. After lifting it to Weir, she drank deeply, inhaling the pollen afterward, running her hands over leaves and mold.

She handed the drained Cup back to Seven Wars. She showed no allergic reaction of any kind.

Floyt supposed that the immunization treatments she'd received over the years, plus her own natural immunities, had protected her. That was the rational explanation. But he found himself thinking, *Who knows? Maybe she's got Agoran royal blood in her. Wouldn't that be a good joke on all of us?*

A hand on his shoulder drew his attention to a grinning Alacrity. "Better let him give you an inhaler," the breakabout said, indicating a doctor with a jerk of his thumb.

"By head's a bit clogged," Floyt admitted stuffily, "but I dod't doe that I really deed a—"

Alacrity was chuckling. "Good God in the Void, man, your head's swelling up like a vacuum tent. Better do it."

Floyt did it. Alacrity wondered if a complete cure for allergies wasn't out there someplace already, like so many other things waiting to surface in or already filtering through the Third Breath.

Seven Wars made a deep bow to Dorraine. Tiajo held her hand up to the bier. "Until we're together again, Caspahr."

A noise began to build in the machinery under the crystal bier. Tiajo moved away, motioning the rest to follow. They did, Seven Wars bearing the Thorn Cup. The entire group entered the shelter of an enclosure of broad, transparent panes.

A glow had started in the projector under Weir's body. It became brighter as the sound indicated a power buildup. It was becoming difficult to look directly at the bier.

Tiajo's voice nearly broke, and she had to strain to be heard. "We're richer for your having lived, poorer for your passing!"

The light was blinding, and the noise reached an eerie, verging pitch. The enclosure's panes polarized.

From the projector a beam of energy shot straight up into the air like an impossibly intense searchlight, roaring and humming. The planes had polarized almost completely, but the glare was still intense. Every plant in the garden was ablaze.

The searing incandescence lasted for a second or two. When it was gone they smelled ozone, even through the closed doors. The panes were too hot to touch. The walls and planters in the garden were scorched and blackened; nothing but ash remained of the plants Weir had tended so carefully. The onlookers blinked.

The bier was empty, Weir's body gone without a trace.

The machinery beneath it was silent again, though Floyt could see that parts of it still glowed white-hot, and little coils of smoke ascended lazily from it.

The panes cleared once more. Stars were appearing in the night sky of Epiphany. Tiajo was staring upward into the infinity that her brother had illuminated for a moment in time.

The doctors withdrew. The old woman shook herself loose from her contemplation. "If you'll follow me to the trams, we'll have the Willreading."

Still dressed in their ceremonial robes, they repaired to Weir's suite. Serving robos and catering automata labored around the antechamber under lavish cargoes of food, drink, and other amenities. As they made themselves comfortable on the sumptuous furniture, Tiajo called for their attention.

"The various endowments and delegations of authority have been made public or will be later this evening. You individual Inheritors will be ushered, one at a time, into my brother's private chamber. There you'll hear his bequest to you. This is as Caspahr wished it to be. Escorts may accompany you if you so desire." She retired to the bedroom with Redlock and Dorraine.

Endwraithe was first. As Floyt and Alacrity slouched on an air-rest sofa, the Earther plucked a cold, scented cloth from a passing service robo and draped it across his eyes and forehead. He tried to collect his thoughts.

The breakabout beckoned to a catering machine for a chilly bottle of the wonderful cream ale brewed on Cindy Lou, and a nasal inhaler of Perkup, for morale's sake. Others were availing themselves of snacks, delicacies, beverages, smokes, and other things.

Maska took up a finger cap soaked with fragrant essences and inhaled it delicately, eyes closed in bliss. Brother Grimm was sipping contentedly on a cup of herbal tea. Stare Skill drank a domestic champagne from an elegant fluted glass.

The Perkup made Alacrity more alert, setting aside part of the sadness of the funeral. He spotted Dincrist on the other side of the antechamber, engaged in earnest conversation with Sir John over steaming cups of chocolate. The breakabout considered asking after Heart, but concluded that it was no time to start anything, especially with Invincibles and Celestials stationed in the room and drones overhead.

Instead he leaned back again. "What do you think they'll do with Inst's inheritance?" Floyt asked. Of course, on Earth, the Earthservice got most of any estate, except that upper bureaucrats seemed to know ways to get around the inheritance regulations.

"Depends on the provisions of the will, Ho. Tiajo's probably got a lot of leeway as executrix. It'll probably go to Dorraine."

"I can't help feeling sorry for him."

"Chin up. This'll be over soon, and we'll be on our way back to Earth." He *had* to see the Nonpareil soon.

Endwraithe emerged from the bedchamber and left without another word or a sideways glance, but he was smiling. Stare Skill and Brother Grimm were called next.

Alacrity took another breath of Perkup and another deep, grateful swallow of cream ale. Had it only been that morning that *Thistle* had slid down the launcher?

Floyt, thinking about Alacrity's reply, supposed that he'd be a Functionary 3rd Class again soon. There'd be no time to examine Weir's fabulous family tree, or look for a bicycle engineered with the technology that had built *Thistle*, or . . .

Stare Skill and Grimm emerged laughing, arms around one another, in a transport of delight. "He gave us Ifurin! The whole planet! Made it a protectorate!" the Djinn rejoiced. "Wait until my family hears this!"

"He provided development funds, a self-help program," Stare Skill added, "which I am to administer." She was beaming. Floyt thought her very lovely in that moment.

Sir John was next, and so it went. Sometimes Inheritors

revealed their legacies. Maska, for example, had been left an island estate deep within Weir territory and the hard copy of the message he'd sent Weir so long ago. He and Alacrity traded a few nose-sung gibes over that.

Others kept their own counsel, like the Severeemish. Nevertheless, Seven Wars and Sortie-Wolf were plainly elated. Floyt deemed war unlikely.

Billy Risk, who'd withheld any reaction to Stare Skill's news, left the bedchamber with a face-creasing grin. "The nervy old bastard named me to be in charge of the Djinn's defense forces until they get on their feet." He shook his head, chuckling at himself and Weir and life. Then he went to find Brother Grimm and Stare Skill.

Dincrist entered the bedchamber and came out again in a very short time, looking content. He ignored Alacrity and Floyt. It gradually dawned on them that Floyt was being left until last.

When his name was called he crossed to the door with Alacrity hanging back uncertainly. A captain of Invincibles was on guard. "You'll be going in alone, Citizen Floyt?"

"Hm? No, my . . . my friend's coming with me," Floyt found himself answering automatically. The captain inclined his head to them politely and stepped aside. Alacrity joined Floyt; they entered.

The scene in Weir's bedroom was much as it had been the first time, except that First Councillor Inst was absent and the Weir family tree was fully activated. Every tiny point of light gleamed and flashed.

They halted before Tiajo, Alacrity a pace or so behind Floyt.

"Citizen," the old woman said tiredly, "it came as something of a surprise to me, to all of us, that my brother saw fit to include you in his will at the last moment. I still wonder if he had any idea how much trouble he was starting. It gives me pause, how events here might have resolved themselves, absent Hobart Floyt and Alacrity Fitzhugh."

Everyone was watching him now, but Floyt made no comment.

"Ah, well. You weren't consulted on the matter either, I know," she resumed. "I thought that the nature of your inheritance might shed some light on the subject, but it hasn't."

More formally, she proclaimed, "Citizen Hobart Floyt of Terra, you've been bequeathed the full and unencumbered title of ownership of the starship *Astrea Imprimatur* and all that she contains."

If Floyt was stunned, Alacrity was faint. The breakabout's conditioning immediately locked in mortal combat with a primeval instinct that welled up inside him chanting, A starship! *A starship! A STARSHIP*! He knew an unquenchable desire to claim her and use her for his own ends, making Floyt fabulously wealthy in the process. Terra, Earthservice, and Supervisor Bear could go twirl themselves. The idea sent sharp pains lancing through his head.

"She's a refitted military vessel of the old *Jaguar* class, a privateer taken as a prize of war near the end of the Turmoils," Tiajo went on, consulting a data readout. "I know very little else about her. Apparently, my brother kept most of the information pertaining to this vessel in his head."

"Let's take a look at her!" Alacrity winced at the throbbing in his skull.

"According to my data," Tiajo told them, "*Astrea Imprimatur* has been grounded, for the last Standard year or so, on a planet called Blackguard, an independent kleptocracy. At last report, a captain and crew were still with her. I know nothing else about her and am enjoined by the will to make no inquiries."

"What's a kleptocracy?" Alacrity asked.

"Government by theft," Tiajo answered.

"Redundancy," he muttered to himself, unaware of the withering glare it drew. Lost in thought, he stared at the floor. *Grounded?* For a year? That might mean mutiny, breakdown, quarantine, impoundment, or any of a dozen other extremely unpleasant things. The pain in his head lessened.

"If you wish, Citizen Floyt," Tiajo was saying, "I can facilitate *your* inquiries. You and Master Fitzhugh are welcome to stay here until such time as you know more about your situation."

Floyt felt an urge to accept, so powerful in him that it very nearly overcame his conditioning. But he knew what the impatient Earthservice bureaucrats would expect of him, and he knew that the conditioning would eat away any temporary impulse or resolve. "I don't think that's possible, Dame Tiajo. Alacrity and I must go to Blackguard."

Her expression told that Tiajo wasn't used to having her invitations rebuffed. Dorraine spoke for the first time. "Hobart, why don't you stay? Weir the Defender *hated* the Earthservice; surely he meant the ship for you! If you take her to Terra, they'll confiscate her, and that's the last thing Dame Tiajo's brother would've wanted."

"It is indeed," the old woman said darkly.

"You'll be stuck on Earth for the balance of your life," Redlock added. "That can't be what you want, can it?"

Floyt and Alacrity were locked in a titanic battle with their conditioning. But one of the primary dictates of that conditioning, one of its strongest compulsions, was against their revealing that they'd undergone it.

"We . . . must go," Floyt got out at last.

Tiajo's mouth might have been drawn with a straightedge. "Very well; as you will." She touched a sensitized bead set in the arm of her chair. The door opened almost at once. Dincrist entered, wearing a smug grin.

"Citizen Floyt, I will now impose my judgment of penalty upon you, as loser of the airbike race," Tiajo announced.

The Earther's mouth was agape. Alacrity yelled, "But Inst sabotaged our ship—no offense. This isn't fair!"

"It is under Severeemish Usages. Captain Dincrist had nothing to do with the tampering," the grandam told them.

"Now wait just a—"

"*Silence!*" There was. She resumed, "Discretionary funds are provided by the will. No doubt some of these were intended for your expenses in locating and taking possession of your inheritance."

Floyt noticed this last, that she had been careful not to mention *Astrea Imprimatur*.

"As penalty, however," she went on, "I am going to withhold those monies, leaving you both to your own resources." Her nostrils flared disdainfully. "Such as they may be."

"Hardly a penalty at all, under Severeemish Usages," Dincrist squawked.

"I doubt Minister Seven Wars would support you in that," Redlock commented mildly. "He is too good an ally."

"Hey, how're we supposed to get halfway across creation, or whatever?" Alacrity demanded. "Sex appeal?"

The breakabout just *might* be able to deadhead in the general direction of Blackguard, wherever that was, with an understanding skipper, but Floyt had only the voucher for a return trip to Earth from Epiphany.

"That is of no consequence to me now, nor do I care if those Terran bureaucrats ever get their hands on Citizen Floyt's inheritance. Of course, if you wish to alter things, you may challenge Captain Dincrist to another contest of some suitable sort. Naturally, as challenged party, he would have the choice of terms."

Dincrist struck Alacrity as being only too eager for such an opportunity. The breakabout said, "We pass."

Dincrist gave him a frosty smile. "So be it; it will do, for now."

"Where's Heart?" Alacrity demanded. "I want to talk to her."

"I sent her ahead, as soon as I got back to Frostpile," Dincrist told him, savoring it. "She's on her way home."

"This doesn't end it."

Now the smile split into a bloodless grin. "Perhaps, Fitzhugh. We may well encounter one another again."

He bowed to Tiajo and the others, spun on his heel, and headed for the door, but paused there.

"Yes. I'd place that well within the realm of possibility, Fitzhugh."

When he'd left, Floyt turned to Alacrity. "Was it my imagination, or did it look like his face was lit from beneath just then?"

CHAPTER 18

BITE THE BULLET

As they waited gloomily for a corridor tram, Alacrity asked, "D'you think Supervisor Bear would send us more cash?"

"Interstellar passage for one, perhaps two? That's more than the budget for her entire project."

"But for a *starship*, Ho! Don't you understand what that means?"

"The *Astrea Imprimatur* might be nothing but junk by now, or she might not even be there on Blackguard. No. No Earthservice supervisor would take a risk like that."

A tram appeared just as a messenger drone floated toward them, chiming. It delivered a printout from Sintilla. Floyt began reading. "She wants us to meet her in the Hall of Remembrances." He lowered the printout. "Why would she choose the Hall?"

"Search me. Maybe she's afraid the rooms are bugged. Ho, all I want to do is go lie down. I never want to live another day like this in my life."

"But Tilla says it's about Dincrist and Heart."

"Hold on tight!" Alacrity hit the manual override and

headed for the Hall as fast as the little cart would glide—not nearly fast enough to suit him.

As they went, Floyt said, "You know, there's still one thing that puzzles me."

"Only one? Rig, you must be a genius."

"No, seriously. If Inst didn't mean to kill me—to kill either of us—why were those men at the Sockwallet lashup going to use guns?"

"Probably thought they could get away with just waving 'em around; they sure as shrinkage didn't know how Foragers react to firearms inside a lashup. Or maybe Inst's orders got garbled somehow and they thought they were supposed to horizontalize us."

"But the woman on Earth only had the styrette. Why should—"

Exasperated, Alacrity threw his hands up from the controls for an instant. "If I knew, I'd tell you, Citizen Floyt. But right now, with your permission, I'm worried about Heart."

With the Willreading completed, many of the guests had already left or were in the process of leaving; the area of Frostpile in which the Hall of Remembrances was located was now very quiet, but they still had to pass two Invincible checkpoints for weapons scans, and a number of drones remained in the air.

The Hall was deserted and partially emptied of exhibits, the more valuable ones having been removed to safer keeping. The lighting had been turned down as a discreet message to any last-minute visitors that the funeral rites of Caspahr Weir were over and lingering wouldn't be appreciated.

They called Sintilla's name softly in the echoing Hall, but heard no response. Alacrity held Floyt back from searching among the darkened, silent maze of display cases and shelves; Frostpile might have been swept clean of unauthorized firearms, but there were limitless ways to improvise a weapon. Besides, the illuminated floor strips and floating holos had been extinguished, and it would be easy to get lost. They called her name again.

"Don't bother," advised a voice behind them.

Endwraithe! The Spican banker had changed from his robe to an inconspicuous shipsuit and was no longer wearing his Inheritor's belt. Leaning on Weir's floater chair near the Hall's entrance, he carried no weapon, at least as far as they could see. They knew that he had to have passed at least one checkpoint to enter the Hall.

"The little lady is off somewhere, running after a story," Endwraithe said casually. "But I thought the message would bring you. We can talk with little danger of being overheard here."

"About what?" Alacrity asked. Possibly it was the conditioning that had him easing in front of the Terran in a protective way; possibly it was a more fundamental reflex.

"I wanted to find out about Citizen Floyt's inheritance, of course," Endwraithe said. "Oh, there's no need to squint, Fitzhugh!"

"Why do you care?" Floyt wanted to know. "And why here?"

The man laughed. "You don't know much about Spican bankers, do you? We are a competitive breed, sir! An opportunistic breed. I wanted another chance to talk to you about venture capital, and about investments."

"So you send us a phony note?" Alacrity snapped, recalling now that Endwraithe had been aboard their tram earlier and heard Sintilla call out to them. "Or *do* you know something about Heart?"

"Only what everyone else knows," the banker admitted smoothly. "Dincrist sent her home—had to be quite forceful about packing her off, I understand. I'm obliged to deal with him in matters of business, but candidly, the man can be such a rustic at times."

Floyt was weighing what Endwraithe had said. He and

Alacrity had to find a way to get to Blackguard; perhaps Endwraithe would stake them to the money in return for a portion of the proceeds from the *Astrea Imprimatur*'s sale, or her earnings, or whatever.

But Alacrity, warning senses shrilling, told the banker, "Thanks anyway, but he's got nothing you'd be interested in."

Endwraithe gave them an urbane smile. "That's something for Hobart to decide, Alacrity."

The Earther had come to a certain respect for the breakabout's judgments. "I'm afraid he's right, Board Member Endwraithe. The inheritance is a confidential matter."

Endwraithe shrugged, chubby, beringed fingers toying with his meticulous white beard. "It is also a secondary one." He brought his hand out from behind Weir's floater chair with a snubby energy pistol in it, and fired.

Endwraithe had taken into account Alacrity's reflexes, but not the breakabout's already being in motion when the banker made his move. Alerted by the drift of the conversation, Alacrity had correctly read Endwraithe's controlled expression and body kinesics as something much more than a simple shift of posture.

The breakabout had thrown himself at Floyt, bearing him over backward. They went flailing into the darkness between rows of exhibits as a narrow green pinbeam cooked the air where they'd stood. It was, in a way, a vindication of Supervisor Bear and the theory behind Project Shepherd.

They knocked over a display case in a crash of delicate old glass blown 150 years earlier on Éclat; Alacrity was on his feet instantly, yanking the stunned Floyt deeper into the shadows. They heard Endwraithe pounding toward them.

The breakabout cursed the fact that Endwraithe had lured them to where the surveillance equipment had been shut down and Invincibles would no doubt patrol infrequently. And the odds against a drone drifting by up here, high in

Frostpile, were long. But the Spican had overlooked one thing—Alacrity hoped.

"Very good! You're very quick!" the banker chuckled. "But not as fast as a beam, I daresay." He moved around a case, pistol ready, but saw no target.

"So how did you get your hands on a persuader?" Alacrity yelled up one aisle as he led Floyt into another.

Endwraithe wasn't fooled, but he elected to play the same game. "It's been here all the time. I concealed it in Weir's chair the night he died." He stopped to listen for their movements, then tiptoed up an aisle a meter or two. "I very nearly killed him with it, out there in the fields, in a thunderstorm he had whistled up."

He turned his head slowly, concentrating on his ears. He thought he detected the whisper of their slippers. "But that turned out to be unnecessary." He reversed field and leapt to the end of the next aisle, gun raised. It was empty.

The words made frightening sense to Alacrity. Weir's chair was an object that the Invincibles would expect to give off power readings, and it was nearly a holy relic, relatively immune to routine probing or dismantling for inspection.

Endwraithe didn't have everything covered, though, Alacrity reflected, as he and Floyt stopped by the case containing Weir's old Emancipator pistol. Using gestures, the breakabout instructed Floyt to be ready to overturn a shelf. The Terran got ready as Alacrity, making a fist, poised his elbow over the glass. At a nod from his companion, the Terran gave the shelf a shove with his shoulder, tipping it over.

It crashed, and at the same moment Alacrity shattered the case with one blow of his elbow. He hoped the sounds had merged sufficiently that it wouldn't occur to Endwraithe that his victims were breaking into a display. That would make the man more cautious.

Alacrity gingerly plucked the Emancipator from among

the shards of glass, blowing and brushing away the bits that clung to it as best he could in his frantic haste. He checked it; there was a round in it, a metallic slug of some kind, but the power pack that supplied its propulsion unit was deader than a year-old economic forecast.

"Clumsy!" Endwraithe chided. "Or are you inviting me into a trap, gentlemen? Let's find out, shall we?" They heard his footsteps.

Some of the display cases were antiques, Alacrity knew. The lights in them were off, but at least some of them must have fed off leads rather than broadcast power or storage packs. He hoped.

He lowered himself as quietly as he could. Floyt crouched, listening with an animal intensity for the banker's approach. The breakabout located an outlet by feel, slicing his fingers on a stray piece of glass in the process. He mated the Emancipator's adaptor to it. Power flowed as Alacrity waited, dreading an explosion that would blow his hand off; the pistol had been inert for something like seventy-five years. The Invincibles hadn't even felt the need to keep it locked away securely.

But it was a durable old relic; it accepted a charge. He got to his feet with an assist from Floyt, praying that it would still fire. *One shot, just one*, he reminded himself, as with a mantra.

He padded toward Endwraithe as silently as he could, with the Earther close behind. They had to ambush their would-be assassin before he came across the shattered case and discovered that they were armed, or they'd lose their main advantage.

The breakabout came to a section without even the dim illumination thrown by the ceiling panels. An oversize cabinet extended beyond the others in its row, offering concealment. Farther along was a lighted stretch of aisle. They hid themselves. Endwraithe's footfalls became louder.

Alacrity began a slow, controlled breathing, gripping the

unfamiliar handgun. Floyt scarcely breathed at all. Both were perspiring freely. Alacrity peeked around the cabinet with one eye. He saw the figure of Endwraithe, silhouetted by some light source behind it, appear, pistol clearly outlined. The breakabout waited for the best possible shot that he could get while holding on to the edge that surprise would give him.

The banker paused to kick off his shoes. Then the man came on, keeping to one side of the aisle. The breakabout thought for a moment about making a flanking run and heading for the Hall's main door, but he was no longer sure of the direction. In addition, there was the possibility that their enemy had secured it somehow, which would make them exposed, easy targets.

Endwraithe eased into the lighted area, cautious but confident, pinbeam raised, eyes flickering in this direction and that. Alacrity already knew that the man's speed and accuracy merited respect; he steeled himself for as fast a move as he could make.

Floyt tapped his shoulder. The Earther was holding up a plaque silently lifted from a display case; he made gestures. Understand:ng, Alacrity nodded. The Terran skimmed the plaque off into the darkened aisles.

It landed somewhere with a clatter. Startled, Endwraithe looked off somewhere behind him for the source of the sound.

Alacrity didn't stop to wonder why; he brought his right hand up, gunbutt cupped in his left palm. Endwraithe caught the movement and spun toward him, wide-eyed, bringing the pinbeam around. The breakabout, centering the Emancipator's crude, open sights on him, fired.

The pistol made little noise, its propellant unit hurling the slug with an acceleration field rather than a chemical explosion. The slug left the barrel with a *chuff*.

Then the banker seemed to fragment, spiderwebbing, the

projectile's impact point centering low on his torso. Nevertheless, he fired.

But his green pinbeam never reached Alacrity and Floyt. It splashed, deflected, and dispersed halfway to its mark. The banker appeared to come apart, his fragments dropping to the floor in a glittering shower.

"It was a mirror!" Floyt yelled. He was only partially wrong; the banker and the breakabout had seen one another in—and fired at—one facet of a display booth in the center of a rotunda, at the confluence of several aisles. Its sides had been highly reflective.

The difference between them now was that Alacrity's weapon was empty.

"C'mon!" Alacrity and Floyt dashed away in the opposite direction, expecting a pinbeam to find their backs at any moment. They cut abruptly into a side aisle, the soles of their tabi giving them fair purchase on the slick, reflective floor. A beam hissed though the air where they'd been.

They came to an aisle that stretched away in either direction, offering no concealment or cover. But the cross aisle continued, leading to an exit door. Hearing Endwraithe's running, heavy-footed pursuit, they plunged through the exit like two startled hares—

—And found themselves on a broad, pourmelt ramp that spiraled into the distance up and down the cylindrical well. But the way down was blocked by a locked security gate. They sprinted upward.

After traversing a half-dozen coils of the ramp, they came to a large access door only to find that it too was locked. No amount of pounding, yelling, or leaning on the door signal produced any result.

"If this keeps up, he'll corner us," Floyt puffed.

"He sure can't afford to forget about us," Alacrity replied, panting. He added, "I think there's still power in the gun; if only we had another round for it."

But they had nothing except their soft robes and slippers,

and Floyt's Inheritor's belt, which, given the available tools, was practically indestructible. They even checked the folds of their clothing and the soles of their tabi, searching for a fragment of glass from the Hall, but found none. The ramp and walls were smooth and featureless.

Then Floyt exclaimed, "Alacrity! The light!"

The breakabout saw what he meant: high overhead was an illumi-plate two meters long and half as wide. Alacrity hurled the Emancipator up at it.

But the builders of Frostpile had meant for their creation to last; the pistol bounced off the resilient plate without even scratching it. Alacrity barely caught the rebounding weapon, nearly losing it and himself over the ramp's railing, dragged back from the abyss by Floyt, who seized fistsful of his robe.

"No good," the breakabout judged.

"We've got to keep moving," Floyt whispered.

They raced on. In another minute they came to a halt on the roof of the tower. The air had become cold, the unfamiliar stars clear and bright since Weir's remains had been projected away across eternity.

The tower was set apart from the others. Their shouts and waving drew no response from distant windows and terraces. The roof was a circular area nearly a hundred meters across, perfectly flat, without railing, and featureless except for the rampwell opening. A quick, desperate reconnaissance showed them that the tower walls were smooth, offering no chance for a climb, dead drop, or hand traverse.

"We'll have to jump him when he shows up," Alacrity concluded grimly.

"But there's nowhere to hide, Alacrity." Floyt glanced around for a pebble or bit of appropriate debris to use as a bullet, but it was hopeless; domestic automata kept the roof as clean-swept as an operating room. He couldn't even think of a way to leave some message naming Endwraithe as their assassin.

"Ambush, just the same," Alacrity maintained as he paced back toward the ramp head. "Unless you know how to flap your robe and *fly* away."

The breakabout began to consider assorted ploys and tactics, none of which promised anything but a more strenuous and protracted death. He reversed his grip on the Emancipator and edged closer to the ramp, prepared to throw the pistol if the unlikely opportunity presented itself.

He circled the ramp head, looking for the best vantage point. "You'd better get back, Ho. If I don't stop him, I might manage to slow him up. It'll be up to you after that."

"Alacrity, I think there's another way!"

"What, give up and make life simple for him? Damn it, Citizen Floyt, I'm not—"

He stopped, staring in amazement at the Earther, who was grinning a bizarre and unnatural grin, eyes bulging, lips drawn back in exaggerated humor.

Alacrity's own eyes widened as he understood. "They still breed 'em nutty and daring on Old Earth, don't they?"

Lines of tension bracketed the breakabout's mouth; the muscles along his jaws jumped. He dropped the pistol, clamped his left hand on Floyt's shoulder, and swung a long right to the Earther's face.

Endwraithe advanced slowly up the rampway, watchful for an ambush. Aware that his two prey had the Emancipator, he was certain that they were out of ammunition; they'd had several opportunities to use the gun but hadn't. He went guardedly nonetheless, knowing that the breakabout was athletic and unpredictable. The pistol itself would make a dangerous missile at close range.

But as he emerged onto the roof, he saw the two, one standing, one stretched out flat, not far off. A few glances told him that there was no one else around, no patrol craft overhead or watchers on other roofs or in windows.

He was relieved in some measure, though still cautious.

The banker had cringed inwardly when his *own* deep and thorough conditioning had been activated by commands from his superiors, moving him to immediate and drastic action, the assassination attempt in the Forager lashup on Luna having failed. He'd been astounded to discover that someone else was making attempts on the two companions, and content to let that third party handle things. But with Inst's death—Endwraithe had received word of it through his own sources—matters had fallen to him once more.

Alacrity Fitzhugh now stood over the limp body of Hobart Floyt. Floyt lay with his face in a pool of blood. The breakabout held the little Emancipator in his hand, offering it to the banker, glowering at him. He held it with grip extended.

Empty, registered Endwraithe, smug that he'd been fairly confident of that all along. He stepped a little closer.

Alacrity tensed. "I'll make you a deal," he said.

Endwraithe almost guffawed at the man's naiveté. Still, it might be an opportunity to learn Weir's enigmatic bequest to Floyt. And that could be worth quite a lot. He took a few steps closer, keeping in mind that he must finish things quickly. "What sort of deal? Toss the pistol over here!"

"All right, Endwraithe: you get the gun and the groundling, then you let me go and we're quits."

Only too promptly, the banker responded, "Very well, it's a bargain. But throw down the gun right now!" He wasn't too afraid of the weapon; the breakabout held it by the barrel.

"Anything you say," Alacrity agreed, seeing that the man could be lured no closer. His hand swung down and back, preparing to toss. But when it came up, it gripped the pistol normally and Alacrity was taking aim.

Endwraithe's pinbeam began to rise. Remembering that his weapon had fired low the first time, Alacrity aimed higher. The projectile passed through Endwraithe's left eye in an eruption of blood and aqueous humor.

The banker reeled backward, dropping his weapon, clapping hands to his face, falling. He convulsed, blood running between his fingers. The spasms and kicks were weakening even as Alacrity got to him, pistol reversed again, prepared to club him. In moments, Endwraithe had stopped moving.

Alacrity scooped up the pinbeam. "It's over."

But Floyt had already sprung up and charged in to back up his companion. Now he slid to a stop. The Terran's mouth still streamed blood and froth. He looked down pensively at Endwraithe.

"I guess we won't be needing this," he remarked, holding out a palm in which a bloody tooth lay, his own upper left cuspid.

"Nope. Your bicuspid did the trick. A little light for distance work, though, I'd say. How's your mouth feeling?"

Floyt spat out a gobbet of blood. "*You* try it sometime. And my nose hurts again, too."

"I'm sorry, Ho. I truly am. But it *was* your idea, after all."

Alacrity started for the ramp. Floyt fell in with him. "What about his body, Alacrity?"

"It's not going anywhere."

They'd barely walked three coils of the ramp when they encountered a mob of Invincibles bearing heavy weapons, hand-held spotlights, detectors, portable shields, and loudhailers. They were instantly surrounded and disarmed. It was clear that they'd receive a thorough pummeling at the first sign of resistance. Officers shouted a barrage of questions at them.

"They never told me this was in my job description," Alacrity sighed to Floyt.

"Mine either."

CHAPTER 19

STRANGE ATTRACTORS

FROM THE HILL ON WHICH THE ALPHA BUREAUCRATS' CONference villa sat, virtually every part of Kathmandu could be seen, and the great valley in which it sat. The city had escaped destruction in the Final Smear.

The gathered Alphas looked out on buildings of redbrown brick made in time-honored style, side by side with glassy domes; millennia-old stupas next to permacrete minarets. The rainy season was over, but the hour was too early for the heat of the day to have begun blowing the city's dust about.

Ranged along the outdoor breakfast table, Terra's ruling public servants dined on shell eggs, fresh meats in unlimited quantity and genuine coffee, tea, and juices. They were waited upon by attractive, well-trained human servants.

The Alpha Bureaucrats gave their meal appropriate attention; no one else on the planet rated food of such quality. All the Alphas had aged beyond the ability of Earth's medicine to fight off signs of catabolism; all contemplated retirement with great joy.

Their meetings were characterized by a conspicuous, even forced casualness. They maintained an informal clubbishness to set themselves aside from the tightly controlled masses they ruled and to mask the wary and unrelenting competitiveness among them.

"One last thing," Cynthia Chin said around a mouthful of coddled egg, as if she'd just remembered it—though the subject had been hovering in the air all morning.

"There's the matter of that Weir bequest. The one in which that delightful Supervisor Bear person of yours has embroiled us, Raymond."

Stemp contemplated a gorgeous fruit cocktail, pretending to smile. Eyes went to him. The Alphas waited, dressed in their uniforms and ceremonial outfits and eccentric, one-of-a-kind costumes from Earth's past.

"That situation has been dealt with," Stemp assured them with elaborate calm.

"Surely you'll forgive our being curious," Chin pursued. It looked like an afterthought when she added casually, "I understand that there are rumors to the effect that Weir had become aware of certain Blackguard information."

Stemp hid the impact of that warhead by languidly sampling the fruit cocktail, but he'd been rocked. *Blackguard information!* He wondered where she'd obtained her data— who might be allying with her against him.

Yielding to Chin's probe would be surrendering an Alpha's right to privacy and autonomy. The others might take it as a sign of vulnerability or decline—a very dangerous thing for Stemp.

On the other hand, if he refused to reassure, to keep them abreast of a matter potentially disastrous to all, it might bring about a consensus against him.

And occasionally the predators fed on one another.

He elected to cut his losses and salvage all he could from the skirmish. "Well then, let me put your mind at ease, dear

Cynthia. We should never hold back pertinent information, don't you agree?"

Although she tried to avoid answering, showing a non-committal expression, he went on congenially, "Yes, of course you do." He'd nailed it down, making it awkward for her to refute, since she'd done the asking. He vowed to use it against her one day.

He continued, making strong eye contact with the others as he spoke. "Our agent, the Spican banker Endwraithe, is in place and has been activated. He has orders to discover what he can about the bequest, but his primary mission is to execute Floyt and his escort. He will then transmit confirmation to me on the fastest available ship."

"Ah!" Cynthia Chin toyed with a dish of sherbet. "What if—unthinkable, I know, but isn't preparedness-in-depth always a good idea?—what if the banker fails you?"

Fails *you*. Stemp considered the possibilities in an instant's hesitation. Endwraithe was one of their most capable operatives. Surely, with his long-established position in Frostpile and the advantage of surprise, he'd have no trouble carrying out an assignment against a minor functionary and a nameless space tramp.

Stemp gave Chin a blasé look. "I can give you my personal guarantee: the matter will be dealt with."

"So." She appeared to go back to her egg. "If Alpha Bureaucrat Stemp promises to see to a problem personally, there's nothing more to be alarmed about."

That wasn't what he'd said, as everyone at the table knew. But retrenching and redefining would be tactically unwise, indicating confusion and lack of confidence. Little as he intended to become personally involved in the affair, he let her distortion stand.

The thought of those two idiots, Floyt and Fitzhugh, on the loose with some unnamed Weir legacy and a valid Earth-service letter of Free Import in their possession chilled him. But Stemp forced down his misgivings and exchanged small talk with the other Alphas. After all, Endwraithe was a capable, rigorously conditioned agent.

And his prey? Two hapless pawns. Insignificant nobodies.

This time, it was Tiajo who favored shooting them.

And, oddly, it was Governor Redlock who intervened, with the help of Dorraine and Maska. But all the furor over Endwraithe's death was deflected when, in grudging response to the claims of Floyt and Alacrity, Tiajo had Endwraithe's suite and personal effects examined. Among the personal commo codes of the deceased were several no one could identify. A canny, squint-eyed old house cryptographer vouched that they were not commercial codes nor anything recognizably Spican. At about that same time, an Invincible forensic officer reported that the story told by Floyt and Alacrity checked out; the banker had attempted to kill them, and they'd ambushed him in self-defense.

"But why would a Spican banker care what happens to us?" Floyt repeated. Medics had stopped the bleeding of his gums and lips, controlled the swelling, and taken away most of the excruciating pain. They'd also removed the sharp-edged roots of his missing teeth, but replacement or regeneration would have to wait.

He was just thankful that he'd had the presence of mind to open his mouth at the last second to minimize the damage done by Alacrity's big fist. Still, the analgesics and the gap in his dentition made his speech lispy, distorted, and a bit sloppy.

Alacrity stood with folded arms, not answering Floyt's question. The doctors had seen to his wounds and tended the fractured knuckles in his right hand, disinfecting the deep lacerations made by Floyt's teeth.

No one else had an answer for the Earther. Finally, Dorraine said, "If you two still intend to go to Blackguard to claim the bequest, I think you'd be well advised to go at once, as quickly as you can."

"But how?" Floyt demanded.

"My wife and I are departing in half an hour, in the *Blue Pearl*," Redlock answered. "We'll take you as far as Epiphany's spaceport. From there you're on your own."

The two companions looked at Tiajo. The old woman made no objection to Redlock's offer of minor assistance. Neither did she relent on the penalty she'd imposed on them. "If you remain here, I'm reasonably certain that my legal staff can present a number of serious indictments. Spican observers would be present at any legal proceedings."

The pair instantly abandoned any thought of pleading for further aid. Their Earthservice conditioning and their instincts of self-preservation had their hair standing on end; their irresistible urge was to get into motion. Bowing and backing toward the door, bumping into one another, they were gone in moments.

"Strange Attractors," Admiral Maska mused.

"How's that again, my Lord?" Dorraine asked.

"Strange Attractors," the Srillan said again, louder. "Something of an interest of mine. Enigmatic forces affecting the turbulence around them. The subject held a certain fascination for Director Weir, as you know."

"Is *that* how you perceive those two blatherskites, Admiral?" Tiajo exploded.

"Wouldn't you say that that's been their impact here on Epiphany, madam?" He looked at the door through which Alacrity and Floyt had disappeared.

"And now they're on the loose together in the grandest turbulence of all: the chaotic dynamics of the Third Breath of humankind."

A contemplative silence settled over the chamber.

There was no time to wait for automated valets or household servants. Their suite became a whirlwind scene of hysterical packing, of yelling, accusation, and counteraccusation. Nevertheless, they were in too much of a hurry to be angry with one another.

Out in the corridor again, they glanced at the door to Sintilla's suite. "I forgot all about Endwraithe's phony message," Floyt said. "You don't suppose he hurt her, do you?"

"We'd better check. Besides, she might have some advice."

Prolonged leaning on her door signal produced no result. Finally, Floyt pressed out the entry code. "I couldn't help noticing it the other day." He blushed.

"Don't apologize to me; I do it all the time."

She was not inside. On a hunch, Floyt went and hit the playback on her answering unit. On a table lay his and Alacrity's proteuses; they'd completely slipped his mind. He shoved them into a pocket.

No messages were recorded, but in her answering recording, Sintilla said that she would be at funeral rites slated to be held by some of the non-Inheritors.

"So she went straight there after we left her in the corridor," Floyt concluded with relief, "and she won't be back until midnight or so. She's all right, then. Alacrity? What are you doing?"

The breakabout was bent over the journalist's personal, desk-model proteus. "Oh *no*! Oh, God, Buddha, and Freud in the Void!"

"What is it?"

"Read for yourself!"

Floyt leaned over the screen and read the message on which Sintilla had been working.

TO: ANDRAX MIXTO, MANAGING EDITOR, FIRST BURST PUB-
    LICATIONS
FROM: SINTILLA
    ANDY,
    SIT DOWN BEFORE YOU READ THIS, LOVE! I HAVE THE
PERFECT NEW SERIES FOR PUBLICATION UNDER MY BOM-
BASTICO HERDMAN PSEUDONYM! THE SITUATION FITS THE

READERSHIP-PSYCHOMETRICIANS' REQUIREMENT EXACTLY: VERIFIABLY EXTANT MAIN CHARACTERS WITH AN "EVERY-MAN" TOUCH; VERY LOW PROBABILITY THAT THEY'D EVEN STEP FORWARD TO *IDENTIFY* THEMSELVES, MUCH LESS DENOUNCE THE STORIES; PLENTY OF LEEWAY TO "SWEETEN" THE STORY LINES. IT'S A NATURAL FOR MY READERS!

WORKING TITLE FOR THE FIRST BOOK IS *HOBART FLOYT AND ALACRITY FITZHUGH IN THE CASTLE OF THE DEATH ADDICTS*. OTHERS ALREADY OUTLINED ARE *HOBART FLOYT AND ALACRITY FITZHUGH VERSUS THE BRAIN EATERS OF THE GALACTIC RIM*, AND *HOBART FLOYT AND ALACRITY FITZHUGH CHALLENGE THE AMAZON SLAVE WOMEN OF THE SUPERNOVA*.

IT COULD MAKE US EVEN MORE MONEY THAN THE WEIR BOOKS! I'LL BE WAITING TO HEAR FROM YOU, ANDY!

KISSES,
TILLA

"Well, she *said* we were going to make her rich," Floyt remarked weakly.

"So. She wrote all those Weir books too. No wonder she's a privileged character around here. I'll bet that's how he bribed her into not writing any more of them."

"Alacrity, she can't *do* this to us!"

"What're *you* complaining about? At least your name's first." He settled into a chair, shoulders slumped. "If I sat right here and thought all day, I couldn't think of anything that'd get Earthservice madder, or make things tougher on us. Once this gets out, every mental case in the galaxy's gonna be on the lookout for us."

They both had the same thought in that moment: Kid Risk, and the many kinds of sorrow a similar fate had brought down upon him.

"Alacrity, we've got to hurry." Floyt grabbed his luggage; Alacrity snatched up his warbag. They made for the door.

"Yeah, that's the ticket, Ho! If we can get everything squared away before she gets those books published, maybe we'll be all right."

They spied a corridor tram and hastened toward it. "And if we don't manage that?" Floyt couldn't help wondering aloud.

"The crackpots'll be all over us like a cheap spacesuit. They'll be out to rob us, or challenge us!"

"Or *interview* us!"

"Run, Ho! *Run!*"

ABOUT THE AUTHOR

Brian Daley is the author of seven previous novels of science fiction and fantasy, the most recent being *A Tapestry of Magics*. He also scripted the National Public Radio serial adaptations of *Star Wars* and *The Empire Strikes Back*. His whereabouts are subject to change without notice, but he favors Manhattan.